LOVESICK

Also by Alex Wellen

Barman: Ping-Pong, Pathos & Passing the Bar

NAME _____ AGE _____

ADDRESS _____ DATE _____

℞

LOVESICK

A NOVEL   *Alex Wellen*

THREE RIVERS PRESS • NEW YORK

This is a work of fiction. Names, characters, places, and incidents either are the product of the author's imagination or are used fictitiously. Any resemblance to actual persons, living or dead, events, or locales is entirely coincidental.

Copyright © 2009 by Alex Wellen

Published in the United States by Three Rivers Press, an imprint of the Crown Publishing Group, a division of Random House, Inc., New York.
www.crownpublishing.com

Three Rivers Press and the Tugboat design are registered trademarks of Random House, Inc.

Library of Congress Cataloging-in-Publication Data
Wellen, Alex.
     Lovesick / Alex Wellen.—1st ed.
          p. cm.
     1. College students—Fiction. 2. Pharmacists—Fiction.
  3. Family-owned business enterprises—Fiction. 4. Drugstores—
  Corrupt practices—Fiction. I. Title.
     PS3623.E4665L68   2009
     813'.6—dc22   2008051148

ISBN 978-0-307-33795-5

Printed in the United States of America

Design by Barbara Sturman

Technical illustrations by Richard J. Gathercole

10 9 8 7 6 5 4 3 2 1

First Edition

For Kris +1

1-2-3

"Apprenticeship must not be made too easy for him; he must go the whole way himself. If he could be intimidated, deterred, shaken off, discouraged, he would be no great loss."

—Hermann Hesse, *The Glass Bead Game,*
"The Rainmaker" (1943)

PART ONE

CHAPTER 1

Magnitude 3.0

"ARE you disturbed?"

Standing there in his full-length lab coat, those rosy pock-marked cheeks, the droopy hound dog jowls, the crooked yellow bottom teeth, and that flawless white crew cut, Gregory Day seems to want a response. But I know better.

I don't appreciate the way he talks to me. If he talks to me. Direct questions receive monosyllabic responses. To Gregory, everything I do, say, or ask is unhelpful, asinine, and rhetorical. I clench my teeth and count out thirty pills in therapeutic fashion, sliding the lot into a burnt orange plastic bottle.

"Yeah Gregory, *I'm disturbed,*" I burst out, my voice shaking. "I'm an idiot because I told Mrs. Olivia to take her pills on an empty stomach. I'm an idiot even though *she asked me,* and I told her exactly what it says on the tiny green label. The label *I* put there."

Gregory pulls out his inhaler, awkwardly stuffs it in his mouth, and gives it three quick toots. This is how he exercises. The seventy-four-year-old quit smoking ten years ago, but it was too late. Emphysema had already set in. There's no erasing a half century's worth of nicotine plus some exposure to nasty chemicals in the war.

"No, *you're an idiot* because I've repeatedly told you not to dispense medical advice to our customers, Andrew," he says catching his breath.

For nine months now, Gregory has refused to call me "Andy."

After a long pause, he adds, "And for the record, you didn't just tell her to 'take the pills on an empty stomach.' You went into some long, complicated, totally off-base explanation about how food interferes with the drug's absorption into the bloodstream. For the umpteenth time: you are not a pharmacist."

I know.

3

"You're a pharmacy *technician.*"

I know.

"That's all I need—to break the law and get my license yanked because you have a hankering need to feel validated," he says.

Oh, please.

In terms of all-out destruction, this argument rates low—a magnitude 3.0, tops—mere aftershocks from the 5.0 we had two hours ago over the effectiveness of zinc lozenges. I say they pre-empt the onset of the common cold. Gregory's professional opinion is they're "baloney."

As the crow flies, this tiny pharmacy is about twenty miles northeast of San Francisco and sits on solid bedrock, but the tiny township of Crockett is bordered on every side by precarious fault lines, the most threatening—the Hayward Fault Zone to our west. Of the ten thousand earthquakes that California experiences every year—in the last hundred years—only two have been catastrophic. In fact, most folks can't even sense anything lower than a 3.0. But not me. I feel them all the time. Right here. For Gregory and me, this pharmacy is our epicenter, and anything above a 5.0 generates intense feelings of nausea and vertigo.

Belinda is behind the front cash register too engrossed in *People* magazine and too consumed with the taste of her finger-nails to give a damn about a measly 3.0. Gregory and I bicker all the time, and a mag 3.0 doesn't even break her concentration any-more. Some ripples in her no-foam soy latte. It's going to take at least a 6.0 before anything interrupts "Britney Time."

"Is this a 3 or 5?" Gregory asks with my back to him.

I spin around and realize that he's not referring to our argument at all.

"How do these doctors expect us to read their chicken scratch?" he complains, holding a streaky fax up to the overhead fluorescent lights that turn us all a sickly green hue. "Well, this medication doesn't come in 3 milligram doses," he informs the sheet of paper, "so he's getting 5."

He tosses the prescription in the sink. This is his way of telling me to enter the information into our computer system. By law, we are required to keep original prescriptions for five years, but there are boxes in our storeroom with scraps of paper that go back to the Cold War.

He limps toward me. "We're getting a delivery in about an hour, Andrew. I need you to restock the shelves."

So now I'm a stock boy. I thought I was a pharmacy technician.

"I've got quite a few more scripts to fill. Belinda can handle it," I suggest.

Without taking her eyes off her magazine, Belinda crosses her wrists above her head and wiggles her fingers, hands tied.

Nice.

"I can take care of these orders just fine. You just handle the delivery. I can't have boxes cluttering my aisles," Gregory continues.

If I don't handle the delivery, Gregory will—jamming makeup, toiletries, sunglasses, and worthless knickknacks on arbitrary shelves, wherever they'll fit. When customers ask where we keep the suntan lotion, I have to tell them *over there, over there, and probably over there.*

Between the lighting, overflowing shelves, littered aisles, and vintage dust, this place is closing in on me.

Day's Pharmacy is a Crockett institution. Located at the same Pomona Street address for nearly ninety years, it is the second-oldest independent pharmacy in the East Bay and the seventh oldest in all of northern California. Everyone knows this because Gregory won't let us forget. The only other local business that's been around longer is the California & Hawaiian Sugar Refining Company. C & H is how Crockett became "Sugar Town."

Over the last one hundred years, the sugar business has been bittersweet for Crockett. Behind the walls of that massive Willie Wonka–like factory, you'll find far more machines than men and women. A century ago, it took a thousand employees to churn out seventy thousand tons of Hawaiian sugar each year. Now the plant manufactures about ten times that, but with one-fifth the staff. Among the layoffs: my father, prompting his early retirement with Mom to Vegas. Only half the factory is still in operation. In the late 1990s, the company sold a good chunk of its real estate to Charles Warner, a wealthy local investor. Warner Construction was supposed to convert the old C & H warehouses into lofts, but development has been stalled for years.

There are still a few perks to having C & H headquartered here. First off, every business in town gets a free, complimentary supply of sugar. Then there are the Red Rockets. C & H makes a limited supply of the highly coveted candy rings once a year, to coincide with the Crockett Memorial Day Parade. One of my earliest memories is coming to Day's Pharmacy with my mother—right after the annual Pancake Breakfast and right before the parade—and Gregory handing me my first of those mouthwatering cherry-flavored delights.

Red Rockets have changed slightly over the years. The ones I used to get had a red plastic ring that you slipped on your finger with a missile-shaped sucking candy on top. But then kids started poking each other with them like weapons, we entered the Age of Lawsuits, and as a precaution, C & H lopped off the tops. Now they look like nothing. Technically the shape is called a "frustum," not that Gregory would know. I think he likes those truncated cones because they look like inverted medicine cups. That, and the power this candy represents: the only way to get a Red Rocket is to snatch one up at the Memorial Day Parade or come here.

It's awe-inspiring to think that soon, Gregory will pass the candy baton to me. I haven't done a hell of a lot with my life, but "Gatekeeper of the Red Rockets" is right up there.

THE bell on the front door jingles and in walks the most wonderful eighty-three-year-old in the world. Clunky square wraparound shades, a ratty brown homburg hat with a matted-down red feather, his trademark mint green polyester shorts, and that navy blue Members Only windbreaker—he looks like Mr. Magoo's hipper, tan older brother.

"Sid!" Gregory and I cheer in unison, both of us thankful for the reprieve from each other.

It kills Gregory that Sid and I are so close. It took Gregory and

Sid decades to create the sort of bond Sid and I formed in just eight months.

Holding open the door, Sid goes to greet his fans, but is knocked back a few inches by the most awful eighty-two-year-old in the world. Cookie is on a rampage, again. Her purple ruffled blouse is buttoned all wrong; her thin brown locks are shielded in a hairnet; and she's testing the limits of those electric blue stretch pants. The pug nose, the beady black eyes: the rat resemblance is uncanny.

Seeing her, Gregory and I let out a collective moan.

"You're a quack!" Cookie shrieks, speed-limping toward us, cane in hand.

She's in here every day complaining about something.

"*Quack* is a word reserved for doctors," Gregory says nonchalantly, turning his back to her to grab a tube of ointment.

"Hardy har-har," she yells back.

Following her down the aisle is a small black and gray dog. Loki is more poodle than schnauzer, which is good for Sid, who is severely allergic to longhairs. The tiny schnoodle is full of energy and affection. Cookie lets go of the leash, and Loki races toward me. I bend down to pet her.

"What'd I tell you about bringing that animal in here," Gregory chastises her, pointing to the Shoes Shirts No Pets sign.

This is how the two of them talk to each other. Like family.

The phone rings. It never stops ringing.

Gregory-the-grouch tells me to leave the dog alone, get back to work, and answer the phone, all with one suggestive nod. Get the phone, fill a prescription, file an insurance form, I do the same three or four things all day long, and according to him, I can't even manage to do those things right.

"Boys!" Sid yells. Following closely behind Cookie, he throws open his arms wildly and knocks over my perfectly stacked pyramid of Colgate toothpaste.

"Cleanup on Aisle Four," I broadcast into cupped hands.

"All make fun of the blind guy, why don't we?" he says, bending over to pick up the rectangular boxes.

Sid isn't blind, but glaucoma in both eyes has compromised

his peripheral vision considerably. It's like viewing the world through a slowly shrinking periscope, he tells me. Sid takes eye drops for his glaucoma and an assortment of pills and sprays for his cholesterol, heartburn, enlarged prostate, and allergies.

"You've got a problem!" Cookie cries, shaking one of our pharmacy bottles in Gregory's direction. She's on twice as many drugs as Sid for everything from an enlarged thyroid to high blood pressure to osteoporosis.

"There's something wrong with these pills," Cookie insists, shoving the rubber tip of her dark wooden cane across the counter and in Gregory's face.

"Watch it!" he says, knocking it away. "Now don't get all uppity," Gregory demands, calmly proofing the two prescriptions I just filled.

"I don't *feel* like myself," she says accusatorily.

Peering over bifocals, Gregory gives her a look. "You seem like yourself."

Cookie's pooch starts tearing into a bag of zinc lozenges.

Sid doesn't bother resurrecting my toothpaste pyramid. Instead, he piles the boxes on an already crowded shelf. Stuffing the last one in quickly, it starts a domino effect, shoving the mouthwash off the ledge. Now Sid's chasing two bouncing plastic bottles of Listerine down the aisle.

"Cleanup on Aisle Six," I call.

Cookie shakes her head, ashamed of her husband.

"I swear, if I find out that you're diluting my medication," she scolds Gregory, shaking the container, "or, God forbid, substituting it for . . ."

"Placebos?" I suggest.

"Hey kiddo, the adults are talking here." Cookie whips around to address me. "Mind your own beeswax."

I've grown accustomed to Cookie's put-downs.

"All I'm saying is you should cut Gregory some slack," I insist. "I *personally* filled your prescription myself and I *swear* the pills are legit."

"DO NOT stick up for this man," she hollers, her voice cracking as she pounds her cane on the ground. "I'm on to you, buster," she tells Gregory.

I love that she calls him "buster."

Rattling the bottle, she says, "I'm licking all these pills when I get home, and if I taste sugar, I'm reporting you to the DEA."

"The FDA," Gregory corrects her.

Sid is finding this entire exchange highly entertaining. Cookie and Gregory stare each other down. Belinda stops pulling at the silver hoop-ring in her lower lip long enough to see who blinks first.

"Leash!" Cookie orders me, stretching out her arm, blindly.

I pat Loki softly on the head and then pick up the dog's leash from the floor and hand it to her. The schnoodle still has that pack of lozenges clamped between her teeth. Cookie gives the leash a tug and Loki relinquishes the bag. I wonder if zinc prevents dogs from catching a cold, too.

"Take these," Gregory says, handing her a brown bag of more pills.

She snaps it out of his hand.

"Do me a favor," Gregory yells to her as she waddles away, "make sure you drink lots of water before you launch into your little lickfest."

"Oh, you're a regular Buster Keaton," she mumbles loud enough so we all can hear. "Sidney, let's go!"

"Sweetie, I'll meet you at home," Sid says, leaning on one of the lunch counter barstools. "I'm going to grab a cup of tea with Andy, assuming that's copacetic with G-man?"

"You're your own person," Cookie tells him.

Belinda's ready to ring Cookie up, but Gregory waves her off.

"Door!" Cookie commands Belinda.

Belinda is all skin, bones, and tattoos. She takes her sweet-ass time getting the door for Cookie.

"Do come again," Belinda tells her, and the two exchange phony smiles.

Sid moseys behind the counter and starts playing with the pearl handle on the soda fountain. "Damn shame you disconnected this," he says. "Lydia made the sweetest egg creams," Sid says, trying to get a response out of Gregory.

But Gregory ignores him. Sid and I wait for the go-ahead.

"Can I go?" I ask finally. I'm overdue for a break.

"Go. But fifteen minutes means fifteen minutes."

Gregory then waves me over.

"And one more thing," he whispers sternly in my ear, his voice raspy. "I don't need you defending me to Cookie or anyone else for that matter. I've got everything covered just fine."

Then fill your own damn prescriptions, answer your own phone calls, ring up your own damn customers, and restock your own shelves. You can't pay me enough to endure this abuse. I should walk out the door right now and leave you twisting in the wind. Find yourself a new whipping boy.

I quit you, miserable old man. And I would, too, if I wasn't madly in love with his daughter.

CHAPTER 2

The Engagement Formula

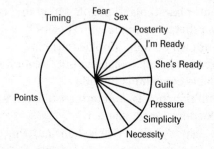

ACCORDING to my calculations, I'm ready to get married.

I've zeroed in on the relevant variables, constructed the proper algorithms, evaluated the empirical evidence, and crunched the numbers. I've checked and rechecked the math, reverse-engineered the process, and charted the results.

No one will appreciate this mathematical certainty as much as Sid.

Sid prefers Langley's Diner next door, but we need some privacy, and I want to minimize the risk of bumping into someone we know, so I persuade him to accompany me to Roy's Gourmet Coffee Roaster two blocks away. Next week they're opening a Starbucks around the block, but I'll never go: the coffee's fine, but I hate that they insist you order in Italian—and I don't need their cheese plates, paninis, or Sting CDs, just some coffee, thank you.

Roy's Roaster is busier than I'd hoped, though it appears the coast is clear. A pleasant enough teenage barista with strawberry blond hair and out-of-control acne waits on us.

To celebrate today's big announcement, I order an extra-foam, vanilla double-latte. This prompts a cockeyed look from Sid.

"Tea for me," he says firmly.

"Lemon Zest, Earl Grey with Bergamot, Earl Grey with Lavender, English Breakfast, Scottish Breakfast, or Irish Breakfast?" she ticks off mechanically.

Sid's completely stumped.

"We also have a variety of green teas and some herbal blends. Or maybe you'd like Darjeeling?"

"No, darling, just tea," Sid says. "You have that, right?"

Sid is regretting our decision to come here.

"He'll have English Breakfast," I tell her, pushing Sid toward a table.

We sit and quietly enjoy our beverages. The age difference has never bothered me before, but sitting here, silently, with more than fifty years between us, I do feel a bit like a volunteer in an elderly assistance program. I shouldn't say "elderly." The elderly hate the term *elderly* almost as much as they hate *geriatric. Senior citizen* is no longer politically correct, either. *Retiree* is about as polite as it gets.

"Were you able to locate that old vacuum cleaner so we can proceed with Operation Jet Stream?" I ask him.

"Uh-huh. It works like a charm. But I know you didn't drag me to this frou-frou place to talk windshield wipers. What's with all the drama?"

I give him a long, affectionate stare. Sid is a good friend. He's smart; he's helpful; he has a lifetime of experiences and all the time in the world to share them. I trust him. Sid was the one who convinced me not to move in with Paige. (As if that would have even been an option with Gregory.) "Living together is a cop-out," he's prone to telling me. "When you live together, you're committed to working things out *until* they get tough. When you're married, you're committed to working things out *when* they get tough."

"I'm getting hitched," I say, trying to downplay the news.

"Congrats! Who's the lucky girl?"

He knows exactly who she is. Sid couldn't be any more immersed in our lives. He watched Paige and me fall in love. Gregory is his best friend; he is mine. Sid and Cookie are Paige's godparents. "Brewster men make boys," Sid is always saying. Paige is the closest thing Sidney and Cookie Brewster have ever had to a daughter, and they spoil her rotten.

"I'm thinking I'll pop the question in the next couple of weeks. I'll need your help with the final arrangements," I tell him.

Sid's eyebrows poke out over his massive sunglasses. Only now does he realize that I'm serious.

"Final arrangements? This ain't a funeral, kid. It's great news, but what's the rush? It's only been a few months. You sure you're ready for marriage?"

Sid has asked me this question before, and this is the first time that I've had a suitable enough explanation.

"Because I've got proof," I say, slapping my pie chart on the table.

Sid's expression swiftly goes from playful to disturbed. Sid lifts his shades and holds the chart up to his nose to get a better look.

"This is horseshit!" he says, laughing and tossing the chart on the table.

"Hold your horseshit," I tell him. "I made this chart for *you.*

Right about now I bet you're wondering why I didn't just do a simple list of pros and cons like a normal person—"

"There's nothing normal about this, Andy."

"Indulge me for a moment."

"I don't like the looks of this chart. I don't even understand it."

"Each slice signifies a different factor influencing my decision to propose, by percentage. Take this slice labeled 'Timing.' It occupies about 10 percent because it's more important to the engagement formula than, say, 'Necessity,' which occupies 5 percent of the pie," I explain.

"Do you have any idea what it costs to throw a wedding?" Sid asks.

"I thought the father-in-law pays."

Sid flashes me a disapproving look.

"*Kidding.* Geez, where's your sense of humor?"

"Be funny. Then I'll laugh."

"Look, I've been saving. We'll be fine. Unless you think we should elope."

Sid reacts to the word *elope* like he's just heard nails across a chalkboard.

"Don't you still have student loans left over from pharmacy school?"

"I've got twenty years to pay them," I say, brushing him off.

"You've got it all figured out, don't you."

"I'm thinking a small wedding."

"Well, then, you're thinking too much. You'll have whatever wedding you'll have . . . within reason. It's not *your* job to figure that part out. Your job is to *help Paige realize her fantasy.*"

Sid lets the words linger.

"You heard me, right?" he confirms. I nod. "I did it for Cookie and you'll do it for my goddaughter." He looks back at my pie chart. "What's this big slice labeled 'Points'?" he asks hesitantly.

On our third or fourth date, for some unknown reason, I started awarding Paige points for various feats. For example, she got points the day she bowled a turkey (a miraculous three strikes in a row); Paige got points that time she split aces and doubled down in blackjack; just last week she got points for slurping down a dozen slimy bluepoint oysters. After "I love you" no three words bring Paige more joy than "You get points" (although "You were right" and "I am sorry" are a close third and fourth).

For me, I explain to Sid, this is how love adds up.

Sid hates this system.

"Does she ever award *you* points?" he asks curiously.

"No, but she could. Paige likes points, *really.*"

"Uh-huh," he says with skepticism. "Okey doke, so I think we're done with this little chart of yours."

"Just indulge me for two more minutes," I plead.

I pull out a thick black Magic Marker. "Take these two slices," I say, using the marker to point to "Pressure" and "Posterity." "I'm not getting peer pressure to get married, and I'm not getting married for show. Then there's 'Sex.'"

"Hold your horses," he tells me, raising the stop signal.

"All I'm saying is monogamy doesn't scare me."

"And 'Guilt'?" he asks of the corresponding slice.

"None whatsoever. I'm not proposing because I feel like marriage is 'the right thing to do.' I'm not caving to Paige's demands. I want this. 'Necessity' isn't a factor, either. Paige isn't pregnant. I'm not proposing because I'm tired of the dating scene. I'm popping the question because I want to marry *Paige.* We're not getting married because it's convenient. 'Fear' doesn't come into play, either. I'm not worried about ending up alone. I'm ready, Sid. She's ready."

"You're brilliant, kid, but a moron when it comes to relationships."

"I don't understand . . ."

"Then let me put this in terms you will: you're trying to solve the unsolvable."

"Tell me *one factor* I've missed," I insist.

"Look at me, Andy."

I look at him.

"No formula, no pie chart, no miracle calculation is going to give you the answers. Take it from someone who thrives on math: there ain't going to be a solution at the bottom of the page that you can place in a neat little box. You want to marry Paige? I'm thrilled. You think she's ready? You're ready? I can respect that. But not this," he says, swatting the pie chart away like a gnat.

He slowly takes off his shades to look at me. The sunlight hurts his eyes like pins and needles. They begin to tear.

"So what does the father of the bride think about all this hooha?" he demands.

"Don't start."

"You *need* Gregory's blessing," Sid says. "That part is *not* up for negotiation."

"The guy doesn't think I'm competent enough to drop pills in a plastic bottle; you really think he's about to consider me worthy enough to marry the 'apple of his eye'?"

"And the alternative is what?"

"He brought this on himself by hiring me in the first place."

"Now you're talking nonsense." He chuckles. "You're punishing Gregory because he gave you the job that landed you the girl of your dreams? We both know Gregory had little to do with it. You had your mind made up when you came back to Crockett in the first place."

"I'm sorry, but I'm not giving Gregory the satisfaction of rejecting me on a whole new level," I tell him. "You're being a total hypocrite. Look at what happened to your own grandson when he asked *his* future father-in-law."

Jordan, Sid's grandson, was ridiculed for asking permission. Something along the lines of: "Our daughter is not a piece of property. We don't treat her like chattel. And please don't tell me you're expecting some sort of dowry. Abigail is an adult. I suggest you ask her yourself." Jordan did, Abigail said yes, and they lived happily ever after, but not before her father struck "obey and honor" from their wedding vows.

"That man is a hippie tree-hugging commie," Sid says of Jordan's father-in-law. "He doesn't count. You ask the father for his blessing because that's what us old geezers expect. Why do you ask for my opinion when you don't even want it?"

"This would be so much easier if Paige were just *your* daughter."

"Don't say that!" he says loud enough to startle the next table.

"Drink your tea," I suggest softly.

Sid is on all sorts of heart medicine. I need him to stay calm.

"What am I going to do with you?" Sid laments, clearing his throat.

"Gregory doesn't make it easy," I mumble, gulping down my latte.

"You're no walk in the park yourself," he responds. "Level with me, kid: how are the two of you getting along?"

"Pretty good," I lie.

"I'm blind, but I'm not deaf. I hear the way you talk to each other."

"Just don't tell him I told you what I'm going to tell Paige."

"And the wedding? The grandchildren? You plan to enter them into a witness protection program?"

My stomach gurgles from anxiety. Everything's starting to unravel.

"I think Gregory hates me," I whisper.

"He doesn't hate you," Sid insists, softly. "Do you know Elie Wiesel?"

"I've seen her around the pharmacy."

"She is a he, and I highly doubt you've seen Elie Wiesel trolling the aisles of Day's Pharmacy. Wiesel is a famous writer and philosopher, a Holocaust survivor. He won the Nobel Peace Prize in the 1980s. He's famous for saying a lot of very smart things, but one of my favorites is 'The opposite of love isn't hate, it's indifference.'"

Sid studies me. "Just *talk* to Gregory," he says. "Gregory is a good, generous man—more generous than you'll ever know. You need to have a relationship with him. It would make Paige happy and earn you—whatever you call 'em—'points!'"

Staring blankly at the table, I run the back of the Magic Marker along a grain in the wood. My chest hurts.

"Do you love her?"

"You know I do."

He snatches the marker from my hand, pulls off the cap, and starts drawing across my stunning masterpiece.

"Can you not do that?" I beg.

"You want the perfect formula? You think you're ready?" he asks.

Sid draws a big, thick jittery "G" around the circumference of my chart. "From where I'm sitting, you missed the biggest factor of all: Gregory. He takes the cake . . . or rather, pie."

CHAPTER 3

ILYs

THE six o'clock news is eleven minutes out. When I see Paige approaching, I punch up a random Web page to hide what I'm doing. *Look busy.*

"Okay, bring it on," Paige goads. "What's tonight's word?"

Paige drags her pointer finger across my back as she heads for the nearby printer. She stands there, sorting television scripts.

" 'Chewbacca,' " I tell her.

"That's impossible," she says with a slight snort.

Paige and I have a long-standing relationship with Han Solo's burly seven-foot four-inch fur-covered *Star Wars* sidekick. I met Paige one unseasonably warm October evening, twenty-three Halloweens ago. I was six. Paige was seven. *Return of the Jedi* was still in theaters and a monster hit. I must have run into a dozen Darth Vaders that night, but I was the only Chewbacca in all of Crockett. Drenched in sweat, the gorilla suit sliding off my shoulder, the furry mask tucked under my free arm, I rang doorbell after doorbell. At one house on Alhambra Street, the door opened, the angels sang, and there she was—a vision in white. The flowing robe cinched at the waist, her hair twirled up like Cinnabons glued to the side of her head, Paige was my Princess Leia.

"Put on the head!" she screamed. Paige enjoyed giving out the candy almost as much as eating it.

I complied, and she shrieked with delight, dumping the whole bowl of candy corns in my pillowcase.

"That's enough of that," Gregory told her. Our fathers nodded to each other politely. Everyone knew Gregory from the pharmacy.

Chewbacca and Leia up in a tree, K-I-S-S-I-N-G. Since then, I've often wondered whether all along, Princess Leia was just using Han Solo to get to Chewbacca.

Our love has always been forbidden.

"Fine, you want a different word?" I tell present-day Paige. "How about 'kumquat'?"

She thinks about it. "Can we go back to 'Chewbacca'?" she wonders. Paige is entitled to a twenty spot if she can figure out a way to surreptitiously slip the word *kumquat* into her on-air report this evening. Last week she managed to sneak in *carnivorous*. A month ago it was *pinky*.

"I love you," she says with a tender kiss on the cheek, and then she's gone just as quickly as she appeared: off to the tape room, to the edit bay, to the voice-over booth, to check in with the line producer. She has six, no, five minutes to get her segment approved, cut, and loaded for the six o'clock news. On the scrap paper next to me, I memorialize her drive-by affection with a small slash mark, adding it to the column with three others.

I'm Paige's ride home this evening. Just like I was last night, and the night before. I'm here because, yet again, her car, affectionately known as "The Vomit Mobile," was, how do you say, "indisposed." Three months ago it was the alternator, last month the exhaust system, and now, Lordy, it's the dreaded transmission. At this point, we might as well just put Ollie's Auto Shop on retainer.

Paige never should have bought that Matchbox car in the first place. I tried to change her mind; I reminded her about the cool-off period, about buyer's remorse, but she wouldn't listen. There *was no* remorse.

"You sure you're supposed to feel every crack in the road?" I pleaded with her as we circled the block on the test drive.

"Aw yeah, they told me that's how the manufacturer sets the suspension on these sport vehicles, tight, like a stock car," Paige said.

Little did we realize this convertible would also get the same mileage and provide the same storage space as a Formula One.

Despite all the headaches, to this day, Paige has never regretted her decision to buy the two-seater, though the down payment did clean out her life savings and place her fifteen grand in debt. It would be so easy to resent the fact that she didn't listen to me, but I don't. For everything there is to hate about this car, I love what it represents: Paige knew what she wanted and she went for it. I wouldn't have had the guts. She bought a manual transmission without a lick of experience driving stick. She signed the final paperwork and didn't even know how to drive her dream car off the lot. Amazing.

"Fine, if this is the Vomit Mobile, then you're Barfman," she told me on the herky-jerky drive home.

"Guess that makes you Hurl Girl."

Paige is so fearless sometimes.

She earned points that day. She got points for buying the car, points for attempting to drive it, and points for having a sense of humor about what was likely an abysmal mistake. Tonight, it's points (and cash) if she manages to insert a coded message to her lover on live television.

TV anchor Pamela Worth takes her seat at the anchor desk. The newscast starts in three minutes. It's *Wheel . . . of . . . Fortune,* and this is her last commercial break to tease tonight's top story. I'm about to be on TV! I am part of the newsroom backdrop—my silhouette is hard at work on a breaking news story. A thin, translucent scrim separates me from Worth. The inference: *Behind me, Andy "Scoop" Altman is doggedly tracking the people responsible for today's cat-up-a-tree. When he knows more, faithful viewers, so will you.*

The lights flip on, the camera rolls, and I'm frozen. I begin pretend-typing.

"Tonight, breaking news: the Food and Drug Administration pulls a popular hypertension pill off the shelves," Worth announces. "Details at six."

I stare at Worth's profile, and Worth stares uncomfortably at the teleprompter. She's overestimated the length of her script. Her eyes dip to her desk, but the camera stays trained on the bald spot of her scalp as she nervously shuffles a few blue sheets of paper.

You've got four more seconds, Pam. Hurry up! The least you can do is tell viewers the *name* of the drug so they don't take it. The depths local news will go to increase ratings. *A common eating utensil could kill you. Find out which one, at six.*

The screen dips to black. Vanna White is back, flipping me the "B." The blinding lights of the flash camera turn off. Worth unhooks her microphone and earpiece, and casually walks away.

As it turns out, Gregory and I got wind of Pamela Worth's "breaking news" ten hours ago. We received the pharmacywide warning that said Simpson Pharmaceuticals was being forced to recall its hypertension medicine, Betapro, after tests revealed that instead of lowering blood pressure, the key ingredient—beta-blockers—actually increased the risk of heart failure. Blood pressure medication that raises your blood pressure. Unbelievable.

"Are the two of you making nice?" Paige asks, appearing suddenly, clasping a few small videotapes in one hand. She musses up my hair, and then gently pats my playmate's flat-screen monitor.

"Please address him as Mac Daddy," I say of the computer.

Paige introduces herself and then informs both of us that her report—Arnold Schwarzenegger is rumored to be reprising his role in the next *Terminator* movie—was bumped to the last news block thanks to this big Betapro story. Paige's story is now "the kicker"—television-speak for that light entertainment story that TV producers save until the very end of the program to keep viewers viewing. Paige's piece on "poodles in poodle skirts" had to be my favorite.

"Do you mind waiting?" she asks.

Where else would I go? What else would I do?

I tell her of course. It's Thursday, which means pizza and Scrabble. Paige is a Scrabble fiend. Everything is set up and waiting for us at my apartment. The board, the racks, the tiles, the lazy Susan, the wine, and the pad memorializing Paige's record: 82 wins, 54 losses. Her first twenty wins shouldn't count—that was before I realized that she was taking one too many tiles. *Show me in the rules where it says you only get seven letters,* she demanded. *Oh.*

"I love you," she adds sweetly and then runs to get makeup.

Hearing these three precious words, I draw a diagonal line through the four slash marks on my pad, and hot key back to the beautiful diagram-in-progress on Mac Daddy's screen.

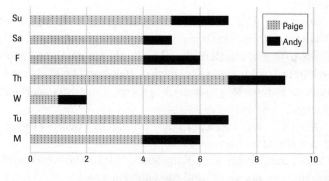

Average Number of ILYs

That's five "I love yous" so far today. Based on historical data and some simple extrapolation, we're on track to hit seven: a typical count despite an atypical Thursday. Most Thursdays, neither of us works, and the ILYs are flowing and plentiful, but today someone got sick at the news station, and Paige agreed to fill in. When you're freelancing, you take what you can.

I'm counting on Mac Daddy's massive left brain to help me figure out which day of the week would be best to pop the question. Before he tells me that, he informs me of an embarrassing truth: Paige averages way more ILYs than I do. Physical meetings, telephone calls, and e-mail, all told, she says it approximately 2.5 times more often than I do.

"Got to get my ILY ratio up," I whisper.

Mac Daddy gives me the silent treatment, his microprocessor always humming, always judging.

The six o'clock newscast launches with the urgency of an apocalypse as Pamela Worth tosses to a reporter in the field, standing outside Simpson Pharmaceuticals. I feel for him, standing there like a jackass. What's he supposed to say? *Thanks, Pam. I'm standing outside Simpson Pharmaceuticals. This is what the building looks like when it's closed. About an hour ago . . . it was open.*

Our anchor needs to lighten up. Nothing a few shadow puppets couldn't fix. *How would Pamela Worth look with bunny ears?* I wonder.

"What's an ILY?" Paige curiously whispers over my shoulder, studying the horizontal lines of the stacked bar chart.

"Yewp," I yip, startled by the visit. My tiny outburst prompts Worth to flub a line on live television. Paige and I clench our teeth in unison. Pamela Worth is such a witch. Paige will likely pay for this later.

"What's what?" I whisper back, frantically covering the screen with a splayed hand.

"Mm-hmm," Paige says skeptically. "Make sure you watch my segment," she demands, and then she runs away.

I study my chart. In Mac Daddy's humble opinion, I should propose on a Wednesday. *Do it on a Wednesday and maximize the surprise.* This makes total sense seeing as Wednesday is generally reserved for Gregory, the other man in Paige's life. Most Wednesdays, Paige and I are lucky if we speak.

With love, romance, and affection at an all-week low, I'll spring the ring. She'll never see it coming.

"YOU'RE quiet," she says as we exit the Oakland Bay Bridge.

"Am I?" I ask her, my eyes fixed on the road.

I prefer Paige in civilian clothes, without all the pancake makeup, the conservative hairstyle, and TV attire. Sitting next to me in low-cut denims and a black tank top, her jet-black hair held in a haphazard updo, bubble-gum-smelling lip gloss, I want to ask her to marry me right now.

"You didn't say anything about my TV segment," she complains.

"What do you mean? I said I loved it, like, three times."

"But what did I say *right before* telling people to catch Arnold in theaters?"

"When you say 'theater,' why do you make it a long 'a'?" I ask her.

"What do you say? *The*ater?" Paige says, hitting the first syllable.

"Yeah, *the*ater, like a normal person. You're not British, you know."

"It's more fun to say the*ater* than *the*ater," she informs me. "Did you or didn't you hear what I said on-air?"

I shrug.

Paige shifts into her broadcasting voice: "*Kumquat may,* nothing's going to stop the original Terminator from telling fans: 'I'll be back.'"

"Bull," I laugh. "You did not."

"Watch it on TiVo. You'll see. Time to pay the piper."

With one hand on the wheel, I reach into my back pocket. But Paige is disappointed to see me pull out my cell phone instead.

"Don't worry, I'm no welsher. I'll pay." I hit number 4 on my speed dial. "Salami, black olives, and fresh *tomahto*?" I confirm.

Paige says "tomahto"; I say "tomayto."

"Hang up, please," she pleads suddenly.

"Three Brothers!" shouts the grumpy man on the other end of the line.

I look to Paige for some direction.

"Hello? Speak!" demands the pizza guy.

Then it hits me: a moment of clarity. I know exactly what she's thinking; I know exactly what she's going to say; and I know exactly how she's going to say it.

Tired of waiting for my pizza order, one of the Three Brothers, presumably the Rude One, hangs up.

"Don't be mad," she insists.

"Don't do it."

"But I have to," she says. "Daddy's all alone. I didn't leave him any dinner. The laundry's piling up."

"And the gutters need cleaning. Firewood that needs chopping. A spice rack that needs alphabetizing," I say.

"Don't be mean."

"No, *you* don't be mean. I thought we had this custody battle all worked out. Gregory gets you Tuesdays, Wednesdays, Fridays, and Saturdays, and I get whatever's left. Now you've got him muscling in on my Thursdays?"

I exit the 101. Paige puts her hand on my lap and starts rubbing my thigh, slowly and seductively. She leans over and kisses my neck. We swerve slightly onto the shoulder.

"Just don't be mad," she whispers.

"And what about Scrabble?"

"I must admit, nothing gets me hotter than a triple-word score," she sighs. " 'Q' me, Andy, oh 'Q' me," she says, biting my earlobe.

I'm going to crash. I take a hard right onto her street, pull over one house short of Gregory's, and turn off the engine. I can see his pudgy silhouette reclining in his ratty olive chair. Paige and I mash faces, grabbing, groping, kissing, tugging, squeezing. We round first base and sprint toward second.

"Don't go in," I huff, my eyes focused on the bay window to his living room. "Come home with me. I'm more fun than he is."

Gregory's silhouette stands. I quickly disengage.

"Sunday . . . I promise," she says, catching her breath and adjusting herself.

I pull the car forward another twenty yards and Paige is home.

"Kiss me," she commands. With one foot already out the door she holds out her cheek.

I present my own cheek and she kisses it.

"No, that's me kissing you." She laughs, longing for affection. "Kiss your girlfriend."

She holds out her cheek again and I rub my cheek up against hers Eskimo-style. Paige laughs a second time.

"I love you, Andy," she says, closing the car door.

I nod, but say nothing. Fifteen paces later, I'm alone.

Seven. Seven ILYs. Seven "I love yous," just like Mac Daddy predicted, and yet his chart is way off: she says it, but I love her more.

CHAPTER 4

Deflected

THE story behind Day's Pharmacy is the story of Ringer's Lactate. Gregory Day isn't the type to reminisce so what I know about this place and his life I've largely pieced together from Paige and Sid.

In the early 1950s, Gregory is drafted into the Korean War. Six months later, his entire platoon is airlifted into the heart of enemy combat, and his troop is given an unenviable task: stall—stall the North Korean Army until American reinforcements arrive. But the U.S. Army severely miscalculates how long and how many men it will take to fend off the enemy. Gregory and the men of C Company, Twenty-first Regiment, Twenty-fourth Infantry Division are greatly outnumbered. Gregory's battalion is decimated, but Gregory is among the few survivors, sustaining severe shrapnel wounds to his left leg. He is losing a lot of blood. Airmen helicopter him to the nearest M.A.S.H. unit, where he receives one of the very first applications of a new miracle drug called Ringer's Lactate, now a common electrolyte fluid used to resuscitate the wounded. Gregory receives a Purple Heart and a Bronze Star. Ringer's saves his life.

Following an honorable discharge, inspired by the power of medicine, Gregory returns to northern California to attend college. The army pays for the first three years until he drops out in 1955 to play ball for a now-defunct minor league baseball team. The San Francisco Seals are willing to overlook Gregory's slight limp because he's a true slugger. During the third day of spring training, Gregory is hit—literally—with a stroke of bad luck when a wild pitch smacks him square in the chest, cracking three ribs. He sits the season out.

Six months later, the San Francisco Seals relocate and become the Phoenix Seals, but Gregory isn't invited to join them. His career is over before it begins. A medical degree seems too far off and too much work, so instead, he chooses pharmacology. In those days, you could get a pharmacy degree straight out of high school in just three years. Pharmacy school takes twice as long today.

In 1958, Gregory moves back to his hometown of Crockett to work at the only pharmacy in town—Ace's, owned by one of Crockett's most famous residents, Barnaby Rothschild. No one seems to know why Barnaby called it Ace's. (I'd heard Ace was his poker name, but that's probably folklore.) Barnaby, come his late seventies, decides he's tired of running a pharmacy and agrees to sell the business and transfer the long-term lease to Gregory and his new bride, Lydia—Gregory's high school sweetheart. But there's a catch: Barnaby isn't ready to retire, so Gregory must keep Barnaby on part-time. For ten long years, the Days are held hostage to a dying man and his endless demands.

Barnaby Rothschild lives to see man step foot on the moon, but only by a few hours. He dies the next morning. With Barnaby out of the way, Lydia finally convinces her husband to change the store's name. It costs them $500 to purchase the defective neon sign out front. A picture screwed into the wall near the front register still shows six brawny men with a crane struggling to mount the cherry red, four-hundred-pound, fifteen-foot sign on the side of the building. It was only after they got it up there, and flipped the switch, that anyone noticed the punctuation error—it was missing that crucial apostrophe. That's when "Day's Pharmacy" became "Days Pharmacy."

The early 1970s brings the national pharmacy chains. To stay competitive, Lydia persuades Gregory to borrow some money from her parents and rent the empty barbershop space next door. They knock down the dividing wall, nearly doubling the pharmacy space. Gregory and Lydia add hundreds of new products, extend the pharmacy workbench, build out a lunch counter, install a soda fountain, and lay down that magnificent honeycomb tile floor.

Gregory, so proud, and Lydia, so pregnant, with her second child, Paige, invite the entire town to the ribbon-cutting ceremony.

There are plenty of pictures of the celebration on the wall. One of the photos shows Paige's sister, Lara, not even two years old, resting her head on Lydia's belly. There is another picture where—if you squint—you can make my parents out in the crowd. (My mother tells me that it is entirely possible that I am conceived later that evening.) *Gross.* It is at the pharmacy opening that Crockett's townsfolk crown Gregory Day "The Mayor of Pomona Street," a title he embraces to this day, perhaps a little too much. Soon thereafter, the town council appoints Gregory grand marshal of the Crockett Memorial Day Parade, a responsibility that never interested his buddy Sid.

For the next twenty-five years, Gregory handles the prescriptions and Lydia does the books. The hours are long. Neither Paige nor her older sister, Lara, are born in the pharmacy, but Lydia's water breaks here both times, nearly two years apart to the day. Exactly where, I don't know, and I've repeatedly asked Paige not to tell me (even though she's dying to). Paige and Lara have always worked here. First as child labor and then over many a summer break. Paige never had much interest in more than part-time work, but Lara worked here full-time while going to college at night, and then again when she was studying to get her CPA. The sign out front should probably have read "Days' Pharmacy."

Unlike most Bay Area towns, Crockett's population has only grown modestly in the last one hundred years. Gregory still handles the prescription needs for just about everyone here, the vast majority of them senior citizens of Italian and Portuguese descent who at one time or another were employed by C & H Sugar.

In the nine and a half months I've worked here, Gregory has always been the first person to arrive at the pharmacy and the last to leave. Although he is hardly the picture of health, best I can tell, he's never missed a day of work. Paige tells me that Gregory even came to work after Lydia's funeral. *Being here makes him feel closer to Mom,* she tells me.

Paige's mother, Lydia, died before I moved back to Crockett. I really only have one memory of her. I was twelve, and a future felon by the name of Anthony "Bunky" Bianco dared me to steal some Hubba Bubba watermelon-flavored bubble gum. I must have walked back and forth past that candy rack twenty times before stuffing two packs in my Levi's jeans and booking. "Excuse me," Lydia shouted politely as I bolted out the front door with bulges in my front pocket. If she wasn't sure what happened, she definitely figured it out moments later when Bunky high-fived me. We ran like hell. I didn't return to Day's Pharmacy for years after that, even if that meant forgoing those precious Red Rocket candy rings and taking my chances at the parade. To this day, those two packs of gum have been the only two things I ever shoplifted in my life—a childhood memory that still sickens me.

I often wonder how happy Lydia would have been to learn that her daughter ended up with a hoodlum. I can only hope she would've been forgiving.

It's not stealing now when I snatch a candy bar or pack of gum off the rack. Like Belinda and her magazines, we consider it more like back pay for all the uncompensated overtime Gregory expects from us. The truth is that us stealing chocolate and gossip rags is the least of Gregory's problems. Gregory has dozens of customers who have gone years without settling enormous pharmacy tabs. Around here, "tab" is code for "free." Every once in a while Gregory says or does something that suggests he's ready to collect, but he never follows through. What's most important to him is that his customers get the medical attention they need, when they need it.

"No need to do the math. Our customers will never cut a pill in half"—that's the Day's Pharmacy credo.

EVERYTHING I find dreary and dilapidated about this place, Paige finds charming and quaint. She uses words like *authentic* and *warm* to characterize the faux wood paneling on the pharmacy counter. *Retro* is how she describes the now-unused marble-top lunch counter and the red vinyl chrome barstools where Lydia used to serve fountain drinks and hand-dipped milkshakes. The number 4 key on the cast iron cash register sticks, *but we can't get rid of that, it's a collector's item,* she insists. Mixed among the modern plastic pill containers are empty antique glass bottles, oddly shaped, some with corks and some without. In all the time that I've worked here, not a single customer has ever asked me to unlock the small glass display case filled with knock-off Montblanc fountain pens and dusty magnifying glasses.

To me, this place is a death trap: a dying town with a dying generation of clients, and Gregory's glorified but dying legacy. If not for Paige, I would have managed a Houdini escape long ago.

OUR delivery guy, Manny Milken, is thirty minutes late and Gregory is annoyed, which is good news for me—anything to deflect attention from our latest argument, somewhere on the order of a magnitude 4.0. (Gregory was mad because I forgot to slap a red "Do not take this medication with antacids" label on one of our orders. I don't see the big deal—all of our prescriptions come with an instruction booklet. But Gregory thinks no one reads those. He's probably right. I never do.)

Manny has an excuse for everything. Today it's FedEx's fault.

"Sorry, Mr. Day, I was, like, 'Where are these guys?' and when they showed up, trust me, it wasn't pretty. We were close to coming to blows. But it's a blessing in the skies seeing as it gave me time to pick this other package up for you," he says, holding up a shirt box wrapped in brown paper and twine.

Manny Milken isn't the sharpest knife in the drawer. He's more like a spoon, or possibly a spork. I suspect he sustained too many blows to the head playing high school football. Last week, he told me that my point was "mute." At our five-year high school reunion, he asked a roomful of alums what they thought of his "chick" jeans. Manny wouldn't know chic if it smacked him upside the head. I told him white dungarees aren't appropriate after Labor Day, but that he still looked "fetching." Manny told me to shut up, then went home and "prolly" looked up *fetching* in the dictionary.

I sign for Gregory's packages. The box secured with twine has neither postage nor a sender's return address, just Gregory's name.

"Gimme," Gregory says about as nice as you can say that.

I reach over the counter and he quickly snaps the box from me with a shaky hand.

"Emmanuel, pull your truck around back. Andrew will help you unload."

I meet Manny in the back alley. It takes him ten minutes to back up ten feet. He can't risk scratching his baby—our love for cars may be the only thing we have in common. Right after we graduated from high school, Manny bought, repaired, and re-painted a vintage 1965 Superior Cadillac ambulance and launched his own delivery service. Gregory gave him his first break. Soon, another independent pharmacy in Hercules signed on, along with a few grocers and a handful of restaurants that wanted to do take-out. It's been nearly eleven years now, and to his credit, Manny's carved out a decent little business for himself. Over the years, Gregory's made plenty of cutbacks, but he'll never drop our pre-scription delivery service. Partly out of loyalty to Manny and partly because Gregory thinks that it's the little things that distin-guish his independent pharmacy from the evil corporate chains.

Emblazoned across the side of Manny's ambulance and em-broidered on every white cotton short-sleeved shirt he owns is that lame slogan: "Milken Deliveries: Delivering More Than Milk-In California." He thought that up all by himself. Just ask him.

If he backs his car up any slower, Gregory will have my head.

Let's go, let's go, I wave my hands.

Since his years as high school lead tackle Manny has let him-self go. He now sports one of the biggest potbellies I've ever seen on a thirty-year-old. These days, Manny must be pushing 280.

He pops the trunk and taps on the boxes with his clipboard. I begin unloading the toiletries and prescription meds. Manny, of course, supervises.

"The original version of *The Haunting* was on Turner Classics last night," he says, scribbling something down—I can only as-sume smiley faces or basic geometric shapes. "Man, is that movie terrifying. Paige would have loved it."

Paige does love her horror flicks.

"I was going to tell her to watch it, but I didn't have her number handy," Manny explains.

Gotcha. Why don't I hustle those digits right up for you?

"Just tell her that we need to talk."

"I'm writing that down," I say, pretending to record the urgent message in thin air.

Manny Milken has spent the better part of his life pining away for Paige. It's Manny's fault that Paige and I didn't get together years ago.

Back in the early '80s, Paige and I went from *Star Wars* to star-crossed, seeing very little of each other in the decade that followed that fateful Halloween. It wasn't until ninth grade that we actually became true-blue friends: Paige being "Day," and me being "Altman," we shared homeroom together, but it was Madame Kuepper's French class where things really came together.

Madame Hedwig Kuepper still teaches at Willow High, a fireplug of a woman from Normandy, France, no taller than Dr. Ruth, with streaked blond hair tightly pulled back and pasted to her head like a sculpture.

I remember the first day of class. Paige was sitting right there behind me. It was first period. I was half asleep. Madame Kuepper turned to write something on the chalkboard, and I leaned back over Paige's desk and silently let out a huge yawn. At the height of my stretch, Paige playfully poked me in both armpits. It was petrifying, really. I blurted out the only sound one *can* make when he's been unceremoniously stabbed in both underarms during high school French.

From that day forward, Madame Kuepper considered me *"très bizarre."*

Paige sat directly behind me during all four years of high school French, and over time, we developed a system of signals to help each other with vocabulary. For example, when Paige mistakenly used the masculine form of a feminine noun, I might start massaging my neck and biceps. (I'm sure these idiosyncrasies played right into Madame Kuepper's impression of me.) By sitting behind me, it was easier for Paige to tip me off if I made a mistake.

One swift kick to my chair and I knew: *Mais oui, naturellement, j'aime la . . . LE chat noir.*

By sophomore year, I still hadn't worked up the courage to ask Paige on a date; somehow I'd convinced myself that I'd only be ready to pop that question when I could order dinner for her in fluent French. But then the Crockett Indians were playing the Piedmont Highlanders. It was the last high school football scrimmage of the season, and out of the blue, Paige wondered if I'd like to accompany her to the game.

On paper, it had all the markings of a legitimate date—just the two of us (and the rest of the student body) . . . at night—but then Paige suggested we meet there instead of me picking her up, and when I arrived at the game, there were "others," among them Paige's older sister, Lara, and Lara's best friend, Tyler Rich, both seniors.

It was five minutes into the first quarter of the game—Paige and I locked in an intense conversation over whether the first word or words in the Peter Gabriel song "Big Time" was "higher," "hi there," or "hey la"—when it hit me. The football. Or at least that's what I'm told.

I would learn later that while it was the Piedmont Highlanders' star quarterback who was responsible for launching the pigskin, it was *our* defensive linebacker, Emmanuel Milken, who, in attempting to block the shot, tipped the ball slightly upward, causing the torpedo to hit me smack-dab in the right temple. What happened next happened quickly. Through various witness accounts, computer simulations, and expert testimony, I believe the magic bullet then ricocheted off my noggin, smacked Paige square in the forehead, knocking her off her bench and across two rows of bleachers, and then returned off Paige's face to pop me in the nose before coming to rest.

The crowd gasped. The game stopped. It all happened so fast, I think Paige thought I head-butted her midsentence.

"You okay?" I managed to blurt out before Lara and Tyler jumped on Paige, all Secret Service–like.

Paige said nothing. We were both seeing stars. Lara and Tyler helped Paige to her feet.

"Let me help . . . ," I said, stumbling to rise.

"You've done enough!" Lara insisted.

Through tunnel vision, I can still see Paige's protectors dragging her away toward the on-site nurse, Paige crying, "Wait, wait, wait. Hold up one sec. I'm fine. I think Andy's the one who's hurt."

"I'll be no problem," I screamed back, one hand cupping my bloody nose, the other rubbing the side of my head.

Paige and Tyler were tight after that, though she rarely mentioned him in French class. They dated off and on for the rest of high school and possibly beyond. It would take me ten years before I'd get a second date with her. Had Manny just kept his right meat hook to himself, everything would have been so different.

"Know what these are?" Manny says, reaching inside his delivery truck and dragging a medium-sized box closer with his fingertips.

My eyes widen. The orange and light blue lettering on the box is a town trademark. The red ribbon unmistakable. Memorial Day is only two weeks away. Crockett's Red Rockets are back, baby!

"I've got Gregory's supply right here. Can I interest you in a few freebies?" he says, tapping the contraband.

"No way," I lie. "Those are for the children."

"What-ever. You're such a wuss. I got my own stash anyways. One box always manages to fall off the truck, if you catch my drift."

"Nice," I tell him. "So you literally steal candy from babies."

"You should shut your piehole. I'm sorry I said anything to begin with."

Once I've moved all the supplies, drugs, and candy inside, no thanks to Manny, I take my California-sanctioned fifteen-minute break.

The storeroom is windowless and I nearly break my neck tripping over Gregory's boxes. The overhead fluorescents in here flicker uncontrollably, so I flip them off, pop on the computer monitor, and begin mocking up a simple diagram of what I plan to give Paige for her birthday. I draw the quadrilaterals. The one on the left is exactly five inches tall at its highest elevation.

I can hear Gregory in the next room talking to a customer about cough syrup. *The generic is the exact same thing,* I lip-synch along with him. I know this monologue by heart. *If you want to pay twice as much for the brand name, be my guest, but they both contain the SAME dosage of dextromethorphan.* Gregory gets too much pleasure out of saying words like *dextromethorphan, pantoprazole,* and *fluvastatin.* Actually, who *doesn't* like saying *fluvastatin.*

Paige is feeling tremendous anxiety about turning thirty later this month. She's made it abundantly clear that she cannot be held responsible for what happens the next time someone asks her if she's excited about turning "The Big Three-Oh."

I complete the third and smallest quadrilateral and inspect my work. Paige is going to love this one.

Homemade gifts have gone over well in the past. Paige still uses that custom makeup case I built her for Valentine's Day. The makeup applicator worked just fine up until the accident. (Three words: temporary eye patch.) Then there was the automated plant watering system. It took me three freaking weeks to snake those tiny hoses through the walls of Gregory's living room, affix the timers and sprinklers, and install the elaborate irrigation system. Gregory was such a sourpuss about the whole thing, but Paige was quick to call the project a "moderate success." Most of her plants were dying, anyway. Plus who paid the rental cost of the wet/dry vac? Me.

It's going to take a few days to track down the supplies I need to build a proper prototype of my gift in time for Paige's birthday. Meantime, Sid and I have some other collaborative projects to attend to.

The door to the storeroom wildly swings open. White light pours in like a portal to the afterlife. I fumble to find and eventually hit the on-off switch on the computer monitor. It's hard to know how much Gregory's seen.

"Altman! What are you doing in here? Are you disturbed?" he asks, clearing his throat and shaking his head, dumbfounded by my oddness. "Why are you sitting in the dark?"

"I'm not" is all I can think to respond.

"You're not sitting in the pitch-dark?"

"I wasn't. At that exact moment I just finished catching up on some Medicare stuff, shut the computer, and you walked in."

Neither of us believes me. We stare at each other. *Hey, quick question: Could I have your daughter's hand in marriage?*

"What?" we both ask at the same time.

"Your lips were just moving, but you weren't saying anything," he says.

"Sorry."

"We've got a line of customers and you're in here doing who-knows-what. I need you back on the floor," he barks. "I'm going to be here late enough as is."

CHAPTER 5

Reversing the Polarity

THE deal: I supply the car. Sid supplies the vacuum cleaner.

The car: My car—"Hulk." A swamp green 1995 Oldsmobile Series II Cutlass Supreme coupe complete with worn pleather bucket seats, one functioning fog light, multiple dings, dual air-bags, and a 3.1 liter 3100 V6 engine. This beauty can go zero to sixty in about twenty-eight seconds—roughly twenty-five seconds longer than it takes a Ferrari. The 1995 Cutlass Supreme is among the least stolen cars in the country.

The vacuum: Sid's vacuum. A red and chrome 1952 Eureka Attach-O-Matic swivel-top canister unit. Most of the original clip-on tools for this flying saucer went missing decades ago, but Sid's garage is a treasure trove—a destination hot spot at the annual Crockett townwide yard sale—and he managed to dig up the original flex hose and upholstery nozzle, its ragged brush hanging by a thread.

This is what Sid's thinking:

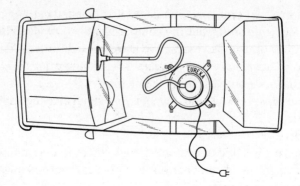

"Flat screwdriver!" Sid demands, holding out a shaky hand.

He's just about managed to pry off the vacuum cleaner's chrome top.

"Hammer," he says with a surgeon's tone.

A bachelor's degree in electrical engineering plus four decades of building naval ships, and the man's literally bent over a vacuum cleaner in his driveway smashing it to bits with a hammer.

"Why don't I take that," I offer, grabbing the hammer's handle in the upswing. "You're sure Cookie's cool with us using this?"

"I just bought her a new one from Target, like, five years ago. She thinks I threw this hunk-a-junk out decades back."

I loosen the lid with my bare hands; fifty years of coagulated gook comes undone.

"Nice job, small fry," he says.

"Small fry" is Sid's nod to my hero, Linden Fry, the inventor of the Bellowing Big Mouth Bass. At the turn of the twenty-first century, it wasn't flying cars or nanotechnology that captivated the country's fascination, but a reanimated trophy fish that could sing and dance the "La Bamba." The Patent Office has this rule about inventions being "useful," and Linden Fry's bellowing bass suggested the bar is pretty low, but the potential rewards, infinite.

One of Fry's millions of singing trophy fish graces the wall of the pharmacy. Belinda started calling him "Corey"—as in the singer Corey Hart–the-one-hit-wonder—after she heard the big mouth bass belt out "I Wear My Sunglasses at Night." Gregory happens to be pretty fond of that fish. That's because Lydia gave it to him for Christmas years ago after seeing it on *The Tonight Show*. When Lydia was alive and the two of them were healthy enough, Paige says her parents loved to fish together—neighboring Boone offers some decent fly-fishing. If Gregory's in the right mood, nothing makes him happier than seeing Corey swing his head forward, wag his tail, and perform Johnny Cash's "I Walk the Line."

"There it is," Sid whispers, squinting into the dusty guts of the vacuum like he's spotted pirate booty. "Electric current powers *that fan* right there and the blades force air and debris toward the exhaust port into the vacuum bag."

"Uh-huh," I say, pretending to understand.

"We need to change the direction of the fan so it blows the air *out* the *intake* pipe," he explains.

"So we're reversing the polarity," I conclude.

"Come again?"

"Reversing the polarity: making something negative positive," I explain.

Sid impatiently waits for me to recant.

"Yeah, I'd be making that up."

"Just unscrew that fan unit and flip it 180 degrees. We need to lower the level of air pressure outside the fan," Sid says.

I'm more confused than ever and he knows it.

"We need the fan to *blow*, not *suck*," he says simply enough.

Sid goes inside the garage to find an extension cord. Meanwhile I jury-rig the vacuum to his specifications by screwing in the fan the other way around and reattaching the swivel top. With one heave-ho, I lift and mount it on top of my car. As I duct tape the metal pod to the center of the car roof, I ignore the little voice inside my head telling me this is a terrible mistake. Then I run the flex hose along the roof, and I duct tape the upholstery nozzle so it hovers just above the windshield.

Inside the garage a rack of hubcaps crashes to the floor.

"Oopsy-daisy," Sid chuckles as the last disk takes forever to settle on the concrete floor.

I ask if him if he's okay; he's fine.

"Small fry, I'm thinking this one's PMP-worthy," Sid yells from inside the garage.

"Exactamundo," I scream back.

Gone are the days when an inventor needs tens of thousands of dollars and a deep familiarity with arcane law to patent an idea. A few years back the Patent Office came up with an invention of its own: the Provisional Patent, or as Sid and I call it, the "Poor Man's Patent" or "PMP." Nowadays, if you've got an idea, all you need is three hours to fill out a simple three-page application plus about three hundred bucks for the filing fee. A PMP buys you exactly one year to experiment with the idea, make and market it, and decide whether it's worth patenting for real. The best part about a PMP is it entitles you to start using two of the most powerful words in the English language: "Patent Pending."

I remember our first PMP fondly. It was September. Sid designed a ladder stabilized on three sides like a camera tripod. Then in November it was my dog umbrella. In March: side-access Velcro sneakers. Both of our names appear on every application; it's just a matter of which inventor is the headliner. Neither of us is made of money, so nothing gets filed unless we're in total agreement. For example, I couldn't convince Sid to PMP "Urine Bed." *Who needs the bathroom in the middle of the night?* I pitched him. *When you're in bed . . . "Urine Bed."* Sid stopped me right there. We now have a standing rule: all bladder-control devices are off-limits.

I tear off a piece of duct tape with my teeth. Just then the Vomit Mobile pulls into Gregory's driveway across the street. This clown car has been out of the shop for all of seventeen hours. The driver's side door slowly swings open and a bleary-eyed beaut climbs out. She's just finished a killer shift—4:00 A.M. to 12:00 P.M. Tack on the forty-five-minute commute each way plus a quick workout and Paige is toast by 2:00 P.M. Ready to slink back into bed, Paige slowly throws a gym bag over one shoulder and a garment bag over the other.

"Yoo-hoo!" I scream. "Come here!"

With her back to me she weighs her options: *Maybe I can pre-*

tend I didn't hear him. I yell over to her again. Paige does an about-face and trudges across the street like a pack mule. Sid appears from the garage dragging one end of an infinitely long, thick yellow extension cord. I plant a kiss on her cheek.

"Why aren't you at work?" she asks, doing her best not to sound too judgmental.

"Yeah, I decided to take the day off. Stanley from Walgreens filled in."

Stanley and I dropped out of pharmacy school a week apart. We're both about three hundred practitioner hours away from becoming fully certified pharmacy technicians.

"Sid and I really need to nail down this invention, and today worked best for Sid, isn't that right?" I prod him.

He doesn't react.

"Sid's retired," she reminds me. "Every day works best for him."

"You'd be surprised how busy retirement gets," he chimes in, finally.

"So what do you think?" I ask her, giving the device strapped to the roof of my car an exaggerated "ta-dah."

"My dad could *really* use your help at the pharmacy, Andy," Paige replies. "And Stanley is . . ."

"Stinky?" I suggest.

Stanley's not big on showers.

"Stanley makes him uncomfortable," she says. "Let's leave it at that."

Stanley also has this habit of breaking into a human beatbox machine every time he counts out pills.

"He's fine," I assure her. "Five bucks says your dad doesn't even notice he's not me."

"You're wrong," she insists. "He *needs* you, Andy. You *get* him. Stanley doesn't. Daddy likes having you around."

Sid nonverbally seconds that.

Maybe there was a time when Gregory liked having me around, but not anymore. That ended the moment he learned I was dating his daughter. No one has ever been good enough for Paige. In

French class, Paige used to regale me with stories about how much her father detested the guys she dated. I think that's part of the reason it took me years before I asked her on that second date. Baseball players, budding actors, and future business leaders of America, to Gregory, they were losers, lemons, and future failures. Even that All-American good-looks-Porsche-driving-girlfriend-stealing Tyler Rich didn't cut it.

"What?" Paige asks me.

"What?" I ask her.

"What?" Sid asks us.

"You're looking at me funny," she says.

"I'm thinking. This is my thinking face," I explain.

"Is it my sweats?" Paige is wearing a velour powder blue running suit. "If you hate them, just say so. I promise I won't be mad," she swears.

This is the oldest trick in the book and I'm not falling for it.

"And this is not a trick," she assures me. "So you won't be falling for anything."

Saying that it's not a trick is also part of the trick.

Sid shakes his head begging me not to do it.

"I really wasn't thinking about them; I was thinking about something else and they happen to be in the space where I was thinking. But if you're asking me my opinion, then it's a no, they're not my *favorite*."

I hate them. I was just thinking that I hate them.

Sid flips his head back and starts whispering *why* to the sky.

"But they're just workout clothes and they're so J-Lo!"

No one speaks.

"Fine. How much?" she asks.

"Ten dollars," I offer quickly.

Sid raises an eyebrow.

"Ten? Are you disturbed? These cost me thirty. Twenty," she counters.

"Fifteen," I say, fishing the bills from my pocket.

While Paige deliberates over my offer, I dangle a Hamilton with one hand and a Lincoln with the other.

Once in a while I buy Paige's clothes. Not to wear them but to burn them. Paige has a standing offer to do the same with mine but, like our points system, has yet to exercise the option. There are rules, of course. Paige has to initiate the ritual and I have to be certain that she's "in the mood." Previous purchases have included short shorts, sandals, and last month, a lovely pink mini-T with diamond sequins. I used it as a car rag and scratched my hood. Karma, she insists.

Paige snaps up the two bills.

"Fine," she says flatly, stuffing the cash into her gym bag.

"Good!" I spit back.

We hate to argue, but for some peculiar reason we love to pretend.

"Fine!"

Sid is completely perplexed.

"Thanks," I tell her. "You get points."

"I do?" she says, blushing.

Paige offers to change out of my new clothes here, but I tell her it can wait.

"We'll destroy them Thursday," I suggest.

Paige turns to leave and I grab her around the waist with both hands.

"Stay! *We need you.* It'll take three minutes. All you have to do is sit here. Promise," I say, theatrically holding open the driver's-side door for her.

Paige indulges me, and I squat down beside her.

"What is this contraption?" she asks, rubbing her eyes.

Contraption sounds like *harebrained scheme,* but I let it slide.

"This is Stage One of Operation Jet Stream," I tell her. "You'll need to use your imagination a little. On the roof above you is a rudimentary prototype of our newest brainchild—the bladeless windshield wiper."

"I don't get it," Paige says.

She's uttered the four most devastating words to an inventor's ears.

"It's no longer a vacuum cleaner," I explain quickly. "We've reversed the polar . . . We've altered the direction of the fan. Here's what will happen: You'll turn on the car. Then Sid will turn on the hose and spray water onto the windshield, simulating rain."

Sid gives Paige a shy smile and waves hello. He's in khaki shorts, a white V-neck T-shirt, his homburg hat, black dress socks, and black leather sandals. Paige waves hello back. Eyeballing the height he's holding his hose, I tell him to lower the nozzle a couple of inches; that's all I need, some blind guy shooting water directly into an electrical appliance. Sid complies.

"After the water starts flowing, I'll turn on the-appliance-formerly-known-as-a-vacuum and tiny jet streams of air will shoot out of this upholstery nozzle, in turn pushing the water off the windshield. What I'm looking for from you is a sense of whether the air jets properly disperse the simulated rain. This sort of trial run is what's known in my profession as 'reducing the invention to practice.'"

"Mm-hmm," she says with an abundance of skepticism.

"Our system could make the conventional windshield wiper obsolete!" I scream, realizing I need to take my enthusiasm down a notch. "All I'm saying is this could be big. We really may be on to something."

Keep using possessive plural pronouns like "we," "us," and "our," I remind myself. *Make sure Paige feels a sense of ownership.*

I reach across her, key the ignition, kiss her on the mouth, and then scream to Sid, "Initiate the water!"

Sid loosens the nozzle on the hose and adjusts the spray stream so it hits the windshield just below the vacuum upholstery nozzle.

I shut the car door and steady the black flex hose with my elbow.

"Behold, the first bladeless windshield wipers!" I yell.

Then I flip the switch on the vacuum.

The vacuum motor slowly revs after being inert for so many years and I instantly smell smoke. The machine is clearing its throat. The vacuum coughs three times and out floats black gunk from 1952. My gag reflex kicks in. *Do not vomit.* As I reach over to turn off the motor, it suddenly finds a comfortable place in the twenty-first century and begins purring.

With things under control, I cautiously lean over to see whether air is blowing out of the vacuum and onto the windshield. Paige catches my attention and begins frantically waving her pointer finger back and forth across her neck. The "kill signal"—a familiar hand gesture to the seasoned television broadcaster. But does her pantomime refer to the vacuum or me?

Two things happen very quickly: I hear the sound of metal crushing metal and then everything goes black.

I'm on the ground. In a blind stupor, I hear the sound of duct tape coming undone; then the sound of what can only be a heavy metal vacuum cleaner tumbling off the roof of a car. The Eureka Attach-O-Matic crashes down and in its wake takes out my passenger-side mirror and my left ankle. *Am I wetting myself?* No, Sid hasn't let go of the hose and he's kneeling over me fumbling to find the off switch on the vacuum cleaner. Finding and flipping it, the contraption slowly winds down.

"What the—?" I say standing up, wiping hairballs and black dust from my eyes, nose, mouth, and ears. I'm a human ashtray.

"We should have emptied the vacuum bag before starting," Sid concludes contemplatively. "It took a few seconds, but I believe the entire contents inside the vacuum bag hit you in the face."

I spit. I cough. I pick mystery crud from my tongue.

Paige gets out of the car.

"It was terrifying and thrilling all at once," Paige says, wiping tears of laughter from her eyes. "Sweetie, are you okay?"

"No, I'm grotesque! Don't look at me," I say, dusting myself off.

"Should I call Poison Control?" Paige jokes.

"I wonder if you've released some sort of airborne virus," Sid speculates.

"Yeah, and I'm the host," I say, rubbing my bruised ankle.

"And . . . scene," Paige says with director's authority. "I'm off to bed."

Paige goes to kiss me, but unable to find a safe place to plant one, pats me on the butt like a football chum.

"Give us one week!" I yell to her as she crosses the street. "One week!"

Once she reaches her door, she looks back, and throws us both a kiss.

"She'll be conked out for a good two or three hours," I whisper out the corner of my mouth.

"Well, we're running late," Sid says, tapping his Timex. "You can take a quick shower here but then we *have to go*. My guy leaves at four."

CHAPTER 6

The Blind Leading the Blind

SID and I glide over the Al Zampa Memorial Bridge from Crockett toward Vallejo.

"Twenty-five thousand tons of steel," he marvels.

From the moment I stuck the key in the ignition, Sid's been issuing moving violations.

"No radio," he told me as I reached for the knob. "No speeding," he said as we pulled out of the driveway. "No sudden turns," "no abrupt stops," and in general, "no horseplay of any kind." We're driving to the nearby ferry because long drives make Sid carsick, unless he drives, which isn't about to happen anytime soon. Cookie took away his license fifteen years ago after he inadvertently sideswiped a gasoline pump at Ollie's Auto Shop. An ophthalmologist visit later, Sid was diagnosed with glaucoma.

From the passenger seat, Sid bobs back and forth, window to windshield, inspecting every angle of the bridge with the wonderment of a child. Bridges are a big deal in Crockett.

In Carquinez Middle School, one of the first things they teach you is the history behind the Carquinez Strait Bridge. At the ribbon-cutting ceremony in 1927, the Carquinez became the longest suspension bridge in the world, serving as the final link in the Pacific Coast Highway connecting Canada to Mexico.

But that's where the fairy tale ended. California then erected a second Carquinez bridge in 1958 to alleviate the traffic congestion from the first bridge and the new off-ramps ended up covering huge swaths of Crockett. Then the first Carquinez bridge started falling apart a decade ago, and they began building a *third* bridge, this one called the Al Zampa Memorial, in honor of the well-known iron worker Alfred Zampa, who miraculously survived a fall off the Golden Gate Bridge after slipping on a wet girder, flipping backward three times, and landing in a safety net, breaking four vertebrae. At the opening of the Al Zampa Memorial, the governor promised us that the "Golden Gate Bridge's Little Sister" would deliver tourism and prosperity to Crockett, but that never happened. Instead of bringing people here, this sleek third bridge now helps them bypass it.

About then, I, too, took that bridge, right out of Crockett to San Francisco. After enduring too many mind-bending years of traffic jams, jackhammering, and pile driving, I managed to get off the waiting list and into pharmacy school. It only got worse for Crockett after I left. The final version of the Al Zampa ended up covering even more of our tiny town. "Sugar City" unofficially became "Shadow City," the population leveled off, construction stopped, and the local housing market froze.

I roll down the window to pay that ungodly expensive Al Zampa toll and hear what sounds like a deadly car accident minus the screeching skid. Our peaceful reprieve from decades of construction ended two months ago when demolitionists arrived to begin dismantling the original Carquinez bridge.

Smash! goes another metal girder as it hits the bottom of the metal bin on the flatbed boat.

Sid doesn't share my resentment. He doesn't see the shadows or hear the destruction. As the Zampa shrinks in my rearview mirror, he twists up in his seat belt to get a final look.

"The concrete towers, shaft foundations, aerodynamic steel deck." Sid is talking to himself. "Truly awesome."

Ten minutes later, Sid and I are boarding the Vallejo Ferry. The fact that I'm paying and he's getting a senior citizen discount still doesn't prevent Sid from complaining about the expense. But this is chump change compared to what I'm about to spend.

The ferry shoves off, and Sid and I take to the top deck, where we're told the ride is much smoother. Standing at the railing, shoulder to shoulder, Sid smells pretty good. Irish clean. Or maybe that's me. Following Operation Jet Stream, it took three shampoo rinses to get the vacuum soot out of my hair. Sid has lent me one of his pink polo shirts, which is two sizes too small, and I look ridiculous; I spent the entire car ride here playing peek-aboo with my navel. This gut was a gift to myself six months ago for my twenty-ninth birthday.

Sid is dressed to impress. A trip to the city is a special occasion. He's got on yellow polyester pants, brown leather slip-on dress shoes, a black-and-white-checkered short-sleeved button-down, and a blinding white linen newsboy cap.

We need to discuss important, pressing issues, but all Sid wants to talk about is the weather and the view.

"One-tenth of one percent," he says, reminding me that of the 6.7 billion people on this planet, only one-tenth of one percent get the "privilege" of living in the Bay Area. Bay Area natives are prone to brag about things they have no control over, like its scenery and climate.

I go to speak but he shushes me again.

"Just soak it in," he pleads.

The San Francisco skyline is spectacular.

"Look where we live"—that's what Paige would gush if she were here right now. Television has taken her to markets all over the country, but like Sid, to Paige, nothing compares to the beauty of the Bay.

Halfway there, the temperature drops fifteen to twenty degrees, and the ferry itself vanishes as we float on thin air. The warm East

Bay temperatures are mixing with the cold Pacific Ocean, creating the city's trademark midafternoon fog.

"You need a story," Sid instructs me, frustrated by the low-hanging clouds. "My only goddaughter deserves a *legitimate* engagement story."

"I know," I say with a hint of indignation.

A quiet moment passes.

"I'm not an idiot, you know," I tell him.

"Of course you're not. You're a resourceful, creative chap. So what's your plan?" he asks.

There is nothing casual about Sid's question. This is the guy who invented the big, showy, romantic engagement story nearly sixty years ago.

Sid's story is the stuff of legends.

Sidney Brewster and Clarice "Cookie" Schwartz's first date was blind and chaperoned. The two teens lived three city blocks apart and went to the same high school in Brooklyn, but had their mothers not played canasta together, different blocks may well have been different coasts in Flatbush.

Their second date was the Lincoln High School prom.

Three days later, Sid's draft number came up. Six weeks in boot camp and he was shipped off to an American air base in North Africa. This is where Sid repaired aircraft, among them, the B-24 bombers used to invade and capture Sicily and force Italy out of World War II. For the next two years, Cookie and Sid were prolific and passionate pen pals.

Following the formal surrender of Japan in 1945, Sid telegraphed Cookie: "How about dinner Thursday? STOP. My treat. STOP."

The reunion began with an elegant seven-course meal at the Pierre Hotel, followed by a horse-drawn carriage ride through New York's Central Park. At the end of the evening, the young couple found themselves at the top of the world. "This is our third date in two years," Sid told a stranger. "Can I trouble you to take our picture?" he asked, handing the man his box camera. It was there on the observation deck of the Empire State Building that Sid pulled out a dark jewelry box from his back pocket, knelt down, and popped the question.

Click!

The sepia-toned photo memorializing, no, immortalizing the two of them hangs over Cookie's plastic slip-covered lime-green couch. For their fiftieth wedding anniversary, the Brewster grandchildren had the image made into a poster. The curls, the short fur, the flowing silk gown, standing there, one hand touching her face, Cookie is a dead ringer for Rita Hayworth. With her free hand she reaches out to her soon-to-be fiancé. Sid on one knee, in a military peacoat, diamond in hand.

This is how Sid set the standard for future generations of Brewster men. Sid's son, Oliver, managed to measure up. He rented a catamaran, packed a fancy picnic lunch, and asked his wife, Katherine, to marry him while calmly drifting on Lake Tahoe. Sid's grandson, Jordan, was much more showy. Four and half hours into the New York City Marathon, nearing the twenty-six-mile marker, Jordan slogged toward his future fiancée, slightly weighed down by a small, virtually colorless stone in his back pocket. Barely catching his breath, he took Abigail's away when he stopped running, bent down, and proposed. She said yes and the crowd went nuts, pulling out premade signs that said stuff like "Congratulations" and "Now the Race to the Altar." Jordan's stunt even got a mention in the *Daily News.*

To remain in Sid's good graces, I, too, need to be faster than a marathon runner, more powerful than a catamaran, and able to propose on a tall building in a single bound.

The engagement story is important—all men know this. Women put your engagement story right up there with how you met and your first date. You can't tell your children *I met your mother in prison.* You can't tell your family your first date was at the dentist. You can't tell your friends you proposed in the Burger King drive-through. *I'll have a Whopper Jr. and your hand in marriage.*

"Our engagement story is still in the planning stage," I assure Sid.

"Of course it is, but how about a taste? Indulge a poor old man," he says, smacking his lips. "Just a morsel."

"Fine," I say, wishing he'd drop the whole matter. *"Hey mamacita. What do you say you and me get hitched, shack up, and squeeze out a few pups?"*

"Fan-tabulous!" Sid cheers with two raised fists. "Short, simple, and honest. You've got your short-term goals in there and your long-term ones. But that's the payoff. Where, when, and how do we arrive on such poetic genius?" He sighs and gazes out across the bay. You can tell the warm breeze feels good on his face.

Before I can say anything, Sid butts in: "And seriously, kid, no food," Sid demands, patting down a flyaway. "None of this malarkey where you drop the ring in a fancy drink or plant it on a cake."

"Totally," I agree quickly, mentally purging any and all food-oriented proposals. "What about one of those propeller planes with a banner? I did some research and it only costs, like, three hundred bucks."

"No! No propeller planes! No electronic billboards, no ticker tapes, and no JumboTrons! No professional sporting events! You need to light up a blimp or shoot off fireworks without lighting up a blimp or shooting off fireworks." He gathers his thoughts. "The key to a good romantic engagement story is *creativity*. A little creative flare and the romance will pay off in spades," he insists.

THE MUNI bus takes us from the Ferry Building to downtown San Francisco. From there, Sid and I embark on foot. San Francisco doesn't have an official diamond district. No sketchy side streets where vultures swoop in on unsuspecting future grooms only to swindle away their life savings. All San Francisco really has is Union Square, where the crooks wear Armani suits and stand behind counters at upscale chains, ready to take pity on you and your paltry credit line.

But if we intend on finding a deal, we won't find it at the likes of Shreve's, Cartier, Bulgari's, or Tiffany's. We need a back room. We need someone on the inside.

Enter Igor Petrov, Sid Brewster's personal go-to-guy. The Petrovs have been supplying Brewster men with diamonds for generations. Sid bought his first diamond from Petrov's father, Dmitry. More recently, Igor hooked Sid's son and grandson up with gorgeous stones.

"What sort of engagement ring would Paige like?" Sid asks.

"I'm not sure."

All I know is what I have to spend. Between both my credit cards, some emergency funds in my savings account, and Friday's paycheck, I have a total of about $4,500. This assumes I go a few months without paying down my student loans. I don't know what this gets me, but I'm hoping I know it when I see it.

"Do you know her ring size?" he asks.

"I don't." *Boy, I stink at buying engagement rings.*

"Okay, you're just going to have to eyeball it," he determines. "You can have it resized later."

Sid knows San Francisco much better than I do. I read the signs for him as he drags me around Union Square. We take a right off Sutter Street onto Grant, and then a left down a quaint alley called Maiden Lane. Our undisclosed location is manned at the front door by a brawny, bald militant-looking security guard who checks our names against a visitor's register (or a watch list), scans my license into a computer, and then walks over and punches in the six-digit code to the elevator.

We're let off at the end of a long, completely white hallway. There is no floor directory. None of the offices display business names, just gold-plated suite numbers. To the right of the door to Room 304 is an intercom system. After a brief authentication argument, the man on the other side of the wall buzzes us through the double steel doors. I brace myself for the sudden blindfolds, black hoods, and cavity search. You'd think I'm here to pick up the Hope Diamond.

The teeny-tiny two-room office is bubbling with life. The prospective groom to my left taps his left foot nervously; he pinches the inside corners of his eyes to make the headache go away. To my right sit two couples. One couple is busy ignoring each other—him thumbing away on his BlackBerry and her yakking it up with a friend on her cell. The other young couple leans back shoulder to shoulder, half-asleep. In the center of the room there is a well-dressed, middle-aged woman and her teenaged daughter—they're not speaking.

Igor Petrov's assistant, an emaciated man in his twenties with a thick five o'clock shadow, looks up long enough to scowl and then goes back to crunching numbers feverishly on a ribbon-printing calculator.

Sid and I take a seat. An open doorway separates this room from Igor Petrov's office. Sid peeks around the corner and gives his friend a quick wave hello. Leaning against the dividing wall I can hear the men next door arguing over—if I'm not mistaken—koala bears.

"Small fry, you ever play Texas Hold 'Em?" Sid whispers.

"That some sort of Southern sex act? Zinger!"

Sid is stone-faced.

"You're talking about 'making whoopee,' right?" I ask.

"Never say 'making whoopee' again. Even *I* don't say 'making whoopee.' Texas Hold 'Em is a card game. When we start negotiating for this sparkler, I need you to put on your best poker face."

"No problem," I say, rehearsing that face.

Sid is appalled.

"For crying out loud. Here," he says, handing me his wrap-around shades. "Wear these, leave the talking to me, and we're in like Flynn."

Where would I be without Sid.

"If you're so ready to get married, then tell me about the Five Cs," he quizzed me the other day.

"The five keys to marriage. You bet. There's closeness . . . commitment . . . caring . . . compassion, and, uh . . . credit cards? Is that five or six?"

The diamond industry would be devastated to learn that I'd gone nearly three decades without knowing that diamonds are judged according to their color, clarity, cut, number of carats, and of course that fifth C—cost. But now, thanks to Sid, I did.

They're sitting ten feet apart, but Igor still uses the intercom system to beckon his assistant. A moment later the assistant returns, walking right up to the mother and daughter in the center of the room. He cracks open the red jewelry box and sparks fly. Diamond earrings. The teenager is so delighted she throws her arms around her mother and cries.

I'm in the right place.

Petrov is now screaming at someone who has insulted him somehow. Before long, an overweight man in his forties, in heavy jewelry, storms out. Enraged, he tugs at the door violently; it's locked. The assistant finally buzzes Mr. Bling out.

"Send in my dear, dear friend, Sidney Brewster!" Igor bellows.

We stand, take three steps to our left, and we're inside his office.

There sits Igor Petrov in all his sweat and glory. The springs on his brown leather chair let out a desperate squeal when he shifts in his seat. He is forty, fifty, sixty; it's impossible to tell behind that bushy red mustache. The three top buttons on his white dress shirt are left open while the rest are poised to pop. The black suspenders from his black pants bow out over his shirt. Igor's toupee, dark brown and matted, is a few degrees off center.

Seated next to Petrov is a dead ringer for Mr. Bling—presumably Bling's twin. Strewn about on the disheveled desk are hundreds of thousands (millions?) of dollars in diamonds and a gold scale.

Igor Petrov has on itty-bitty reading glasses, and his head is buried in a *Wielder's Beginners Crossword Puzzle Book.*

"Iggie!" Sid greets him.

"Quick, Brewster," Petrov yells without looking up, "A five-letter word for Australian native dog. Third letter is an 'N.'"

Sid closes one eye. The other bounces wildly around in his massive noggin in search of the answer.

"DINGO!" Sid declares with a raised finger.

Igor fills in the answer. In pen.

"Last one," Igor pleads. "A seven-letter word for deer. Last letter is 'U.'"

Igor, Mr. Bling #2, and I study Sid like sport spectators. Sid mentally flips through the possibilities, and then squeaks out: "Caribou?"

"CARIBOU!" Igor celebrates, penning the answer and tossing the book onto his desk.

Igor takes his time getting up, but then pulls Sid toward him, swallowing Sid whole in a bear hug.

"So this is the grandson you mentioned on the phone?"

Sid is old enough to be my grandfather, but there is no family resemblance whatsoever. I've got reddish brown hair. Sid has none. I have a fair complexion and tend to blend in with eggshell-colored walls, and Sid is perpetually tan. I'm tall and soft. Sid is little and lean.

"God Almighty, you didn't mention the kid was blind," Igor cries.

As I reach to take off the clunky shades, Sid lunges for my hand.

"Birth defect," Sid laments. "He can see, but just barely. Not much of a speaking voice, either," he says, helping me to my chair. "Hasn't uttered a word of common sense in years. Now those ears . . . that's a different matter altogether," he adds. "Super hearing the kid's got. A regular Aqua Man."

"Your grandfather's a good man." Igor talks to me like I'm a simpleton.

"You need to set this kid up real good, Iggie. The boy is proposing to my only goddaughter," Sid says authoritatively.

"So what are we talking about here?" Petrov asks, slapping both hands flat on the desk and leaning in.

The oversensory experience, the stress, the sunglasses—I'm having a "senior moment." I can't remember anything Sid's taught me about precious gems.

Sid answers on my behalf. "Andy is thinking a one carat, VS2 with no inclusions or blemishes, virtually colorless, round, ideal cut."

I nod in agreement.

Petrov tips back in his chair and plays with his mustache, thinking it over. Mr. Bling #2's cell phone starts playing Bruce Springsteen's "Born to Run." He answers the call. Cupping the phone, Bling #2 asks Petrov whether he'd be willing to knock two grand off on a three-carat G stone.

Petrov slowly leans over and smacks Bling #2's head smartly, causing Bling's slim cell phone to fly across the floor.

"Richie, that's going to be a no," Bling #2 yells, searching for his phone.

Digging through his desk drawers, Igor finds what he's looking for.

"Here," he says, carelessly tossing Sid a small plastic envelope. "One point five carats, colorless, no flaws, no fluorescence. You won't find better."

Sid studies the stone through the plastic the best he can.

"Given your condition, and seeing as you're family," Petrov tells me, "I'll throw the setting in, for free."

Igor reaches for a stack of gem certificates and starts paging through them.

"Gorgeous stone," adds Mr. Bling #2, tucking his phone back in his breast pocket. Then he hands Sid some tweezers and swings the magnifying lamp as close as possible given that it's bolted to Petrov's desk.

Petrov is back to his crossword puzzle.

Sid isn't ready to take the stone out of its plastic bag just yet. He slides the rock over so he can read the card inside that lists the diamond's specifications. Holding the baggie two inches from his face, he twists it so I can read it. The diamond is priced at $11,500. I am speechless.

"Pay no attention to the price," Igor says, penning another answer in his crossword book. "All Brewsters get $1,000 off the top."

"That's very generous of you, Iggie, but I think this is still a little outside our price range," Sid says politely.

I give Sid a subtle, shocked nod in agreement.

"What do you want me to tell you? Maybe you want to try Wal-Mart. I don't think I carry the type of stone you're looking for."

Mr. Bling #2 dumps the $11,500 stone on the table, locks it in a pair of tweezers, and holds it underneath the magnifying lamp so we can see. I raise my shades to look. This is the sweetest, clearest, whitest stone that I've ever laid my eyes on. I bet Sid can talk Igor down to just under $10,000. It would be the deal of a life-time and I still can't afford it.

I'm inadequate.

"It'll be sold by end of business today," Petrov says matter-of-factly. "This guy's brother Richie is coming back for it. I shouldn't have even shown it to you."

Mr. Bling #2 nods in agreement.

Sid knows the drill. He thanks Petrov for his time; we get up and head for the front door. But like Mr. Bling #1, Petrov's assistant won't buzz us out. Petrov then calls us back to show us what he calls "the irregulars." With each stone, I lift and lower my shades. These diamonds are a bit more reasonably priced, but they all look the same—smaller, duller, and yellower than that first breathtaking stone. Mr. Bling #2 does all the work showing us each stone one by one while Petrov projects frustration at us over his puzzle.

Ten minutes later, Sid's really fed up.

"You're showing us complete rubbish. Let's go, Andy, plenty of other people will be happy to take your money."

I don't want to leave without a stone. Maybe I'll just get this one, or that one. Either is fine. I'm ready to spend whatever it takes. You only get married once. *How do you say "$6,000, one carat, S1, F stone" in sign language?*

Sid helps me to my feet.

"Your father would be so ashamed of you," Sid scolds Petrov.

This snaps Igor Petrov out of it. Mr. Bling #2 and I exchange worried looks. Sid and Igor stare each other down.

After a nervous moment, Petrov speaks first: "Always a pleasure to see you, Sidney," he says, rising from his chair and extending a meaty mitt.

They shake.

"One more before you head out?" he asks.

Thank goodness. The bluffing is over. Petrov is ready to show us Paige's ring. Then he reaches across his desk and picks up his puzzle book.

"Fifteen across. A six-letter word for 'spotted South American feline.' Second letter is 'L,'" Petrov says.

"Enough already," Sid demands impatiently.

Then someone blurts out the word "JAGUAR."

"JAGUAR" hangs in the air. Sid, Mr. Bling #2, and Petrov are looking at me, astounded. Apparently I said it.

"Well, I'll be a monkey's uncle!" Sid cheers, slapping his hands together. "It's a goddamn miracle. The boy can speak. Is your vision back as well, Sonny?"

"Why, yes, I can see, Grandpa," I say, ripping the glasses off dramatically.

"Praise the Lord," Mr. Bling #2 screams sarcastically.

"What's wrong with you?" Petrov screams. "There's no 'L' in *JAGUAR*!"

Who cares? I can see and speak now.

"Wait!" Petrov shrills, his eyes darting around the puzzle. "I think I spelled *gazelle* wrong. There two 'Ls' in *gazelle*?"

"Yep, two," Sid tells him flatly.

"Of course, the clue was 'Loves antelopes' and I wrote 'gazelle,' but it's 'hyenas,' hyenas *eat* antelopes," he says writing and rewriting his new answer. "That makes 'jaguar' work for fifteen across. Brilliant!" Igor yells.

It's the first time I've seen Igor Petrov smile, dentures and all.

"Paige is crazy about the Animal Planet Channel," I whisper to Sid.

Sid gives my arm a supportive squeeze. Petrov closes his puzzle book. Now that I have my vision back, Igor and I can finally see eye-to-eye.

"I have an idea," he says, staring thoughtfully through me.

Petrov plops down in his chair, spins ninety degrees, hunches over, and begins unlocking a small safe on the ground.

"You fill in the blanks, I fill in the blanks," he mumbles.

Then Petrov hands me Paige's diamond. This is the one—and the platinum setting sounds perfect. I give him a deposit and arrange to bring the rest of the money when I pick up the ring tomorrow. I've drained my savings and maxed out my credit cards, but right now I feel like the richest man in the world.

Then it hits me like a ton of bricks: I know Paige's engagement story.

CHAPTER 7

If the Shoe Fits

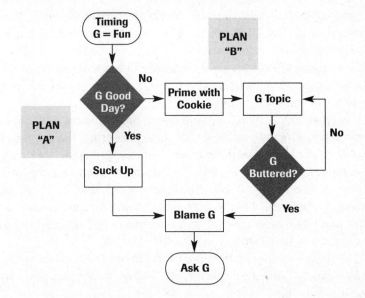

THE way my voice bounces off the porcelain tiles, the pulsating warm water on my back, only now do I feel truly relaxed, invincible. If I could just lure Gregory to this shower stall, it would be so easy. Then again, maybe I don't need to be stark naked when I ask for his blessing.

My plan is to corner Gregory tonight at Paige's birthday party. I've put this off for far too long. *If I practice this speech one more time it's going to sound too rehearsed.* I twist the shower faucet off. *When in doubt, flip to the flowchart.* I drip-dry for a moment. *Flip to the flowchart in your mind's eye.*

Step 1: Hit Gregory at the zenith of fun: right around birthday cake time.

Step 2: Lure him into a false sense of security. "Business was good today, wouldn't you say?" *That's how you remember your opening line, Andy—it rhymes.* As it turns out, business *was* good today; there were plenty of paying customers and none of our arguments registered above a magnitude 2.0.

Step 3: Suck up. Tell Gregory how much you love your job, how much you've learned, and how you're ready to take on new responsibilities. *Teach me, oh Mayor of Pomona Street.* If that doesn't work, go with Plan B: lighten matters by poking fun at Cookie. Then butter him up. *How about those Oakland A's? Don't you just love the chicken and portobello mushroom alfredo at the Olive Garden? Tell me again how you drove the North Koreans back past the thirty-eighth parallel?*

Step 4: Blame. With his guard down, finish him off with a one-two punch. First a body blow with some pandering: *You've always believed in me* (Mental note: this would be a good place to insert his name). *I just want to thank you again for giving me this job, Gregory.* Then a right hook with some accountability: *If you think about it, Paige and I really have you to thank for our reunion.* At this point he'll be dazed and confused, in a public setting, unable to react, and that's when you drop him.

Step 5: *With your permission, I'd like to ask Paige to marry me.* The lights will dim, he'll say yes, she'll blow out the candles, and we'll all eat cake.

I ATTEND the party fashionably late. There's no room to park in Sid's driveway so I pull into Gregory's across the street. With her back to me and her hands full, Paige bounces open the screen door with her hip. But when she turns toward me, I realize it's not Paige at all, but Lara, her older sister, in from Los Angeles.

Lara is her father's daughter in every way. She has the same oval-shaped face, pointy nose, and cleft chin. I suppose Lara's attractive, but all I see is Gregory.

Lara thinks I'm a loser. I wish it were more complicated than that. Lara made up her mind about me long before that football careened into my skull sophomore year. The fact that Paige was wearing an eye patch (thanks to my makeup applicator) the first time Paige introduced me to Lara as her boyfriend didn't help, either. "You'll see," Lara told Paige loud enough for me to hear. "This thing with Andrew Altman is already on CPR: you're dating him out of 'convenience,' 'proximity,' and because you're on the 'rebound.'" Lara's never gotten over the fact that Paige and Tyler Rich didn't go the distance.

"Party's across the street," Lara apprises me as if I didn't know.

"Welcome home," I say, tucking my shoebox-sized present underneath my arm and offering to take something from her.

"I've got it," she says. "Can you believe Cookie reuses her plastic utensils?"

"You should see her paper plates after one cycle in the dishwasher," I reply.

I wish I were kidding.

Lara and I cross the street and we walk up the Brewster lawn. There are cars everywhere. We can hear the music from here. The house is packed.

"Why am I not surprised that it takes all of Crockett to celebrate Paige Day's birthday?" Lara remarks.

I hold the door open for her.

"Expensive?" she rhetorically asks me of my gift. But before I can answer, Lara tells me how *absolutely* thrilled I'm going to be with her present.

Inside, the party is hobbling. The median age is about sixty-five, but this is a lively group. In the dining area there are good cold cuts from Concord's Deli. Balloons are taped at various heights in arbitrary spots along the light blue walls of the living room. Whether it's because Sid was feeling lazy or maybe Cookie decided the decorations were high enough, partygoers are forced to duck underneath a crisscross of purple streamers located at eye level.

We've been transported to the early 1930s. The turntable inside the antique console blares "Ain't Misbehavin'" by the incomparable Louis Armstrong. Mounted above the hi-fi console are two shelves of recordings that go back to the mid-1920s. For Sid's eighty-third birthday, I bought him the remastered CD box set of Armstrong's 1931 performances with the New Cotton Club Orchestra. Sid appreciated the gesture, but promptly returned the gift: *You can't listen to Louis on anything but vinyl,* he insisted. We used the cash to buy him some 78s on eBay. (I still feel a tinge of guilt for introducing Sid to the online auction world. His obsession with eBay got so bad at one point that Sid spent an entire Social Security check on an original scat recording of Armstrong's platinum hit "Heebie Jeebies." Cookie went berserk and has since cut him off.)

Competing with the virtuosity of Armstrong's trumpet playing is the unmistakably gravelly voice of the play-by-play TV announcer for the Oakland A's. Gregory and Sid are on the couch. When the Kansas City Royals score a run, the two of them slowly tip away from each other like bowling pins. Above Sid is that sepia-colored photograph immortalizing the perfect marriage proposal.

The picture calls out to me. It takes me to task.

I spot Paige in the corner. The warmth in her face lights up the room. She, too, feeds off the energy and attention. The back of her black dress plunges low and she manages to exude both grace and sensuality. In between swatting away streamers, Paige chats politely with the only other two members of Cookie's book club: Mildred, a seventy-six-year-old, thrice divorced, bespectacled spitfire with a new hip and walker, and Beatrice, a tall, big-boned blue hair with nothing to contribute to a conversation besides repeating whatever Mildred just told you. Both are frequent patrons of Day's Pharmacy.

Over by the vegetable dip, our cashier, Belinda, is here with her film school boyfriend, Cleat. (Cleat's very particular about his nickname. One time, I mistakenly called him "Pete." You'd think I'd burned down his house and called his mother a whore. I love it that his real name is Albert.) The two twenty-something twigs seem totally out of place with their tattoos and piercings, and yet somehow they've settled in comfortably. I'm surprised to see Belinda here. She and Paige are acquaintances at best, but I suppose Belinda wants to earn some points with her boss. It would seem everyone wants Gregory's blessing.

Cookie, cane in hand, swipes the hors d'oeuvres plate from the young couple. I can read Cookie's lips from across the room. *These are for the guests,* she scolds them. Belinda laughs, and Cleat snaps up one more pig in a blanket before Cookie whisks the tray away.

Paige is excited to see me. She waves hello and excuses herself from her conversation to run over and take the eating utensils from Lara. Seeing Lara and me anywhere near each other makes her uneasy.

Paige has a secret to tell us: "Did you know that Mildred is big into online dating? Last week she went on *two* dates: a seventy-two-year-old retired prison guard and a seventy-five-year-old limo driver. And yes, if you're wondering, both can drive at night. Apparently that makes you quite the catch in the senior scene."

"Andrew, why don't you tell Paige what you bought her," Lara pries.

"And ruin the surprise?" Paige complains, taking my present and placing it on the end table with the other gifts.

"Daddy, what can I get you to drink?" Paige asks, giving him attention.

The game goes to commercial.

"A beer, thank you, sweetheart," he says, reaching down and gently petting the Brewster schnoodle, Loki.

"Let me get it for you, Dad," Lara insists.

No, I want Paige to get it, Gregory seems to suggest, shaking his head.

"One-two-three," he tells Paige. This is Gregory's equivalent of "ILY."

Paige bends over and Gregory gives her a quick peck on the lips.

Ick.

"Why don't I get you that beer?" I say as if we're competing for whose kidney he'll take. Paige is delighted by my offer. Before I can react, she whips around and kisses me right on the mouth.

Great. I basically just kissed Gregory. Gregory isn't thrilled, either.

"I'll come with," Sid says as he jumps up.

The fact that Gregory has his two adoring daughters by his side should be enough, but he doesn't appreciate Sid leaving him for me.

To counter any hurt feelings, Sid informs his pharmacist, "If we're having dessert, I need to take my meds."

Once the kitchen door swings closed behind us, Sid's all up in my face.

"You're killing me here. I thought you asked him for his blessing already," he screams in whispers.

"Were you just eating M&Ms?" I confront him.

He knows that chocolate is a no-no.

"Yes," he confesses sheepishly.

There is a brief pause before he goes back to yelling at me. "Seriously, what's wrong with you? You were *supposed* to ask him *yesterday*. The man walks into my house this afternoon and I cry, 'Congratulations,' he says, 'On what?' and then I spend the next ten minutes complimenting his shirt and celebrating his military record," Sid says rubbing his head. "I felt like a complete imbecile."

"Yeah, yeah, yeah, sorry about that."

"Get with the program, kid. If you really plan to propose in the next couple of weeks, then you *need* to get his permission *now*."

"I'm doing it tonight," I promise. "Trust me, I've got a plan," I say, tapping the mental flowchart seared into my frontal lobe.

I make myself a strong gin and tonic.

"Limes?"

"In the Frigidaire," Sid says.

"You're making me nervous," he continues. "This may be a formality to you, but you have to understand . . ." Sid's always telling me that I "have to understand." *You have to understand, back in the fifties, there were no socks. You have to understand, in those early skyscrapers, you couldn't take oxygen for granted. You have to understand, in my day, we treated most medical disorders with a stick of butter and bed rest.*

"You have to understand," Sid says, "Gregory needs to feel like you legitimately *need* . . . no, you legitimately *want* his approval."

In walks Lara. How much has she heard?

"I need to do the cake," Lara says, all business.

Gregory's ordered Paige's favorite—midnight chocolate with fresh strawberries.

I gulp down my drink, make another, and grab Gregory's beer from the icebox.

"I need you to run interference tonight," I inform Sid.

The shock washes over Sid. I don't know who's more nervous. Bug-eyed, he agrees. Lara can barely hide her curiosity.

In the living room, I hand Gregory his beer.

"Finally," Gregory says, taking it from me.

"Daddy, say thank you," Paige commands.

"I just did," he says.

Sid asks Paige to help him clear the table for dessert, and as she gets up, she lovingly brushes my shoulder with her hand and I take a seat beside Gregory. In a single move, Sid's put me one move from checkmate.

I wait for a commercial before speaking.

"Oakland is having a decent season," I try.

Gregory and I have never talked sports before. He looks at me like I'm asking for a raise. Then he quietly takes a swig from his bottle. *Where are we in my flowchart? What was my opening line again? Something like "work was good, don't you think?" But that doesn't rhyme. What rhymes with "good"?*

The ball game's back on.

"The A's are getting clobbered tonight," Gregory complains.

"Hey, I was thinking. Tomorrow is Memorial Day. Would you mind if I helped hand out those Red Rocket candy rings?"

"Already did it," he says flatly, eyes trained on the screen.

"Really? You did it early?"

"I did it when I always do . . . a couple of days beforehand. You were off that day." He sips his beer. "I'll handle the last few myself on Monday."

The screen to the front door violently flies open and in walks a six-foot fluffy white teddy bear. The door smacks the wood-paneled wall with such force it literally causes the needle to dig a deep scratch across the album.

"Louis!" Sid squeals, holding both hands out in desperation.

I quickly scan the room to confirm everyone else, too, sees Big Foot outside its natural habitat. Gregory slowly places his beer on the coffee table. Everyone else is frozen in place except for Mildred, who loses her balance. Thankfully Paige is there to catch her and her new hip.

This teddy bear is Macy's Thanksgiving Day Parade big. Someone has gone to great lengths to fit Teddy in a tiny red T-shirt that says "Happy Birthday." The dancing bear has Beatrice in his sights. She is speechless, overcome with this sort of big-teddy-bear-in-the-headlights look in her eyes.

From my proximity, I can see that someone is behind the bear operating its stubby white arms. The ventriloquist's first two words come in Marilyn Monroe slow motion. "Hap-py Birth-day," he says all cuddly and creepy at once. "To—you!" he adds with two quick, darting ninja steps forward.

Crash go the birthday gifts as Teddy takes out the leg of the end table.

Beatrice screams bloody murder.

"Cheese and rice!" Cookie yells. "Beatrice, can it!" she demands. "Emmanuel, put down the bear!"

Manny Milken slowly lowers the tender animal to the ground. Seeing them side by side, the resemblance is uncanny: Manny and Teddy are both furry, doughy white, chubby creatures with the same vacant look in their eyes and stuffing for brains.

"I'm so sorry, Mrs. Brewster," Manny pleads, getting down on one knee to pick up the birthday gifts scattered across the floor.

Bent over, Manny's loose-fitting jeans give the room quite a view.

Mildred begins wheezing.

"For heaven's sake," Cookie says, poking Manny in the small of his back with the rubber end of her cane. "Pick up your pants."

Manny quickly complies and I walk over to inspect the end table.

"He ruined it, and it's part of a matching set!" Cookie laments, pointing to the other end table near Gregory.

"It looks salvageable," I tell her with a doctor's bedside manner.

Sid dashes to the garage to get some tools.

Lifting the snapped-off leg from the floor, I lean over and whisper in Manny's ear: "Another thirty seconds and I would have put you down with a tranquilizer gun."

"You're so hilarious," he fires back.

"I can't believe you broke Cookie's beautiful table," I tell him.

"Manny, you're such a sweetheart!" Paige says, running over to give him a hug. "I can't believe you got me this," she coos, patting Teddy on the head.

"Sorry to break up the party, Mr. Day," Manny says, embarrassed.

"Most excitement we've had all night," he says, getting up from the couch to pat Manny on the back.

Lara flips off the lights and orders everyone into the dining room for cake. I sidle up to Gregory.

"Why so many candles?" I whisper to Lara.

Paige contemplates her wish.

"I bought two boxes and just used them all," she mutters.

"I count . . . forty."

"Ten for good luck!" Lara explains.

Paige glares at her sister and then smiles lovingly at Gregory, or me, or both of us. Then she blows out all forty.

Everyone is having chocolate cake except Sid. Cookie tells the room that Sid's bad cholesterol is too bad and his good isn't good enough. It's so unfair. Half this room is on anticholesterol medication, including Cookie. Sid puts down his toolbox, and I slip him a serving, encouraging him to devour it in the privacy of the laundry room.

Gregory is in the corner inhaling his slice. Both of us have a decent alcohol-sugar buzz going. I can finally visualize my get-Gregory's-blessing flowchart. *Okay, Andy, it's time for Plan B: Mock Cookie. Then butter him up.*

"Man, she sure loves cake," I observe of Cookie.

Cookie seems to be competing in some sort of secret cake-eating contest.

"Who doesn't?" Gregory says, polishing off his.

"No, but she *really* loves cake," I say.

Cookie picks some crumbs from her lap and pops them in her mouth.

"How's your mom feeling?" Gregory yells across the table to Manny.

Manny interprets this as *I love you. You're an interesting person.*

Manny's mother, Margaret, suffers from Parkinson's. Manny speaks quickly; he's nervous that Gregory might lose interest at any moment.

Standing there like a schmuck, I eventually excuse myself for the gift giving.

In the living room, Sid is now on the floor next to the bad end table. He's flipped it upside-down and is trying to distinguish between two different-sized wrenches. Annoyed, he waves off my help. Nearby, Belinda and Cleat have found a cozy spot on the floor and are huddled together so they can share one heaping portion of chocolate cake. As we gather around, Paige agrees to open my gift last.

Mildred and Beatrice have chipped in and bought Paige a crystal vase.

"That gift calls for a crocheted doily," Lara goads.

"It would be my pleasure!" Mildred cries.

Paige politely squeezes Mildred's hand.

Gregory and Manny rejoin the party and Manny reminds everyone that he gave Paige the teddy bear, as if anyone could forget. Gregory's gift is the party. Belinda and Cleat bought Paige a massive aromatherapy candle and Paige insists on everyone smelling it. Cookie's gift is next. The gift-wrapped lump contains a ghastly, hand-knit, light blue sweater. Mildred finds it stunning. Beatrice finds it stunning. When Cookie's not looking, Sid slips Paige a savings bond.

As Paige unwraps each present, she expresses gratitude and remarks on the beauty of each gift, kissing each gift giver.

It's Lara's turn and she's chock-full of gag gifts. A mug that says "Look Who's 30!" An "Over the Hill" parking hangtag. Even a gaudy greeting card celebrating "The Big 3-Ow."

"This next one's from Andy," Paige brags, reaching for the box. "It's a puppy!" she concludes, rattling the tightly wrapped gift. Beatrice doesn't think that's funny at all.

I've wrapped Paige's gift in a Nine West shoebox. Paige opens it and is thrilled to find a pair of strappy cream-colored high heels.

"I love them, but I think I have a pair *just like* these already," she says, inspecting them.

"No, those *are* your shoes," I tell her, "but I've redesigned them so they're *adjustable*. Now you can change the height of the heels to fit any occasion."

I dramatically present one of the shoes to the room like a card trick.

"You just pop this off," I say, tucking the base under one armpit, wrestling to separate the heel. I'm perspiring. "And a different heel can snap into place. You see, different male parts slip smoothly into the female keyholes."

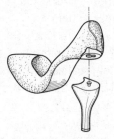

The room is silent.

Gregory stopped listening a while ago. He's back to his ball game.

"Genius," Paige tells the room.

"It really is," Beatrice agrees, confirming her decision is okay by Mildred.

I dump the remaining heels on the floor. There are three complete sets. I begin handing out the wooden blocks to partygoers. Sid studies his; Cookie and Gregory politely pass. I snap the five-inch set in place. Paige straps them on and I help steady her to her feet. While Paige gingerly models the pair, parading around the room, I launch into the details of the design.

"The heels snap in and *away* from the toe to create a differential force in the opposite direction. With each step, Paige locks the heel more tightly in place."

"I have a question," Sid says, raising his hand.

"Yes, to your question, I do think we should PMP it," I say, anticipating his next words.

"Actually, my query is more one of stability," he says.

But before he can finish, Loki darts in front of Paige. Paige shifts her weight to get out of the way and one of the wooden heels snaps. There is a collective, audible gasp as we watch Paige tumble forward. In that split second, Gregory's paternal instincts kick in. With all his might he punts the gigantic white teddy bear toward her. Paige and Teddy embrace in midair and the good end table breaks their fall. Once again, Cookie has a matching set.

"You have got to be kidding me," Cookie hollers.

Her head buried in Teddy's furry chest, I can hear Paige laughing hysterically. I run over to her.

"I'm so sorry. I'm so sorry. Tell me you're okay," I beg, trying to get her to lift her head. "Say something," I plead. I turn her face toward me and I privately realize that these are not tears of joy. She's holding her ankle; it's starting to swell. "Oh man, you're hurt. Is it broken?" I whisper.

"Sprained," she assures me.

I offer to bring her ice, but she wants to come with me to the kitchen.

"Just Andy," she says, kindly fending off advances from everyone.

"I can't believe you broke Cookie's table," Manny says with a shit-eating grin.

"Just as I suspected, the screw split the wood," Sid says, inspecting the broken heel.

I throw Paige's arm around my neck and we slowly limp off the field. In the freezer, Cookie and Sid are stocked to the gills with ice packs. Gently applying the cold compress to her bruised ankle, I keep my head down out of humiliation.

"I'm such a jerk. I ruined your party," I mumble.

"Don't flatter yourself," she kids.

"How does that feel?"

"Cold. I don't care about my foot." Paige wipes away a tear. "The shoes are a beautiful gift, Andy. I'm upset because I'm old, because I feel ugly, and because I don't know what I'm doing with my life."

"A regular spinster," I agree.

"You watch: I'm going to wind up being the Crazy Old Cat Woman of Nob Hill."

"You don't even like cats," I remind her. "I thought you said thirty was the new twenty."

"That's a load. Twenty is the new twenty."

I move the ice pack. Paige lets out a slight moan. I am on bended knee. It would be so easy to fix everything right now and propose.

"I haven't given you your *real* gift yet," I decide.

Igor Petrov's ring may be stowed away in the floorboards of my apartment, but right now, it's burning a hole through my pocket like kryptonite. I can't wait two more weeks. I can't wait two more seconds. I think back to Mac Daddy's ILY chart and his recommendation on the perfect day of the week to spring the surprise.

"How is your availability this Wednesday?" I ask her.

"Uh, not great. I work. Day-side, I think."

"I'm picking you up afterward and we're going on a romantic escapade."

"I dunno."

"It's too late. I've already made the reservation at an expensive B and B and it's nonrefundable." All lies. "We both have Thursday off. We'll go up, sleep over Wednesday, and take our time coming home."

She studies me thoughtfully.

"I guess," she relents softly.

"Yippee. 'You guess!' That's what I was shooting for."

I've done it—I've initiated an irreversible launch sequence.

CHAPTER 8

Medicine Men

IF ONLY people still called them "apothecaries" or "chemists," maybe I would have stuck it out in pharmacy school. Even "druggist" has a certain retro flare to it, though Gregory despises the moniker—says it feels too much like "drug dealer."

Pharmacists generally get a bad rap. Doctors think we're illiterate if we can't read their writing. Patrons think we're gouging them if we say insurance won't pay. It really is appalling how people treat the world's second-oldest profession. I'll admit, for the better half of my life, I didn't have a lot of respect for pharmacists, either. Count, pour, lick, and stick. Does it really take a rocket scientist to slap a label on a prepackaged tube of ointment?

But then I met Paige.

Back in high school, Paige compared her father's work to that of a saint. She described a time, not so long ago, before the greedy insurance companies and parsimonious Medicare, before the insatiable pharmaceutical companies with their superprofits, when your small-town pharmacist was the local hero, and patrons were treated like family. That's when folks *only* went to the doctor for one of the three B's—bleeding, babies, and the big stuff—and the rest was reserved for someone like Gregory, the Mayor of Pomona Street, who happily dispensed medical advice from behind his mighty pharmacy bench.

Maybe it was my recollection of how Paige lovingly described Gregory's work, or perhaps the job just reminded me of Paige, but the more I searched for the right career, the more I kept coming back to pharmacology. After a couple of moderately successful years of community college, I finally managed to gain admission to the UC–San Francisco pharmacy program. When it came time to find an internship, second semester, second year, I immediately thought of Day's Pharmacy. When I heard Paige had returned to Crockett, I made landing a job there my mission.

This was my chance to reunite with Paige plus see a real pharmacist in action, crushing pills daily mortar-and-pestle–style. I learned that Big Pharma produced the drugs and doctors prescribed them, but it took a gifted pharmacist to figure out how to deliver them to a patient's bloodstream. Someone like Gregory—a devotee of a dying breed of medicine men known as compounding pharmacists.

The compounding pharmacist is a practitioner of a lost art, one dating back to medieval times when medicine was made from scratch. When Gregory entered the profession decades ago, he was still responsible for physically shaping most of the pills, filling the capsules, preparing the salves, and mixing the suspensions. Compounding isn't even taught in pharmacy school or tested on the Boards anymore. Nowadays, most drugs come in standard forms, strengths, and dosages. When you go to chains like CVS, Rite Aid, or Walgreens, you're basically stuck with whatever flavor the commercial drug maker is currently mass-producing.

But not at Day's Pharmacy. And not with Gregory.

Gregory is old school. His customers are not beholden to any pharmacy chain or pharmaceutical company. The folks who come here keep coming in large part because they know that Gregory can tailor-make medication to their specific needs. Like a magician, he can extract dangerous dyes, remove unnecessary preservatives, and steer clear of additives that may cause allergic reactions. The man is an artist, always nurturing his craft. You can see it on his face: Gregory is most fulfilled in his work when he's compounding.

Many of our elderly customers, about two-thirds of them women, have trouble with pills. For example, the Widow Riggs can't take her arthritis tablets without her ulcer acting up, so Gregory pulverizes the pills and transforms them into a transdermal gel that she can apply topically to her wrists and ankles. Former lightweight boxing champ Mickey "Bulldog" Bratton doesn't have the strength to swallow his cholesterol capsules, so Gregory mashes them up, mixing in syrup, and converts the whole suspension into a sweet cocktail. When the Rally sisters, Rhonda and Fay, kissed the same infectious man in a two-week span, Gregory concocted an antibiotic lip balm. Gregory compounded a nasal spray for Sally C's bronchitis. Conrad Callahan, who used to play catcher on Gregory and Sid's old softball team, insists on taking his pain medication in lozenge form. And Lucille Braggs, that spitfire, prefers a suppository to pills.

At the other end of the evolutionary continuum are the children. Thanks to a generous free supply of C & H sugar, Gregory is a regular candyman, routinely turning out lollipops, sugary drinks, and gummy cures.

"QUIET around here today," Gregory says with a mix of relief and anxiety.

Gregory is unusually upbeat today. I think he's still riding Monday's high as grand marshal of the Memorial Day Parade. Crockett is about the only town left in the East Bay that still goes gangbusters for the holiday. The afternoon kicks off with an air show; people build elaborate floats; every generation from every arm of the military and every conflict since World War II marches; and bands from all over Contra Costa County perform their little hearts out.

This week is notoriously slow for business, Gregory reminds me again.

"All those lamebrains are freezing their asses off at the beach right now," I say.

Gregory manages a grin. In the last two hours we've had six customers. I think Belinda is on her tenth magazine.

"By the way, I stuffed a half-dozen candy rings under the register. Extras. Feel free to distribute them to worthy recipients," he says generously.

Alas, I already know about the rings and I've already found at least one worthy recipient: Gregory had chili at Langley's for lunch and I had two Red Rockets.

"These need to cool," Gregory warns me as he carefully sets down a tin of confection masterpieces.

Today's special is penicillin-infused dark chocolate. The recipient of these mouthwatering candy bars is Adrian Mackowski, the most miserable six-year-old this side of Marin County. Two months ago I singed all the hair on my left arm when Gregory forgot to turn off the propane Bunsen burner he uses to melt the chocolate. The near-work-related accident provided some leverage. Gregory took my advice and replaced the open flame with a cheap portable electric range. Since then Gregory's candy bars have started looking a lot less like blobs, and a lot more like slabs. Today's batch looks particularly delectable.

"Yummy," I say, rubbing my belly. "Can I?"

"If you do, you'll want to refrain from operating any heavy machinery. And stay out of the sun," he says. "Penicillin can cause blotchiness."

"Maybe a Three Musketeers Bar instead," I say, walking out from behind the counter, grabbing one, and wiggling it in Belinda's direction.

Belinda nods, mentally adding it to my nonexistent tab.

"You could make these," Gregory assures me, squatting down at eye level to inspect the candy bars for lumps.

"You think so? I learned from the best." *I am such a miserable suck-up.*

I haven't so much learned from the best as I've learned *nearby* the best, picking up tips and tricks as best one can. Before I dropped out of pharmacy school, before I befriended his best friend, and before I fell in love with his daughter, Gregory showed signs that he might take me under his wing. One time, he even sat me down for a compounding lesson.

"I'm impressed," he marveled that day, as I popped the pristine handmade pills out of the mold. It was beginner's luck. We both knew it.

But then I started dating Paige, and he lost complete interest in my career, and I lost complete interest in him. When I ultimately bailed on pharmacy school halfway through my second semester,

Gregory didn't say a peep. It was just as well. The coursework was only going to get tougher, the student loans higher, and what I really came for was within reach. The only thing standing in my way now: Gregory.

I've had all day to do this. I've had weeks to do this. I've put this off for far too long. Paige and I leave for wine country in less than an hour.

I step right up to Gregory and tap him lightly on the shoulder.

CHAPTER 9

His Blessing in Disguise

"GREGORY, can we talk?"

"Isn't that what we're doing?"

"No, I mean *privately*," I whisper.

"But there's no one here."

Belinda cups her ears to give us space.

"Andrew, how about we talk-and-work? We've got, like, two dozen scripts that still need filling."

"Talk-and-work, sure thing," I say. *Deep breath.* "You know we're headed out of town this evening."

"We who?"

"Me and Paige."

"Yeah, yeah, yeah."

"It's part of my birthday gift to Paige."

Gregory starts reliving last night. "You're not going to make her wear those ridiculous shoes, are you? She nearly broke her neck."

"No," I say, offended. "I'm not going to make her wear the shoes."

"Good."

The bell on the front door jingles.

In walks a petite blonde in a tight-fitting, above-the-knee blue pinstriped suit. She's dragging a big black leather briefcase on wheels. Brianna McDonnell is hardly the typical insurance collector. Silky golden locks cropped just above the shoulder, Ivory-girl skin, angelic features, and a bright, energetic smile, she might as well have just walked off a movie set. So splendid a specimen, one is inclined to stare, and that's when you notice something slightly off. Leaning this way and that, Brianna hides it well, but at equilibrium, she can't manage to stand up straight. Brianna has chronic back problems.

"If it isn't my favorite deadbeat druggist," she calls out to Gregory.

"Go away," he tells her, kindly.

She walks right up to me at the counter. "It's Andy, right?" she says leaning in, making direct eye contact. That citrusy scent is intoxicating.

"Andy I am," I say. Whenever I get nervous I somehow turn into Dr. Seuss.

"Is he always this grumpy?" she asks.

"Always."

I assume she can see my heart pounding through my button-down. Brianna delicately bends down to retrieve something from her briefcase, but her body won't cooperate. A pinched nerve, a herniated disc, a pulled muscle, whatever it is, it's killing her. As she grabs her paperwork, there is a shooting pain and she moans in agony.

Gregory is concerned.

"I thought we had an agreement," he demands.

"I *have* a chiropractor."

"No, you need a doctor-doctor. No acupuncture. No physical therapy. No stretching. None of this holistic crap. It's enough already."

"Humph," she says.

Brianna starts flipping through a stack of papers.

Manny Milken arrives. He holds the door open for Dr. Brandon Mills, a general practitioner in his early sixties who works around the block. Milken and Mills give each other mixed messages, prompting them to enter the pharmacy at precisely the same moment. Their shoulders collide in the doorway, knocking Mills's brown leather medical bag out onto the sidewalk and Manny's packages down two different pharmacy aisles.

I expect as much from Manny—the type of guy you're amazed still has all ten fingers—but there's nothing quite as satisfying as seeing that balding, smug, pretentious Dr. Mills look like such a stooge.

"Doctor Mills!" Gregory says, genuinely thrilled to see his friend and primary physician.

"Doctor Day, always a pleasure," Mills replies politely, clip-clopping across the tile floor in golf cleats.

It kills me that Gregory lets Mills call him "doctor."

"Brandon, I need you to recommend a good back doctor for Ms. McDonnell here. She's twenty-six and falling apart."

Dr. Mills gives Gregory's request some serious consideration.

"Tess Mayor. She's an orthopedist in Vallejo."

Brianna playfully snaps the pen I'm using from out of my hand, flips over her stack of papers, and starts writing. Mills spells out the doctor's name for her.

"Tess is always completely booked, so you'll need to tell her I sent you."

Brianna writes this down, too.

Good ole Brandon Mills: always looking for the goddamn referral.

"The last doctor said I needed *surgery*," Brianna complains.

"Go see Tess, she'll make you right as rain," Mills assures her. "Which reminds me, you're due for your seventy-five-thousand-mile tune-up," Mills tells Gregory. "I'll need you to make an appointment with Diane *soon*. I'm on vacay part of June and most of July."

Gregory nods, and then goes back to filling prescriptions.

"Mrs. Mills and I saw that gorgeous daughter of yours on the eleven o'clock news last night," Mills says. "The camera loves her."

Gregory raises both eyebrows in agreement.

"Have to make today's trip quick," Mills says, as if he's doing us a favor.

"Whatever you need," Gregory casually replies and, with a majestic gesture, grants Mills free rein of the pharmacy aisles.

So begins Mills's biweekly shopping spree. Forgoing the stack of red plastic shopping baskets near the doorway, Mills starts sliding Tylenol, toothpaste, and dental floss directly into his medical bag in apocalyptic fashion.

Only now do I notice that Manny's spent the last five minutes staring breathlessly at Brianna. He, too, is intoxicated by her pheromones. I bob my head in his eye line, whistle loudly like a parrot, and wave to get his attention.

"Sometimes Manny goes on little vacations without telling any of us," I inform Brianna. "Idn't that right, Manny?"

Brianna blushes slightly.

"I'm ignoring you," Manny tells me, stepping behind the counter.

He introduces himself to Brianna as "Emmanuel."

"Nice to meet you," she says, sticking out her hand.

They shake, and Manny doesn't let go, but Brianna doesn't seem to mind.

"Emmanuel!" Gregory yells. "Let's get with the program."

"This everything?" Manny says, lifting the cardboard carton of brown bags.

"Give me those, you ignoramus," I demand.

I snatch the delivery from him. Gregory slides a pile of octagonal-shaped pills into a wide, burnt-orange cup, twists the cap shut, and hands it to me. I check it over, rubber band instructions around the bottle, drop the goods into a small brown bag, and place the contents with the others.

"Say it," I command, playing keep-away with the carton.

"Are there special instructions?" Manny mumbles in Gregory's direction.

Manny is required to ask this question ever since he inadvertently delivered Ms. Rothkin the wrong heart medication. She caught the mistake, and decided not to sue, but it's the closest Gregory has ever come to firing Manny.

"One note," I say on Gregory's behalf, finally relenting the carton. "Roy Crane needs his insulin shots. He has a physical therapy appointment at 3:30, and I promised him that you'd wait until he arrives home."

Manny knows it's against California state law to leave medication on a doorstep or in a mailbox. That means he either needs to get a signature, redeliver, or wait, and Manny hates to wait: "That *so* kills business," he whines.

Manny places the carton on the counter, slicks back his thick oily black hair with one hand, and pulls out a handheld electronic organizer with the other.

"Check this out," he brags to Brianna, as if she's interested. "It tracks all my deliveries irregardless of who sent what. Do you have one of these? Because if you don't, you can have mine."

Maybe he doesn't say that last part.

"I do have one," she says politely.

"Oh good," he says, relieved to hear they're compatible.

Manny uses the organizer to remind himself that he needs to wait for Roy Crane, but as he goes to press a button, the organizer slips out of his left mitt and crashes to the ground.

"Oh my God!" he screams.

He picks it up and tests a few buttons at random.

"It's fine, it's fine," Manny reassures us. "I'm still figuring out how this thing works."

"You're still figuring how the Clapper works," I tell him.

Mills laughs from two aisles away.

"I know how the Clapper works," Manny shoots back.

"Okay, Mr. Day, you and me, we need to talk turkey," Brianna says, all business. She checks her list. "I've been asking for those prescription records for three months now. You don't want me to lose my job now, do you?"

Gregory ignores her. Manny is studying his deliveries.

"One of those is for your mother," Gregory tells Emmanuel. "She needs to take the *entire* course of antibiotics. I'm not kidding here."

Manny nods obediently.

Brianna is struggling to stay upbeat. I feel for her.

"This place is a mess, but if you tell me exactly what you n
I can probably pull those records for you," I offer kindly.

"No!" Gregory thunders. "Andrew, I'll handle this. Ms. McDonnell," he lectures her. "I'm trying to run a business here, and if
you people had your way, I'd be spending my days filling and filing insurance forms."

Brianna's back is acting up again.

"Blue Cross will have to wait. Sue me," he says.

She shakes her head and starts packing it in. I check on Dr.
Klepto in Aisle Three. I watch as he slides six of our most expensive toothbrushes off a spoke and into his bag. This from a man
who is married with no children.

"Do you *really* need six?" I yell over.

Mills didn't realize anyone was watching. He freezes, mortified.

"My—God, shut—up—Andrew!" Gregory screams, stretching
out the words. "Brandon, pay no attention to him. Please accept
my personal apology."

Mills has what he needs and heads for the door, booking past
Belinda just like I did to Lydia Day when I stole those two packs of
Hubba Bubba bubble gum seventeen years ago. Belinda doesn't
even attempt to ring Mills up. He doesn't have a tab and even if he
did, it's not like we'd ever dare collect.

Manny follows Mills out, waving good-bye. Now it's Brianna's
turn.

"Thank you again for the doctor referral, Gregory," she says
politely, trying to get his attention. "I'll be back *next Wednesday*.
Please force him to put that paperwork together," she begs me
softly. "I'm running out of time."

Brianna is barely out the door before Gregory is all over me.
He's boiling. The ground beneath us begins to shake. The overhead fluorescents swing wildly side to side. Toiletries vibrate off
the shelves. A magnitude 7.0. We're talking October 17, 1989, Loma
Prieta big.

"Talk to a customer that way again and you're fired," he screams.

"How could you apologize to Brandon Mills?" I'm incredulous.

oping crap into his medical bag like a game-show

ess is it of yours?"

en care?"

clearer can I be? Mind your own goddamn business!"

Gregory takes a step toward me. His hands are shaking.

"I'm just trying to help," I say. "You're giving away *expensive* stuff."

"I know exactly what I'm doing. I'm the one paying the bills around here."

"But you're handing out toothbrushes and pills like they're candy."

"I'm not going to stand here and be lectured on how to run my business from a pharmacy-school dropout half my age."

He's more like three times my age, but I don't correct him.

"You don't understand," I tell him softly.

"Just stop, Andrew," he insists, flashing his palm at me. Gregory gives me a long, forced, cigarette-stained smile. "Our little talk is *over*. How 'bout I take care of my life and you take care of yours. Can you manage that?"

I press my lips together and nod.

CHAPTER 10

The Gregory Factor

I DETEST wine country. This makes me a deplorable person.

Only a monster could resist the gorgeous countryside, those charming trinket shops, the hidden outlet stores, the homey beds, and those home-cooked meals. If you're not capable of appreciating northern California's exquisite wine and the exhilarating journey these brave grapes make each season, then you must be dead inside.

And yet, to me, wine country is one giant buzz kill. All I see are tourist traps, unmanageable crowds, and overpriced Brie. I see pretentious foodies intoxicated by their own palates and wine snobs intoxicated behind the wheel. There are great big Lyme-diseased ticks in these woods. Who needs to drive all the way to Sonoma when you can get the same damn bottle at the nearby Safeway? And there aren't any real hotels up north, just "quaint" B and Bs. In other words, camp for big people.

Then again, after decades of watching people use Crockett as a pit stop on their pilgrimage north, perhaps it's just sour grapes. But this trip is all about Paige. Paige loves wine country, so this is where our engagement story begins.

I've handled all the arrangements. The overnight bags are packed and stowed in the trunk. I've made us dinner reservations at an upscale restaurant in Healdsburg, the heart of Sonoma wine country. The Thistle Dew Inn was Sid's suggestion. He went there years ago and boasts that every room has its own fireplace, and no communal bathrooms.

The sky is a magnificent deep pumpkin color. I've managed to get rock star parking across the street from the television studio exit. As Paige approaches, still limping slightly from the adjustable heels incident, the sun dips below the horizon.

Leaning against my car, arms crossed, I greet her with an enormous grin.

"We're not going," she concludes.

"Why would you say that?" I screech.

"Something's not right. You look deranged."

"Deranged in a bad way?"

"Let me guess. You were fired."

If only she knew.

"I quit," I correct her. "Gave the boss a piece of my mind."

Paige studies me.

"Get in, we're behind schedule." I pretend to check my wristwatch.

Paige gives me a kiss and then holds out her cheek. Instead of kissing her back, I rub my cheek up against hers until she laughs.

The San Francisco Embarcadero runs along the waterfront,

and as we pull onto the roadway we catch a flawless glimpse of the Oakland Bay Bridge, its beauty and fame unfairly eclipsed by its more popular sibling, the Golden Gate. Paige cranes her neck to catch a glimpse of Coit Tower. Set against the orange sky, the white monument has a supernatural glow.

I can read her mind.

"Look where we live," I tease her.

Paige rolls her eyes at me yet can't resist.

"Well, *look at it,*" she demands, enthralled by the beauty of the bay.

Once we break free of city traffic, it's a straight shot to wine country.

Most men want to get married, though few will admit this to themselves or say it out loud. People tell you how important timing is, but that's a load. *You won't meet Miss Right until you're ready.* I've always been ready to meet Paige. Maybe that makes me a sap. I just don't think you should go on a first date with someone if there's no chance you'll ever marry them. This doesn't make me a romantic, just practical. This would also explain why I've had so few dates and even less sex.

The moment I realized I was ready to propose to Paige wasn't anything like the epiphany I have with a good invention. A lightbulb didn't go off. It was more like a dimmer, brightening steadily and more quickly over time, until I could see clearly.

For every woman before Paige, it started off pretty much the same. I never bothered to graph it out, but I can visualize it easily:

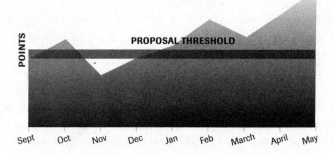

The excitement that came with a first or second date produced elevated levels of possibility; for the relationships that lasted a bit longer, we occasionally crossed that critical "proposal threshold," but invariably it went downhill from there.

Except with Paige. In the nine months leading up to this decision, the points kept coming. The highs kept peaking—until one day, I realized I was comfortably above the threshold.

It was a Sunday afternoon at Ocean Beach. We still try to go there once a month to drink good coffee, read the *Chronicle,* and walk along the Pacific. At one end of the beach, tucked away in the lower level of the Cliff House, is the penny arcade, Musée Mécanique, a San Francisco institution. "Laffing Sal"—a six-foot animatronics clown with bright red curls and a sinister smile—greets tourists at the door. Amid the circus music and Sal's maniacal laugh, we bypassed the antique viewfinders, fortune-telling machines, and vintage games, in pursuit of the Holy Grail tucked in the far corner—Ms. Pacman and a slew of other 1980s classics.

I've always been impressed with Paige's dexterity at destroying asteroids, racing around pixilated tracks, and hopping barrels, but it was the grace with which she obliterated insects that sealed the deal. Spinning that roller ball, sweeping across the screen, wiping out that quickly descending centipede with master firepower, Paige stole my heart. She got points when she got points.

I think that's when I started planning this trip, or at least some form of it.

The roads are clear. Paige is absorbed in her own thoughts. Paul McCartney is singing about Desmond, apparently he has a barrel or a barrow in the marketplace, and some Molly girl is a singer in a band. I turn up the volume on the radio. Resisting the chorus would be impossible:

> *Ob-la-di, ob-la-da, life goes on, oh!*
> *La-la-la-la life goes on.*

Paul launches into the second verse and Paige is impressed that I know every single word of the peculiar lyrics.Then she realizes I know none of them—that I'm "singing Chewbacca."

Two months back, I caught Paige massacring Michael Jackson at the top of her lungs. "Why would he tell Billie Jean the 'chair' is not his son?" I asked her curiously. Paige tried to deny it, but caved. That's when we agreed that if either of us was ever at a loss for lyrics, we would sing Chewbacca.

The Beatles chorus is upon us again. We give each other a knowing nod and scream in unison:

> *Chew-bac-ca, Chew-bac-ca, Chew-bac-ca, oh!*
> *Chew-bac-ca, Chew-bac-ca, Chewy.*

Laughing to tears, I swerve into oncoming traffic. At the very last moment, I quickly jerk us back into the proper lane. The Mercedes driver blares his horn after the fact. *Drunk driver!* A shot of adrenaline hits my bloodstream and my hands begin to shake. I turn the radio down and confirm Paige is wearing her seat belt.

Maybe the lodge is truly hidden or maybe I'm in denial, but I drive past the entrance to the Thistle Dew Inn twice before spotting the dumpy ranch house buried in the crabgrass. Our room is cold, small, dank, and depressing. The fireplace that looked so toasty on the Web site is actually powered by gas and activated by a light switch. There is no TV, no phone, and definitely no mint on either of the two scratchy crocheted pillows. They promised me the perfect room to propose. But this won't do at all.

I'm incapable of hiding my disappointment.

"It's cute," Paige reassures me. "I'm going to get ready for dinner."

"You do that and I'll go see if they have a Scrabble set."

"Genius," she tells me.

There is no one at the front desk. On the bookshelf next to the wood-burning fireplace is a stack of board games, among them Scrabble. But I don't need theirs—our set is sitting in the trunk of my car.

I go to the dining room for some privacy. *It's now or never.* I press the speed dial for "Gregory Home." While the phone searches for a cell tower among the sticks, I confirm the coast is clear. Reception here is spotty. My phone flickers between one and three bars. *You can't do this with anything less than three out of five.* The quality of the connection is crucial. *"Come again, Andrew? Why on God's green earth would you want my dressing?"*

I've got two bars. It's ringing. *Holy crap! Holy crap! Holy crap! I'm getting married.* I should have done this in person. I should have taken him to Applebee's or bought tickets to an Oakland A's game or just asked him over lunch at Langley's Diner. This should be easier. Doesn't every man secretly want a son?

"Hello," Gregory says, bracing for a telemarketer.

"Dad! It's me." *No.* "Mr. Day, Andy Altman here." *No.* "Gregory, we need to talk." *No.*

"Is anyone there?"

"Hi, it's Andy," I say finally.

"Hello, Andrew," he says, still concerned I might sell him something.

I can hear him tearing paper like he's opening mail.

"Everything okay?" he says suddenly.

"You bet. We arrived safely in Sonoma," I assure him. "Paige is getting ready for dinner." His daughter may have just turned thirty, but a father never wants to be reminded that his unwed daughter is on a sleepover with a boy. "Ignorance is bliss," "plausible deniability," this is how a father deals with his daughter's virginity, Paige tells me.

"After dinner, it's bingo at the Baptist Church, a mug of hot cocoa, and straight to separate sleeping quarters," I want to tell him. "How are things?" I ask, scanning the reception area, working up the nerve.

"Same as they were two hours ago," he says coolly. Gregory clears his throat: "What can I do for you this evening?"

"So I wanted to call," I say, taking a deep breath.

"Let me stop you right there. I don't need an apology about before. Just don't let it happen again. I want to put this whole evening behind us. Tomorrow's another day."

"You want to put this evening behind us?"

"Yes."

I let out a long sigh. "God, I've never done this before," I say. *Was that my inside voice or my outside voice? Calm down.* "I wanted to call you," my outside voice says. "You know Paige and I have a wonderful time together. I love her very much and I would like to ask her to marry me. I have such great respect for you and I wouldn't feel right not checking with you first."

It sounded better in the shower.

A tumbleweed rolls through the dining room. Crickets chirp.

"Hello?" I ask.

Gregory speaks, finally. "I appreciate that, Andrew," he says kindly. "I do." He seems genuinely touched. "When did you want to do this?"

Didn't I say "tonight"? I swore I said "tonight."

"Tonight."

"Tonight!" He's appalled, his voice rising. "You're proposing tonight and you're asking me *now*?"

"You're totally right. I screwed up. I'm sorry. I was just worried about spoiling the surprise."

"You don't trust me to keep a secret?" Gregory demands.

"No, not at all, I trust you. I bet you're the best with secrets."

Gregory takes a deep breath. Then another. He clears his throat.

I'm blowing this.

"Wait," he commands finally.

"Okay. No problem."

I lean against the dining room wall, sandwiching the cell phone between my ear and the window. I close my eyes, bracing for what Gregory might say next. Nine long hours pass in silence. Then I hear him take three short hits of his inhaler.

"Hello?" I ask.

"Hello?" he asks.

"Oh, hey, you're back."

"What do you mean 'I'm back'?" he asks.

"You're back, you told me to wait. Didn't you just go somewhere?"

"I'm just sitting here. I was waiting for you to say something."

"I thought you wanted me to wait," I say.

"I do. I want you to wait to ask Paige to get married."

It's as if Paige and I are back in the car and I've narrowly missed that head-on collision. My blood vessels widen. The adrenaline kicks in. *What is he asking me? Is he saying no? Is he saying maybe?*

"If this is about money," I prod, "I've got savings."

"That's not it at all."

"You think a year is too short to get engaged," I conclude.

"It's been more like nine months, and that's not it either. Listen," he begins.

"I don't want to pressure you, Gregory," I jump in, "but I love Paige. We're a *good* couple. I'd be honored to be a part of your family."

"Just wait, Andy," he says, his voice shaky.

It's the first time he's called me this.

"I have my reasons and I'll explain when I see you. I promise. But you need to make me two promises, son: keep this between us . . . and wait."

CHAPTER 11

The Toes Have It

ALFRED Hitchcock style, men fantasize about scaring the living bejesus out of their future bride. If we could, each of us would rip open the shower curtain, clutching a diamond ring. Our future fiancée would scream bloody murder and we'd scream back: "Marry me!" Now *that's* how you *pop* the question. On your wedding day, men promise to love, honor, respect, cherish, and trust. Men sincerely promise to be faithful, loyal, and honest. And yet we spend the weeks leading up to the marriage proposal lying, cheating, and deceiving a woman, all in the spirit of preserving the surprise.

The surprise is how I've justified the torture and trickery. My need to keep Paige guessing makes it okay to caution her against slipping into the future tense or discourage her from reading the wedding announcements in the newspaper or pretend in some subtle way that I'm not ready. Just last weekend we were lounging on the couch, watching a movie, and Paige jokingly suggested that we have a wedding just like the people on TV. That's when I reminded her that we are neither big nor fat nor Greek. *What do you say we take this relationship one step at a time.* Every great magician needs misdirection. I'm going to hell.

For Paige, a majestic wedding is only the beginning. In Paige's fantasy, we'll barbecue chicken every Fourth of July in Alexander Park. Next door is the Community Center where we'll decorate the Crockett Christmas tree. Our daughter will attend Rodeo Hills Elementary. Our son will pitch in at the Boy Scout Fish Fry. I'll be on the Chamber of Commerce. Paige will join the Lions Club. On weekends, we'll go antiquing and attend local car shows, art exhibits, and yes, even that ridiculous psychic fair where Tarot card readers, palmists, and healers gather from all over the Bay Area. The Altman family will trek across the Al Zampa Bridge every summer for Second Sunday Stroll. And every fall, we'll play competitive bocce ball on one of those teams with cutesy names like "The High Rollers" or "The Be-Occe Ballers." When we're empty nesters, too old and gray to lawn bowl, we'll retire to the rolling hills of the Carquinez Vista Manor. If it were up to Paige, we'd spend the rest of our lives together in Crockett.

"Wait," he tells me. Does Gregory think this marriage is too sudden? Surely he wouldn't have us live together first. Living together is a "cop-out"—just ask your buddy Sid. *I should call Gregory back and invoke Sid's advice.*

I whip out my cell phone, toggle over to my outgoing calls list, and redial Gregory. The call connects instantly.

"Hello," he says.

I hang up.

Gregory doesn't have caller ID. Gregory may have caller ID. I don't know if Gregory has caller ID.

He knew it was me. He has my number. If he thinks something's wrong, he'll call back. I wait for the phone to ring, but it doesn't. I try to imagine what he's doing. I envision him playing computer solitaire. He's reading a World War II thriller. He's reheating leftovers from the party. He has no reason to suspect that I just called or that we still need to talk. In his mind, we made a deal: I'm waiting. *But should I?*

I prop my feet up on the dining room table, pry off my sneaks, and slip off my socks. What I wouldn't do right now to have Mac Daddy here to help me.

What if I ask now? Claws for cons. Toes for pros.

Toes						Claws		
Market Little Piggy	Home Piggy	Roast Beef Piggy	None Piggy	Wee-Wee Piggy	Other Market Piggy	Thumb	Index Finger	Middle Finger
Ask now. Avoid Gregory ruining the surprise.	Ask now. Lower the risk of losing the ring.	Ask now. Reduce chances that someone else asks.	Ask now. Change Gregory's mind later by thrilling Paige now.	Ask now. Roll out your existing engagement plan.	Ask now. Before Gregory is able to change her mind.	Wait. Use the time to make Gregory like you.	Wait. Use the time to convince Gregory you're ready.	Wait. Use the time to convince Gregory Paige is ready.

The toes have it over the fingers, six to three. There's no resisting simple math: I've got twice as many reasons to ask than to wait.

I swing by the car and grab our Scrabble set. When I walk in the room, Paige is adjusting the strap on her black cocktail dress. A few loose strands of hair hang like bangs. I shake the familiar scarlet game box in her direction.

"Yes!" she says jerking her fist down as if she's just scored a goal.

CHEZ Canard is located about twenty minutes north of the Thistle Dew in Healdsburg, the quaintest of Sonoma towns. I selected the four-star restaurant not so much for its soft lighting, vaulted ceilings, or subdued atmosphere, but for the Parisian cuisine.

Tonight I will finally deliver on the pledge I made to myself more than a decade ago: order a complete meal for Paige in French. I downloaded the menu off the Internet last night, but very little of it was actually in French (or English for that matter). I'm still not sure what Kaffi Lime, Saffron Nage, or Salt-cured Torchon with Rhubarb is. Still, I did my best to translate the menu from Chinese to English to French.

"The lady will start with the *hairy cot-verts aveck pasteek et Bookerone,*" I say, butchering Paige's appetizer.

The garçon nods his head confidently, but nothing's registering.

I give him a hint by pointing to the Green Beans with Watermelon and Anchovies on the menu.

He tells me that I've made an excellent choice, but neither Paige nor Frenchy can stand much more. Halfway through ordering her entrée, the two of them beg me to surrender like Napoleon at Waterloo.

I rush us through the most expensive dinner of my life so we can get back, and get started. As we coast past Sonoma's tree-lined plaza packed with small shops, restaurants, and historical buildings, Paige can't help herself.

"Let's walk dinner off," she implores. "It'll be romantic."

"We can do that when it's light out. Let's go back to the room. It'll be plenty romantic there," I assure her. "I brought red wine. We'll flip on a fire."

Before she can answer, I'm turning into the rock driveway of the Thistle Dew Inn. I pull the emergency brake, pop the car in neutral, and turn off the ignition. The car slowly winds down. The crickets chirp loudly.

Then the first tremors strike. This is the real thing: something on the order of a magnitude 5.0 earthquake.

"Did you feel that?" I cry.

"Feel what?"

"There it is again."

"I think my cell phone's vibrating," she realizes, digging through her purse.

She's right. The muffled hum is emanating from her purse. My heart is thumping. I'm cracking up. Gregory is calling so he can spoil everything.

"Let the call go," I suggest calmly. "We're on vacation."

I place my hand on her bare thigh and strangle the pleather steering wheel with the other. She produces the phone. The tiny green cell phone light illuminates the cabin like kryptonite.

"Hmm, it's Lara," she says, studying it.

Lara knows! Paige looks at me. The phone vibrates again. *Please don't answer it,* I plead with my eyes. I kiss her on the lips. The phone buzzes. I kiss her neck until the phone stops. Thirty seconds later, the device alerts Paige that she has a voice message.

"How about we Jacuzzi before 'The Sex'?" Paige asks.

"Why not," I tell her. A dip in the hot tub and a couple of glasses of wine might smooth things out.

The whirlpool is a sliver of paradise. A crescent moon pokes through a fortress of cedars and oaks. We have the tub to ourselves and we cook in silence. Arms resting on the ledge, eyes closed, bubbles frothing, jet streams pounding, I am convinced that everything is going to be all right. I often feel this way in Jacuzzis. Maybe this inn *will do,* after all.

I'm about to become someone's husband. *Have you met my wife?*

When I open my eyes, I'm staring face-to-face with the innkeeper.

"Evenin', sailor," she greets me in wire rim glasses, a floral button-down blouse, khaki shorts, and ratty gray hair. She knows exactly why we're here.

Please go away, I think.

"Warm enough for you?" the woman asks.

Suddenly, with striking speed and force, she submerges her hand into the hot tub only inches from my rear. A second later she pulls out a stringed thermometer.

"One-oh-three," she says, inspecting it carefully. "Perfect soup!"

"Perfect," Paige kindly repeats with the same inflection. "Thank you so much." Paige is always thanking everyone for everything.

"Goodnight," I tell Chatty Cathy.

"Nighty-night," Cathy chirps back.

It's time.

Back in the room, while Paige is busy setting up the Scrabble board, I subtly drag my duffel bag into the bathroom and fish out the rings, jamming one in each back pocket. Then I grab the California Syrah by its neck, pinching two plastic cups between my fingers. *Does it get any more romantic than this?* Paige is just about done flipping over the tiles when I return. I take a seat across from her on the floor and begin picking my letters.

"You get seven, not eight," I remind her.

"Yeah, yeah, yeah, I know. Ready?" she asks.

I am: in my back pockets, both rings, and in my front pocket, the seven letters that I've been carrying around all day.

After four plays each, the board starts opening up. I still haven't quite figured out how I'm going to get the crucial letters from my pocket to this rack without getting caught.

"You're peeking at my letters," I complain.

"Are you mental? How am I looking at your letters from over here?"

"Cheaters never prosper," I remind her.

I grab my rack of letters, crawl over to the bed, and pull down one of the large crocheted pillows with my free hand. Retaking my seat across from her, I reposition the pillow so it shields my tiles from the board. I lean forward and give Paige a big smile, readjusting the ring box poking my left buttocks cheek.

"You've completely lost your mind," she determines.

It's Paige's turn, but I see my window of opportunity—the "E" in "LEFTY." My heart begins to race. At all costs, I must prevent her from playing that "E."

"If you don't use the 'Y,' then I will," I threaten her.

"Hold your horses." She's trying to concentrate.

"The 'Y' is four points plus the double-word score . . ."

"I know. I know," she says with a hint of anxiety. "But I don't have anything."

"Take your time," I encourage her.

While Paige contemplates the "Y," I slide all the letters on my rack into one hand and casually drop them behind my back. Then, from behind the pillow, I slowly reach into my front pocket, and pull out the replacements.

"I think you've learned your lesson," I say, tossing the down pillow aside and moving my rack closer to the board. "Whose turn is it?"

"Fine!" she says. "I'll go!"

"Good!" I say theatrically.

"Fine!"

Paige uses the "Y" and plays "YAWN" for twenty points. Not bad for someone who said she had nothing. I score it. I always keep score.

"My turn," I say, steadying my hands. Using the "E," I lay out my letters—

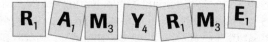

I begin tallying up my score.

"Ramyr-me?" she asks. "Is that a word?"

"Two, five, ten, fourteen, plus a double-word score," I whisper to myself.

"Use it in a sentence," she demands.

"That's twenty-eight points," I say, adding the figure to my column. It was all fun and games until I wrote "28" on the official score sheet. Now Paige is irritated.

"Ramyr-me is not a word, Andy."

"Are you challenging?"

"How can I challenge? We have no dictionary. Just tell me what it means."

"Oh wait," I say as if it's only just occurred to me. I slide my tiles around on the board, rearranging them to read "ARMMY RE" and then finally "MARRY ME." I let the words sink in. The blank expression on her face is priceless.

"You're not allowed to play two words," she says softly.

"Can we make an exception?"

"This isn't a game," she says.

And yet it is.

"Can I be your husband?" I say tenderly. "Will you be my wife?"

I suspect that this is at least the second member of the Day family whom I've made cry in the last two hours.

"Of course, definitely, absolutely! Did I say yes?"

She moves toward me on her knees, crossing the board and losing her balance as she slips on one of the tiles. We tumble backward and that's when she notices the letters discarded behind me.

"And *I'm* the cheater?"

"But all I have is this," I say, pulling out a Red Rocket candy ring from my right pocket. I tear open the packaging with my teeth and beckon her left hand. The red candy jewelry clumsily slips down her tan ring finger.

"It's lovely," she says, holding it high, batting her eyelashes. Then she brings her hand to her face and pops the candy in her mouth.

"Don't eat it!" I exclaim. "Fine, eat that one, but don't eat this one," I say, pulling out a small red jewelry box etched in gold fabric.

Her eyes widen. The candy ring makes the perfect popping sound when she removes it. Paige hesitantly opens the red jewelry box, the Red Rocket still awkwardly hanging from her left hand. She stares at it. Staring back at her is a one-carat, virtually flawless white diamond with a small diamond baguette on either side in a sparkling platinum setting. Indeed, Igor Petrov sold me the most beautiful stone.

RAMYR ME for JAGUAR, seven letters for six . . . plus six weeks' salary.

"Of course I'll ramyr-you," she says.

I pull off the Red Rocket and slip the diamond ring in its place. It's two sizes too large for her.

Hugging me tightly, she rests her head on my shoulder, and lifts up her hand to study the sparkler.

"My father is going to be so happy," she whispers across my nape.

CHAPTER 12

You're Going to Fix This

THE engagement bliss lasted six minutes. Then Paige started ripping the room apart for her cell phone. I'm willing to bet she doesn't look for it powered down and stowed away in a sock at the bottom of my duffel bag. I couldn't risk Gregory interrupting the deed or Paige playing back Lara's voice message.

"I had it right here," she cries, referencing the nightstand.

Got me, I pantomime.

"No pressure, and this is *not* a trick question, *seriously,*" she says innocently enough. "Did you happen to ask my dad before you asked me?"

"I did ask your dad," I reply.

Paige lets out a sigh of relief.

"You didn't have to, but I appreciate it," she says, dragging the antique cast-iron bed away from the wall. "Can you call my phone with yours?"

"Just take mine," I relent.

I pinch the inside corners of my eyes to help make the approaching migraine go away.

He'll hear her voice and he'll change his tune, I pray.

Paige dials Gregory, then puts her cheek up against mine so we can both listen and speak together. I can hear it ringing. She glances over at me as if to remind me that this is the part where we both scream: "We're getting married!"

"You talk," I lip-synch, pulling away as it rings a second time.

We stare at each other, both holding our breath. Paige tucks a strand of hair behind her ear. There's still time to confess everything.

Why isn't Gregory answering? Is it because he sees my name on the caller ID? He's avoiding me. He thinks I'm calling for a third time. He's irritated. He's going to pick up and start screaming into the other end.

Hang up!

"Your daughter's getting married," Paige says like peekaboo. "You Sneaky Pete, how long have you known?"

Paige starts pacing around the room as she listens. Gregory does all the talking. Paige turns serious. Then she smiles. She nods. She nods again.

"Uh-huh, uh-huh, uh-huh," she says.

Now she's thanking him . . . *thanking, thanking, thanking, nodding, nodding, nodding.* This is good. Confidence building. Future brightening.

"Of course, hold on, Daddy," she says handing me the phone. "He wants to congratulate you *personally.*"

"Hello?" I say playfully, as if I don't know who it is.

Utter silence.

"Gregory?" I ask, checking the line.

Paige beams a smile in my direction.

I whisper to Paige, "I think we lost the cell signal."

She shrugs.

"Are you disturbed?" Gregory asks. He is beside himself.

"There he is," I inform Paige, with a forced grin.

A few seconds pass.

"What's wrong with you?" he asks. "Just smile and nod your head."

I'm way ahead of him.

"Listen here. I'm not going to be the one who ruins this day for my daughter. I thought I made myself perfectly clear. We were going to wait." He pauses to cough. "Why on earth would you ask my permission if you were just going to do whatever you want, anyway?"

Paige can tell something's wrong.

"I don't care what you say. We're more excited than you are!" I cheer.

I'm about to vomit our expensive dinner.

"You and I are going to have a long talk at work tomorrow," he says.

"Well, the wedding planning will have to wait one more day. I'm off tomorrow, and your daughter and I are touring wine country. There must be something we can bring back for you."

Paige is delighted by my generous offer. I can read her mind: *Go ahead. Just do it. Call him "Dad."*

"Friday then!" he says, catching on. "You're going to fix this," he says in no uncertain terms.

"The ring is beautiful. She can't wait to show it to you, too," I say.

Gregory hangs up, and I tell the dead air to have a good night.

Lying head to toe on the bed, passing the phone back and forth, we start calling everyone we know. The more people we tell, the more the lie becomes true. First we wake up my parents in Vegas. Then we break the news to Lara in Los Angeles. Apparently she didn't know anything. All of our friends ask the same questions. The men look forward: When's the big day? The women reminisce: How did he do it? Did he ask your father? With each phone call I fine-tune the fib. I'm caught up in the excitement. By the time we reach Sid, I'm pathological.

"Aw, that's great news, small fry. See what I said," Sid tells Cookie. Then he's back to me: "I just knew Gregory would give you the go-ahead."

"I did just like you suggested, Sid," I tell him, giving Paige a loving grin. "Gregory and I had a long talk, and he's excited to discuss the next steps."

Now Cookie is screaming in the background. "For Christ's sake, they'll be engaged in the morning," she cries.

"Sorry kids, Cookie needs her beauty sleep."

"Hang up," she yells a second time.

I promise to call Sid tomorrow.

We've called everyone, even a few wrong numbers. It's time for the engagement sex. Paige crawls on top of me and flips over so we're both facing the ceiling. We stare at the intricate ceramic molding where a chandelier once hung.

"This is comfy," she says.

I grunt back. To be crushed like this feels good.

"I'm tired. You tired? Because I'm tired," she says quickly.

The alcohol buzz and engagement adrenaline have worn off and I'm feeling drained too.

"I am."

A tacit agreement has just been reached.

"But just so you know, I want to," Paige swears, turning her head slightly to kiss me on the cheek.

I close my eyes and start making snoring sounds. She adds her own snores to the beat.

"We have to promise to have sex in the morning," she mumbles.

"I'm totally there," I say monotone.

And before long, we're out, one mattress on top of another.

Daybreak arrives and through a series of unconscious gymnastic moves, we've miraculously slipped into our customary snoozing configurations.

Paige is going to be a good sleep partner. Like any couple, we have our occasional land grab issues in bed, but aside from the occasional, terrifying psychotic laugh in the middle of the night, Paige doesn't snore, move, or even speak in her sleep.

The bed is still crooked from when Paige was looking for her cell phone, and I never bothered to close the wooden shades, so now my face is sunburned. Paige is fending off the light by holding a folded pillow over her head with both hands. I roll my head toward her, hesitantly opening one eye for fear of bursting into flames. As the room comes into focus, I realize that Paige's gorgeous diamond engagement ring is only inches from my face. It's about to slip off. I gently push it back down her finger and close my eyes.

The ring may be the wrong size, but between the lighting, the brilliance of the stone, and the startling contrast against her tan skin, it most certainly is the right fit.

"I LOVE you," she reminds me as if there's a chance I've forgotten.

I pull out of the Clos du Bois compound, our third and final winery. Her eyes are fixed on the dirt road.

"Then I love you, too," I kid as we turn onto the main thoroughfare.

We're both a little tipsy. Paige is somewhere else. In the last fifteen hours, I've lost track of the number of ILYs exchanged back and forth, but now that we're engaged, it seems silly to count.

"Everything is changing," she says with mixed emotion.

We pass a bunch of lazy cows lounging in a grassy field. If they're lying down, is that a sign it will or won't rain? I can't recall. The looming clouds confirm my suspicions.

"I wish you could have met my mother," she tells me.

Lydia died of leukemia nine months before I returned to Crockett.

"Me, too," I tell her, but my answer only seems to make her feel worse.

"She was so funny." Paige turns to me and chortles, "She would have *loved* you."

I just nod. But Lydia wouldn't have liked me at all. Unbeknownst to Paige, Lydia wrote me off as a hooligan years ago. A bubble-gum-stealing goon. I wish Lydia were still alive. I wish Paige had given me a proper introduction; then I could have apologized and won her over. *I was young and foolish then,* I would tell her. *Bunky was a bad influence. Do you know his current rap sheet is this long?* Gregory has no right to withhold his blessing, but if Lydia were alive today, she would.

Then, as if it's just occurred to her, Paige says, thrilled and slightly anxious all at once, "I'm going to be your *wife.* You're going to be my *husband. My husband!* That sounds so weird."

"We're a team," I explain.

Hearing this makes her happy. I should say things like this to her more often. Five minutes pass silently before either of us speaks again.

"You're my best friend, Andy."

I'm touched. I privately award her points. We're headed back to reality, back to Crockett, where the weather forecast is gloomy with a high likelihood of shit storm. Whatever happens in the next twenty-four hours, I want her to promise me that she'll feel the same way afterward.

It's getting late. We're both a little drunk. We need to head home. I'm sure Gregory's already starting to worry. I turn down a dirt road.

"So you're up for one more?" she asks, surprised.

The entrance to the vineyard is quickly approaching on the left, but I take a hard right, and park fifty yards away underneath a large oak tree. Then I stick the sun reflector in the front windshield, flip on the CD player, and awkwardly climb into the backseat. Paige takes my hand and joins me.

"We need to sober up," I tell her in between kisses up and down her neck.

We pull off each other's clothing, multiple layers at a time, until we're both naked. I love her. And I love wine country.

CHAPTER 13

Time Constraints

THE phone rings twice and each time I expect it to be Paige crying hysterically because Gregory's spilled the beans. But alas, both calls are from Sid, who wants the real scoop on how everything went down. I'm screening calls. Each time his digits appear on the display I let it go to voice mail. I'll patch things up with Gregory. Then I'll deal with Sid.

I hate the thought of Paige and Gregory together right now. I seriously doubt Gregory is capable of perpetuating this charade. I want Paige to call every five minutes and confirm that everything is status quo. I would call, but I can't risk getting Gregory—the slightest provocation might set him off.

I am out of control. I'm exhausted. I'm wired. I need something to occupy my mind. I check my watch. It's midnight. I have an idea for an invention, but I'll need some special software to draw it properly. I find a trial version you can download for free off the Web and work into the wee hours. *Sid is going to love this.* At some point, I drift off to sleep.

When my clock sounds at 7:00 A.M., I nearly fall off my chair. Touching my face, I feel the slight indentations across my left cheek from the keyboard. Untold volumes of drool lay between the keys.

It's pouring outside. If it rains twice a summer in Crockett, that's a lot, and because we live below the snow line, we haven't seen snow in over a century.

I'm not accustomed to being the first at work, and by some great miracle, I manage to remember the alarm code on the third and final try. I use the quiet time to fill some new scripts and rework mine:

"You have every reason to be angry and I'm sorry," I'll begin. He'll be expecting a magnitude 5.0 or 6.0 and the apology will take him off guard. At that point, I need to say things that make it utterly clear there is no undoing this. *So what do you think of the engagement ring? My parents can't wait to see you again. Sid is so happy for us. Paige will make such a beautiful bride. I'm a lucky man. It's big of you to forgive me. You're handsome. Nice tie.*

The bell on the front door jingles and my heart skips a beat. But it's only Belinda. She shakes off her umbrella, jams it in the nearby pail, and then asks me about my trip to wine country. She mustn't know that Paige and I are engaged; I can't have Belinda congratulating Gregory before he even sets foot through the door—or maybe she should.

For the first time, in all the time that I've worked here, Gregory is late, by at least twenty minutes, and Belinda and I are beginning to worry. She tries him at home, but there's no answer. We make a collective decision to open the pharmacy for business. By now, my stomach is doing somersaults. Somehow I'm responsible.

Forty-five minutes later and still no Gregory. I can't take it. I call Paige and leave a cryptic message. As I hang up the phone,

Gregory walks in. He's dripping wet. Wheezing and coughing, he ignores Belinda's concerned questions, and heads straight for the storeroom. I try to make eye contact with him, but he won't have it. The temperature in the room drops forty degrees.

I can't take the anxiety. I poke my head in the back room.

"Everything okay?" I ask.

He flashes me a look to kill, his eyes watering more than usual, or maybe it's the rain. He awkwardly peels off his wet baby blue windbreaker.

"What do you say you give me a sec?" he asks sternly, frustrated, shaking, barely catching his breath.

He pats his eyes and forehead with a handkerchief.

"Sure, sure, you got it. No worries," I say as cheerily as possible.

I hesitate briefly before leaving. *Let me start off by saying that you have every reason to be angry with me . . .* But the words don't come.

"Where is my future husband?" she shouts. *Oh God.*

I pop my head back out onto the pharmacy floor. But it's only Ruth Mulrooney. She's been calling me her boyfriend from the moment we met. The eighty-year-old Crockett socialite and real estate tycoon is impeccably dressed in a long pink raincoat. With shiny white latex nails, she daintily pulls the plastic rain bonnet from her head. Her hair is dyed sherbet orange.

I compliment her scarf—it's green paisley and I tell her that it brings out the hazel in her eyes. Ruth coos. My wedding news could end up hitting Ruth the hardest. I'll let her down easy, but another day.

"That daughter of yours sure is lucky to have landed this catch," she reminds Gregory as he enters from the back room, buttoning up his long white coat.

Gregory shoots me a look. It's uncanny how people can say the kindest things at the most inopportune times. I hand Ruth her antiaging drugs—anticholesterol pills and antidepressants.

Earlier this year, Ruth buried her third husband, Harold. Her first, Joseph, was killed in World War II. Her second, Samuel Mulrooney, died of a stroke thirty-five years ago. Then there was Harold S. Warner, husband number three. Before he died, Warner was considered Crockett's wealthiest resident. Now Ruth is. Warner Construction is known throughout the Bay Area. Harold invested all of his construction money in real estate. Among the properties Ruth Mulrooney inherited: Ollie's Auto Shop, the Carquinez Manor retirement home, and a block of unused warehouses originally owned and operated by C & H Sugar. Ruth is fond of saying Harold died in bed, but not peacefully and not in his sleep.

"Too much," she complains, studying the contents of one of the bottles through cat-eye reading glasses.

I tell her that a thirty-day supply is minimum. "You don't have to wait a full month before visiting us again," I reassure her. Ruth is among the pharmacy's many do-drop-ins, something Gregory encourages.

I come out from behind the counter to escort Ruth to the front door. She hooks her arm around mine and squeezes it tightly. At the register, Ruth pays in cash. She always pays in cash. Then I give her a kiss on the cheek, pop open her umbrella for her, and send Ruth on her merry way.

Gregory's "big talk" never happens. In fact, Gregory doesn't speak to anyone all morning, just grunting and gesturing. I finally work up the nerve to ask him whether he can talk, but he pretends to ignore me. After Gregory refuses to acknowledge the question a second time, I decide that he is no longer entitled to my apology. *Who cares why he originally asked me to wait.* He's right: I *am* going to fix this. I've decided that after work I'll end the misery, drain him of all his power, and come clean to Paige. *Then what are you going to do, Gregory?*

By lunchtime, I'm ready to break down and beg him for forgiveness.

It's a welcome relief when I see Sid and Loki walk through the front door. I run over to Sid like a Death Row inmate: *Any word from the governor?*

I'm flattered—he's using that stupid dog umbrella I invented a few months back.

"It still needs improvement. I'm sort of sorry we PMPed it so fast," he adds, clumsily folding the contraption up and jamming it in the umbrella bucket.

"You look good, Sid," I say, flattening out his raincoat. *Help me.*

Sid knocks away my hands. Loki races up and down Aisle Three.

"You can't bring that animal in here." It's the first thing Gregory's said in hours.

"But Sid's potty trained," I remind Gregory.

Sid raises his fists and silently cheers *good one.*

Gregory is nonplussed.

"This is a place of business," Gregory demands, raising his voice. "No dogs!"

"Come on, G-man, why the long face?" Sid chirps. "Your daughter is getting married. You're about to gain a son-in-law!"

Gregory shakes his head in disgust. The ground begins to shake.

"It's not sanitary to distribute medication around pets," Gregory yells in between coughs. "All I need is someone tripping over that creature. "

We both look at Loki, then at each other, and then back to Gregory.

"Seriously?" Sid and I ask in unison.

"OUT!" Gregory yells at the tiny pooch, startling a customer one aisle over and sending himself into a total hacking fit.

Gregory tries to hold his mouth closed to muffle the coughs. Then he pats down his lab coat for an inhaler, but can't find it. Once he catches his breath on his own, he goes back to crushing pills with his mortar and pestle.

Sid and I know better than to antagonize him further. Sid picks up Loki, who is terrified, and we move the conversation a few feet down Aisle Three.

"What's going on here?" Sid whispers.

"It's complicated," I whisper back. I'm convinced Gregory can still hear us.

Sid studies me stone-faced while Loki licks his cheek. I wish we could step outside, but it's still pouring.

"Please, Sid, just talk about something else. Anything."

"Okay. I've been giving your bladeless windshield wipers concept some more thought," he replies at normal speaking volume. "I'm not convinced we can get those jet streams blowing hard enough to clear away heavy snow or mud."

I stop him. "I've come up with something even better," I tell him. "Do you have the time?"

"Time for what?"

"No, what time do you have?" I ask, tapping my wristwatch.

This prompts a peculiar look. *Check for yourself.* He hesitantly plays along. Sid awkwardly hands me Loki, pulls up his sleeve, and squints to read his Timex.

"Three . . . no four-fifteen," he says.

I place Loki on the floor and unfold a piece of paper from my back pocket.

Sid has become conditioned to worry when I do this. I hand him the technical drawing I spent all night drafting.

"I call it a 'tactile timepiece,'" I say proudly.

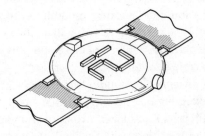

Gregory clears his throat. If he has something to say, I wish he'd just say it. His nonverbal signs are driving me crazy.

Sid is intrigued. He traces the lines with his finger.

"Study the diagram and tell me what time it displays."

Sid's eyes dart around the picture. "Twelve o'clock," he concludes.

"Yes. The digits in the middle represent the hours. But what about the minutes?"

Gregory starts coughing again. I brace myself for the yelling.

Sid studies the drawing. "A quarter to one!" he cries like eureka.

"Nice!" I scream, smacking him smartly in the chest with the back of my hand. "The hour is big so you can read it with your eyes *or* your fingers. All you have to do is rub your thumb over the raised numerals."

"And the minutes are represented by elevated markers at each quadrant around the circumference," Sid determines. "North, south, east, and in this case, west, representing forty-five minutes."

"Like a compass," I cheer.

"Hmpf. But don't Braille watches already exist?"

"They do, but that's the beauty of this timepiece, it works for the sighted as well as the visually impaired, and requires no special training whatsoever. Business meetings that go long, dates that stretch on for eternity, now you can reach under the table and surreptitiously check the time with your fingertips."

"Not bad," he admits.

"I've even got a slogan. Ready for this? 'The Touch Ticker: Changing the Face of Time.' "

Sid rubs his chin and studies the drawing some more.

The crash is loud and sudden. Sid and I cringe as if someone has botched up that trick where you pull a tablecloth from underneath six place settings. Chunks of glass and pills glide across the floor and come to a sudden stop.

Has Gregory snapped? Oh man, where's Loki?

No one is standing behind the pharmacy counter. I call out to Gregory, but there is no answer. I rush over, smashing open the saloon doors and leaping to the raised platform. Gregory is on the floor, eyes shut, his vintage porcelain mortar and pestle shattered to bits. White powder is everywhere.

I yell out to Belinda, "Call 911!"

"I'm on it," she screams back.

Sid is crouching next to me now.

"Is he breathing?" Sid asks anxiously.

"I can't tell." He's gasping, I think. "Sid, go to the end of the aisle right behind you, second shelf from the bottom. I need one of the inhalers labeled 'ipratropium bromide.' "

Sid springs into action. Once he's back there, he needs me to repeat the name of the medication. My mind is racing. I took a beginner's first aid course three years ago. It included the basics on nutrition, fractures, burns, and the Heimlich maneuver. We worked on dummies. I've never attempted to save anyone's life.

The color has drained from Gregory's doughy cheeks. He's perspiring. I gently sit Gregory up and pat him on the back—maybe this will clear his throat. I listen for breathing.

"Please, Gregory, come through this," I beg him.

Belinda rushes over.

I gently lower him, tipping his head back, and try mouth-to-mouth resuscitation. I'm not sure I know what I'm doing, but I'm blowing air, pumping his chest, and counting. Sid uses my tactile timepiece drawing to cradle a heaping pile of inhalers. He drops everything next to us.

"Tell me what to do," I ask Sid urgently.

"An ambulance should be here any moment now," Belinda yells.

"Just hang tight, kiddo. Don't get yourself all worked up," Sid says.

Only then do I realize that I'm crying.

"He's going to be fine, Andy," Sid promises.

I wring my hands.

"I'm sorry, Gregory," I say softly. "I'm so sorry."

R

PART TWO

CHAPTER 14

Cold, Hard Numbers

GREGORY died.

I still can't believe it.

The ambulance arrived two hours later. (Sid tells me it was more like ten minutes.) Brandon Mills, Gregory's primary physician, says it was a massive coronary due to chronic emphysema. At a loss for air, Gregory's heart gave out. He never made it to the hospital. Mills assures us Gregory didn't suffer, but this is something doctors always say. I killed Gregory.

In the waiting room of the Veterans Affairs Hospital, Lara pressed Mills for more answers. Most of Gregory's medical problems were irreversible, Mills told us. Gregory relied heavily on quick fixes. He used medicated inhalers when oxygen therapy was called for. Paige tried, but the Mayor of Pomona Street had too much pride to cart around a tank of oxygen. Even at home, getting Gregory strapped in was a feat. The few times he did capitulate to Paige's pleas, I was always refused admission to the house. *Daddy needs his privacy,* Paige would tell me, closing the front door behind her. The only person who ever managed to convince Gregory to really take care of himself was Lydia.

Losing Gregory is the most awful thing that has ever happened. People say time heals all wounds, but it's hard to imagine that happening in our lifetimes. Nothing will ever be the same. Inserting arbitrary words into a live television newscast, pretend arguing, burning clothes, awarding points, singing Chewbacca— nothing will be funny again.

I am no comfort to Paige at all. She cries. She is doubled over in pain. *Hold her,* Sid tells me. *Leave her alone,* Cookie insists. *Love her,* says everyone. I try, but nothing works.

The last week has been a blur. Gregory asked to be cremated, and Lara and Paige privately dispersed his ashes in the Pacific.

People are always dropping by the house. One thing Crockett does well is death. People die here all the time. Unlike me, everyone seems to know his or her role. They know what to say and they usually say it with chicken—the refrigerator is jam-packed with chicken casseroles, grilled chicken, and chicken Parmesan. The countertops are always crowded with baked goods and bagel spreads.

The pharmacy has remained closed ever since. Every afternoon I try to meet Manny at the pharmacy to sign off on a few deliveries, and forward any outstanding prescriptions to the Walgreens in Benicia.

It's hard to be in the pharmacy for too long, particularly now that Lara is there all the time. She's co-opted the space, splitting her day between her accounting responsibilities out of Los Angeles and Gregory's affairs. To hear Lara describe it, sorting out everything could take months.

Paige hasn't returned to work and hasn't decided if she will. Within the last week, I can count on one hand how many times she's left the house. When her mother passed away, Gregory refused to let anyone go through Lydia's belongings. That was nearly two years ago. Now Paige talks about the dread of going through two lifetimes' worth of stuff.

Paige floats around the house, not so much cleaning it, but moving items from one side to the other. She has yet to go into Gregory's bedroom. Lara sleeps in there; I sleep in Lara's room; and Paige sleeps in her own room. I keep waiting for something to happen, decisions to be made, but nobody seems to be talking about anything.

When I'm not ineffectively comforting Paige or irritating Lara, I'm bored to tears. I busted my ass for Gregory in those final days. Fifty- to sixty-hour workweeks were typical. I used to complain so much about that job—about how it was distracting me from doing what I really wanted in life—and yet now I don't find any of the other things I used to do very fulfilling. Yesterday, Sid and I spent a few hours tooling around in his garage, but all of our ideas fell flat. Our hearts aren't in it. Only now do I realize that, in short, Gregory and that pharmacy came to define who I am.

A few days ago, Paige took off her engagement ring. The next day she caught me eyeing it on the bed stand. *We need to get it resized; it keeps slipping off. I don't want it to get scuffed up when I clean. It doesn't mean anything. I love you.* The lady doth protest too much. That ring represents happiness. Hope. A future with me. I get the impression that Paige is ashamed to feel any of those emotions right now.

Paige is alone in her childhood bedroom lying in a fetal position on top of the covers. She is in jean shorts and a tank top, her hair is in a ponytail, and she's covered in grime. There are small purple bags under her eyes. Every light in the house is on and the place is empty. She seems to be staring straight across the hall at the door to her parents' bedroom. I block her view suddenly and she invites me in with her eyes. I can barely spoon her on this single bed.

When the phone rings, neither of us moves.

"Leave it," Paige says after the second ring. "No more condolences. Plus someone's been calling here and hanging up. Twice in the last hour."

After the third ring, the answering machine picks up downstairs. Despite Lara's pleas, Paige hasn't had the heart to change the outgoing message. Suddenly Gregory is back—his raspy voice echoing through the hallways.

"Leave the message and we'll call you," he says simply.

Leave the message, as if there could only be one, proper way of saying something.

The answering machine beeps and the caller hangs up.

"This sucks," she says flatly.

"It does."

"I can't go in there. It's too painful."

"There's no rush," I tell her.

"But it might be time."

"There are no rules," I say.

What am I, a goddam fortune-cookie dispenser?

"Aren't we entitled to some privacy even after we die? I'm just going to rifle through their most personal belongings?"

I give her a squeeze around the waist and kiss her thick black ponytail. The sweet scent tickles my nose, causing me to sneeze directly into her lustrous mane.

"You've got to be kidding me!" she complains, springing to her feet. "Couldn't you turn away? Right in my hair?" she says, completely grossed out.

There is a familiar look on her face. She wants to laugh, or at least grin.

"It came up on me too quickly," I joke defensively.

I run to the bathroom, ball up some toilet paper, and hand it to her.

"Your lease, it's month to month, right?" she asks, patting down her ponytail. "Maybe it's time to give your landlord notice."

"Move in together because I sneezed in your hair? If I cough in your face, will you put the engagement ring back on?"

"Don't be cute."

"Is that really what you want? For us to live together?" I ask.

Personally I don't want to start our life together here, amid the musty carpets, dark-wood paneling, minichandeliers, memories, sickness, and sadness.

"I'm just trying to be practical."

I'm not sure what to make of this. Living together was never an option, but if we're engaged—assuming we still are—I suppose it's different.

The screen on the front door slams. It's Lara.

"Oh, good," Paige says. "We need to get Lara's okay before we do anything. I want her to feel comfortable in her own home."

"I'm sure she'll be over the moon when she learns that we'll be bunking together."

"She'll be fine with it. I'll find a way."

Paige grabs my hand, dragging me down the hall, and then down the steps.

The door slams again, and through the window I see Lara reach into her trunk and dig out a pile of papers.

Out front, a black Lincoln Town Car cruises our house, then speeds away.

"Sis, we've got problems," Lara tells Paige, balancing a tall stack of papers.

I've haven't left Paige's side since it happened and yet every time Lara sees me, she seems surprised I'm still here.

"Andrew, would you mind giving us some privacy?" Lara asks. "Paige and I have some family matters to attend to."

"Be civil, Lar," Paige says. "Andy *is* family. Just talk."

Paige takes a seat on the couch. I stand. Lara plops down in Gregory's olive armchair and a plume of dust kicks up. Paige doesn't approve of her sister's choice of seating: Gregory's chair marks hallowed ground.

Lara starts shuffling through the papers on her lap. She hands Paige a legal-sized document.

"The mortgage on the house," Paige says, inspecting it. Paige turns to the last page of the packet. "Is this right?"

Lara hands Paige a preeviction letter and then a notice of foreclosure. Standing over Paige's shoulder I can read it: "Mortgage in Default Due to Nonpayment." Lara is baffled.

"Dad hasn't made a house payment in *six months*. Last year, he took out two lines of credit," Lara complains. "He has completely sucked the equity out of this house. I did his taxes five years ago; back then, Dad's mortgage was within striking distance."

"Five years ago Mom was alive," Paige says.

Lara doesn't want to talk about Lydia in front of me.

"Should I go?" I ask Paige.

Paige and Lara say no and yes in unison.

Lara takes a deep breath.

"It gets worse," Lara says. "Dad used credit cards to pay for *everything*—pharmacy rent, overhead, prescription drugs. He would go through the burger drive-through and use VISA or MasterCard."

"Oh, Daddy," Paige scolds him. "How much does he owe?"

Lara licks her index finger and pages through her pile some more.

"Over six different credit cards? Conservatively?" Lara estimates, "About fifty grand. But the interest and fees constantly add up to a lot more."

"Seriously?" I blurt out.

"Seriously, Paige, does he *have* to be here?"

"Sorry," I say.

Before Paige can respond, Lara hands her a pile of collection bills.

"Didn't he ever say anything to you?" Lara asks her kid sister. "I'm surprised the phone hasn't been ringing off the hook with creditors."

Paige and I share a sheepish grin.

Headlights blast through the living room blinds. Someone is here. I walk over to the window and peek outside. Some guy in an old Chevy Impala is using our driveway to turn around. Gregory's driveway is a popular turnabout.

"I haven't the foggiest idea what we could get for the pharmacy," Lara admits.

The blood drains from Paige's face. Reality is sinking in.

"Who said anything about *selling* the pharmacy?" Paige panics. "You're kidding, right?"

"*I'm* kidding?" Lara asks, cocking her head to one side.

No one's kidding.

"We don't have to sell the pharmacy," Paige pleads. "We just need to keep it open long enough to pay down some of these credit card bills."

"Oh, I see. You get to be the sentimental one and I get to be the ice-queen-bitch-from-hell," Lara roars back. "That way *I'm* the one flushing our birthright down the toilet, not you. That's not fair, Paige, and you know it. Don't punish me for saying what needs to be said, for doing what needs to be done.

"And, by the way, who's going to run the pharmacy?" Lara cries. "I certainly can't."

"Andy can help. So can I. We'll find people," Paige replies.

"This isn't a charity carwash. We need a pharmacist, a *licensed* pharmacist, and that certainly isn't Andrew, unless somehow he secretly reenrolled in pharmacy school and miraculously obtained a degree."

I refuse to dignify this with a response.

The antique clock on the shelf pounds out the seconds.

"I have a tiny bit of savings. Maybe I can get us back on track with the mortgage payments on the house," Paige suggests.

"So you have a spare $12,000 lying around?" Lara asks.

Paige shakes her head no. She still owes a fortune on the Vomit Mobile.

I have nothing to offer by way of cash. The engagement ring wiped me out, not to mention I still have plenty of student loans and this wedding to pay for.

"Wait a minute," I say. "If Gregory is no longer . . . with us . . . I'm not sure we're responsible for paying down his credit cards."

"Already thought of that. We need to foot the bill if we don't want the creditors to go after Dad's assets," Lara says. "One of Dad's VISA card companies has already put a lien on the pharmacy."

Lara waves the letter in my direction.

"How can they put a lien on property you don't even own? Your father rents that pharmacy space," I say.

"But the business itself is worth something," Paige's sister replies. "And if we don't pay, first they'll take the pharmacy and then they'll take . . ."

"No way," Paige cries. "No matter what, *we are keeping* this house."

"The creditors will go after the house unless we figure out a way to repay all of Dad's debts," Lara says. "It's that simple."

Paige and I think, but Lara's already there.

"I have one idea," Lara continues, all impressed with herself. "Apparently Dad had a bunch of running tabs with customers. There are at least a hundred patrons with accounts receivable of at least $500 each."

"Yeah, that's not going to happen," I quickly interject.

"Why would you say that?" Lara viciously snaps back.

"First off, those tabs are totally incomplete." It's the first time I've raised my voice to Lara. "Belinda doesn't even write half that stuff down. I don't even want to think about how long it would take for someone to reconstruct exactly who owes what."

"What do you think I've been doing for the last week? Need I remind you that I'm a certified public accountant."

I know.

"I've been comparing the prescriptions filled with the insurance forms, receipts, and deposits. I have a ledger with everything spelled out in painstaking detail. Most of the pieces of the puzzle are right there," Lara insists.

"You're going to retroactively bill people for stuff you're not even sure they did or didn't pay for?" I cry.

"No. I'm just talking about the deadbeats," she starts.

"You mean the customers?" I interrupt.

"Customers pay, Andrew. These people hardly qualify as patrons of Day's Pharmacy. What I'm suggesting is more than fair. Listen, I'm generously writing 50 percent of the tabs right off the top. But the rest is gettable."

"This is bad news, Lara. You should rethink this plan," I tell her. "No offense, but your father would never—"

"No offense, but shut the hell up. I'm not about to be lectured on what my father would or wouldn't do. Especially by you," Lara yells.

This conversation has the look and feel of a magnitude 4.0.

Paige jumps in. "Yeah, I don't love the idea of shaking down seniors for cash," she says softly. "These people are our friends. Our community. We're eating their chicken!"

"That chicken has cost us nearly six figures!" Lara insists. "All I'm saying is that we get half of that back to cover the credit card bills and mortgage payments. It's not even our money, Paige. I don't get it. How do you plan on getting the bank and credit card companies off our backs so we can keep the house? Our neighbors wouldn't want us to shoulder this burden."

Paige and I think.

Tick, tock, tick, tock, the clock on the shelf is killing me. If we sell anything, we need to sell that clock.

"You show me your list and I'll figure out which ones can really afford to pay," I suggest finally. "Just let me do it."

"Be my guest," Lara says. "Hit them up the next time they come into the pharmacy for a free refill. Which reminds me, I think we need to reopen for business as soon as possible, even if it's reduced hours. Overhead alone is killing us. Every day we stay closed we go about $400 deeper in debt."

"We'll need to bring Belinda back, on a part-time basis," I inform her.

"No, we're not paying anyone, especially Belinda. I used to baby-sit that girl, and she's got problems," Lara says. "We'll be fine without her."

"Belinda is a conscientious, loyal, and reliable worker, and we need her help," I demand, looking to Paige to back me up.

"We'll see," Lara mutters.

"This is all too much, too quick," Paige says somberly.

I rub her back softly.

"These problems have been coming for some time, sis," Lara says.

Lara puts the rest of her papers on the ground. She gets down on her knees and reaches for Paige's hands, clasping them between hers.

"It's just stuff, Paige. It's not Mom. It's not Dad. For me, all these things are just painful reminders that they're gone. For you, it's different; it represents your life. I understand that. I love you. I hate to see you like this. But you have to let some things go. *Change is hard,*" Lara adds softly.

Paige stares blankly at her sister; both of them have their father's crystal blue eyes. There is a long pause before anyone speaks next and it's Paige. She pulls out her hands from in between Lara's and reverses the configuration.

"Change *is* hard," she says. "Which reminds me, Andy's moving in."

CHAPTER 15

Slow Down

TONIGHT we're having fresh crabs at The Dead Fish. Why the finest seafood restaurant in all of Crockett thought it would be funny to give its establishment such an unappetizing name is beyond me. But the food is delicious, and The Dead Fish has stunning views of the Carquinez and serves Paige's favorite—midnight chocolate cake with fresh strawberries, the same as we had for her birthday. It's hard to believe that was just two weeks ago.

Paige needed to get out. There is nothing to eat in this house. The condolence meal train trailed off days ago. I managed to convince her to leave by systematically eliminating everything in the refrigerator.

"Something reeks," I declared, handing Paige the kitchen wastebasket like a challenge. Then I got down on my knees and began inspecting the shelves of the fridge for the foul culprit, handing her suspicious items, one by one. There was unanimity on the first three entrées: chicken cacciatore, chicken Parmesan, and deviled eggs—dump, dump, dump. I tossed her a plastic bag of iffy salami. Paige poked her nose inside and handed it back.

"Really?" I asked.

"Cured meat can stay forever," she insisted.

"But it was sitting out on the counter for like . . . two hours."

Paige hasn't been to pharmacy school. She can't appreciate the spectrum of chemicals, parasites, fungi, toxins, and viruses that can infiltrate meat.

"There are at least twenty different types of bacteria that cause food poisoning," I informed her.

"The meat's fine," she said, surprised by my squeamishness. "Those deli labels are a scam to make you buy more salami. Put it back."

"Something doesn't smell right," I told her, urgently sniffing the fruit bin.

"Get up," she commanded, handing me the garbage pail.

We switched positions. She grabbed the half-and-half.

"The expiration date is yesterday," I piped in.

"That's the 'Sell By' date. You've got at least three days after that," she said authoritatively. "Cream keeps. Smell it. If it smells bad, then we'll toss it."

I smelled it. It might have smelled fine. I think it smelled fine.

"Not all bacteria have a scent," I theorized.

Paige rolled her eyes and laughed. I was breaking her down.

Cheese is supposed to mold. She tried. *Butter can stay out for days.*

"You win, queasy peasy," Paige said. Then she threw on a blue sundress, some heels, and a happy face, and we headed out.

The hostess at The Dead Fish, Maggie, greets us with a warm smile. Paige and I casually know her—she graduated a year behind us and runs with Belinda and Cleat's crowd. I didn't recognize Maggie at first. She dropped the Goth look, took out the obvious piercings, and let her hair go long.

Maggie tells Paige how sorry she is to hear about Gregory. She gives Paige a tight hug. I want to brag that Paige and I are engaged and show Maggie the ring, but there is no ring to show, and not since our telethon at the Thistle Dew has either of us boasted to anyone about getting married.

Maggie seats us by a bay window overlooking all three bridges: the Al Zampa, the second Carquinez, and what's left of the first. Over the last week or so, I've heard Sid speak of the loss of his best friend and the demolition of the 1927 Carquinez Bridge in the same breath, as if somehow the timing was more than coincidence. Gregory and the bridge happened to be about the same age. "The end of an era. The loss of a legacy," Sid remarks wistfully of both friends.

Deconstruction of the Carquinez is over for the day—thankfully— or Paige and I wouldn't be able to hear ourselves think.

From our seats, I have a clear shot of the C & H Sugar factory. The largest smokestack in the center sputters white puffs. Further down the river, you can just about make out those undeveloped warehouses that Ruth Mulrooney inherited. Early in our relationship, Paige and I used to park in the deserted lot next to these old wooden buildings and neck.

The Dead Fish's polished blond woods, mellow lighting, small plastic palm trees, folksy service, spectacular view, and tasty meal only modestly raise Paige's spirits. She and I need to talk about everything and we discuss nothing. The pharmacy, the house, the debt, the wedding, our future—all on hold. To fill one of the lulls, I tell Paige that Sid and I now have nearly a dozen PMPs. Sid's been sending out query letters to major manufacturers all over the country, I tell her. *You never know,* I remind her. Paige listens politely, nodding at most of the appropriate points in the conversation. Her swollen, sleep-deprived, makeup-camouflaged eyes are fixated on the scenery. She is a million miles away. It breaks my heart when she passes on the chocolate cake.

As we coast down Crockett's main drag, the radio fills the silence with country music. I see our turnoff, and as I reach for my turn signal, Paige waves me through.

"I'm not ready to go home yet," she says softly, slinking deeper into Hulk's bucket seat.

Before long Pomona Street turns into Eckley Drive, a ten-mile unlit windy, narrow, scenic road that runs alongside the Carquinez Strait.

"Maybe we should just elope," she kids.

"Totally," I agree all surfer-like. "If we stay on this road another fifty miles we'll hit Interstate 5 South. From there we can take Route 58 East to I-15 North. Two bathroom breaks and we could be in Vegas by sunrise. We could crash with my folks or stay on the Strip. I've always wanted to try the Venetian."

I'm talking too quickly.

"It sounds so easy," she says faintly. Paige closes her eyes.

"Here's what I'm going to do. I'll keep driving in this general direction, and if at any point you determine I'm headed the wrong way, just say the word."

I remember wanting to marry Paige Day in 1983. Something happens to a man when the first time you meet a woman she's dressed as a princess in a white flowing gown. I received complete confirmation a decade later in Madame Kuepper's high school French class. Paige was the only reason I kept taking French, despite my C average. Because of Paige, I joined French Club and eventually ran for treasurer. Paige was vice president, and my first order of business was suggesting we stage a coup. But Paige was far more diplomatic. Drunk with power and now directly hooked into the French Club's funds, she arranged a field trip to San Francisco so all eight of us could spend the afternoon eating chocolate fondue.

After graduation, Paige moved to Sacramento to work for a local television station. She did TV stints in St. Louis, Reno, Omaha, Los Angeles, and eventually returned years later to Crockett to tend to Lydia.

We stayed in touch after high school, but over the years, the letters and e-mails trailed off. The first time I saw Paige again was on my first day of work at Day's Pharmacy. She popped in to see her father. Gregory was so busy showing me the ropes, he didn't even notice Paige and I exchange a quick, friendly wave hello, and a familiar smile. It was as if we'd been planning this ten-year reunion all along.

I kept looking for opportunities to ask Paige out, but Gregory was always lurking. Then one day, I called the news desk where she works and managed to pry her schedule out of an unsuspecting intern; I drove all the way to San Francisco that day, and waited outside the studio, all stalker-like, with a bouquet of tulips. She agreed to go bowling with me that weekend. To avoid tipping off her father, we took separate cars and met at the alley.

This was our first, second, or third date depending on whether you counted the French Club fondue trip or the high school football incident. Lacing up my bowling shoes that night, Paige asked me, for the first time, if I knew what really happened the night Manny Milken tipped that pigskin in my face.

"Everyone thinks it hit me directly in the face, but it really ricocheted off yours first, didn't it?" Paige prodded, taking a swig of beer.

"It did," I confessed. "I cushioned the blow. Thanks to Manny, I still can't remember anything before my seventh birthday. I still have the bump to prove it," I said, taking her hand and rolling her fingers over the lump.

"No way!" she screamed. "Me, too. Feel mine," she said, guiding me to the tiny bump near her hairline.

We tried to keep our forbidden love a secret for as long as possible with winks and nods, hand signals and kicks, SMS messages and Facebook. But then one day Gregory walked in on us in the storeroom. We could have been doing anything, but as it turned out, we were just talking and—gasp—holding hands. It was all the confirmation he needed. Earthquake-wise, I was anticipating "the Big One," but there were no blowups or lectures. In fact, he never brought it up again. "Plausible deniability"—I think that's how Gregory used to deal with most aspects of our relationship.

We coast down Eckley Drive. We're five minutes closer to Las Vegas than we were five minutes ago. There are no streetlamps on this back road. It's pitch-dark aside from the occasional clearing in the trees where the moonlight bounces off the river. I check to make sure that Paige is wearing her seat belt. She is, but I still take the country road slow. I'm not familiar with these parts.

"I don't want a Vegas wedding," she concludes suddenly.

"Neither do I," I fib.

"I don't want any of this," she says.

I try not to take that personally. She gently bunks her head against the passenger side window.

"Tell me what you *do* want," I whisper.

"I love you," she says. "You're such a good person."

No, I'm a terrible person. I asked you to marry me and it killed your father.

"There *is* one thing that would help me," she says, taking a deep breath. "Can we agree to put this wedding on hold?"

I pull over to the shoulder of the road and stare at the steering wheel.

"Say something."

"Indefinitely?" I ask.

"No, 'on hold,' just for a while."

"Three days ago you convinced me to break my lease," I say, confirming no cars are coming in either direction. I begin turning the car around. "They've already started showing people my apartment, you know."

"*I must sound like a crazy person. I know I've been out of my mind, but I'm thinking clearly right now. I want to be with you. I want you to move in. I want us to be married. But I can't think about a wedding right now. I don't want to think about all the things this wedding can't be.* How my mother won't be there to see me in my dress. How my father won't walk me down the aisle. All my life I've dreamed of this day, but right now, planning this whole event fills me with . . . dread. Who knows, maybe tomorrow I'll feel different. Maybe we'll elope. Maybe we'll get married next Thursday. I promise you that you'll be involved in the decision, but it would be such a relief, right now, if I knew that you were okay with this nonplan . . . plan."

Far off in my rearview mirror I can see a car approaching. Hulk is now pointed toward Crockett, but we're sitting idle, in the middle of the road.

"All I'm asking you is that we . . . wait," she says.

That word. The crabmeat, green beans, vodka, and tonic become unstable in my stomach. It gurgles, breaking the silence. Paige asks me whether I just said something. I'm going to be sick. I need some air. I need to get us out of the middle of the road.

I roll down the window and put Hulk in drive. The air feels good.

Paige puts a hand on my knee. I speed up. The other car's headlights fall off my rearview mirror, but the next turn comes up on us quickly. We skid slightly and right before we slam into some random roadside car, the driver flips on his high beams.

Paige screams, slamming her hand down and bracing for impact.

We miss him by what must be millimeters, and after a moment, I manage to get us off the shoulder and onto smooth pavement.

"Sweetheart, you're upset and you're driving erratically," she informs me.

"I'm driving fine. You saw how that car jumped out of nowhere."

The car in question pulls out behind us and I hold my breath for the inevitable siren.

"He's following us," I inform her.

"Oh, no. Did you hit him? Were you speeding?"

"Like it's possible to make out a speed limit sign on this road."

As I slow down, he speeds up. The car is right on top of us now, and through my rearview mirror, the make and model look oddly familiar. This looks like the same blue Impala I saw turning around in Gregory's driveway the other day.

"I think that's Principal Martin," I inform Paige, glancing quickly over my shoulder to confirm.

Our high school principal Harvey Martin retired right after we graduated.

Martin is waving his hands wildly. He cuts back and forth into the neighboring traffic lane. The sixty-year-old hothead is making signals like he wants to pass.

Yeah, right. I gas Hulk and we take the next two curves fast. My car fishtails. Paige squeezes the door handle for dear life with both hands.

"What's wrong with you!" Paige yelps. "Maybe he's trying to tell us something, like we have a flat tire!"

Paige could be right. I let go of the wheel.

"WHAT ARE YOU DOING!" Paige cries.

"We're on a straightaway. If something's wrong with the tire, Hulk will pull to one side," I inform her.

"Yeah and yank us right into that ravine. Ten and two!" she cries.

I grab the wheel with both hands. There is another car quickly approaching in the opposite direction.

Now Principal Martin is laying on his horn in long, irritating blasts.

"Just let him pass," Paige yells.

Paige straightens up in her seat and wrenches her neck to see the deranged yahoo herself. Suddenly, Martin slams his brakes. A moment ago, he was tailgating us, and now he's far off in the distance, frozen on the road. The approaching SUV whizzes past us in the other direction. I double-check the rearview mirror and Principal Martin and his blue Impala are gone as we glide into Crockett.

What the hell? Paige and I wonder, pulling over.

"That was strange," I laugh nervously.

"Ya think?"

"That was definitely Harvey Martin."

"Do you think he's okay?" she asks.

"Has he ever been 'okay'? Maybe we need to call the police."

"And say what? I think he *is* the police," Paige realizes. "Didn't Principal Martin join the sheriff's department or something after we graduated?"

"I didn't see any sirens." I shrug.

After a long pause, Paige asks: "Are we okay?"

Is she referring to our heart-to-heart or the latest episode of *America's Craziest Car Chases*?

I pat myself down. *"Très bien. Et tu?"*

"D'accord. But are *we* 'd'accord,' you and me?" she asks tenderly.

"Let me get this straight," I say, shaking my head. "You want to move in together, but we put the wedding on hold?"

She nods.

"So you want the milk for free?"

"Yes. I want the milkman for free."

I nod.

"You get points, Andy Altman. Big points."

WE PULL into Paige's driveway. Parked in my spot is a tan Merce- des I've never seen before. It's a sedan, probably from the 1970s. I can now make out the green bumper sticker across the back fender: POWERED 100% BY VEGETABLE OIL.

Paige unbuckles her seat belt and leans over to kiss me softly on the lips. I can hear Lara's obnoxious laugh from here. We aren't even through the front door before Lara screams, "Finally! He was about to leave."

Tyler Rich stands up to greet us. He is unshaven, and taller and thinner than I remember. But maybe he's always looked that way. Despite his crunchy-looking exterior, a few details divulge his inner richness: jeans ripped in just the right places, a designer T-shirt, that perfect auburn tan, and plenty of hair product. I wish I had Tyler Rich's shiny black hair. But the tiny patch of hippie whiskers under his lower lip I can do without.

"Pay Day!" he cries with joy.

Paige protectively reaches for my hand.

He steps closer, lowering his voice. "I don't know what to say. I came as soon as I heard."

Gregory died two weeks ago.

"Where *were* you guys?" Lara asks, as if we've done something wrong.

"Tyler, this is Andy," Paige says, raising both our hands to- gether in the air like I'm a prizefighter. "This . . . this is the man who kicked your scrawny little ass in the contest for my love."

She doesn't say that last part.

Tyler reaches over to shake my right hand, but Paige hasn't let go, so I'm forced to reach out to him with my left hand and squish together his fingers all unmasculine-like.

"Hi, Tyler Rich."

To Paige and Lara, he's Tyler. To me, he'll always be Tyler Rich.

"Andrew was two years behind us," Lara jogs his memory. "You remember senior year: he was there when Manny Milken creamed Paige in the face with that football."

"It wasn't Manny's fault," Paige corrects her. "And Andy got hurt, too."

Enough about me. I squeeze her hand tightly.

"Nice to see you again, Andy. After all that, who would have thought you two would end up together," Tyler Rich concludes. "This really is incredible news."

"It's really not news at all," I inform him. "Paige and I have been dating for, like, ten months and a week." *What am I, three and three-quarters years old?* I want to add that we're engaged, but I'm not sure we are.

"So how long you back for?" Paige wonders out loud.

"Maybe for good," he informs us.

"Tyler's renting a luxury houseboat at the marina," Lara coos. *Lame-o-rama.*

"A forty-footer," she adds. "He gave me a walk-through this evening."

I'm sure he did.

"What's the boat's name again?" Lara begs.

"The *Lobsta Mobsta*," he crows.

Lara thinks that's hilarious.

"Does it run on vegetable oil?" I ask him.

"Excuse me?"

"It's just I saw your veggie machine in the driveway and I didn't think forty-foot houseboats were exactly eco-friendly."

"Go Andy Altman," Tyler cheers. "Just for that, I'm going to buy some carbon credits online. You know it's important that we all take steps to minimize our carbon footprint."

Lara nods.

This guy is full of greenhouse gas.

"You three are invited over for dinner anytime. I've got plenty of room. The place sleeps six," he says.

We'll pass, cabin boy.

I grab Paige's wrist with my free hand, and I extricate my crushed hand from her death grip. She doesn't even seem to notice.

"I'd love to," Paige says. "Right now, though, we have so much to do, settling Dad's affairs and all."

Lara shakes her head. "Sis, you're being a bad host. Sit!" Lara directs Paige. "The guy's been waiting here for you for like an hour."

"More like thirty minutes," Tyler Rich corrects her.

Tyler Rich tells us about how he dropped out of Cal State Sonoma after his sophomore year to work as a copywriter at an Internet startup company in San Jose called Sort. The company invented a search engine that could list your search engine results starting with the most recently added links. It was such a good idea that Google gobbled up the company, laying off—but paying out—all of its employees.

Tyler Rich has never had to worry about money, but Sort's golden parachute gave him permission to spend a few years roaming the Earth. As I listen to him babble on about months of living off the fat of the land, sleeping in the wilderness, and hitchhiking through Washington State, he sounds less like a mountain man and more like a homeless one. And still, the Day sisters are completely enamored with Tyler Rich's au naturel lifestyle.

"A few weeks back, it felt like it was time to come home," he informs us.

I thought you rushed back as soon as you heard about Gregory.

Job-wise, Tyler Rich tells us he's weighing his options: the *San Francisco Bay Guardian* is looking for a new "greener living" blogger, and the Bay Area cooperative, Rainbow Grocery, is accepting applications at its new Berkeley location. Tyler Rich has the *Lobsta Mobsta* through the end of August.

The phone in the kitchen starts ringing. Nobody makes a move.

"I should go," he tells us, reaching for his jacket. "Lara caught me up on her life. We've hardly seen each other since . . ."

"Prom." Lara remembers affectionately.

The telephone keeps ringing.

"I'd love to get an update on your world, Pay Day. But you probably have plenty of things to do . . . like answering that phone."

"Andrew, would you do me a *huge* favor and grab that," Lara asks politely. "We've received three hang-ups since I got home and there were four more on the answering machine. Maybe you'll have better luck."

I fling her a curt "sure" and head for the kitchen, snapping up the phone seconds before Gregory's answering machine does.

"Hello?" I roar into the receiver.

The breathing at the other end is slow and heavy.

"Hello?"

More breathing.

"This is the part where you hang up on me," I remind the caller.

"Oh Andy, sorry, I got distracted," Sid says, his voice shakier than usual.

"Hey, there. Everything okay?"

"Dandy. What's with you?"

I peek into the living room. Tyler's got the Day sisters giddy with laughter.

"I'm about to be blindsided for the second time tonight," I mutter.

"What's that?"

"Nothing. What can I do you for?" I stay as upbeat as possible.

"I'm fresh out of cholesterol medication and Cookie won't give it a rest. Any chance I could persuade you to make a late-night run to the pharmacy?"

I'm about to say yes when I hear Gregory's voice: dispensing medical advice or medication without supervision is a no-no for a pharmacy technician. I check my watch. It's after 10:00 P.M. Everything's closed.

"Gee, Sid," I begin, studying the three of them in the living room.

"You'd really be helping me out," Sid urges.

"What if I grabbed you *one* pill, just to get you through the night, but tomorrow we switch your prescription over to the Walgreens in Benicia. Okay?"

"Whatever you say, chief."

"I can get to the pharmacy and back in, say, fifteen minutes?"

"Why don't I meet you there? It's a beautiful night and I could use some fresh air. Give me twenty minutes. I need to finish watching *Antiques Roadshow*—Cookie's convinced the remnant collecting oil underneath our car in the garage is a priceless Navajo blanket. Are you sure you won't be missed?"

"Positive," I say, studying the reunion.

"Good," he adds. "We need to talk."

CHAPTER 16

The Day Co-Pay

THERE are boxes everywhere. The pharmacy was closed a full week before I realized Manny Milken was storing all of our deliveries at his mother's condo. In return for subletting the space, the Milkens helped themselves to some of our inventory. Manny thinks I won't miss the rolls of toilet paper, vials of mineral oil, or bottles of shampoo, but I will gladly add Manny to Lara's collections list.

With the future of Day's Pharmacy in question I figure it's pointless to bother restocking the shelves. For now, I simply place the new toiletries in the appropriate aisles next to their displayed brothers and sisters. If I were a guessing man, I'd say we end up returning most of this stuff.

Our medicine shelves are bare. We're fresh out of Sid's cholesterol medication, but we may have a new sealed supply in the back.

Lara's stink is everywhere. Along every countertop, there are small mounds of paper: Bank of the West, Bank of America, Citibank, GM, and MBNA—each one of Gregory's credit cards gets its own pile. Some of our biggest debtors have stacks, too.

The largest pile is simply labeled "Dad" and includes all sorts of medical records, insurance forms, and doctor's prescriptions.

I am no closer today than I was two weeks ago to understanding why Gregory wanted me to wait to ask Paige to marry me. I may never know. Maybe it had something to do with all his money problems, maybe he never thought I was worthy enough for his daughter, or maybe there's a clue in this neatly assembled stack.

It feels less intrusive if I flip through his papers quickly. Nothing really jumps out at me. You spend ten months with a guy in a pharmacy, and you quickly get to know what sort of pills he's popping. Sprays, capsules, inhalers—Dr. Brandon Mills was prescribing Gregory anything he could to help the Mayor of Pomona Street breathe. Gregory was also taking Lanicor, which is no shocker: you can't swing a dead cat in Crockett without hitting someone on anticholesterol medication.

Which reminds me, I still need to find Sid that pill.

At the end of the aisle, I find lots more of Lara's handiwork. She's co-opted five new whiteboards from Aisle Two and hung them along the back wall where there's room to walk. On each board she's pasted dozens of insurance forms, co-payment records, and prescriptions. She's drawn Magic Marker lines connecting people as if she's mapping out some sort of terrorist network. I've seen Lara pace back and forth past this display, narrowing down her suspects. Lara is a determined woman. She'll crack this case. Collar her old man. She's already got some strong leads.

I study the scraps, scribbles, and dot-matrix printouts. I'm equally enamored and sickened by Lara's masterpiece. I hate being the designated muscle around here: the guy charged with knocking over walkers, kicking out canes, breaking hips, sending a clear message to the community.

I grab a sealed, commercial-sized plastic bottle of Lanicor out of a box on the floor and head back down the aisle, inadvertently plowing into a delicately stacked pile of unopened packages. I inspect one. It's one of those packages Gregory used to get, wrapped in brown paper, with no postage and no return address.

There is a large box nearby addressed to the pharmacy, in care of Sidney Brewster. Wrapped a dozen different ways with black electrical tape, the package is about the size and weight of a small boat engine. I slide it across the honeycomb tile floor with the side of my foot. The floor is uneven, and as it drops two inches, it sandwiches and crushes my flip-flop-exposed pinky toe. There is a short delay before the pain signal hits my brain.

"Son of a—" I scream.

"Gun?" Sid lip-synchs from the sidewalk, pantomiming a gun with his fingers.

The bell jingles as Sid pushes open the door. This is the first time we've both been back in the pharmacy since Gregory died.

I rub my toe in agony. He shakes his head.

"What sort of clown are you?" Sid asks.

"I dunno, the sad hobo type," I guess. "It's *your* freaking fault. Now my toe's broken. This big, stupid package has your name on it."

I hop over two aisles, grab an instant cold pack, and crack it in half. If only I could sue my employer for worker's compensation.

"Who's David Bloomington?" I yell as I bounce back over.

"You got me," he says, putting his nose right up to the box to read the label. "Oh, you mean David *Wallingford* from Bloomington, Indiana."

Like that helps. He kicks the box with his safely protected sneaker.

"I bought this for you," he announces. "Get some scissors."

I cut away all the tape, tear the box open, blindly jab both hands into the Styrofoam peanuts, and pull out a red GE canister vacuum.

"Seven bucks!" he exclaims, as I fish out the hose, nozzles, and dusting brush accessories. "You'd be amazed what some people auction online."

"I thought Cookie cut you off from eBay?"

"Why do you think I shipped it here," he says tapping his temple.

"Operation Jet Stream take two?" I ask.

"Bingo!" There still may be hope for our bladeless windshield wipers after all.

I hop behind the counter, drop the ice pack on the floor, and step on it lightly, to relieve the swelling. My pinky and big toe are about the same size now. It may be broken—it's so hard to tell with pinkies.

I pop a single cholesterol pill in a small bottle, fasten the plastic top tightly, and hand it to Sid. But before I let go, I warn him, "The first hit is free. But after that, you come to me. Got that, buddy? You want your fix, *you come to Andy.*"

Sid is not entertained.

"Tomorrow we'll call Walgreens in Benicia and get you the rest of your refill," I say.

"What's all this?" Sid asks, changing the topic.

He's poking through one of Lara's little piles of paper on the counter.

"Evidence from a crime scene," I confess. "Lara's on to you. Your tab and Cookie's put you on Lara's most wanted list."

"I suspected this might happen," he says. "Let me explain."

"No need, I'm the thug tasked with collecting, and in my book, Brewster, we're even Steven."

"That's not it, I want to explain about the hang-ups at the house."

I'm confused.

"That was you?"

"No."

"Oh, then you know about the creditors?"

"Those aren't creditors. At least not all of them," he says confidently. "I also know about what happened tonight on Eckley."

Now I'm completely lost.

"Eckley Drive . . ." he repeats. "Harvey Martin . . ."

"So you know that maniac almost ran us off the road?"

"Harvey was confused."

Sid slowly takes a stool at the lunch counter. I hobble over to the other side of the bar. I wish I could make us milkshakes, but the soda fountain doesn't work and Sid is lactose intolerant.

Sid searches for the words. "I have a sense of your money problems," he says, pulling a handkerchief from his pocket and dabbing his forehead. "Gregory never went into detail, but I suspect you have lots of bills, and that house of his is probably mortgaged to high heaven."

"It's not good," I admit.

"Gregory had too much pride to accept money from us, and I

for one didn't have much to give. But we tried to find other ways to help."

Sid's throat is dry. I grab him a bottle of distilled water from the nearby minifridge and unscrew it for him.

"We owed Gregory," he says, taking a big gulp. "We still owe him."

"Gregory would have done anything for you and Cookie," I say.

"No, not just us. . . ."

"I know. I'd do anything to get that time back, too. To make some sort of connection with Gregory," I say with deep regret.

My nose tickles. My eyes are watering.

There is someone tapping on the front windowpane. I lean over to look and realize it's that crazy fucking lunatic Harvey Martin. Principal Martin is wearing red flannel pajama bottoms and a white T-shirt. A few grayish wisps of hair jut out in different directions like a madman. Martin greets us with a maniacal grin and a slow, creepy wave hello, fingers fanned out.

I'm awestruck. *Sid, you see him too, don't you?*

Sid spins slightly on his stool, lays his eyes on Harvey Martin, and waves the man inside.

"What the hell?" I mumble.

The overhead fluorescent lights flicker slightly. Time slows. Then the rest of the zombies start pouring in, one by one. First there's Cookie Brewster; cane in hand, she limps toward me in satin purple pajamas. Mildred Pritchard is right behind her, in a neon pink jogger suit. She uses a walker to inch closer. That blue hair, Beatrice Lewis, looks even more like Big Bird than ever in her yellow nightgown and bouffant do. She holds her back in pain as she steps closer, dragging one foot. Harvey Martin is more like Frankenstein's monster, rocking side to side. They're all tired. In pain. Moaning in agony.

"I love that color!" Beatrice says, inspecting Cookie's evening wear.

Cookie shakes her head in disgust. "It's eleven o'clock. I should be asleep picking daffodils in la-la land right now," she says.

When Cookie reaches her husband, she hands him her cane,

and regally extends her hand. Sid then helps his wife take a seat at the counter.

"Let's do this," demands Cookie.

Mildred and Harvey catch their breath while the rest of the crew look on with anticipation.

"Fair enough," Sid says, lowering himself off the stool.

He claps his hands twice and clears his throat. Then he pulls out a folded-up piece of yellow-lined notebook paper and addresses me directly.

"Our government has failed us!" Sid yells with a raised finger. "As drug prices continue to skyrocket, outpacing inflation, seniors on modest or fixed incomes struggle to gain access to critical drugs." Sid loses his place. He flips between the first and second page.

"For Pete's sake, I'll be six feet under before you get to the point," Cookie interrupts him.

Cookie slaps both hands flat on the lunch counter and leans in close. Her pajama blouse hangs loosely open, revealing some sort of heavy-duty bra. I uncomfortably concentrate on her eyes.

"A bunch of us old fogies haven't been able to afford our meds for some time now. For years, we'd come in here with no money, no insurance, no nothing, and Gregory, God bless him, would give us our pills and charge us some token amount. We started calling it the 'Gregory Day Co-Pay.'"

Mildred adjusts her hairnet. Harvey Martin scratches his back with an unopened toothbrush.

"First it was just drugs, but then Gregory started giving away the farm—Q-tips, aspirin, whatever we needed. He tried to keep track with tabs, but this godforsaken town is teeming with in-grates and everyone started piling on. Before long, Gregory lost track of who owed what, and he went into debt. Deep debt. That's when 'we,'" she says, motioning over her shoulder wildly toward Martin and her book club, "started 'subsidizing Gregory's cause.' Capeesh?"

"You lost me after 'Pete's sake,'" I say flatly.

"Prescription drugs, Andy," Sid chimes in. "We'd get him free drug samples. Whatever, wherever, and however we could and he'd distribute them."

"Digoxin, Monopril, Viagra, Lanicor, you name it," Mildred shouts.

"But no narcotics," Beatrice chirps. "And no amphetamines."

"Yeah, no class two narcotics," Harvey Martin assures me.

"How responsible of you!" I cry. "These pills just dropped out of the sky?"

"No, we've got a system," Sid explains calmly. "The free samples come from local practitioners. Cookie pressures Dr. Mills. Mildred's assigned to Dr. Platt. And Beatrice works closely with that nice ear, nose, and throat gal on Hudson, what's-her-name."

"Hardy," Beatrice pipes up. "Dr. Cynthia Hardy."

"Right, right, right. The doctors would put together brown box collections and Manny Milken would pick them up and deliver them here," Sid explains, pointing to the stack of generic packages I just knocked over.

"Jesus, Manny knows?" I holler.

"No, Manny's clueless. He just delivered the stuff to Gregory," Sid assures me. "Gregory would give us the packages and then Cookie's book club would meet once a week and sort the sample pills."

"We're not big readers," Cookie says on behalf of Mildred and Beatrice.

"There is *absolutely no way* Gregory was okay with this," I insist. "The guy wouldn't let me prescribe water."

"Before he handed out the samples, Gregory would stay here late and check our work. It was totally on the up-and-up," Sid insists.

"Up-and-up?" I yell. "He commingled legitimate pills with free samples that were *clearly marked* 'Not for Sale.' Then *we* distributed them and"—panic strikes—"and we filed the forms and committed insurance fraud!"

"I didn't realize we were dealing with such a prude," Cookie ridicules me from her stool. "Down!" she commands her husband.

Sid helps her, handing Cookie her cane. "Clearly this ain't happening."

But Cookie isn't going anywhere. Mildred and Mildred's walker stand in her way.

"And what about Looney Tunes over here?" I ask, pointing my thumb at Harvey Martin. "You're a cop, for Christ's sake!"

"Volunteer peace officer in the Contra Costa County Sheriff Department's Reserve Program," he clarifies.

Like that makes a difference, I say with my hands.

"It's no big whoop," he assures me.

He steps right up to me. Harvey Martin has always been a close talker.

"I'd go to the Veterans Affairs Hospital, they'd give me whatever I need, and I'd hand it over to Gregory."

Then he starts with the theatrics. Harvey clutches his heart and puts on a thick Italian accent: "Ooh, ahh, ooh, my chest. *No problem, Mr. Martin, here's a prescription for Lipitor.* Ooh, ahh, ooh, my head. *Take some Frova, Mr. Martin.* It's my bones, my bones I tell you. *How about this 90-day supply of Boniva?*"

"You realize you almost killed us tonight!" I scream.

"And for that, my friend, I apologize," he yells back like he means it. Harvey Martin places one hand on my shoulder. "Since Gregory passed I got all these drugs piling up in my house. I thought maybe I could drop them off at the house, but you're never alone. I saw your car tonight, and thought 'bingo, here's my chance,'" Martin cries, snapping his fingers. "I chased after you, but then Paige poked her head up, and I guess I panicked. Sorry."

"Harvey gets a little overexcited sometimes," Sid explains.

"None of you can afford drugs? What about Medicare?" I insist.

"Medicare sucks!" Cookie blurts like some adolescent.

"It's too complicated. Too pricey," Beatrice echoes.

"That stupid jelly doughnut ruined everything," Mildred complains.

There is a slight pause before Sid gently reminds her: "You mean *doughnut hole.*"

Mildred nods, warmly. Cookie doesn't appreciate Sid showering attention on another woman.

The dreaded Medicare "doughnut hole." The doughnut hole is the government's legal loophole in the Medicare prescription coverage plan: it represents the span of time or "hole" during the year when a senior citizen has to pay for drug benefits in full, but receives none. During the doughnut hole, Medicare folks fork over twenty times what they're accustomed to paying.

"Gregory was an American hero, small fry," Sid says. "Like a soldier, he always covered everyone 'in the hole.'"

I start thinking about how many people this might mean.

CRASH!

I've been conditioned to panic when I hear this sound . . . especially here. But this time, the commotion isn't coming from behind the pharmacy counter, but the front of the store. It sounds as if someone's thrown a brick through our window. There is glass everywhere. The front door is hit with such force the bell flies off, sliding all the way down Aisle Five and landing right in front of our group.

"Nobody move!" the bandit commands.

From where I'm standing, I can't see him, but I spot another dark figure file in quickly. Beatrice screams and then squats down to get out of the line of fire. Mildred knocks a shelf full of aspirin to the floor, but her walker is there to catch her. Neither Sid nor Cookie moves a muscle. Harvey Martin seems the most terrified of all. He's frozen, next to me, arms by his side, chanting "Oh-my-God." I don't have a lot of faith that Sid's gang is capable of taking these thugs down in a rumble.

I take a few steps to my left, peer down the aisle, and watch as a member of the local sheriff's department struggles to free his foot from the door frame he just kicked in. The Keystone Cop can't be more than twenty years old, five feet tall, with rippling muscles and a wide-brimmed hat. His gun pointed straight out, Sparky finally loosens his leg and tells everyone to "get down on the ground. NOW!"

In the split second that I realize that we're being raided by the police and not robbed by desperados, I go from rattled to relieved and then back to rattled again. The last thing we need right now is the fuzz, and if Lara hadn't just told me that our pharmacy insurance was three months in arrears (*arrears,* fun word), I might even welcome a break-in right now.

I throw up my hands and Sid slowly starts bending at the knees.

"Go ahead and shoot me," Cookie advises the officer once he's behind her. "Put me out of my misery. I'm too tired to get down. And this floor is filthy."

"Sweetie!" Sid says, all concerned, but then he grabs his back in pain.

How are we going to explain this? How much did they hear? The last thing I remember saying before Sparky barged in was "insurance fraud."

"Aw crap," the police eyewitness shouts once he sees us. "False alarm. False alarm. Put down your weapons," Manny cries.

In a panicked fit, Manny awkwardly reaches out and lightly swats down on the barrel of the officer's gun.

"Dude, what the hell are you doing?" Sparky yells, spinning around. "You almost made me shoot this lady."

Beatrice is still on the ground, her hand clutched to her chest. Mildred's eyes dart around the room. We all have this guilty look on our faces.

Manny begins: "Sorry, sorry, I was driving by, saw some suspicious activity, knew the pharmacy was closed. I was worried you guys was being burgled."

Manny squares off with the young officer who doesn't know what to make of this pajama party. "Nothing to see here," Manny repeats. "Andy *works* here."

"Did you have to kick the door in?" I complain to the officer.

"We had 12-11 in progress," Sparky says. "You expect me to knock?"

"Damn it, man, the door was open," I lecture him.

"You really should get a burglar alarm," the officer advises me.

"We have one. It wasn't set because we were in here, you moron. Did you even *try* the door?" I ask.

He has no response to that.

"Someone tell me what the hell is going on here," a second officer asks.

His nametag says "D. Fielding." I'm pretty sure Paige and I graduated with this guy. He played baseball or football—definitely a sport where you throw something. *Danny, Donny . . . Dudley!* Dudley Fielding. It's the thick brown mustache that threw me.

"Why are you all dressed like that," Officer Fielding demands.

"It's an orgy," says Cookie.

Sid buries his face in his hands.

"We're having a book club meeting," Mildred insists suddenly.

"That's right!" Beatrice remembers.

"Book club?" Dudley Do-Right asks skeptically. "I don't see any books."

"Who brings books to a book club?" Mildred complains.

"And what book are you reading?"

Like possessed game-show contestants, Beatrice, Mildred, and Harvey shout out different titles: *Love in the Time of Cholera, He's Just Not That into You, Who Moved My Cheese?*

"You're reading *He's Just Not That into Cholera Cheese?*" Dudley asks.

"No, dum-dum, we're all reading different books. That's how this club works. Then we gather here in the dead of night and discuss them," Cookie explains. "I bet the last thing you read was an eye chart."

Dudley flashes her a look that would intimidate anyone but Cookie.

"All right, fellas, you've done your job here. Time we call it a night," Martin informs them.

"Not so fast," Dudley says, taking off his hat and patting down his bushy brown hair. "With all due respect, Mr. Martin, we're not in high school anymore, and you're not the boss of me."

Dudley Fielding doesn't say that last part.

With a mobster's nod, Sid tells Harvey to get rid of them.

Principal Martin walks right up to Dudley. "Listen here, Mr.

Fielding," Martin says, dropping his voice two octaves. "I don't think your parents—or rather, your supervising officer—would appreciate learning that you barged in here and terrorized a group of helpless elderly women during their book club meeting." Mildred wags her finger at Dudley. "I think you and I need to have a little talk outside. Let's go," he demands.

Uh-oh, I smell detention.

Harvey pats both young bucks on the back and shows them out the broken door. Then he turns to us, shrugs his shoulders, and delivers a big wide grin. Manny, Sid, and I follow right behind.

"My bad," Manny apologizes to us, daintily stepping over the shards of glass.

It's hard to be too angry with him. He did what I hope any concerned Crockett resident would do, even if it was overkill.

"Oh man," I say, wiggling the door side to side. The top hinge is busted. "That cop trashed it," I complain to Sid. "It was *unlocked,* ya dumb ox!" I scream over to the officer.

From across the street, Harvey shushes me with his hand. Cookie, Beatrice, and Mildred make their way over to examine the damage, too.

"Who's going to pay for this?" I mumble.

If we weren't susceptible to a burglary before, we are now.

"I know this is a lot to take in," Sid whispers to me.

"It's broken. Geez, now we need to buy a new door."

"Forget the door for a minute. We'll patch that up in a jiffy. I need you to focus," Sid informs me. "Gregory did a lot for this community, and we did what little we could to pay him back."

"So the late-night phone calls? The house drive-bys?" I whisper back.

"People who need your help. Folks that depended on Gregory."

"How many are there?"

Sid shrugs.

"Seriously, Sid, you're good with numbers. Make an educated guess."

"Twenty?"

The ladies exchange dubious looks. Harvey gives us the all-clear thumbs-up, and the two officers head back to their patrol car.

"Eighty?" Sid tries again.

"You don't know how many, do you?" I ask him.

"I don't. I'd have to give it a good, hard think," he admits.

Gregory's late nights at the pharmacy, the free tabs, the doctors' shopping sprees, the financial problems—I get it.

"And what exactly do you want me to do?" I ask the drug ring. The motley crew stares back.

"We'll walk you through the logistics more carefully," Sid says, finally. "We'll take your lead, but you've got piles of precious free samples stacking up in the corner there . . . you've got people who desperately need them . . . and you need money. We can all help one another."

"Why would Gregory destroy himself like this? And how could you continue to take advantage of him?" I wonder out loud.

"Some of us were desperate, and Gregory was our life support," Sid insists. "Misguided, maybe. But we tried to help."

"I have to talk this over with Paige," I say.

"No way," Cookie yells.

"No one knows about this besides the people in this room," Sid explains, firmly. "Not Lara, not Paige, no one."

"Yeah, no one knows except every other senior citizen in town," I reply flatly.

"The recipients of the co-pay assumed Gregory paid for the drugs out of his own pocket—that he was just being his same old generous self," Sid says, tenderly. "After all, he was the Mayor of Pomona Street. He was beloved by this community. Let's keep it that way. Help us or don't, but do me one favor: preserve the man's reputation, if for anyone, for my goddaughter."

CHAPTER 17

Drug Mills

I HAVE this recurring dream where I'm Chewbacca.

It's a beautiful fall afternoon in Crockett and I walk into Day's Pharmacy. Gregory is busily working behind the counter. He zips around leaving streaks of light in his path. When my turn comes, to my surprise, Paige is standing at the register. She's very polite, but doesn't recognize me because of my costume. I try like the dickens to tell her it's me, but nothing registers. My bad temper, or rather Chewy's, gets the better of me. I moan and roar. I tug at my outfit, but soon realize *this is no outfit—I am in fact a hairy brown monster.* That's when I ask Paige where they keep the aspirin (which is a silly question really, because everyone knows we keep it in Aisles Two and Five). In my head, the question is so clear, but apparently she doesn't understand.

Then Gregory steps in. He's healthier than ever. Wide-eyed, rosy-cheeked, and twenty pounds lighter, he demands: "You leave her alone, you fur ball. How many times do I have to tell you: we don't serve your kind here."

Somehow Gregory knows it's me—me in Wookie's clothing.

THE new normal is setting in. Having run out of rooms to clean and tears to cry, Paige has returned to her TV career, at least part-time, mostly working the daybreak shift. It's been three days since Lara first came to us with her pathetic plan to collect on Gregory's pharmacy tabs, and forty-eight hours since Sid's drug ring approached me. I wonder if his crew has gang signs or a handshake.

Sid and I haven't spoken or seen each other since the pajama party in the pharmacy, which is saying something. Normally we talk two or three times a day. I haven't made a decision on whether to help him with the Day Co-Pay program. He told me to take my time, but I know I can't take too long. Every minute I wait, someone, somewhere is getting sicker—or worse.

I hate not being in constant communication with Sid. These days I'm filled with anxiety. My instinct is to fear the worst. Gregory kept a pair of binoculars next to his chair. Probably the same ones he used to spy on me with Paige. Like a baby sleeping, I check on Sid all the time, to be sure he's all right. Each time I peek through the blinds at his house, I half expect to see an ambulance out front.

For Cookie, it's business as usual. Sometimes I catch her in the golden hour, stumbling around the block with a blue handkerchief tied around her head, walking Loki. Cookie still gardens, but less so now—we're experiencing a rare heat wave. The only other times she leaves the house are to food shop around 2:00 P.M., and of course, to walk the dog one more time before dark.

This morning, she nearly took out a jogger's eye with her bamboo cane. Cookie is half asleep, shuffling down her walkway with Loki. A jogger approaches from the west, iPod-oblivious. Moments before they collide on the sidewalk, Cookie swings the rubber tip of her cane millimeters from his face and tries to scream something, but her voice goes hoarse.

The near miss gets me thinking: Cookie needs a better cane. It's the first dose of inspiration I've had in weeks. I've since begun working up ideas.

Last night, Lara came to me with her definitive list of pharmacy deadbeats. Lara thinks the biggest freeloaders will be first to show up when we reopen the pharmacy on Friday. She may be right. I managed to talk her down from 120 people to 60. In winnowing her list, I still couldn't manage to eliminate key members of the Day Co-Pay drug ring, among them, Mildred Pritchard (no. 6), Sid and Cookie Brewster (nos. 13 and 26), and Beatrice Lewis (no. 33). According to Lara, every person on the list owes us between $500 and $2,000.

As for the stragglers in need of a free fix, but too afraid to show their faces at the pharmacy, I'm expected to chase them down. I don't know what I'm going to say to these people. I assume the first shakedown is the hardest—probably something akin to "whacking" someone. At least that's what they say in all the authentic mobster movies—*it gets easier after you've offed your first,* the thug reminisces wistfully. From there I suppose you go numb.

Maybe I just need a stiff drink. Or maybe I just need an easy mark—someone who I know can pay, even if he isn't on Lara's list.

THERE are no drug prescriptions, no insurance forms, no receipts, and no records for Lara to trace back to Gregory's primary physician, Dr. Brandon Mills. But Mills gave Gregory heaps of free samples, and in return, Gregory allowed Mills to ransack this pharmacy at whim. It was hardly a fair trade—that bastard took ten times as much as he gave, stuffing some of our most precious toiletries in that brown patent leather medical bag of his. I bet the disposable razor blades alone could cover three mortgage payments.

Dr. Mills, I regret to inform you that you are no longer a recipient of the Day's Pharmacy lifetime shopping spree.

With a few keystrokes on my pocket calculator, I estimate the average cost per grab bag and multiply it by the total number of likely visits Mills made over the last five years. I'd put Mills's bill as high as five grand, but I'll ask for a thousand.

It's Monday and apparently Dr. Mills has the day off. Semiretired, Mills keeps office hours two days a week at his Crockett office and one day a week in neighboring Martinez; he spends the rest of his time at the Mira Vista Golf and Country Club, where Gregory was Mills's guest and golf partner; that is, until Gregory's health deteriorated, and the golf outings became luncheons.

Getting to Mira Vista Golf and Country is a fifteen-minute drive southwest to the bedroom community of El Cerrito. This is my first visit to the clubhouse. The spectacular Old English Tudor mansion sits atop the Contra Costa hills. It has a decadent entrance with dramatic vaulted ceilings supported by mammoth oak beams. The club prides itself on its exclusivity.

I inform the clerk at the pro shop that I am Mr. Free Razor Blades' nephew. "Philippe" expects Dr. Mills to be finishing up a round of golf any minute now and encourages me to grab some lemonade in the members' lounge. I thank him and plant myself in the golf cart return area.

Before long, Mills approaches. He's yukking it up with the driver, a young, fit, blue-eyed, blond-haired Hitler-youth type. There is a faint family resemblance; unlike me, this teen could actually be Mills's legitimate nephew.

I try to get their attention all businesslike, but regrettably the hand gesture has the look and feel of a Nazi salute. Even up close, Mills doesn't recognize me in the slightest.

We say hello to each other and in the awkward silence I remind him of my name, occupation, and relationship to Gregory.

"I know," Brandon snaps. He's so annoyed already. "Are you a guest?"

Guest, trespasser.

"I need a few minutes of your time."

"Is this a medical emergency?"

"No."

"Then you need to set up an appointment through my office," he says firmly.

Mills steps out of his cart and instructs his nephew to grab the golf bags.

"You can't just meander onto club grounds."

And yet here I am.

"I need to talk to you about Gregory Day."

"Richard, what do you say you get us a table for lunch," says Mills.

"Will it be two or three?" he asks.

"Definitely two," Mills says. "I'll be less than a minute. Time me."

The real nephew throws the second bag of clubs over his shoulder and heads for the clubhouse. Dr. Mills crosses his arms and waits for me to speak.

"I was wondering," I say, working up the nerve. "I came across a prescription you wrote for Gregory. I know he had breathing problems, but I didn't realize he also had bad cholesterol."

Mills bends down to pull up his left sock. I'm talking to this man about serious matters and all he's thinking is: *Man, my sock feels loose. I need to pull up that sock. I'm going to pull up my sock.*

"Is there a question?" he asks from down there.

"How bad *was* his cholesterol?"

"I have no idea, and I wouldn't tell you if I could." Mills rises. "Doctor-patient confidentiality survives death. Plus that information is reserved for family."

"Paige and I are engaged to be married."

"Good for you." Mills shakes a fist in frustration. "Is that all?"

I want to push him. I want to knock him to the ground.

"Just one more thing," I say, all Columbo-like. "We're updating our books. How do you plan on settling your pharmacy tab?"

Mills's eyes narrow, his nostrils flare. I think he's about to punch me in the nose.

"I'm sorry if this makes you uncomfortable," I say, uncomfortably. "But our records show you owe us money for Schick razor blades, Reach toothbrushes, and uh, toilet paper," I say from memory.

"Toilet paper?"

"I can get you specifics, but over the last five years, you owe Day's Pharmacy roughly"—I shoot high—"$3,000."

"This had better be a joke," Mills yells, drawing attention to himself. "This is grotesque. I've tried to be polite, but I've had enough," he says walking away.

I catch up to him and we dance as I block his path.

"Look, I know about your arrangement," I say in a conspiratorial tone.

"Excuse me?"

"You invited Gregory to this club as your guest—I'm sure he appreciated that—but those samples you gave him were *free,* and the toiletries you so generously helped yourself to cost Gregory thousands of dollars," I whisper.

His face is beet red. Mills is about to blow a gasket.

"It's what's fair," I say with gusto.

"It's what's fair? You are *way* outside your depth, son. You haven't a clue of what's fair! I could still lose my medical license for giving Gregory those pills," he whispers with pure vitriol. "Not to mention that I never charged him for a *single* office visit. I never charged *anyone* in that family. Neither did my father. The fact that it took you three weeks before cashing in on his death, was that out of respect or a lack of resourcefulness?"

Dr. Mills pokes me in the chest.

"I don't know what that lovely daughter of his sees in you. But Gregory is spinning in his grave right now. Spinning!" Mills yells.

Mills shoves past me. I'm numb.

"He was so right about you," Mills adds smugly, his back to me. I just stare.

"I'll pay the $3,000 in toilet paper," he says, addressing me one last time, "simply because this whole episode is a steaming pile of horseshit. But expect an invoice from me, too: for Gregory's doctor visits covering the same five-year span."

CHAPTER 18

Comfort Food

I SHOVEL Honey Nut Cheerios into my mouth with one hand and use the other to shield my squinty eyes from the atrocity on the television screen. HBO is running a *Real Sex* marathon. A hairy, overweight middle-aged man with a beer gut, dressed in a brown bear costume, tells the camera that "furry fetishists" are more common than one might think. The man bears an uncanny resemblance to the Cal Berkeley mascot, Oski, minus the cute golden cardigan, plus the easy-access aperture to conduct, uh, business. A woman dressed like a white bunny rabbit bounces up and down on top of him. He is about to have a heart attack and HBO is there to catch the nightmare on video.

The phone receiver is sitting right next to me on the couch so I pick it up on the first ring. It's Paige, again. She called ninety minutes ago promising she'd be home "within the hour." Does that mean before the current hour is up or within the next sixty minutes? I'm never sure.

"Yeah?" I answer, oddly enamored by the bestiality on the screen.

"Whatcha doing?" Paige chirps.

"Research." I'm hypnotized.

"You sound like you're mad."

This snaps me out of it. I mute the sound.

"No, I'm fine," I say, relieved to hear her voice. "Where are you? Are you okay?"

"Yeah, everything's grand," she says, drawing out the words. This is what Paige sounds like when she's drunk.

"Uh, I can smell your breath from here," I say.

"Those mojitos sneak up on you." She laughs. "I had, like, two"— code for three—"but I should have eaten something."

"You're probably fine to drive. If it were me . . . I'd risk it," I advise her.

"Really?"

"Of course not really. I'll come get you."

"That's okay, sweetie. I think I'm going to stay in the city tonight. It's late and I have to be back at work early tomorrow. I can buy something cheap to wear at Ross's."

"You're going to stay in the city? Stay where?"

Paige pauses briefly. I can hear her thinking.

"Tyler sailed his houseboat over to San Francisco from the East Bay. He docked it in the marina and invited a bunch of us over for drinks," she blurts.

"Tyler who?" I pretend. "You said you were having drinks with 'work friends.'"

"I was. I did. But then we all came here. It's a lovely boat, Andy. I really think you'd like it. He has a small whirlpool and a full kitchen. It's spacious. I'll have my own bedroom. I swear it's no big deal."

"He has a whirlpool?"

"Uh-huh." She sounds distracted.

"He's standing right there, isn't he?"

"No, I went into his bedroom for privacy."

"Why are you drunk in Tyler Rich's houseboat bedroom at ten P.M. on a school night?" I demand. I hate that she made me ask.

"Andy, sweetheart, calm down," she whispers loudly.

"Who else is sleeping over?" I ask like a protective parent.

"There is nothing to worry about," she says.

"I'm picking you up."

"You can't."

"Excuse me?"

If I concentrate, I can make out the reggae music in the background.

"Okay, so like, we're not in San Francisco anymore. We're about three-quarters of the way back to Crockett. Tyler thought it might be nice if we slept 'at sea.'"

"Name *one guy* who would be okay with this, Paige?"

"A guy who trusts his girlfriend and is secure in his relationship."

"So a chump?"

"I know you're upset."

"I have to go. I'm watching a movie and this is the climactic scene."

"Don't be upset, okay?"

"Uh-huh," I say, mumbling good-bye and poking the off button on the phone, hard.

This is the beginning of the end. No, me killing her father, her taking off her engagement ring, and us placing this wedding on hold was the beginning of the end. Bunking with your high school boyfriend in his high-tech houseboat is the end of the end. How did this happen?

I channel surf for the next seventy-eight minutes, mulling over my options. Then suddenly, with conviction, I wiggle on my sneakers, swipe my car keys off the glass coffee table, and throw on my leather jacket. I plan to be there the moment the SS *Lobsta Mobsta* docks at the Crockett Marina. If that means I need to crash all night in my car, so be it.

As I open the front door, I notice a car pull up to the curb. I assume it's Lara until I realize it isn't.

Paige and Tyler Rich stop one house away. Despite any attempt to be inconspicuous, Tyler Rich's veggie machine comes to a loud, puttering halt. The nerve of this guy: *Doesn't he know that*

I'm the one who invented the parking-one-house-away shtick? I dart inside, grab Gregory's binoculars, and peek through the blinds. In less than a month, I've become Gregory and Tyler's me.

The two of them are talking. With the interior car light off, it's hard to make out faces, but Paige seems dead serious. Her body language is all wrong. Arms pinned to her sides, she's not making any of the big, animated gestures I've grown to love. She shifts from side to side, never looking toward the house. This goes on for another five excruciating minutes.

By now, she must know I'm watching, but she won't look at me.

The conversation winds down. Tyler Rich manages to give her a peck on the cheek before Paige scurries out of the Mercedes and up the lawn. Tyler Rich waits for her to spin around and wave good-bye, but she doesn't.

With lightning speed, I leap over the couch, grab my soggy bowl of cereal from the coffee table, and power on the television. My friend *Real Sex* is back. The women on the screen appear to be attending some sort of orgasm camp.

When the front door swings open, I poke a gross spoonful of Cheerios in my mouth.

"Hi," Paige says apologetically.

I don't turn around, greeting her only with a raised cereal bowl. Paige sits down next to me on the couch, real close.

"Why are you wearing your coat indoors?" she asks.

I ignore the question, remaining focused on my program. Paige tries to kiss me hello on the lips but I pull away.

"Why won't you kiss your girlfriend?" she complains.

"I'm eating," I sputter with food in my mouth.

Multiple moans of ecstasy blast from the television speakers. The women in the workshop appear to be overachievers.

The phone rings. It's been ringing off the hook all night.

"Can we just rip it out of the wall?" she asks.

"It's wireless," I inform her.

The person hangs up a split second before the machine answers.

"Can we go to the kitchen?" she yells over the chorus of orgasms. "I'll make you a proper snack."

"I'm watching this," I complain, convulsing in agony as the scene unfolds.

Paige finds the mute button. Then she cups her hands around my face, forcing me to look at her.

"I'm sorry," she says.

"For what?"

"For being late. For drinking too much," she says. "I have no tolerance for alcohol, you know that."

The phone starts ringing again. *What the hell.* It's after eleven.

"I'm also sorry if you're upset," she says.

"Excellent apology," I respond, giving her the big okay sign.

Paige studies me. She considers amending her statement.

"I'm not sorry I went. But I *am* sorry I didn't tell you the first time I called," she concludes. "Tyler and I are friends. We'll always be friends. But that's it. He knows that. As soon as I told him you were upset, he brought me right home."

"Stop saying I *was* upset. *I'm pissed.*"

I can't take the ringing anymore. I'm determined to pick this phone up before Gregory's voice does. That's all I need right now—him butting in posthumously. I grab the wireless sitting between us and hit "talk." But I'm too late. Gregory and I answer the phone at the same time. I march into the kitchen for some privacy. I have a sneaking suspicion it's Beatrice; she's been driving me bonkers about her blood pressure medication.

"What can I do for you?" I holler into the phone.

"Can you talk?" Beatrice asks, her voice trembling. The conversation bounces off the hallway walls. Only then do I realize the answering machine is both recording and broadcasting every word.

"Not now," I tell Beatrice and slam down the phone.

"Who was that?" Paige asks, meeting me in the kitchen.

"Telemarketer."

"At this hour? Weird."

"You're telling me."

Paige grabs a stick of butter, a few slices of Velveeta, some bacon, and a tomato from the fridge. I take a seat in the breakfast nook. She flips on the burner, lays out a pan, and begins making me grilled cheese.

"I'm not hungry," I lie.

Paige works silently for the next few minutes. When the bread is golden brown, she slides the sandwich onto a plastic plate, cuts it diagonally, adorns it with some barbecue-flavored potato chips, and sets it down in the center of the table. Then Paige takes a seat across from me in the booth.

I refuse to look at her or the butter-encrusted cheese delight.

"Hey, I love you," she reminds me softly.

She lowers her head so our eyes meet. Paige tilts her head slightly, touches my chin with her fingertip, and proposes. "Will you marry me?"

"Haven't we been-there-done-this-before?" I ask.

"This is *my* engagement ring to you," she says, sliding the dish a few inches closer. "What's it cost to make a sandwich like this?"

"I don't know," I mutter, "not including labor, overhead, or tax . . . wholesale, maybe forty cents."

Paige calls for both my hands, but I only relinquish one. She clasps it between hers. That's when I notice she's wearing our engagement ring.

"I don't know what you paid for this," Paige says, adjusting the sparkler slightly, "but I'm ready to reciprocate in grilled cheese, forty cents at a time."

I think about it. Assuming two sandwiches a week, one hundred sandwiches a year. "That could take you sixty years," I say.

"Fine, in sixty years we'll reassess this relationship."

"You're only doing this because you feel bad about your Carnival Cruise with Tyler."

"Yeah, I'm committing the next sixty years to one man because I feel guilty about stepping foot on his houseboat. I love you," she tells me. "I want to be married to you. I want you to be married to me."

"Like I'm going to commit sixty years to one woman because she made me a grilled-cheese sandwich."

"I can see your mouth watering from here," she says.

Who am I kidding? I want the sandwich.

CHAPTER 19

A Quiet Implosion

IT'S on. Oh, it is *so* on. Paige and I are in major wedding mode. In forty-eight hours, we've rejected no less than a dozen wedding locations. Hotel ballrooms, gardens, churches, gazebos, golf courses, you name it—if they're not too dumpy, they're too expensive or too decadent or just too preposterous to be considered seriously.

Real men are supposed to hate this process. Wedding planning is notorious for testing the will of young couples, bringing out the worst in them. But if that's true, I'm not experiencing it. Still temporarily unemployed—we're finally ready to reopen the pharmacy tomorrow—I'm finding this wedding planning stuff sort of fun, especially because we seem to see eye-to-eye on the basics.

Consider the location of the wedding: neither of us wants anything too elaborate or exotic, so this rules out your cathedrals and petting zoos. I refuse to be at the mercy of the weather, so everything needs to take place *indoors*. Paige agrees. Paige's principal concern is accessibility, so the location has to be easy on our guests—many of whom will be senior citizens. I concur.

When it comes time for us to discuss the potential price tag for this shindig, I can't imagine we'll be *that* far apart—both of us keep using words like *small, simple,* and *elegant* to describe the finished product. Lara characterizes our desire to sponsor a wedding as "fiscally irresponsible." But Paige says a good party is exactly what we all need right now.

As far as our finances are concerned, I've been crunching numbers for days. We need to raise about $75,000 to cover Gregory's debts. The hope is we make a decent dent in that figure by collecting on some of his outstanding pharmacy tabs, but even that won't be enough. If we really want to, one, pay off all of Gregory's debt; two, keep this house; three, have this wedding; and four, live day to day, Paige needs to get a grip and we need to sell this pharmacy.

To cover some of our mounting wedding expenses and living costs, I bit the bullet and applied for another credit card. I've already maxed out my other two on that engagement ring, I have student loans up the wazoo, and still VISA jumps at the chance to overnight me $3,000 in credit.

One thing is for sure: the last thing any of us needs right now is to get mixed up in an illegal prescription drug scheme. That's how Gregory got himself in financial ruins in the first place. I'm not a licensed pharmacist. I shouldn't be dispensing medication. Not to mention risking legal action, fines, or even worse, prison. It's a small miracle that the feds have never shown up with a warrant for Gregory's arrest. Isn't it enough that we've already got Brianna McDonnell poking her perfect little button nose in our business?

I elect not to traffic in narcotics. I want to help Sid and this community, and I want to make Gregory proud. But not like that. I haven't got a good answer on how we're going to get all these folks off the Day Co-Pay, but we need to and we will. My pending nuptials to Paige are already premised on a lie. I went when I promised to wait. I don't want any more lies.

"LAWRENCE Hall of Science!" Paige shouts, catching a glimpse of the partially obstructed sign near the bushy shrubs.

I take a hard left onto a narrow road, and we wind our way up the Berkeley hills. I haven't been up this way since I was a kid. For years, my folks would take me to the old-fashioned carousel in Tilden Park. We'd eat caramel corn, and Mom and I would ride the antique hand-carved wooden horses. Dad never liked the merry-go-round much. Between the pungent smell of popcorn, the blaring organ music, and all that spinning, my father found the whole experience trippy. That's when the Berkeley visits stopped.

"This is nuts," I tell Paige as we cautiously maneuver the narrow, windy road.

On the next sharp turn, an approaching school bus nearly knocks us off the cliff.

"Maybe we should forget this," Paige says, catching her breath. "We can't expect our sort of guests to manage this trip."

A children's science museum seems like the last place you'd want your wedding, but *Here Comes the Guide* gave it four stars. The parking lot is jam-packed with yellow school buses just like the one that nearly killed us. It's midafternoon and the museum is hosting dozens of student field trips with elementary- to high-school-aged kids.

We walk toward the main building, across the concrete plaza, and past the fountain and DNA double-helix jungle gym to the ledge. What we see next changes everything. It is enough to make us forget about the hyperactive kindergartners screaming bloody murder or the preteen who just stepped on Paige's big toe.

We're much higher up than I realized.

"We're screwed," Paige says, letting out a long sigh.

We gaze at the spectacular, unobstructed panoramic view of the Bay Area on this warm, sunny afternoon. It's breathtaking. We're outside our price range, way outside, and yet nothing we see after this will ever compare. It's like buying Paige's engagement ring all over again.

"It can't hurt to ask how much," I say. "It might hurt."

Sheila, the events coordinator, a lovely, bookish woman in her midforties, with a Dorothy Hamill 1970s bob and a great big smile, greets us at the front desk. She gives us the nickel tour, walking us past the earthquake simulators, the ocean waves display, and the insect zoo. Elementary school children charge through a gigantic maze like rats. As we walk, Sheila tosses around wedding terms of art like "preferred caterer," "hired security," and "nonrefundable security deposit." Paige and I are total frauds. We're wasting her time.

As we reach the doors to the private outdoor Science Park, Paige and I are pummeled by a sweet, sickly odor. I follow the scent to Exhibit Hall B, where I see a group of kids gathered inside a giant papier-mâché nose. Following a loud blast, the children are gently expelled out one nostril.

The fruity fragrance is overwhelming.

"What is this?" I blurt out with disgust. "It smells like a boiling vat of Jell-O."

"It's an exhibit on the human senses," Sheila says.

Sheila points to the far wall intended to simulate human skin. Small children use cantaloupe-sized protrusions to climb it.

"That one concentrates on the sense of touch," she says.

The enormous nose sneezes again.

"This one explores the sense of smell," Sheila explains. "It was supposed to smell like peanut butter and jelly, but because some children are allergic to peanuts, we kept it just jelly."

"You can have an allergic reaction to the *scent* of peanuts?" I ask.

"We weren't about to take any chances," Sheila says, walking us outside.

Not the scientific answer I was expecting.

The Science Park has a beautiful sprawling lawn with abstract sculptures, a man-made rock garden and small creek, picnic tables, and some strategically planted telescopes around the perimeter.

If we rent the museum, our guests will have exclusive use of the entire building and all the exhibits, Sheila tells us. For dramatic effect, she conducts the entire transaction with her back to the magnificent Bay Area backdrop. Sheila's coy with figures, but she tells us the most reasonable rates are in the off-season, November through March, and if we're willing to do a Sunday evening, she might even be able to knock off a thousand dollars.

"Over the next year, the museum doesn't plan on sponsoring any other aroma-themed exhibits, does it?" I ask.

Sheila needs to check and leaves.

I sneeze a couple of times.

"I think you're allergic to the smell of jelly, if that's possible," Paige says, handing me a tissue from her bag.

I tell her I'm considering suing.

Paige and I walk back inside and stroll through the museum. Opposite the "Nose-Aroma" exhibit is "The Real Astronomy Experience," where students can learn how to measure the size of a planet and track the trajectory of an asteroid. Outside the planetarium, there is a massive bronze head-and-shoulders sculpture of the hall's namesake, Ernest "the Atom Smasher" Lawrence, inventor of the cyclotron—a device used to create the original atom bomb.

"When protons collide," I say, reading the steel plaque to Paige, "just prior to a nuclear blast, there is a massive inrush of air known as 'the quiet implosion.'"

"Nuclear proliferation, sounds like a good wedding theme to me," she suggests.

"It would be quite 'the blowout,'" I say, elbowing her lightly in the rib.

"We're being silly. We totally can't afford this."

"You only get married once," I tell her.

I love seeing her this happy.

"I could sew my own dress," she suggests, "and maybe we could skip dinner and just do cocktails and appetizers, right out here."

Sheila waves us over. She has good news.

"There was a message on my voice mail." *Yeah right.* "We literally just had a cancellation for Sunday, August 12th," she says, excitedly.

"August twelfth of what year?" Paige cries.

"Seven weeks from yesterday," I calculate quickly.

"Are you serious?"

"How much?" I ask Sheila.

"I'd need to get a sign-off from my supervisor, but given the short notice, I could probably give it to you for $4,000."

Is she going to give it to us or does she want $4,000?

Sheila reminds us that this figure doesn't include the cost for the preferred caterer.

"Do we have to rent the *entire* museum? Couldn't we just rent this patch of grass over here?" I ask her.

"Oh, but that would be such a waste," she says. "I suppose I can ask about *just* the Science Park, but I'm telling you now, they're never going to dip below $3,000."

"Seven weeks is *too* soon," Paige says, not even considering the price.

"I completely understand," Sheila says.

"A shotgun wedding," I conclude.

"I'm not pregnant," Paige quickly reassures Sheila.

"Of course you're not, darling."

Both Sheila and I study Paige, who studies the tile floor.

"Can you give us twenty-four hours to think about it?" Paige asks.

"Take your time, but I can't guarantee the date, or rate," she replies kindly.

So you can't give us twenty-four hours? Say what you mean, woman.

"If you're going to just rent the garden, given the short notice, I can do $3,000." All of sudden Sheila has all this authority. *What's it going to take to put your wedding in this children's museum today?*

For $3,000, we can have our dream wedding.

Help Paige realize her fantasy, Sid told me. Paige wants this.

"Oh, to your other question," Sheila adds, "the 'Nose-Aroma' exhibit leaves next week. So you're safe. Next up is 'Legos.'"

Legos! Who doesn't love Legos? I tell Paige with my eyes.

But Paige can't take her eyes off the view.

"I don't think we need twenty-four hours," I tell Sheila.

Paige pretends to be stunned.

I pull out my wallet, and right before I hand Sheila my new VISA, I covertly pull off the validation sticker and quickly stuff it in my pocket. *Mental note: Use the men's room before we leave. Activate this card.* We pay the $500 deposit now, and the balance is due the day before the wedding. Eighty percent of the deposit is refundable if we cancel within nine weeks of the event, but we're getting married in seven. Sheila makes an imprint of my credit card using a pencil across carbon paper. I sign the contract. Then Paige does.

We'll be fine, I tell myself. *You just bought your fiancée the ultimate wedding. We'll sell more toothpaste. We'll eat more Top Ramen. We'll shake down more seniors. The money will come from somewhere. When you owe seventy-five grand, what's seventy-eight?*

CHAPTER 20

Eureka!

THE garage door is partially open. I duck underneath and spot my best friend, planted on a stool, bent over his workbench. Sid is staring into a swing-arm magnifying glass not so unlike the one we inspected diamonds with in Igor Petrov's office.

I take a step closer and he slowly spins toward me. His batlike hearing compensates for poor eyesight. Sid doesn't look like himself without the dark wraparound shades, but he is as upbeat as ever.

"Wait 'til you lay your peepers on this," he cries with delight. "I've just about got it flush!"

He and I haven't lost a step. I want to give him a big bear hug, but I softly put one hand on his back and lean into the lens. It's too dark in here. I remind Sid that this magnifying glass has a built-in lamp.

His cloudy green eyes widen. "Much better," he affirms.

Sid has gutted his sacred pinky ring of its blue topaz gemstone and replaced it with a clear, loose-fitting plastic top.

"See right there . . . that's where you store the nitroglycerin tablet," he explains, nudging the lid delicately with a pair of tweezers. "The first sign of a heart attack and BAM! You pop that little puppy."

In pharmacy school they teach you that a small dose of nitroglycerin dissolved underneath the tongue can sometimes be used to increase blood flow to the heart and preempt angina. The inspiration behind Sid's idea isn't lost on me.

"You could also store a little breath mint in there," I gently hint, taking the tweezers from him to study the prototype.

The façade crudely fits over the opening.

"Sidney!" Cookie screams, nearly causing both of us to pop nitroglycerin.

Cookie is standing in the doorway separating the kitchen from the garage. She has on a wide-brimmed gardening hat and blue jean overalls.

"I'm going to kill you!" she shouts, ready to leap through the air and tackle him to the ground.

But instead, cane in hand, she gingerly descends the two steps to the concrete garage floor. Then she hobbles toward us with a small brown package tucked under her arm.

"I thought we had an agreement," she demands.

Cookie tosses the package onto the table, causing Sid's blue topaz gemstone to disappear into oblivion.

"No more eBay! No more online! You promised!" Cookie cries.

"Where'd you find that?" Sid wonders.

"In your bottom dresser drawer."

"Well, aren't you the nosey parker? Can't a man have some privacy? That's not mine," he insists like a teen busted for weed. "It's Andy's."

"Yeah, and I'm Ava Gardner," she says, leaning her cane against the workbench. Cookie rips off the small piece of Scotch tape holding the package closed. She's already rummaged through the contents. Tossing the packing on the floor, she pulls out a ream of personalized stationery.

"This letterhead has *our* address and *our* phone number on it," she yells at Sid. "Plus the invoice has *your* credit card number. How is this Andy's?"

"Are you *positive* that's *my* credit card number?" Sid bluffs.

That's when Cookie notices Sid's disassembled pinky ring on the countertop.

"For crying out loud!" Cookie hollers. She picks up the empty gold setting. "I gave this to you for your sixtieth birthday. Where's the goddam gemstone?"

Sid begins frantically looking around for the blue topaz.

"*Why* would you *do* such a thing?" she pleads.

Realizing this is my big chance, I casually reach inside my breast pocket and squeeze the record button on the handheld device.

"It was my idea," I jump in. "I wanted to see if we could stick a pill in there for emergency's sake."

I show her how the little lid barely fits over the top.

"You are a dumb person," she says, pointing at me with both hands like an air traffic controller. "You ruined a perfectly good piece of jewelry for what? Nothing. And besides, there is no way that idiotic lid will ever stay on. Where is the original stone?" Cookie demands. "Show it to me now!"

She snaps up her cane and takes a step closer to Sid.

I block her path to protect him.

"Move!" she yells, inches from my face.

"Come again?"

We dance to the right, and then to the left.

"What part of 'get the hell out of the way' don't you understand?" she cries.

"I think you need a time-out," I tell her.

"Listen, buster, I've had just about enough of you." She eyes me up and down. I'm at least a foot and half taller than her. "You think just because I'm two thousand years old that I can't take you?"

We stare some more. She throws up her hands in defeat.

"This is why you have no friends your own age," Cookie concludes.

Cookie does an about-face and heads inside, addressing Sid once more before slamming the door in our faces: "If that stone is missing or I learn that you bought that stationery on the Interweb, I will beat that computer of yours senseless with this cane."

I reach into my shirt pocket and shut the tape recorder. Sid is already on his hands and knees looking for his missing topaz. It's gone. I help him to his feet.

"Cookie's got a point," he says, dusting off his bare knees, and then grabbing his back in pain. "That lid is never going to stay on the ring. I thought maybe a screw top, but that might be tough to disengage."

"That would be bad," I say. "There you are, having a heart attack and all, millimeters from the very pill that will save your life, and you can't get the blasted thing open."

I yank a sheet of personalized letterhead from the paper ream. On the backside, tucked in the lower right-hand corner, is a tiny advertisement.

"What do you think? Nifty, huh? Totally free if you agree to let them include that ad," he says.

"But the invoice here says you paid thirty bucks in postage and handling."

"Rush ordered them. Had to. We need to get serious."

I hold the letterhead underneath Sid's magnifying glass to inspect it.

"Do you like the company name and slogan?" he asks.

It reads: "Euraka Productions: Why Didn't I Think of That?"

"I do. But I think you spell 'eureka' with two *e*'s, not two *a*'s," I tell him.

"You're kidding!"

I show him.

"Crappity, crappity crud!"

The business card also has the company's online address.

"You actually registered eurakaproductions.com?" I'm impressed.

"How can you go wrong for $25?" the future mogul says.

"Well, for starters, Cookie could stab you in the neck. You heard her."

"The Web address came with lots of free storage space and up to twenty free e-mail accounts," he boasts. "I'm going to do the Web site myself. Signed up for a Beginners Web class at the Community Center. First session is Monday."

"Haven't you been the busy beaver," I tell him.

I don't care about the tacky advertisement on the back or the typos on the front, I want this letterhead. I've never had my own stationery. Sid carefully deals me ten sheets, licking his pointer finger with every page.

"This gives us the legitimacy we need when I send out all those query letters," Sid says. "Between the bladeless windshield wipers, adjustable heels, dog umbrella, and tactile timepiece, someone will bite. Maybe one day we'll even have enough dough to buy ourselves a real patent."

"I think you're going to love my next invention," I say, patting the tiny tape recorder in my breast pocket. "But it's not ready for prime time yet."

Sid raises a curious eyebrow. "Can't wait," he says, lowering himself from his stool.

We walk out of the garage to the driveway. It's another exquisite summer afternoon in sunny northern California.

"Thanks for getting this stuff," I say, shaking my share of letterhead.

"Didn't do it for you. Did it for me," he says, pointing over at Gregory's house. "Can't have you selling that place and some unruly new neighbors ruining this neck of the woods. We'll figure something out . . . something we all can live with."

"I owe you an answer about the other night," I begin.

"Hold that thought," Sid commands, whipping out a cell phone. *When did he get that?*

"Free," he brags, wiggling the shiny silver phone.

He has yet to peel off the thin protective plastic that covers the display screen, and I highly doubt the cell phone service that accompanies this "free" phone is free. Sid excuses himself and walks over to the side of the garage to speak privately. In three days, he's gone from homebody to Hollywood agent.

My pants start vibrating. It's my cell phone. Sid's calling me, I assume, until I realize the caller ID says "Paige Home."

"So lemme guess. You're having 'buyer's remorse.' Stop worrying. The hall is beautiful," I tell her. "The money's spent."

"What money's spent?" Lara asks curiously.

"Oh, hey."

"What money?"

"What money?" I repeat.

"You just said 'the money's spent' . . . oh, Jesus, forget it."

This is when I realize that the Vomit Mobile isn't even in the driveway.

"Can I please speak with Paige?" she insists.

I tell Lara to look out her living room window. She does and I wave. I inform her Paige dropped me off a half-hour ago and left for work.

"Have you tried *Paige*'s cell?"

"Don't you think I thought of that?" Lara says, frustrated to the max. "I called, and what happens? Her cell phone starts ringing ten feet away from me."

"I wonder if Paige realizes her cell phone is wireless," I tell Lara.

This is the first time I've made Lara really laugh. She gets as frustrated as I do about Paige's forgetful habits.

"Well, I might as well tell you," she decides. "I'm not sure how easy it's going to be to sell the pharmacy. Apparently Walgreens *and* Longs Drugs made competing offers on Dad's place about two years ago, and both times, my father passed. I haven't heard back from Longs yet, but the Walgreens offer is definitely withdrawn." Lara sounds worried. "Paige'll probably be thrilled."

Man, I always figured the pharmacy would cover at least forty grand of Gregory's debt. Plus now we've got this ridiculous wedding hall to pay for.

"Just tell Paige to call me," Lara says, interrupting my revised computations.

I tell her I will, and we hang up.

Sid eventually returns from his fictional phone call.

"Someone drown your puppy?" Sid asks me.

"I don't have a puppy," I say distantly.

"I know. You okay, small fry?"

"I'm not sure."

Sid tries a different topic. "*You* wanted to know how many people there are on the Gregory Day Co-Pay?" I nod. "I've been asking around, compiling a list, checking it twice. An educated guess? About fifty."

I now make it a practice to keep Lara's Most Wanted list in my wallet just in case I run into a deadbeat. I unfold the sheet of paper and hand it to him.

"Uh-huh," he says, ticking through the names. "Uh-huh, uh-huh. This looks awfully similar to my list," Sid concludes, shaking his head.

"So you're saying Lara's hit list and Gregory's Co-Pay match?" I guess I shouldn't be all that surprised.

"Like father, like daughter," he says, mildly entertained. "Listen, Andy, a lot of folks on these lists haven't got a bedpan to piss in. We're not talking about dipping into someone's retirement nest egg; we're talking about real people, with real money problems. You get me?"

"Trust me, I know plenty about money problems."

"That's just it," he says. "We can help you. I was thinking about it: I say we can scale back, *way back*. Gregory lost track of all those tabs. I can help you figure out which folks *really* need the Day Co-Pay bargain."

I can only assume this includes Sid and his wife.

"Meantime, Cookie and the girls can still get you samples," Sid adds, checking his watch. "You'll get a little money from the insurance folks, some from the pharmacy sales, and even make a few collections on Lara's list. This way you'll be able to give Paige that wedding she's always wanted."

So I'm supposed to help Paige realize her fantasy at any cost?

"Let's assume I agree to do this for a little while, we need an exit strategy. We need to figure out a way to get these people on the up-and-up. No more samples. No more insurance claims. I'm not kidding, Sid."

"I promise," he beams. "But we're also going to need to enlist some help."

"Your drug cartel isn't enough?"

"No, some *special* help," he says, trying to see behind me.

Sid checks his watch against the arrival of the 1965 Cadillac ambulance.

Manny Milken pulls up to the curb, waving hello from inside the cab. His car stereo is blaring the Kansas classic "Carry On Wayward Son." He sings along, completely off-key and mangling every word he meets. (He'd be better off singing Chewbacca.) Manny climbs out, opens the trunk, places two small boxes on a dolly, and wheels it up the driveway, stopping every so often to pull up either side of his pants.

"Four minutes, thirty-five seconds," he says, all proud of himself. Manny shows Sid the timer function on his personal organizer. "You're just lucky I was in the neighborhood," Manny says.

"Aren't you always in the neighborhood?" I ask.

"Hey, man," Manny greets me warmly.

Something's wrong. "Why is he calling me 'man'?" I ask Sid suspiciously.

Sid's too busy inspecting Manny's boxes to pay me any attention.

"Emmanuel, what we got here?" he says, squatting down.

"Product from Dr. Hardy, Dr. Mills, and Dr. Platt. Mostly Prazex, Celebrex, Diovan, and Lanicor. "

"Wait one-cotton-picking-minute," I yell. "You swore Manny just did the deliveries."

"Since we spoke, circumstances have . . . changed," Sid explains.

"Oh, crap. I'm already regretting this."

"Margaret Milken needs us." Sid lays it out there plainly. "She's on all sorts of medication. Parkinson's has many complications."

Manny stares at his sneakers.

"My mom loved Gregory," he mumbles.

I forcibly rub my face with both hands. Sid studies the two of us.

"Come on—you two knuckleheads are a match made in heaven," Sid laughs. "No one's got a better sense of who's on the Day Co-Pay than Manny. And Andy, you're going to need someone to continue with the pickups and deliveries. Someone who will work *free of charge,* idn't that right, Emmanuel?"

Manny nods.

"Here," Sid says, pulling a two-way Motorola radio out of each of his back pockets. "These have a range of five miles. That means, no matter where you are in Crockett, the two of you are only a walkie-talkie click away."

Manny eagerly takes his. I pretend not to want mine.

I stole two packs of Hubba Bubba chewing gum from Day's Pharmacy a half a lifetime ago. This is how I'll make up for it: not by working for Gregory, but by stealing for him.

CHAPTER 21

Aches and Pains

I'M LIABLE to kill someone. I'm liable if I kill someone.

It was so much easier when Gregory yelled at me. I never appreciated the sense of security that comes with having a skilled pharmacist available to check your work. Filling prescriptions *should be* a cakewalk. Janus is right here if I have any questions. She's familiar with the side effects, allergic reactions, and drug interactions associated with more than seven thousand drugs. In fact, the Janus software suite is so smart it even self-updates, twice a day. That's how we knew, for example, ten hours before Paige's news station did, that Simpson Pharmaceuticals was pulling its hypertension pill, Betapro.

But even with Janus at my fingertips, I'm still on edge. I don't know how Gregory managed to keep up. Every day, it seems the FDA or a drug manufacturer or an investigative reporter or a class action lawsuit or a scientific journal is issuing some sort of new warning or drug withdrawal. These days, the unthinkable has become probable: osteoporosis meds that actually cause bone deterioration; arthritis drugs that prompt heart attacks; and now the latest atrocity—antidepressants that actually *increase* the risk of suicide.

This business is fraught with danger. Combined, Gregory and I used to fill about a thousand scripts a week, and this is one of the only jobs where you need to be 100 percent correct 100 percent of the time. The wrong medication, the wrong dosage, the wrong instructions to the wrong customer, one sloppy prescription, one misplaced decimal place, and . . . DEAD.

It just so happens that I could also go to federal prison for filling scripts without a license. Lara knows this but couldn't care less, so long as the cash registers.

It's the pharmacy's first day back in business and Lara promised me—*she promised me*—we'd stick to selling candy, food, magazines, toiletries, and over-the-counter drugs. Then Selma Patterson came in wanting her blood pressure pills, and Lara said *do it,* so I did it. More folks came in looking for basic refills and I did them, too. This morning alone, I filled about a dozen prescriptions. But when it came to Lucille Braggs, I put my foot down. She demanded her medication, and I told her, in not so many words, that when it comes to making suppositories, I don't know my ass from a hole in the wall. Lara could insist all she wanted, it just wasn't going to happen.

I wish Gregory were here.

All things considered, though, reopening the pharmacy turned out to be pretty uneventful. About thirty customers came through this morning. We might have had more patrons if the front door weren't still busted. Until I finally propped it open, feeble humans found it impossible to operate. Many of them never even bothered—I think they assumed we were still closed, seeing as half the door is boarded up. Of the customers who forced their way in, many of them dealt with Gregory's death in a similarly obtuse manner: he or she would walk up to one of us, express heartfelt condolences, pause, and then ask where we keep the Tylenol.

All of today's customers had medical insurance or paid in cash or credit, so the topic of tabs or shakedowns never came up, though you can feel Lara eyeing every customer like they're walking dollar signs. For someone who's spent the better part of her life in Crockett, Lara doesn't seem to know anyone. If we were to put all sixty people on her deadbeat list in a lineup—something Lara would jump at the chance of doing—I'd be surprised if she could identify ten. I'm not ready to confront anyone since my episode with Mills.

It's so empty in here without Gregory. If it's possible, the lighting feels poorer. The dust feels heavier. Lara's presence infuses this place with an uncomfortable library vibe. She and I don't argue like Gregory and I used to. I'm not sure we've said more than ten words to each other.

It's only after the royal arrival of the Brewsters that Day's Pharmacy begins feeling anything like it did before Gregory died. Loki announces their visit by bolting down the aisle, picking up too much speed, and sliding and slamming right into the sunglasses rack. Three pairs crash to the ground.

"Poor thing," Cookie cries.

Her compassion takes me by surprise.

"Don't you worry," Sid comforts his wife. "She's fine. Look."

He's right. The puppy regains her bearings and races off.

If it were up to Cookie, she would avoid even the simplest pleasantries, but Belinda won't have it. Belinda provokes Cookie out of sport.

"Afternoon, Mrs. Brewster. Lovely to see you," Belinda says, accentuating every word as she ducks down to make eye contact with Cookie.

Cookie takes a red plastic shopping basket.

"You should have that looked at," Cookie says casually of Belinda's lip ring. "It looks infected to me, unless that blister's always been there."

Belinda narrows her eyes. Then gives Cookie a forced smile.

Sid is early. He's carrying a small brown box, not so unlike the anonymous packages piled up right behind me in the corner. He brazenly hands me the contraband right in front of Lara; thankfully, she's too self-involved to notice. Then he gives me a long, hard wink and takes his favorite seat at the lunch counter while Cookie shops.

"How is your sister feeling?" Sid asks Lara.

"She's doing okay," Lara answers. "Everybody is always so worried about Paige. I'm coping here, too," she mumbles.

"Of course I want to know how you're doing, too, honey. I thought because you're the big sister and all . . ."

"Sid, lemme ask you a question," I say suddenly. "Why don't you get your medication from the VA Hospital?"

"What? My money's no good here?" he asks.

"What money?" Lara mutters.

"All I'm saying is the Veterans Affairs Hospital is literally one town over and you'd get most of your meds for free."

"It's a hassle," he says, swatting the idea away like a fly.

"Uh-huh," I patronize him.

"I'm not going to make Cookie drive me there every time. Plus I don't like their doctors," he complains, "and they force those generic pills down your throat."

"The horror!" I yell, pushing past Lara to get ointment from the far corner. "If you change your mind, I'm here for you, Sid, and I'd be happy to drive you."

The walkie-talkie clipped to my belt belts out a loud irritating beep.

"Andy, Manny, this is Manny. Over," he yells over the two-way radio.

As if he could be Andy.

I unhook it. "Go," I tell him.

"So I'm doing my deliveries, and I get to Ada Winchester's house, and I realize that I haven't got her osteoporosis pills," he says.

Only now do I realize that I forgot to refill Ada's prescription. I press the button on the radio and apologize, "Sorry, the day got away from me, Man."

"Yeah, well, she was pretty upset," Manny says. "She kept saying: 'Where's my Boniva?' 'I need my Boniva.' 'Boniva this and Boniva that.'"

I tell Manny that if he comes back now I'll give him the pills.

"That's just it. Okay, so don't be mad, but I'd just picked up a bunch of Boniva samples at Dr. Platt's office and they were just sitting there on the seat."

I frantically search for the volume button and turn Manny down, missing the last part of what he says. I'm trapped—whether it's coincidence or on purpose, Lara is cutting off my only exit, and she's doing everything in her power to eavesdrop. I huddle in the corner. Cupping the speaker, I slowly turn up the volume. Manny is still talking.

"Stop talking," I whisper loudly. He does. "Please don't tell me that you gave Ada Winchester drug samples. Please, Manny, I'm begging you."

"Not all of 'em," he insists. "Just a box of twenty-four."

"Are you serious?" I cry. "People are supposed to take those pills once a month! You just gave her a two-year supply."

"Aw, crap."

But we may have bigger problems. I jam the walkie-talkie in my pocket.

"Move," I tell Lara.

She steps away from the pharmacy computer terminal and I feverishly punch a few keys. *Janus*, I ask, *does Boniva come in different dosages?* Janus scours her memory banks. *Please, please, please.* Manny's muffled voice emanates from my pants. *No, Glaxo-*

SmithKline only makes Boniva in one dosage, Janus tells me. *Ada is safe.* The samples match her prescription.

I burrow myself back in the corner of the room.

"What do you want me to do?" Manny pleads.

"No more deliveries for you. You're cut off. Return to the mother ship. Repeat, *return* to the mother ship," I tell him, turning the radio off.

"Andrew!" Lara yells, urgently. "Can you stop doing whatever you're doing? You have a customer."

Waiting for me at the register is Brianna McDonnell. She has a Blue Cross of California white plastic clipboard tucked under her arm. She smiles at me with those big brown eyes and perfectly tweezed eyebrows.

"Hi."

"Hi," she says back, with an awkward pause. "Everything okay?"

"Oh, totally," I try.

"You're sure?"

"Indubitably." All of a sudden I'm the Queen of England.

"I don't know what to say," Brianna begins. "I was heartbroken to hear about Gregory."

Brianna leans in closer than I'm comfortable with. I love the way she smells. I quickly check to see if Lara's watching, and she is.

"I still can't believe I'll never see him again. That I'll never pester him again," she kids.

"We all miss him," Sid chimes in from the lunch counter.

Lara comes up behind me.

"I don't think we've met," Lara says.

"Brianna, this is Gregory's spinster daughter, Lara Day," I tell Brianna.

I don't say the spinster part.

The two of them shake hands.

"Is this your fiancée?" Brianna asks.

Lara, Sid, and I shout no in unison.

"Brianna is from Blue Cross of California," I tell Lara.

"I knew your name sounded familiar," Lara says. "I have at

least three letters with your signature on them. We owe you some paperwork."

"I was crazy about your father," Brianna says. She puts her hand on her hip and adjusts her crooked stance. "You could tell he really cared about his customers."

Lara thanks her.

Cookie stops in her tracks as soon as she lays her eyes on Brianna. Cookie creeps closer, like Brianna's an endangered species.

"Brianna, here, oversees all the insurance claims for the pharmacy," Sid informs his wife delicately.

"Why don't you stand up straight?" Cookie demands. "I'm decrepit with scoliosis and a cane, and I still have better posture than you. You're a spring chicken. What are you, thirty-four?"

"Twenty-six," Brianna says.

Cookie drops her shopping basket, leans her cane against the shelves, steps up behind Brianna, and places both of her hands on Brianna's shoulders.

Brianna cringes.

"See," Cookie says, pushing down hard on the left side as if she can even them out with a little force. "You're all lopsided."

"What the—" Brianna screams, lopping off the expletive.

Then Cookie clamps on to both of Brianna's arms, squeezing and shifting them up and down like udders.

"Please don't touch me," Brianna commands Cookie, breaking away. Her eyebrows point inward like little daggers. "I have chronic back problems."

"Mankind takes thousands of years to evolve, so how is it that in the last ten years, everybody now has 'chronic back problems'?"

"It's a slipped disk." Brianna's all offended. "I've had my back examined."

"You should have your head examined," Cookie tells her.

Brianna's finished mollifying Cookie. She turns her back to Cookie and asks whether there's any chance Lara could get her that paperwork.

I subtly check with Sid on whether Brianna's request is reasonable. His eyes widen and he slyly shakes his head no. *So this is why Gregory was so unwilling to cooperate with Brianna in the past. This is why he was so annoyed with me the day I offered to give Brianna the records—the very same day I proposed to Paige.* If my yell-fest with Manny didn't spill the beans on our little sample sale, then I'm guessing Gregory's records will.

"If you tell me what you need, I'll start putting the documentation together for you now," Lara assures her.

Brianna starts digging through her portfolio.

"Wait, wait, wait!" I yell, but it's too late.

None of us sees this coming, especially Brianna. Cookie has helped herself to a tube of Aspercreme. I can smell the menthol from here. She's squeezed out a heaping pile of goop, and in one swift motion, Cookie lifts the back of Brianna's blouse and slabs the medicated gel all over it. In that split second, I get a brief glimpse of Brianna's lacy white bra and tan, flat tummy. Brianna is mortified and more concerned with covering up than anything else.

"Why are you torturing me?" Brianna screams, adjusting herself. "Ah!" she yells as her clothes cling to the ointment. "This is silk," she says, pulling at the material. "You've completely ruined it."

"Who told you to pull your blouse down so quick?" Cookie yells.

"Get out!" Lara screams at Cookie louder than any Day has probably ever yelled in this pharmacy, which is saying something.

"I'm so sorry," Lara tells Brianna. "We'll pay to have it cleaned."

Cookie grabs her cane and points at Brianna forcefully. "You'll see. By tomorrow your back will be all better," Cookie insists.

Was Cookie actually trying to help Brianna or help us get rid of her? It's hard to tell. Probably a bit of both.

"Basket!" Cookie commands.

Sid slowly lowers himself off his stool, walks over to Cookie, and hands Cookie her shopping basket of goods.

"I'm so sorry this happened," I say, trying to comfort Brianna softly. "That woman is crazy in the coconut."

"I'm fine." But she's not. Brianna is on the verge of tears. "I'm going to leave now," she says.

But she can't, not with Cookie standing in her way.

"Loki, sweetie," Cookie coos.

But Loki doesn't come.

"We're having a party in six weeks," Cookie announces to the room. "It's our sixtieth wedding anniversary," she says proudly. "Sidney rented The Old Homestead and there will be chocolate cake. You're all invited. Even you, skinny," Cookie tells Brianna.

Brianna manages a meek smile.

"I'll write down my address so you can send me an invite," Belinda suggests, rubbernecking to see what Cookie's got in her cart.

"You just got your invitation, missy," Cookie snarls. "Don't push your luck."

"Be sure you charge her for that tube of Aspercreme," I tell Belinda. "This isn't your personal medicine cabinet," I yell over.

"Add it to my tab," Cookie says.

"We're not doing those anymore," Lara screams back.

But it's too late. Red plastic shopping basket and all, Cookie marches out, knocking backward the bane of my existence, Tyler Rich.

Tyler Rich is dressed to impress in a tan linen sport coat and a black dress shirt with the top two buttons undone. He's got gobs of gel in his hair, all slicked to one side.

"Hi there, Andy," Tyler greets me as if we're friends. Then he turns to Lara. "Ready?"

"Can you give me five? I need to print off these records for the insurance lady," Lara explains. Brianna is at least six years younger than Lara. "And I want to change my outfit."

Lara starts assembling the needed paperwork, but the coast is clear for Brianna to exit safely. Brianna begins gathering her things. Slowly bending down to hook Loki to her leash, Sid gives me the signal to stop Lara.

"Why don't you give us a few more days to get you copies of everything," I tell Brianna. "I'll deliver them to you personally. I want to make sure you get *exactly* what you need, and our records are a total wreck."

"They certainly are *not* a wreck," Lara complains, rushing to prove it.

"Fine," Brianna says, backing away. "What's another week, right?"

"That's not necessary," Lara calls over. "I've got it all right here."

"We appreciate it," I say, walking over and placing a hand on Brianna's shoulder, pointing her to the door.

Lara is beyond pissed. There will be hell to pay, but for the time being, it's over and I've won.

Sid and I follow Brianna to the front of the store. She brushes past Tyler, without returning his hungry stare. Someone's managed to knock the doorstop loose. Sid goes to jiggle it open for Brianna, but Loki's leash gets tangled up in one of the wheels of her rolling bag. Loki lets out a tiny squeal. Brianna can't take too much more drama. I separate them, jerk the door open, and Brianna's free.

Tripping over Loki's leash, I stumble outside and all of a sudden my face and Brianna's are inches apart. On impulse, I almost hug her—Brianna needs a hug, but that would be inappropriate (and would only rub the ointment in more). We stare. The small schnoodle then drags Sid outside, and without a word, Brianna breaks for her car, tossing her heavy bag through the open window and onto her backseat.

"We really appreciate it," I yell over to her and wave.

Brianna waves back without making eye contact. Quickly unparallel-parking, she manages to tap the cars on either side before zooming off.

"What are we going to do about her?" I ask Sid out of the corner of my mouth.

"A fair question indeed," Sid answers.

CHAPTER 22

The Father of Invention

I BRACE for complete meltdown, but it never happens. If Gregory were still alive, I'd be knocked over by a magnitude 6.0 or higher before stepping foot back in the pharmacy, but his eldest daughter would prefer to ignore me.

Who would have dreamed I'd yearn for the days when Gregory asked me if I was disturbed. But Lara won't give me the satisfaction. *The opposite of love isn't hate, it's indifference.*

Tyler Rich has hoisted himself up on the glass display case, feet dangling side to side. It's plenty sturdy to bear his scrawny build, but I warn him anyway: "Please don't sit on that. You'll break it," I demand, wishing he'd fall through.

Tyler hops down. "Uh, oh-kay," he says with an air of disdain.

In the short time it took me to usher Brianna out, Lara has transformed into evening wear—high heels, a fashionable brown blazer, and some pink lip gloss. She looks prettier than ever—more like her sister than ever.

Without a word, Tyler and Lara file out.

"Good night!" Belinda manages to get in as Lara runs, not walks, out.

"If you say so," Lara says from the sidewalk.

Belinda and I exchange looks.

"This job rocks!" Belinda complains with a mild lisp and the peace sign. She just got her tongue pierced and she still hasn't gotten used to the silver barbell.

"Take some magazines. That always makes you feel better," I tell her.

"Lifetime subscriptions wouldn't do the trick."

Belinda snaps up the newest *In Touch* magazine. She scans the stacks some more, stuffing a copy of *The New Yorker* in her bag before flipping the WELCOME sign to CLOSED, and leaving.

I check the cash register. In addition to her lightning-fast wardrobe change, Lara managed to find enough time to clean out the front register. I'll never know exactly what we collected in receipts our first day back. If I had to guess, I'd put the figure around $700.

Paige is working the late shift, so I'm having dinner with the Brewsters. Cookie's making brisket and sweet potatoes, and Sid assured me there'd be plenty of extra. I also promised him that I'd drop by with their refills—between the two of them they take about two dozen different pills, sprays, and drops.

Sid's brown-box delivery is sitting on the pharmacy counter. I unfold the flaps of the box and find two dozen neatly packaged and labeled plastic containers. Each bottle indicates the name and dosage of the sorted pharmaceutical samples. I pull out a small white one that used to hold antacid tablets. On a strip of masking tape, Cookie's book club has written in black Magic Marker: "Amoxicillin/40 mg." I unscrew the top and eyeball the contents. There has got to be at least three hundred pills inside— enough to sustain two dozen seniors for about a month.

From the middle shelf I pull down our container of amoxicillin and give it a rattle—it's half-empty. There is a new shipment of unopened tablets around here somewhere, but for financial reasons, I'd prefer we resell those to the next owner; that, or just send them back to the manufacturer.

I unscrew the large jar of *pharmacy* pills. Then I take Sid's contraband and dangle it. *Am I really doing this? Once you commingle them, there's no going back, Andy. After this, I'll never be 100 percent sure of what I'm prescribing our patrons or submitting to insurance.* I tip the small antacid bottle a few degrees lower, but then stop. *Didn't Sid mention something about Gregory conducting quality control on everything the book club sorted?* I study the contents of both containers: they sure look the same—both pills are pale yellow and octagonal in shape. But are they the same dosage? Maybe these sample pills are old, or expired? *I shouldn't be doing this. I'm not qualified to do this.*

It only then occurs to me: What if Gregory already tainted these pharmacy pills long ago.

I close my eyes and dump the contents of one container into the other.

Bottle by bottle, felony after felony, I contaminate the rest of our supply with Sid's free samples. I'm prepared to traffic in illegal drugs, but I've decided insurance fraud is over the line. We desperately need some income, but now that I know, I want to avoid filing any more illegal claims. Lara thinks she knows who owes the biggest tabs; Sid thinks he knows who needs the Day Co-Pay most; what I need to figure out is who, if anyone, can actually pay. If not the folks on either of their lists, there must be others— maybe Mills won't, but surely some of the other doctors who traded samples for supplies can.

Lara's files may also help. I start poking around her work-station. Sitting on her desk is Target File No. 7—"Louise Rothkin." Rothkin is that woman Manny almost killed after delivering her the wrong heart medication. Thanks to Sid's list, now I know that she is a major recipient of the Day Co-Pay. (That would explain why Rothkin never pressed charges against us.) I flip open the manila folder, half-expecting to see a mug shot of Louise paper-clipped to the pages; instead the dossier contains what one would expect: prescriptions, insurance forms, and receipts.

What would really be helpful is if I could locate that black ledger I see Lara writing in all the time. But Lara's padlocked the top drawer to her oak desk and password-protected her computer. *Boy, is she paranoid.*

I aimlessly pull open and slam closed more drawers looking for anything that might help me assess the liquidity of our customers. Nothing.

Then I notice a rectangular wooden panel just below the counter to the black granite sink. I hook my fingers underneath the bottom edge of the plank, but it's glued shut. I try to wiggle the panel side to side, but it won't pop off. Along the top is a small lip. Pulling down on it gently causes the whole façade to tip forward on hinges to reveal a small compartment.

This is no dummy drawer at all.

I squat down and cock my head to one side to see, but it's too dark inside. Blindly feeling around, my hand smacks into a small plastic box. I know what it is instantly. "Son of a gun!" I whisper as I pull out the organic chemistry set.

I grab a rag, wipe off the thick coat of dust, and unhook the lid. Divided up like a box of chocolates are the key organic building blocks to life. The plastic spheres come in six different colors and represent six different atoms. There are a variety of plastic connectors that signify single, double, and triple bonds. If *Organic Chemistry* were a movie (spoiler alert: *terrible movie, do not see this movie*) it would certainly be presented in 3-D. That's because the only way to truly understand how carbon-to-carbon bonds sit at 120° angles to one another is to fit them together yourself. And as Paige discovered, the blue hydrogen atoms and the red double bonds also make handsome stick figures.

Gregory went gaga for this kit when he first got hold of it. Apparently they never had anything remotely this cool when he attended pharmacy school, back when pharmacists prescribed leeches for bloodletting. I can still picture him rolling his first plastic triple bond between his fingers with surgical care.

It's funny now, but it wasn't so funny then. My o-chem professor would assign homework, and I would try to complete the assignment, but my models would bulge and tip over; they were highly unstable. Gregory, on the other hand, had a knack for "spatial diagramming." His building blocks snugly snapped together like Legos.

This kit was the first and maybe the last thing we ever really had in common. We bonded when we bonded. Gregory loved helping me with my homework. But then he began losing patience, skipping ahead on the itinerary. I'd walk into work and find future assignments sitting atop this plastic case like maquettes. I cut him off, cold turkey, and it didn't go very well at all. I'll think twice the next time I try to yank a toy from a seventy-four-year-old baby. That fight instigated our first magnitude 6.0.

One month later, the course was over. Three months after that, so was my pharmacology career. Gregory loved that organic chemistry kit. I could have easily given it to him—I should have—but at the time, I figured neither of us needed a reminder of what I *hadn't* accomplished. My presence here was reminder enough. Then I learned the local college bookstore was paying fifty bucks for a used set in decent condition. I searched for mine everywhere— even convinced Stinky Stanley that he lost his kit and took mine— but I was wrong. The most obvious suspect was the culprit after all.

"Have you seen my o-chem set?" I asked Gregory.

His reply still makes me smile: "Don't look at me."

I reach back into Gregory's cubbyhole and feel around some more. Amid the scraps of paper and dust bunnies is a black-and-white-marbled composition notebook. A thick brown rubber band holds the water-damaged pages shut. Like a kindergartner, Gregory's printed his name and date across the cover in big, blocky blue letters. I roll the elastic band off, lay the notebook flat on the countertop, and crack it open.

There it is—everything you'd ever need to know from the medicine man himself. From lip balms to lozenges, from capsules to cocktails, detailed descriptions on how Gregory converted tablets to topical gels, and compounded pills into potions. Every entry has a date. Some of the more advanced dishes include diagrams and charts. One page explains all the different ways to extract dangerous dyes; another reveals how to remove unnecessary preservatives. Gregory even wrote out a list of additives most likely to cause allergic reactions.

All in caps, Gregory's written "From B.R." next to certain recipes. Gregory's mentor, Barnaby Rothschild, gets credit for the lollipop and gummy candy formulas—just two of the compounding techniques I always assumed Gregory discovered.

The first entry in the notebook is February 17, 1958—that was about the time Gregory started working at Ace's Pharmacy alongside Rothschild. (It makes me sad that I didn't take the initiative to create a notebook like this when I started with Gregory.) The page describes, step-by-step, how to make a suppository. Lucille Braggs's fanny must be ringing. The most recent entry—one week before Gregory died—explains how to make penicillin chocolate bars. On the left side, he's drawn a simple diagram of that portable electric cook range I convinced him to purchase. Next to the drawing, Gregory's written two familiar initials: "From A.A." I'm touched.

Dyes and chemicals stain many of the pages of this half-century-old notebook. I gently pull apart some of the less referenced pages. Buried between the success stories are the half-baked ideas and the partially realized delivery systems. The drawing entitled "Device for administering drugs with meals" shows a condiment shaker where you grind up pills like pepper. "Flip the top open and sprinkle," Gregory writes. *How unappetizing.*

Another page shows a small thermos with two airtight compartments: the upper chamber stores pills and the bottom chamber houses a small supply of water. The vial is cylindrical in shape, measuring no more than six inches in height and two inches in diameter, and according to Gregory, "easily clips onto a belt or fits inside the trousers." *Is that a combination pill-water storage unit in your pocket or are you just glad to see me?*

A few pages farther in, there is an entry labeled "medicine-dispensing pacifier."

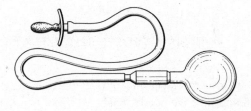

Per the diagram, the medication is initially stored in a squeeze bulb that feeds a plastic nipple via thin tubing. The date next to Gregory's medical pacifier is hard to make out. I lift the composition notebook off the table and hold it two inches from my face.

The moment of conception: January 3, 1977. I do the math—Paige was an infant at the time, no more than six months. Paige must've been sick.

A thin brown passport-sized booklet slides from in between the pages of Gregory's notebook and drops to the floor. I bend down to pick it up. Embossed on the front of it is an image of an old wooden ship. The words *American Trust Company Since 1854* appear around the seal.

The first page says "Savings Account" and it certifies that the original owners are "Gregory Day and Lydia Day." The bankbook is labeled "Book 3," issued to the couple on June 8, 1997. The starting balance is $12,724, and over the next nine years, there is a deposit at the beginning of every month for $30.

I flip through it. Between the deposits and compounding interest, the balance starts adding up. The final entry, dated December 31, 2006, shows a single withdrawal for the full amount: $20,386.23.

The white receipt connected to the wire transfer pokes out of the bankbook like a bookmark. The amount of the withdrawal matches the wire transfer to the penny. The account number of the deposit means nothing to me, but the name is unmistakable.

CHAPTER 23

Registering Complaints

"I'VE got an idea for a wedding gift," Paige tells me the other day.

"Is it something we need?" I ask.

"Not us," she says. "Our guests."

"*We* give gifts?"

"Yes, something sweet to remember the wedding, like a candle with our names and the wedding date on it."

"Tchotchkes?" I confirm.

"Yeah, tchotchkes. But I think it should be something that reminds people of *us,*" she says. "Like a CD with songs that are meaningful to our relationship."

"Why would everyone want a copy of 'We Are the Champions'?"

Paige doesn't flinch.

"It's just . . . isn't this wedding already *all about us.* They spend the whole day *celebrating us* and now they're supposed to go home and keep listening to songs *about us*? It feels like too much."

"Forget it," she says softly, shaking her head.

"Plus we shouldn't go breaking the law," I tell her.

I'm a hypocrite. I'm a fraud.

"Can you repeat that?" she demands.

"Songs are copyrighted like inventions are patented. We'd be stealing valuable intellectual property. You figure: twenty songs per CD, about a hundred guests—that's like two thousand songs."

"But no one's profiting off it," Paige cries.

"Precisely! These artists are entitled to some compensation."

The decision on wedding tchotchkes is still pending.

WHAT I've learned over the last week of wedding planning is that I have strong opinions on topics that I couldn't care less about.

Apparently I think a photographer captures the essence of a wedding, but a videographer distorts the fantasy, meaning we should book the former, not the latter. I think tablecloths and buffet station linens should match, but bridesmaid dresses don't need to (though they should probably complement one another in color and style). Oh, and it's criminal that Mindy's Stationery Shop charges $600 for fifty wedding invitations.

But that's just me. Paige sees things differently.

It was such a promising sign when we agreed to have the wedding at the Lawrence Hall of Science. But we were so young, naive, and flush with credit then. Plus, it's easy to spend $3,000 you don't have so you can get married overlooking one of the most spectacular views in the world. But that was a whole week and a dozen compromises ago. Amid all the fierce wedding negotiations, Paige has never invoked her parents, and still I am haunted by what they cannot give her. No matter what we do, is our wedding destined to come up short because Lydia can't adjust her veil, or because Gregory can't give her away? These tragic realities guide me every time we are forced to strike a compromise—calling out to me to *help her realize her fantasy*—and yet with every bargain, I expect the insanity to wind down, and it never does.

Finding consensus on the guest list is the most formidable challenge we've faced to date. Paige and I are in agreement that both of our families have their share of fruits, but in deciding who receives an invite and who doesn't, how do you compare his apples to her oranges?

Because Paige has more friends and extended family than I do, I surrendered up front. I told her that she could invite three oranges for every two of my apples. I thought that was pretty generous—and it did provide her with a temporary sense of relief until she realized we could only afford to invite half as many guests as we thought, or a total of fifty. Paige's own list was three times that. That's when Paige went underground for twenty-four hours. Behind closed doors, she managed to whittle down her list, but to this day, she is consumed with guilt.

Given this agreed-upon ratio, I still needed to figure out exactly how many guests I could invite so my total number of attendees would add up to twenty. According to Wikipedia, approximately three out of four people accept a wedding invitation. From there, it was simple algebra: solve for apples.

$$.75 \times \text{Apples} = 20$$
$$\text{Apples} = 20 \div .75$$
$$\text{Apples} = 26.67$$

$$\boxed{26.67}$$

I can safely invite 26.67 people, and if I do, 20 will attend. Not only that, but by assigning probabilities to each of my guests, I can figure out *which* 6.67 guests will likely decline and which 20 will accept (assuming a margin of error of +/−2 percent).

I tried to explain all this to Paige; I told her that she could use this same basic formula to solve all of her invitation problems, too, but she wouldn't listen.

"I'm still confused on how you invite 67 percent of a person," Paige says.

"I'll show you," I tell her, sitting at my computer. I pull Paige onto my lap and begin kissing her neck. "I like this body part," I say, moving down the center of her chest. "And these. These body parts would definitely receive invitations."

Once we figured out *whom* to invite, there was still the matter of *how* to invite them. Invites needed to contain invitations—that much we agreed upon. *But how did I really feel about inner envelopes?* Paige wondered. "Redundant" and "expensive" was my thinking. In the end, "elegant" and "negligible" prevailed.

Maybe we should get rain cards, Paige suggested as we flipped through the sample book at Mindy's Stationery Shop. No rain cards, I demanded. Yes, we were risking it all by having this wedding outside, but if it rains, people don't need a card to tell them to go inside. No rain cards, I repeated. Paige relented. It was only days later—when Cookie told me that nobody gets rain cards—that I realized I'd been hustled.

Next came the response cards. I agreed we needed them, but seeing as the vast majority of our guests would end up delivering the response cards to us in person, did we really have to spring for prepaid postage? I never had a chance.

Lara has spent the last week drilling it into Paige's head that wedding invitations *need* to be hand-addressed. "Anything less is frowned upon as too impersonal," Lara told her poor sister. *Frowned upon by whom? By the people we actually invite?*

Thankfully, cool heads, cost, and the Lucida Calligraphy typeface won out. I eventually convinced Paige that I could create attractive invitations using our word processor and printer, and that despite her sister's strenuous objections, most of our virtually blind, computer-illiterate guests would never know the difference. We are now on Emily Post's shit list.

Paige keyed in all the names and addresses, and I agreed to print all the addresses on the outer envelopes. Nothing could have prepared me for the man-versus-machine tug-of-war that ensued. I thought I was doing myself a favor by using the new inkjet printer at the pharmacy. Words cannot describe the profound frustration that comes with clawing at a Hewlett-Packard DeskJet 1310 as it swallows a four-dollar outer envelope, but "god," "damn," and "fucking printer" are a good start.

Despite dozens of test print runs, envelopes jammed, addresses printed crooked, corners creased, and ink smudged. That's how Mindy's Stationery Shop gets you—they give you three measly extra outer envelopes, and I blew through those in ten minutes flat. It's probably a good thing Paige insisted we buy those inner envelopes. She has no clue how many "innies" I ended up using as "outies."

The hall is booked, the invites are out, and this wedding is happening in t-minus five weeks, three days.

Not everything has been a chore. Belinda's mother, Marylyn, was a pleasant surprise. She used to run her own catering business and offered to prepare all of our wedding appetizers and buffet entrées for free. But no good deed goes unpunished. It was only after we accepted Marylyn's generous offer that we read the fine print in the Lawrence Hall contract: "Lessees who elect to use anyone other than the preferred caterer (listed below) will be subject to a $500 penalty fee." We've decided to pay the penalty—it will still cost us less to buy our own food wholesale and hire a few of Belinda's friends as servers than it will to hire one of the hall's hoity-toity caterers.

Then there's Principal Martin. He is a "magnum member" at The Wine Basement on Port Street. With his discount, Harvey Martin says he can get us reasonable wine at cheap prices, and not the other way around. There's something poetic about having your former high school principal purchase your alcohol. With a little notice and cash, Principal Martin thinks personalized wine labels may even be in the cards. Paige and I both love that idea.

As it turns out, my pharmacy school friend Stinky Stanley has far more to offer than his human beatbox rhythms. Known better as "Slick 6" to the Wednesday night crew at a local San Francisco club, I'm told Stinky Stanley's deejay skills are sublime. Lucky for us, his wedding collection is also extensive, he's available, and in our price range: free. Slick 6 only has two, nonnegotiable rules: no chicken dance and no polkas. "I don't play Satan's music," he informed me, placing bended fingers over his head like horns.

There are three of us planning this wedding, and living with the Day sisters, the differences between Lara and Paige couldn't be starker. Lara Day is the type of person who enjoys preparing detailed dossiers on frail, poverty-stricken senior citizens, while Paige Day, much like her father, prefers scribbling down to-do list items on tiny scraps of paper, haphazardly leaving them lying everywhere.

With Paige at the helm, it feels, most days, like we're arbitrarily completing wedding tasks as she thinks of them. We have a pharmacy full of office supplies—I bring home a different organizational tool every day—and yet nothing works. Paige is all over the place. Between the wedding vows, marriage license, music choices, guestbook, seating chart, wedding rings, dance lessons, and cake, something important is going to fall through the cracks. I just know it.

That's why I made her this gift.

Item	Who	Target	Actual
☐ Buy wedding gown material	PD	June 30	–
☐ Register for gifts	AA/PD	June 30	–
☐ Complete centerpiece shopping	PD/LD	July 1	–

It took me twenty minutes to figure out how to print Unicode character 61441, known better by its nickname, "☐." No self-respecting wedding list would neglect to include check boxes. After scouring the house for three hours, I managed to find all of Paige's cryptic notes; decipher, compile, condense, and categorize them into one master list; and print the whole shebang. For every pending item on the four-page list, I designated a lead person, a target deadline, and an actual completion date.

The things men do for love.

TOMORROW morning Paige and Lara are headed to the wholesale market to price flowers for bridal bouquets and centerpieces. But tonight we register for gifts. If I don't go with her, it could be a week before Paige and I spend some quality time together. Now that we live together, we see much less of each other. Paige is the only one around here earning a steady income, and with the living expenses adding up, she's been picking up as many shifts at the television station as possible.

I'd prefer to undergo dental surgery than register for gifts, but the ways things have been going lately—who knows—maybe I have deep-rooted feelings about china patterns.

I haven't been back to San Francisco since picking up Paige's engagement ring from Igor Petrov. Less than two months ago, the pharmacy was open; I was blissfully ignorant of the Day Co-Pay program; Lara was happily toiling away in Los Angeles; Paige and I were dating; and Gregory was alive.

Summer nights in San Francisco, the high hits sixty degrees, if you're lucky. A cable car rattles its bell through Union Square. Misguided tourists stand out like sore thumbs in shorts and T-shirts. Sunday shoppers flood the sidewalks. I take a seat on the park ledge facing Macy's.

The Day sisters are easy to spot in the crowd. Lara and Paige maneuver down the sidewalk, chatting, laughing, and oblivious to my existence. They've never looked livelier, happier, or more alike. Brightly colored shopping bags hang from their fingertips. Worrisome. They were supposed to keep the spending down and find Paige wedding gown material for her dress.

The two of them are absolutely giddy. I wave them over. Paige waves back, but not Lara. *Typical.*

"How'd it go?" I ask.

"Good . . . Fine," Paige corrects herself as our cool lips touch again.

"Then you found what you were looking for?"

"Wait until you see me. You're going to be thinking: 'Va-va-va-voom. I can't believe that's my bride!'"

Her face lights up when she speaks. Her eyes sparkle with pure joy.

"I'm excited," I tell her.

"You ready to do this?" she asks, presenting Macy's to me with both hands.

"Not so excited."

"Come on, it'll be fun, I promise, and if you're good, I'll buy you a cookie."

"More like you'll buy *you* a cookie," I say. "Now I know why you decided to register here—the food court."

"I'll buy us *both* a cookie," she admits.

"We don't need to register. Between my apartment, and your

house, we have everything we'll ever need. Not to mention that our guest list includes some of the biggest cheapskates north of Oakland."

"We're about to exploit the greatest wedding registry loophole ever!" she whispers. "Mildred tells me that if we register for something during the Macy's Fourth of July Sale, and Macy's sells out of that item, we get the equal or higher end product at the same price."

"But we don't even need the equal or the higher end product," I say.

"You'll thank me later," she says all serious. "You *do not* want the likes of Cookie Brewster buying us a wedding gift all by herself. Register now or regret it later. You decide."

Lara walks gingerly across the lawn in high heels.

"I still think we should do my idea," I suggest.

"What idea is that?" Lara asks curiously.

"Andy thinks we should register at Bank of the West," Paige says flatly.

Lara raises an eyebrow. "He's joking, right?"

"Of course he is."

"Think about it," I try. "Guests could choose from any number of denominations of cash, bonds, and CDs. *Looks like Paige and Andy still need a hundred bucks in cash and that high yield money market fund. Let's splurge, Martha, and get 'em both.*"

Lara gives the idea some consideration. Paige doesn't.

I hand Paige her four-page to-do gift. She takes it with a sigh, flipping back and forth between the pages, occasionally holding it up to the light so she can read.

Lara drops her bags and gives her sister the "gimme" sign. Before I can stop her, Paige hands over the computerized wedding list.

While Lara examines it, Paige tells me, "It's very nice."

"It should help," I assure her.

"Help whom? I assume you made this list for *you.*"

"For *me*? Why would *I* need a list?"

"Why *wouldn't* you need a list? You love lists. You *live* for lists.

But not me. I'm going to pass," Paige says. "Where are all my original notes?"

"That's just my point!" I counter. *Now's not the time to reveal that I've incinerated Paige's chicken scratch.* "Your notes are everywhere. It took me forever to find yours and compile this. This is everything."

"Not everything," Paige says.

"Give me one example."

"I'll give you two: Where's the caterer? Where are the invitations?"

"She's right," Lara pipes up, tapping the paper. "They're not on here."

"Yeah, I know they're not on there," I snap. "This is a 'to-do' list, not a 'to-done' list."

"But I *need* to cross items off," Paige insists.

"You're mad at me because I'm making you use checkmarks? Do you have any idea how hard it was to find that little box on our word processor?"

"I'm not mad," she says gathering her thoughts. "You don't get it. I like to cross things off. It gives me a sense of accomplishment. That way I can always look back and see everything that I've completed. But I can't do that with this list. You've gone and *deleted all the finished items.*"

"So you want me to add everything back?"

"This conversation is getting dumber by the minute," Lara interjects, gathering up her shopping bags. "I'd stay, but I have plans to do absolutely anything else but stand here. I'm going to let you two lovebirds do your thing."

From inside her purse, Paige's cell phone begins vibrating. Two seconds later we learn it's the news station. Thirty seconds later we know there's breaking news—a loft apartment complex south of Market has caught on fire.

"I have to go," Hurl Girl says, closing her phone and zipping up her purse.

Paige hands her sister her two shopping bags.

"This is my chance to cover some real breaking news even if

it is just a two-alarm fire. Reed's got the flu. Andrea's pregnant. None of our reporters are available and I happen to be twenty blocks away. It's kismet. Don't be mad," she begs us.

If I listen carefully, I can make out the sound of fire engine sirens.

"I'll take you," I volunteer quickly.

"That's okay, honey, I'll take a cab. It'll be quicker," she says, scurrying down the lawn to the ledge of the park. "Just tell me how it goes."

"Tell you how *what* goes?" I yell.

"Registering. Lara knows what I like. I showed her earlier. I promise, it won't take long. Then you can check it off that nifty list of yours."

Lara and I exchange looks. In that split second, Paige hails a cab.

"Let's just do this another time," I yell, running after her downhill and jumping onto the sidewalk. "What's the rush? The wedding's a month away."

Paige is halfway in the cab. She kisses me softly on the cheek.

"Come on, you're the logical one. You might as well just do it now. You're already here," Paige says. Then she looks me right in the eyes and speaks from the heart: "You want to do something nice for me? Don't make me lists; spend some quality time with my sister. I know you two work together, but you hardly speak. You're an only child, Andy. Haven't you ever wanted a sister?"

"I don't think so."

"Well, you're about to get one, and she's getting a brother, like it or not."

Paige slams the cab door shut, sticks her head out of the window, and points, first at Lara and then at me.

"And afterward, buy him a cookie," Paige demands as the taxi takes off.

LARA does not buy me a cookie and I wouldn't take one from her if she did.

We find Ms. Johnson on the third floor in a cubby office underneath a heavy white wooden sign that says WEDDING & GIFT

REGISTRY. Her desk is cluttered with pictures of grandchildren. Ms. Johnson is a nice enough woman in her late fifties, with Brillo short brown hair and deep creases around the corners of her mouth from smiling too much. From her nametag to the way she introduces herself, it is abundantly clear Ms. Johnson wishes to be addressed as "Ms. Johnson." Lara and I comply, seeing as she is about to school us in the art of registering.

"We have an exceptional team of experts dedicated to helping you create the registry of your dreams," she tells us as if she's reading off a teleprompter.

I doze off somewhere between "experts" and "dreams."

Ms. Johnson hands me a clipboard and Lara politely listens to the rest of her spiel while I take a few minutes to fill out the necessary paperwork. Why Macy's needs *my* Social Security number so other people can buy *us* a hotplate is beyond me, but I comply.

"He is so good to come with you," Ms. Johnson adulates, checking over the forms. "So few grooms take an interest now, but complain later."

"I just want to make Paige happy," I say, slapping Lara's back gently.

Lara can go either way here.

"My Andrew *is* certainly one of a kind," Lara says with a big, fake grin.

"I want a big family, Ms. Johnson," I announce, likening us to her family portraits. "Trust me, this woman is going to be a regular baby maker."

"What do you say we take this one baby at a time," Lara suggests.

Ms. Johnson is delighted. You can read her mind. Lara and I are a solid, long-term investment. *Can you say "baby registry"?*

Ms. Johnson hands Lara a detailed map of the store and then unhooks one of the UPC scan guns from the wall and presents it to me like a samurai sword. It's the oldest trick in the registry playbook: shape the purchasing device like a weapon and hand it to the man. It's not even Lara's wedding, but she's green with envy. Lara needs that gun.

"Point and shoot," Ms. Johnson kindly instructs me.

She walks around her desk to show me how.

Tipping the gun down toward the floor, Ms. Johnson points to the LED display: "Then confirm 'yes' on the keypad."

She escorts Lara and me to Glassware and I test the gun on some crystal.

I shoot. "These things should come with a safety," I tell Ms. Johnson. "You know, to avoid impulse purchases."

"Aren't you the clever one!" she chirps.

"Oh, come on. Andrew's just being his regular jackass self," Lara cries.

"Do *we* need to go back to couples' therapy?" I ask Lara.

Ms. Johnson abruptly leaves to file a police report for domestic violence or get the paperwork for a divorce registry.

"Great, Einstein, so what happens when my sister shows up next week?"

"I bet Macy's still allows people to spend money on us," I say.

Lara pulls a Post-it-note-infested store catalog from one of Paige's bags. We've already wandered into the Bath department, so we start there.

"Okay, we're looking for The Charter Club Hotel Collection," Lara says all business-like. She scrutinizes the sale signs. "Paige says you need wash towels *and* hand towels. She's narrowed the colors to buttercream, sagebrush, or sable."

"What's sagebrush?"

"Muted green," Lara answers.

"What's sable?"

"Grayish brown."

"What's the difference between a wash towel and hand towel?"

"A wash towel is tiny. A hand towel is somewhere in the middle."

Lara graciously holds up a few examples. The overhead speakers play the Muzak version of "Don't Worry, Be Happy."

I place the barrel of the UPC gun in my mouth and pull the trigger.

"Oh, that's sanitary," Lara says.

It takes us forty-five minutes to nail down the towels. Operating the gun is trickier than first thought: when I'm not shooting the wrong brand, I'm pulling the trigger one too many times. In both cases, I need Ms. Johnson's help canceling the requests. Lara thinks I'm an imbecile until she tries. Ms. Johnson assures us that we can correct everything at the end.

We'll be lucky to get through Bedding before Macy's closes. Dining, Cookware, Kitchen Appliances, Home Decor, Luggage, it will all simply have to wait until our next visit. As a reward for getting this far, I add two white terrycloth bathrobes to the registry. Maybe Paige won't notice.

"So that pesky woman from Blue Cross called *again*," Lara tells me as she scrunches a pillow like she's playing an accordion.

"Brianna? She's just doing her job," I say, cradling a pillow with both hands before violently head-butting it repeatedly.

"You clearly have a thing for her."

"And you love Tyler Rich, nah-nah-nah-nah-nah-nah."

"Don't be juvenile."

"Am not. Infinity."

"You know, just because you're getting married, it doesn't mean you stop being attracted to other women," Lara explains. "Brianna is very pretty."

I'm not falling for this.

Lara hands me a pillow. I reject it immediately as too firm.

"Why don't you try drooling on a few," she suggests.

It's not such a bad idea.

"Can we just give Blue Cross the records they need and be done with it?" Lara asks. "This insurance business is hanging over any sale we make of the pharmacy."

"So Paige is fine with us selling?" I confirm.

I wrap a large down pillow around my head.

"If she wants this elaborate wedding, something's got to give," Lara insists.

I carry some samples over to the Calvin Klein display and toss them on the bed. Then I lie down at an angle so my shoes hang off the edge.

"We're not going *that* overboard," I say, rolling my head side to side.

I place another pillow over my face.

"Yeah, right. I know *all about* your fancy-delancy wedding hall. And now this $2,500 wedding gown."

"What!" I scream into the pillow and jump out of bed.

"I promised her I wouldn't say anything," Lara says.

"I thought she was making her own dress."

"Yeah, and she's churning the butter for the dinner rolls, too," Lara quips.

"This is bad," I say.

"Andrew, my sister was dressing up Barbie dolls in wedding dresses before Barbie was ready to get married. She wants this showy wedding. The money's got to come from somewhere."

I study Lara. "I can think of one place," I suggest.

Lara's listening.

"Actually one person, and one amount: $20,386 and 23 cents to be exact."

The color drains from Lara's face.

"I knew you were a waste of time," she says, snapping up her bags and booking down the aisle toward the exit. "I am so out of here."

I chase after her. "Seriously. Six months ago, Gregory gives you twenty grand and this never comes up in any of our financial conversations?"

Lara isn't speaking to me.

"Does Paige know about the money? Seriously, Lara, does she?"

"You have some nerve," she hisses.

I block Lara just as she gets to the escalator.

"Why did you just say I was a waste of time?"

"I said *this* was a waste of time," Lara insists, gesturing toward the showroom.

"No, you said *I* was a waste of time."

Lara can't decide whether to say what she's obviously going to say.

"Look, I'm sorry that I have to be the one to tell you, but it's just not going to work out with you two."

"What's that supposed to mean?"

"Ask Paige."

"Enough with the drama, Lara. Speak!" I command, allowing a few anxious patrons access to the escalator.

"She's been seeing someone else."

"You're talking about your environmentally unfriendly pal Tyler Rich. I know all about the houseboat. Paige told me everything. *Nothing happened.*"

"So then you know about Thursday?"

"Now you're just making shit up to be mean."

"Last Thursday, when Tyler came by the pharmacy to pick me up, he and I weren't having dinner. Paige and Tyler were. I was her alibi."

"Puh-leeze."

"I'm sorry, Andy," she says as I let her go. "It is what it is."

Lara slowly descends to the second floor. When she hits the landing and turns the corner, I slowly bring the UPC gun to my temple and pull the trigger.

CHAPTER 24

Drug Deals

THERE is Zoloft in the wheel well of my trunk. Stashes of Celebrex underneath the seat cushions of our couch. Remicade in my right pocket. Lanicor in my left. The tiny plastic drawers above Gregory's workbench no longer store odds and ends but heartburn medicine and blood pressure tablets. For the privileged few still in the Day Co-Pay program, the pharmacy is always open for business.

The late-night phone calls and customer drive-bys occasionally raise suspicions at home, but Lara is too consumed with our finances, and Paige is too consumed with our wedding to pay much attention.

Collecting from our deadbeats has been slow going. Sid was right: when you cross-check Lara's Most Wanted against Gregory's bloodsuckers, there aren't many people left who can pay. At the pharmacy, Lara's become more adept at recognizing the freeloaders on her hit list, mostly because she's created a cheat sheet with pictures. (When Lucille Braggs finally won BINGO in December 1997 and got her cheery photo in the *Crockett Quarterly*, I doubt she ever dreamed Lara Day would one day use that headshot as part of a criminal watch list.)

"You're Mickey 'Bulldog' Bratton, aren't you?" Lara asked the former lightweight boxing champ just the other day.

"I am," he said, embarrassed to be recognized. "Your father was a standup guy. You can't put a value on what he did for this community."

"I can," Lara said, sucker punching him. "Thirteen hundred dollars. That's the total on your tab. Please settle up with Belinda at the front desk."

All Bulldog wanted was some toothpaste and a can of shaving cream, but that visit cost him a fortune. The check bounced, but I still give Lara credit.

All in all, Manny's been the biggest help. He calls our new collecting system "full proof." I call it the Home Court Disadvantage. We stumbled across the idea a few days ago trying to collect from seventy-something Conrad Callahan. There I was on Conrad's steps, struggling to figure out a diplomatic way to tell him that he owed us $2,000 in shampoo or Doritos or something, when Manny got an urgent call informing him that he missed another FedEx pickup. Without any warning, Manny screeched off, leaving me stranded on Conrad Callahan's stoop.

"I guess you'd be wanting to use my telephone," Conrad said, scratching his bald head with a cereal spoon.

Once inside, Conrad was done for. First I cruised his family portraits. Then I complimented the hell out of his velvet Jesus paintings and ceramic elephant collection. I told him our sob story. I asked him to imagine what it might be like if his beautiful grandchildren inherited our problems instead of all these priceless possessions. It took a good half hour, but eventually he caved, coughing up only a third of what he owed, but a decent chunk nonetheless.

Empathy can be a wonderful thing. Manny abandons me all the time now.

Gregory's doctor, Brandon Mills, never did pay. He did, however, send us a bill (that, thankfully, I intercepted before triggering a magnitude 7.0 with Lara). Despite crediting us $3,000 for "T.P.B.S," Mills is under the impression that *we still owe him* $2,000 in unpaid doctor visits covering the last five years. But toilet paper isn't the only thing that's bullshit about Mills's bill. He won't be paying ours and we won't be paying his. I welcome him to get in line behind the rest of our creditors. The queue is around the block.

The remaining doctors wrapped up in Gregory's lurid swap meets were far more cooperative. That ear, nose, and throat physician, Cynthia Hardy, was in here once a week, stockpiling spring water, makeup, and snacks. Dr. Richard Platt quit smoking thanks in large part to a continuous free supply of nicotine patches. When I laid out the facts—along with all the potential federal crimes in question—both doctors quickly settled for $1,500 apiece.

So far, all told, Manny, Lara, and I have managed to rake in about $12,000—a ninth of what people owe Gregory, and a sixth of what we need to cover the back mortgage payments and Gregory's credit card debt in order to keep the house.

WHEN I'm not illegally dispensing drugs or shaking down seniors for security deposits, I'm conducting patent research online. We've begun vetting Gregory's composition notebook. Sid's taken 1958 through 1972. I've got 1973 on.

Recipes aren't patentable, but chemical compositions, methods, and devices are. Between all of Gregory's capsules, candies, and compounding contraptions (yes, contraptions), Sid and I are hoping we find something PMP-worthy, but nothing so far. Paging through his notebook, there is no shortage of "protectable" ideas—

problem is, Gregory never bothered protecting them while others did. With so many of his inventions now on the market, you have to wonder whether plants posing as patrons spent the last fifty years infiltrating Day's Pharmacy.

Gregory's notebook has come in handy around the pharmacy. I've been experimenting with some of his recipes. The other day I replaced Gregory's porcelain mortar and pestle with a vintage set that Sid found on eBay. Last week I made my first suppository, though Belinda and Lara greeted the achievement with deafening silence. Today I attempted to turn cough syrup into gummy candy and got gook. Tomorrow I'll try my hand at lozenges. It's occurred to me that mastering even a handful of Gregory's most basic compounding formulas could make a big difference in people's lives.

Even if nothing more comes of Gregory's notebook, that Euraka Productions letterhead has still come in handy. Sid and I have plenty of our own Poor Man's Patents, and every day, Sid's sending out query letters to potential manufacturers and licensees. We'll see. Let's hope.

BUSINESS today is slow. It has been all week. With Gregory gone, our peculiar hours, and that busted, boarded-up front door, I think most Crockett folks think Day's Pharmacy went out of business. Either that or they're avoiding us because they know we're looking to settle some debts. On Saturday, I broke down and had the door replaced. Principal Martin suggested I send the $400 bill to the Contra Costa Sheriff's Department care of Dudley Fielding, which I did.

Mildred is here shopping with Beatrice. She spent the last twenty minutes snaking through the aisles with her walker, occasionally tossing toiletries over her shoulder into Beatrice's red plastic basket.

Ruth Mulrooney is quietly browsing, too. She's not her flamboyant self. I can barely make out her face with that massive white kerchief smartly fashioned around her head, and the big black Jackie Onassis sunglasses.

I'm filling scripts at the counter when Ruth walks right up to me.

"It feels impossible that Gregory is gone," she whispers.

"I know. I miss him more than you know."

"He was right there," Ruth says, pointing to where I'm standing. "Alive and well, and now he's gone. Everyone keeps dying."

It's not Day's Pharmacy without Gregory, and yet it's hard to know where to go from here. It feels wrong to keep this place open, or close it down, or sell it to someone else. This pharmacy is sacred ground: Paige and Lara were nearly born here; Gregory died here. In my dreams, our children dart up and down these aisles.

It's been three days since the Macy's Day blowup with Lara and she hasn't been back to the pharmacy since. I have yet to confront Paige about any of Lara's allegations. I keep trying to put Tyler Rich and that excessive wedding dress out of my mind. *Stay focused on the good. There are so many signs you're still on track to be married.* Take today, for example: Paige and I have a food tasting with Belinda's mother. I've starved myself because I know Marylyn's spent all day preparing delicious finger food, appetizers, and potential entrées for the reception.

With Lara away, I can freely dispense freebies. I hand Beatrice her osteoporosis and heartburn pills. Mildred needs a couple of asthma inhalers and medication for type 1 diabetes. Seeing as Doctors Hardy and Platt have settled, I've forbidden Mildred and Beatrice from hitting up either of them for any more free samples. This, I pray, is our first stop on the long road to legitimacy.

I walk Mildred to the front, arm in arm. Ruth stops paying at the register long enough to give me a jealous look; she then peels off two twenties from a wad of bills. These days I'm always surprised to see anyone pay in cash. The last person to pay cash was probably . . . Ruth. I want to nominate Ruth to be President of the Day "Can-Pay" Club.

Neither Beatrice nor Mildred has a red cent.

"Add these prescriptions to their tabs," I instruct Belinda.

"Lara's not going to like that," Belinda says, making a notation.

"Well, Lara can go . . . ," I stop midsentence, noticing Brianna McDonnell standing on the sidewalk just outside the pharmacy.

With a friendly smile, she waves hello.

I'm not entirely surprised to see Brianna, but I was hoping she'd give me a few more days to pull together the insurance records.

Brianna is as stunning as ever in blue jeans that accentuate her long legs and a simple, snug, long-sleeved T-shirt.

"You must think I'm a little obsessed," she says, tucking both her hands in the back pockets of her jeans.

"With who? Me?" I ask nervously.

"No," Brianna laughs, reaching out and touching my arm, gently. My heart is racing.

"With getting this paperwork. It's my day off and here I am harassing you about an audit," she says, adjusting her stance to find a comfortable equilibrium.

This is the first time she's used the dreaded *a*-word.

She arches her back and a shooting pain flashes across her face.

"Did you ever see that orthopedist that Mills recommended in Vallejo?"

"You're so sweet to ask. Never did," she says to the ground, "but *my* doctor says I need back surgery."

"Oh man."

"I know!" she moans.

"Maybe you should get a second opinion."

"I think job stress is aggravating my condition. . . . These records are probably the last thing on your mind," she says, her voice cracking slightly. "But I'm getting a lot of pressure from my boss, and I can't screw this up right now. I *really* need my health benefits."

I nod, biting the inside of my cheek.

"Can you just give me something, anything?" she pleads.

Ruth, Mildred, and Beatrice exit the pharmacy one after another. They can't miss Brianna. All three immediately shoot me disapproving looks. Then Mildred reaches over and plants a long, juicy kiss on my cheek.

"Hi, Paige!" Beatrice blurts.

Beatrice is either confused or thinks she's being clever.

"No," I delicately explain. "*This is* Brianna McDonnell."

"I'm sure she is, but *that's* Paige Day," Beatrice says, pointing to my fiancée approaching ten yards away.

Paige waves.

"Ladies!" Paige greets them, sounding more like her father than ever.

Mildred hugs Paige. Beatrice hugs Paige and Mildred. I hug all three of them while Ruth and Brianna watch. It's weird. From inside this huddled mass, Paige dislodges a hand and introduces herself to Brianna. Everyone finally lets go.

"It's so nice to finally meet you," Brianna says.

"I'm sorry, and who are you?" Paige asks.

"Brianna is the insurance lady," I explain quickly. "Woman."

"Nice to meet you," Paige says unassumingly.

The six of us congregate on the sidewalk in awkward silence.

"Everyone stay right here," I demand, excusing myself.

I race inside the pharmacy to Lara's workstation. It doesn't take me long to find exactly what Brianna needs: Lara's black ledger—unlocked and available, it details every prescription we've filled over the last two years. Lara's even gone ahead and highlighted the transactions subject to the Blue Cross audit.

There is no way I'm handing this over.

Next to Lara's computer is a ream of paper—physical copies of every prescription Day's Pharmacy filled over the last four months. The original scripts were hard enough to read—the Xeroxes are indecipherable. *These hieroglyphics will buy us some time,* I decide, scooping them up.

On my way out, I ask Belinda if she can close out the register and lock up. Paige is waiting outside and we don't want to be late to Marylyn's tasting.

"Sure thing, boss," she says.

How depressing: it's the first time anyone's ever addressed me as "boss," and I couldn't possibly feel any less in control.

I take a few deep breaths, push open our gorgeous new front

door, and hand Brianna the stack. "I'll get you the rest of the paperwork in the next couple of days," I promise her. "We really should go," I tell Paige.

"Just waiting on you," Paige says politely.

Brianna hands me her business card and I promise to call her first thing Monday. Everyone tells everyone how wonderful it was to meet one another. As Paige and I walk to my car, I hear Mildred grill Brianna over why Brianna doesn't have a "nice boyfriend of her own."

Paige must hear this, too.

"It's a good question," Beatrice agrees.

CHAPTER 25

Contents May Upset
Empty Stomach

"MILDRED doesn't want us playing 'dirty music' at the wedding," Paige informs me. Then she tells me to take a right on Second Street. "You know, songs with curse words or sexual innuendo; she says it's vulgar. Beatrice agreed."

I turn up the radio, hoping to drown out this bothersome conversation. The current song is one of Paige's favorites: R. Kelly believes he can fly.

Paige tries to lighten the mood, singing, "*Chewbacca . . . Chewbacca . . .*"

I purse my lips to prevent the words from slipping out.

"Why won't you sing with me, sourpuss?" she protests, lowering the volume.

"I'm trying to drive," I say, checking the clock. We're going to be late.

As Marylyn's home comes into view, Paige demands I pull over.

"I just had an impossible afternoon with my sister, and I feel like you're being hostile. I don't feel like sampling our wedding food angry. What's wrong?"

I yank the emergency brake as we roll forward, the engine still idling. Then I choose my words carefully: "I think the wedding costs are getting out of control. The museum is three grand. The food, plus that penalty fee, is going to run us about thirty-five hundred. I had to talk you *down* on the invites and talk you *out* of the videographer. *It's enough.* Plus I'm sure there are *other costs* . . ."

"You're starting to sound exactly like my sister," Paige says in amazement. "Andy, I never twisted your arm. You've been there every step of the way. We made every decision together. I'm the one who said we could elope."

"You said that as a *joke*," I complain. "Like you'd ever."

"I'm working double shifts to bring in a little cash around here."

"What's that supposed to mean? I'm working for free at your father's pharmacy, bullying the elderly at your sister's beckoning."

"So we'll cancel the wedding hall," she says coolly.

"Is that what you want?"

She shrugs her shoulders.

"Look, we both want that hall," I tell her. "All I'm saying is: why do I have to be punished for being the responsible one? We've got bills coming out of our ears. You want this fancy shindig. The money has to come from somewhere."

Paige studies me carefully. The words are too familiar.

"You talked to Lara. She told you about the gown," Paige concludes.

"You're the one who wanted us to spend more time together," I say.

"I can't believe this."

"Explain something to me: why would you buy a $2,500 wedding dress the day after a romantic dinner with your old boyfriend? Is that guilt or what?"

"I'm going to kill her."

"You're going to kill Lara because she told me the truth?" I say flatly.

Paige tries to take my hand, but I won't let her.

A beep comes over my two-way radio.

"Andy-Manny, are you there?" he says.

"Go ahead. Answer it," Paige says softly.

I grab the walkie-talkie from the tray and lower the volume a notch.

"I'm mad at Lara because she's meddling. I'm sorry I didn't tell you about dinner with Tyler. He kept calling. It's complicated."

"What's so complicated? You just tell him to beat it."

"He's my friend, Andy. Why are you angry about me having dinner with my sister and an old high school friend?"

Manny tries to get my attention over the two-way radio again.

"Why did Lara need to be there? To be your witness? Or your alibi?"

"We're all friends. And Tyler needed to talk."

Just hearing his name makes me sick. *Stop saying it.*

"So what was so important that he had to tell in person?"

She pauses. "Honestly, it doesn't matter."

I want an answer. Now. I stare at her.

"He wanted another chance," she admits, shaking her head. "He said I *owed* it to myself to know for sure, before getting married."

"What do you possibly see in this guy?"

"He's fun . . . a free spirit."

"I'm fun!" I point to myself. "I'm free!"

"You're very fun," Paige agrees. "I love you. I don't know why I went to dinner with him . . . maybe it felt like an escape . . . from everything."

"You want to escape *me*? This is Looney Tunes. I inherited all these problems, Paige," I say, throwing my hands up in frustration. "Tell the truth: you went to dinner with Tyler Rich because you're not sure about us."

I can't believe she has to think about it.

I lean my head against the driver's-side window.

"Andy, please. With all that's happened, are *you* absolutely sure you want to marry me?"

"What's there not to be sure of?"

Paige stares blankly out the window. "You spend a lot of time in Sid's garage tooling around with all those cockamamie ideas," she confesses.

"I do that *for us!*" I yell. "I can't win for losing here," I say, looking around for a referee. "A minute ago I was criticized for not being carefree enough. Now you're saying I'm too irresponsible?"

"I love your inventions, sweetheart, I really do, but inventing stuff is not a *plan*. It's not a future. It just makes me nervous sometimes, that's all," Paige trails off. "And you're just all over the place these days. You get mysterious phone calls at all hours. You randomly disappear for no reason."

Your father was a crook. He was committing insurance fraud on a massive scale. I am carrying on the family tradition.

"Then I see you flirting with some stunning blonde," she adds.

"Are we actually comparing your old boyfriend to an insurance collector?" I scream, banging my fists on the steering wheel. "I am *forced* to deal with her."

"You weren't exactly in agony ten minutes ago," Paige adds.

"I don't like her."

"I never said you did," Paige pretends all surprised.

"So who broke up with whom?" I ask.

"Who? Who? What?"

"You and Tyler. Who dumped whom ten years ago?"

Paige is highly offended by the question.

"I knew it. He broke up with you."

"If you must know, I'm the one who called it quits."

"Uh-huh," I say, not believing her.

The tone of the conversation is turning—you can feel it. Paige and I are done calling one another "hon" or "sweetheart." If I still want to patch things up, I'm running out of time.

"Come on," I say, "Gregory never liked Tyler Rich. You're honestly telling me that the two of you wouldn't be married right now if it weren't for your father?"

"What's wrong with you? I didn't even like Tyler that much. And Daddy didn't dictate who I could and couldn't marry," she assures me.

Finally, something we agree on.

"I don't think either of your parents ever approved of me," I tell her rubbing my forehead slowly.

"What are you talking about? My mother would have loved you, and my father adored you."

"When I was twelve, Anthony Bianco made me steal two packs of Hubba Bubba watermelon-flavored bubble gum from your pharmacy," I spew out. "Your mother tried to stop me, but I bolted out of the store. Bunky is currently serving five to ten in Sing Sing . . . for something else. But I was destined to become his cellmate as far your mother was concerned."

Paige cracks up laughing. "You're being a nutball. Andy, do you actually believe you were the only kid who stole candy from our pharmacy? Why do you think Daddy moved all the sweets to the front register five years ago? Everyone stole candy. I stole it. Lara did. Trust me, you've made up for it plenty in karma," Paige says, cooling down.

Maybe she's right. My stomach gurgles. I'm absolutely famished.

"And why would you have any doubts about my father? He loved and respected you. The man gave you his blessing to marry me, for God's sake! What more do you want?"

"Yeah, about that," I announce. "He didn't."

This stops Paige cold.

"But he didn't *not* give me his blessing, either," I explain quickly. "I asked your dad if I could marry you. I told him how much I loved you and how much I respected him, but he told me to wait. He said 'wait' and he promised he'd explain later, but . . ." I throw my hands up, "there was no later."

I want to cry.

"Did he say 'wait'? Or did he say no? Tell me the *truth.*"

"He said 'wait.' "

"Why would he have asked you to wait?" she asks herself.

I can see her replaying the last seventy-two hours of Gregory's life in her mind: the way he must have responded when she told him the news; the way he acted the night she returned home from wine country.

Then it hits her: "So Daddy told you to wait, but you asked anyway."

"*Your father didn't dictate who you could and couldn't marry,* remember? So yes, I asked anyway, and trust me, I regret it. Profoundly."

"You regret asking me?" she says, putting her hand on the passenger door release.

"Believe me, after the week I've had, I'm starting to!" I yell, gripping the steering wheel tightly with both hands, and rocking back and forth violently.

"I have to go," she says abruptly.

Paige grabs her purse and opens the passenger door.

"Go where? Marylyn is waiting . . . with food. *Gourmet food.*"

Paige slams the door shut and starts marching down the sidewalk. I should chase her down, but I can't manage the strength. I clench my teeth. My temperature's rising. I'm mad at everyone.

"Crap, crap, crap, crap," I chant, pounding lightly on the steering wheel of my car. *What am I doing? What am I doing?*

Paige is nearly out of sight. She hasn't turned back *once*.

"Crap!" I scream once more, smashing the center of the steering column with both fists.

The white airbag ejects like a flash of lightning and everything goes black.

PART THREE

CHAPTER 26

Complications

"HE was unconscious when he arrived," the nurse tells the doctor. "Blood pressure was abnormally low."

"Preliminary tests show elevated troponin levels," says the doctor.

"Vitals are stable. Antiplatelets did not relieve ischemia. The results of the cardiac cath should be ready momentarily," a second nurse reports.

"Let's order an echocardiography, just to be safe. But his HDL and LDL levels look relatively normal." The doctor's puzzled. He turns his attention to the two of us standing in the corner. "Which one of you brought him in?"

"Me," Manny says, thumbing himself.

"Are you family?" the young doctor asks.

"Sid's my uncle," I pipe up. "I'm his nephew."

Manny's shocked. *You are?*

"You don't happen to know what sort of medication he's taking?" the doctor asks.

"Flonase for allergies, Xalatan for glaucoma, Lanicor for cholesterol, Proscar for an enlarged prostate, and Prazex for heartburn," I rattle off. "There may be one more; I'd have to check."

"Looks like I'm talking to the right nephew," he says, scribbling down notes. He introduces himself as Dr. Reid Yeardling. "Are you his doctor?"

"His pharmacist," I say, so flattered to be mistaken for a doctor that it's only then that I realize I may have just copped to attempted homicide—if medication is responsible for Sid's current condition, I'm surely to blame.

Sid looks so tiny lying there in his blue hospital gown. The skin underneath his eyes is black and blue.

"Please help him," I beg the young doctor.

215

I wish I'd gone to med school. I wish I'd I finished pharmacy school.

"Oh, write this down, doc," Manny yells suddenly. "Right before Sid passed out in the car, he said his jaw hurt."

"Discomfort radiating from the jaw, throat, or arm is the first sign of a heart attack," Yeardling explains. Then he turns to me. "What would be of immense help is if you could get me a list of exactly what Mr. Brewster is currently taking, the dosages, and who prescribed them. I don't need to tell you that these medications can interact in peculiar ways," he says, flipping closed the metal clipboard and hooking it on the bedpost.

Yeardling is halfway out the door before he does a double take.

"You're bleeding," he says, studying my forehead. "What'd you do?"

"Something stupid," I admit, touching the bump over my right eye.

"It's what pays our rent around here," Yeardling says.

After Paige stormed out and the airbag deployed in my face, best I can tell, I briefly passed out. The next sound I recall hearing was the low hum of my walkie-talkie. It was Manny trying to reach me again. He'd taken Sid to Kaiser Permanente in Vallejo. I drove the whole way to the hospital with the airbag hanging out of the steering column, thinking: *I've gone and killed my best friend. First Gregory. Now Sid.*

"That's going to need a couple of stitches," Yeardling tells me, gently poking around. "Take a seat."

Manny sits right next to me, a little too close. He is in my personal space. I hop my chair a few inches away.

A nurse arrives with an ice pack and I gently apply it to my cut.

"Glass pane door?" Manny asks, studying me. "Because I've been there."

I dab the cut gently. It hurts.

"You okay?" Manny wonders.

"The cut? Yeah, thanks," I say. "Everything else . . . we'll see."

I close my eyes, curl my lips, and slowly exhale.

"You're always gettin' hurt," he laughs. "You're a total accident magnet. Remember that time back in high school, in the middle of the football game, when the ball smacked you right in the forehead? Man, that was *hilarious*."

"It was your fault. Thanks to you, Paige and I almost never happened," I tell him.

"Oh, please. You have me to thank for it *ever* happening. Like you two would have ever possibly survived high school. The ten-year separation did you good."

Manny's probably right.

"In fact, I think you owe me a debt of gratitude," he says.

I adjust the ice pack. "Thank you for tipping a football in my face."

"My pleasure. Anytime."

We sit some more, staring at Sid.

"You should have brought him to the Veterans Hospital," I say softly. "Medicare will *never* cover this place. They charge $10 for an aspirin."

"I tried, but Sid told me no," Manny whispers.

"Why?"

Manny shrugs.

"What's this?" he asks, reaching for my latest invention.

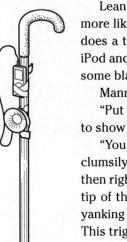

Leaning against the wall, the mechanism looks more like a 1930s Tommy submachine gun than it does a tricked-out walking stick. I've secured the iPod and tiny speaker to the shaft of the cane with some black electrical tape.

Manny picks it up.

"Put it down," I demand. "I brought that here to show Sid."

"You ruined a perfectly good iPod," he says, clumsily flipping the whole thing upside down and then right side up. He's going to break it. I grab the tip of the cane and Manny grips the hook, easily yanking it away from me with gorilla strength. This triggers the playlist.

"You are a dumb person!" the cane yells at him.

"Nuh-uh," he replies. Manny is shocked.

"You think just because I'm two thousand years old that I can't take you?" the cane screams back at him.

Manny jumps out of his seat. "Bring it on, cane," he cries.

Manny hasn't figured out it's Cookie's voice yet. Sid stirs slightly.

"Where's the off switch on this thingamajig?" Manny asks.

"This is why you have no friends your own age," Cookie tells him.

"I've got plenty of friends," Manny insists.

"Move!" the cane yells.

"Where?" Manny asks.

"What part of 'get the hell out of the way' don't you understand?" the voice says.

"Cookie?" Sid mumbles, slowly opening his eyes.

I reach over and hit the pause button on the iPod.

"Cookie's on her way," I promise Sid, standing up so he can see me.

"Who undressed me?" he says all groggy, his eyes fixed on the ceiling.

"Manny."

"Shut up. The nurse did."

"Hand me the bed thingy," Sid says, blindly patting down the mattress.

Sid's eyelids are heavy. His lips are dry.

I hand him the controller, guiding his pointer finger to the "up" arrow. Sid engages the motor, slowly raising the incline of his hospital bed.

On the approach, Sid spots my ice pack.

"Don't ask," I say.

"How about we just swap places?" Sid suggests, livening up.

I hand him a plastic cup of water. He sips from it.

"What happened *to you*?" I ask.

"I'm old is what happened."

"But were you doing anything out of the ordinary when it hit?" I ask him. "And what's this about you not wanting to go to the Veterans Hospital?"

"I *hate* that place," he yells. "They won't take care of me."

Manny and I exchange confused looks.

"Why didn't we invent *this*," Sid laments, adjusting the height of the bed with the remote. *Up, down, up, down.* "I heard Cookie's voice," he mutters.

"That was this," I tell him, proudly handing him the Cookie Cane. "There's a lot of prior art out there on canes," I explain to him. "Walking sticks that double as pool cues and telescopes. Patented exercise canes with snap-on weights. Canes with secret compartments, beverage holders, solar-powered taillights, rear-view mirrors, headlights, even direction signals. I read about this one cane with a retractable jaw that could reposition a golf ball on a tee. But of all of the walking sticks out there, you won't find anything like this one. The idea came to me the other day when I saw Cookie screaming her head off at this jogger."

Sid inspects it carefully. I reach over and hit the play button.

"I will beat that computer of yours senseless with this cane," Cookie's voice yells.

Sid is taken aback.

I press the play button again and the walking stick blares the sound of a car horn. Sid is so startled that he drops the cane and it smashes to bits on the ground. His heart monitor starts beeping.

"That's okay," I say, scooping the pieces off the floor.

"I don't like it," Sid says like "get it away."

"Me neither," Manny weighs in. "I think it's *mean.*"

I scratch my head.

"I don't get it," Manny adds.

"It's a novelty item," I insist. "It's funny."

"I don't get it," he repeats monotone.

"It's not you, Emmanuel," Sid says between coughs. "This is Andy's way. He invents tactile timepieces that can't tell time and snap-on heels that snap in half. For once, I'd like to see you invent something simple, elegant, *or* useful," he cries, inadvertently tangling the bed remote up with his IV.

I go to help him, but Sid starts yelling, "Ow, ow, ow. You're killing me here. You know the war was over years ago."

I don't understand. I back away.

"I want Cookie. I want my wife."

Dr. Yeardling is standing quietly in the doorway. There's no telling how long he's been there.

"Why don't you come with me and I'll patch that cut over your eye? Mr. Brewster needs his rest," the doctor says. "Your uncle's had a tough day."

"Uncle!" Sid yells. "I'd rather be a monkey's uncle."

Yeardling waves me into the hall. "He's obviously confused. That's the medication. You'll be sure to get me a comprehensive list of whatever he's taking, right?"

"Mm-hmm," I nod.

That's when I spot Cookie limping toward us with the original Cookie Cane. She and I make brief eye contact, but before she can speak, I turn around and run in the other direction.

CHAPTER 27

Something Borrowed

I SLEPT in Aisle Nine for four reasons:

1. This is where we display our summer fun flotation devices. Sleeping in an inner tube seemed like a good idea at the time, but as it turns out, honeycomb tile is a poor substitute for water. Trust me, you need the lake.
2. Aisle Nine is also centrally located. Toothpaste is in Aisle Eight. Sleeping aids and breakfast bars in Aisle Ten.
3. The far end of Aisle Nine gets the least amount of direct morning sunlight.
4. The hum of the nearby refrigerator makes for good white noise.

With the phone off the hook, I managed to get three, maybe four hours of sleep, but I awoke this morning to the physical pains and mental anguish that accompany a major automobile accident, or in my case, a series of accidents involving everyone from my fiancée to my best friend.

I break open a box of ibuprofen and then shuffle around the store in my socks, tossing shaving cream, razor blades, shampoo, deodorant, mouthwash, and other necessities into a red plastic basket. The fluorescents in the employee washroom aren't great, but not even Hollywood's best lighting crew could do much with this. I still need stitches and while the swelling under my right eyebrow has subsided, the blood has drained underneath to form a black eye. Somehow I also managed to fall asleep on my cold pack, so now I have freezer burn across the right side of my face.

A delicate shave and awkward shampoo in the tiny porcelain sink helps modestly. When I'm finished with my makeover, I check behind the door. Hanging from the hook is one of Gregory's white lab coats, his name embroidered over the pocket. I turn it inside out and slip on the loose-fitting jacket.

Belinda arrives at the pharmacy late, but I'm not complaining; I'm surprised she still shows up at all.

"Are you wearing makeup?" she screams.

"You can tell?"

"Only in the daylight." Belinda studies me. "Oh man, let's get you some ice. Please tell me that shiner explains why you missed my mother's food tasting. You managed to ruin not *one* but *five* meals."

"I feel just awful. I'm sorry."

"Don't apologize to me. Tell it to the woman who spent three hours baking Paige the perfect chocolate raspberry soufflé. I considered not showing up today—to give you a taste of your own medicine—but that's not how I roll."

"Things are going to get better," I promise her. "They have to."

In walks Lara, wildly swinging open our gorgeous new front door.

"I was wondering when you were going to fix that," she says.

I want to ask her what she thinks she's doing here, and I bet Lara is dying to know where I slept last night and what happened to my face, but instead she tells me I'm wearing my jacket inside out.

Lara takes her rightful place at her makeshift desk, and before long, Belinda is ringing up customers, I'm behind the counter filling prescriptions, and it's business as unusual.

Mindy Monroe of Mindy's Stationery Shop calls. Her daughter, Elaine, has been diagnosed with streptococcus or "strep throat," and apparently "Laney isn't so good with pills." Mindy wants to know whether I can whip up a few of Gregory's trademark medicated lollipops, and seeing as I feel adventurous and we still owe her $600 for wedding invitations (collector's items, I suspect): *Laney gets what Laney wants.*

I flatten out the March 27, 1991, entry in Gregory's notebook entitled "Lemon Lollies." He writes in all block letters:

> IT'S ALL ABOUT THE STICK! MAKE SURE YOU USE <u>CINCH SUPER SAFETY STICKS</u>. KIDS WILL SUCK HARD. THEY'LL LOCK THAT POP RIGHT BEHIND THEIR UPPER TEETH AND PULL WITH ALL THEIR MIGHT. REMEMBER: LOLLIPOPS ENTER THE BLOODSTREAM MORE QUICKLY THAN PILLS, AND YOU CAN'T RISK A CHILD SWALLOWING OR CHOKING ON THE CANDY. THAT'S WHY IT'S <u>EXCEEDINGLY</u> IMPORTANT THE CANDY "STICKS TO THE STICK." CINCH'S SPECIAL PAPER PROVIDES THE STRONGEST CANDY-TO-STICK BOND ALLOWABLE BY LAW.

Everything I need to make the pops is in Gregory's magic chest—a compounding cabinet that contains all his tools of the trade, from the safety sticks to the corn syrup to the circular molds. Today's task is not for the faint of heart; we're not talking about making one lollipop; strep throat requires a full course of antibiotics; that means Laney Monroe will need about twenty. Gregory's recipe makes two dozen, leaving a decent cushion for a few subpar pops.

I tuck the double burner under one arm, steady all the ingredients and utensils with my free hand, and melodramatically push past Lara.

INGREDIENTS

1 CUP OF SORBITOL

3/4 TEASPOON OF LEMON EXTRACT

1 CUP WATER

1/2 TEASPOON OF VANILLA EXTRACT

1/2 CUP CORN SYRUP

4 DROPS YELLOW FOOD COLORING

24 SAFETY STICKS

6000 MG OF TETRACYCLINE

One by one, I slowly drop all the supplies on the black granite countertop. Then I plug in and preheat the stovetop, set out the plastic molds, and systematically position all twenty-four safety sticks.

"Whatcha got cooking, bud-dy?" Manny asks, smacking his lips.

Somehow I missed the entrance of the lumbering woolly mammal.

"You've got to give me a sec," I tell him. "The deliveries aren't ready."

Manny promises to return in one hour.

Lara is whispering over the counter to some guy I don't recognize. The gentleman looks to be in his early thirties, with a long horse face, thick black plastic glasses, and black hair parted to one side. She encourages him to "take all the time he needs."

I pull our supply of tetracycline off the shelf. The recipe calls for 6,000 milligrams—that's twenty-four pills. I begin crushing them with my mortar and pestle, six pills at a time. Then I dump the white dust in a plastic cup. In a small pot, I mix water, corn syrup, and our secret ingredient, sorbitol—Gregory used to use this sugar substitute in all of his candy and cough syrups. I stir the mixture over low heat until all the good stuff dissolves.

CONTINUE BOILING UNTIL SYRUP REACHES
280 DEGREES FAHRENHEIT. BE SURE TO
LIMIT STIRRING—AS TOO MUCH STIRRING
MAY CAUSE THE SOLUTION TO SOLIDIFY INTO
SUGARY LUMPS.

The candy thermometer reads 160 degrees.

There is a small boy no more than four or five years old at the end of the school supplies aisle. Strands of red hair poke out from beneath his crisp new Oakland A's baseball cap, and he keeps saying "he wants": he wants the glossy Batman portfolio and matching pencil case; he wants chalk, paste, a twelve-inch ruler, construction paper, and a three-ring hole-punch.

Standing beside the precocious boy—indulging his every wish (including the hole-punch)—is Grandma. It takes me a moment before I realize that it's Ruth Mulrooney. In twenty-four hours, she's gone from bad to worse. No designer-wear to speak of. No makeup. Just deep, dark creases across each cheek and purple bags under the eyes. It's only now—hatless and handkerchiefless—that I realize she's no longer a redhead. The sherbet-orange hair dye grew out ages ago.

Her companion is running her ragged, but I suspect the gloom runs deeper and outside her control. I check the computer. It's been weeks since she refilled her prescription for antidepressants.

Ruth takes Paxil, but we're fresh out, and seeing as I've managed to cut off most of our legitimate and illegitimate distribution channels, I'm not expecting a new supply anytime soon. I decide to give her Prevos instead. *What could go wrong—they both start with P.* Actually, Janus's microprocessor confirms the adequacy of the substitution. Gregory used to make this swap all the time.

As I count out a one-month supply, I can feel Ruth trying to make eye contact. When I give in, she greets me with a wide grin.

"I understand you've dumped me for a younger model," Ruth says softly.

"Take me back," I beg her as I close the prescription bottle and set it down beside her.

Ruth rests her shopping basket on the counter and studies it.

"You're a peach, but I'm fine, Andrew," she lies.

She speaks so softly and in such monotones it's hard to understand her.

"I guess it can't hurt to have extra, just in case," Ruth admits, shaking the bottle. "You and Paige sure make a lovely couple. She'll make a beautiful bride."

She gives my hand a firm squeeze.

"Now did my wedding invitation get lost in the mail or what?" she asks.

"To be honest . . . you may not be missing anything," I begin.

Lara's ears perk up.

A shelf of tiny tin drums crashes to the ground. Ruth's grandson has gotten to the Pringles potato chips in Aisle Two.

"Uh-oh," the child yells.

"Arnie!" Ruth screams back as only a concerned grandmother can.

"I got it," Belinda volunteers.

Despite the commotion, nothing breaks Lara's horse-faced friend's concentration. He is at the far end of Aisle Eight inventorying how much toothpaste we have and aggressively punching keys on his personal organizer. I assume he's with Longs Drugs or CVS or one of Lara's other potential buyers.

Ruth runs over to check on her grandson.

"Your concoction is boiling!" Lara screams.

Lara's right. The Lemon Lolly brew is bubbling over.

I lift the pot slightly, take the large wooden mixing spoon, and scoop up a small taste, cautiously touching it to my lips. *Needs more sorbitol.* I also add the lemon and vanilla extracts, the food coloring, and all that tasty tetracycline. I'm probably stirring too much, but I'm worried about Laney Monroe licking herself into an overdose. What I don't understand: *How did Gregory manage to distribute the medication so evenly?*

Belinda rings Ruth up. Then she brings her grandson by to say good-bye. That's when Arnie notices Corey on the wall— Gregory's singing bass.

"I want," he says.

Ruth gently asks me whether it's all right. I tell her it's fine if Arnie plays with Corey as long as he's careful. Handing Arnie the mounted bass, I privately mourn Corey's imminent death.

Sensing Arnie's presence, the fish bends his head toward him and begins singing "You've Lost That Loving Feeling."

Petrified at first, Arnie suddenly squeals with laughter.

I stop stirring the lollipop concoction when Cookie calls me a "murderer." She is furiously limping down Aisle Five, teeming with vitriol and disgust. Technically she doesn't just call me a "murderer," she calls me a "murdering wussy loser." I know this because she says it twice, for everyone to hear. The "murdering" part I get. Even "loser" isn't a stretch. But "wussy"? What sort of wussy murders people?

Actually I don't think Ruth heard Cookie threaten my life over Corey's blasted singing, otherwise Ruth wouldn't have greeted Cookie so warmly.

"Zip it, Miss Manners," Cookie hollers, tossing Ruth a vicious glare.

Ruth recoils in horror.

Cookie is wearing the same maroon-colored jogging suit that she was wearing last night at the hospital. I'd be surprised if she's slept a wink.

"You killed him!" Cookie screams, pointing at me with her cane.

I can barely breathe. "Sid's dead?" I manage.

"He's alive, but no thanks to you. You're a danger to society— a complete and utter fraud," she screams.

"But not a murderer," I confirm.

Now everyone's looking, even Lara's horse-faced friend, Sea-biscuit.

"You want to explain what the hell's going on here?" Lara whispers to me.

I'm not sure I could if I wanted to.

"You think that just because you stand behind that counter, you wear his jacket, and you dole out his pills, that somehow you're him?" Cookie yells. "Trust me, you're *no* Gregory."

"No," I mumble, unbuttoning Gregory's white lab coat lickety-split.

"All I know is that something you gave my husband put him in the intensive care unit," Cookie announces to the room.

"You filled their prescriptions?" Lara reprimands me.

I turn to Lara and cock my head in disbelief.

"Just so I'm clear," I ask Lara, "I wasn't supposed to fill Sid's prescriptions because, (a), they owe us money, or (b), I'm unqualified to do so?"

Arnie wants an encore performance. Tripping off the sensor, he persuades Corey to sing: "Great Balls of Fire."

"And you're another one," Cookie says, jamming the rubber tip of her cane inches from Lara's face. "The prodigal child returns!"

Belinda steps closer to get a better view. Seabiscuit, too.

"Even as a little girl this one thought she was too good for us," Cookie tells her audience like a sideshow barker.

The syrup is hardening. The candy thermometer says 310 degrees. I switch off the burner and frantically flip back and forth between the pages of Gregory's notebook for my next instruction.

TO STOP THE SOLUTION FROM COOKING,
BRIEFLY DIP THE ENTIRE POT IN A BIN OF
COLD WATER.

I have neither a bin nor cold water.

"Can you please help me?" I beg Lara.

Lara nods, happy to deflect the crowd's stares.

"In the cabinet behind you, on the second shelf, there's a plastic blue container. Fill it halfway with cold water from the bathroom sink."

Lara finds it quickly and casually holds it up.

"Quick!" I cry, stirring with all my might. "It's crystallizing!"

She bolts into the bathroom.

"Cookie, you have to chill," I whisper, still wrestling with my mixing spoon.

"I don't have to do a goddamn thing," Cookie yells back.

Lara races out from the washroom. Unable to steady the bin, water sloshes everywhere. She sets it down in front of me and I carefully submerge the pot partially underwater.

"You're going straight to jail!" Cookie informs me. Then she turns to Lara: "And *you* . . . I'm suing you for malpractice."

Corey is finishing up the final verse. Arnie cackles and screeches with delight every time the singing bass wags his tail.

"Can *someone* get this toddler a dose of Ritalin?" Cookie yells, pointing at Arnie with her cane. "I can't hear myself think!"

In the instant before what happens next, I'm reminded of Ernest "Atom Smasher" Lawrence—the namesake of where I was supposed to get married—and his subatomic particle accelerator, the cyclotron. In the split second right after protons collide, Lawrence described a massive inrush of air—what he referred to as "the quiet implosion" just short of the nuclear blast.

Ruth Mulrooney is sponsoring today's implosion. She promptly sucks the air out of the room and unfurls, triggering a catastrophic magnitude 9.0 earthquake.

She turns to Cookie and screams at the top of her lungs: "WHO THE HELL DO YOU THINK YOU ARE?"

Cookie freezes, still pointing her cane in Arnie's direction. Ruth smacks the walking stick down and gets right up in Cookie's face, knocking Cookie off-balance and into a shelf of vitamins.

"You are such a bully!" Ruth tells her, jamming her finger in Cookie's face. "You've always been a bully. You think you're the only one who's ever experienced pain? Or suffering? Or loss?"

The Lemon Lollies are solidifying. I desperately page through Gregory's notebook in search of any tips on reversing the process, but find nothing.

Ruth points to Lara, and then me: "This family has taken care of you and yours for *decades,* and this is how you repay them? By threatening lawsuits? By promising prison? You're so pathetic, Clarice! Really."

Corey times his finale with the end of Grandma Ruth Mulrooney's rant. But now Arnie is too quiet. His mouth is wide open and it's his turn to suck the air out of the room. Apparently Ruth has triggered a second, even stronger implosion. *Run for your lives!*

It is that split second—before Arnie explodes and after the sludge has solidified—that I'm struck with a cyclotron of my own. My invention might not be as Nobel Prize–worthy as Ernest O. Lawrence's, but it's not half-bad, either.

The scream that follows is ear piercing. Lara covers her ears as Arnie cries hysterically. That's when I reach underneath the cash register, grab one of Gregory's last remaining Red Rocket candy rings, and pop it in Arnie's mouth.

Silence!

Arnie enthusiastically sucks the candy ring at a ferocious rate.

Cookie's already out of here. Seabiscuit has had enough, too. He waves good-bye to Lara and exits quickly. Ruth gently takes the singing bass from her grandson, collects her bags, and briskly escorts Arnie out.

Lara is frozen in time: she never let go of the blue bin of water, but the dish is ruined. I haven't made Lemon Lollies—I've made a Lemon Lolly. The yellow syrup has completely congealed. The wooden spoon easily separates from the pot along with its entire contents.

I hold the gargantuan pot-shaped lollipop up to her face.

"Now you're going to want to pace yourself with this one," I instruct Lara.

Lara studies it and, after a startled moment, bursts into laughter. This is the first time I've seen her laugh like this, and she laughs and cries until tears run down her face.

I rub her back softly.

"It's going to be okay," I promise her. "Please don't cry."

Lara manages a meek smile.

"It's going to be okay. I have an idea," I tell her.

CHAPTER 28

The Honorable Thing

THE shrubbery lining the Brewster driveway camouflages my presence. Through Gregory's binoculars, I have a clear shot inside the Days' living room. Glimpses reveal a harried woman. This is how Paige looks when she's running late.

That's when I hear him: Tyler Rich and his Mercedes veggie mobile. You can make out Chitty Chitty Bang Bang's diesel engine from a mile away.

Just as Tyler Rich pulls into Gregory's driveway, Paige runs out with a garment bag over her shoulder. He goes to help her, but she dismissively waves him off. Paige is dressed in that velour, powder blue sweat suit that I hate so much—the one that *I* purchased for her and *we* promised to burn together.

Right before getting in his car, she turns to me and waves good-bye.

This has got to be the height of humiliation. I can't even manage to stalk her properly. We haven't spoken since she stormed out of my car all Sandra Dee–like. But I don't want to be rude, so I reach out through the bushes and sheepishly wave back.

Only then do I realize that she isn't greeting me at all. The binoculars have distorted my perspective. I drop them around my neck and realize that Paige is waving to the woman thirty feet to my left. Cookie goes food shopping every day at 2:30 P.M. sharp, but like Paige, she, too, is running behind schedule. Ever since Sid was admitted to the hospital, we're all out of sorts.

Paige and her new beau zoom off with Cookie right behind them. I step out onto the driveway and brush myself off. I haven't got much time.

Both the front and back doors of the Brewster home are locked, but the window to the dining room is wide open—the most common form of air-conditioning in the Bay Area. Bending the aluminum frame of the screen beyond repair, I pop it off its track and slither my way through the kitchen window.

Loki cocks her head to one side, trying to make sense of the burglary in progress. What looks and feels like a quiet "dog implosion" is a false alarm. Lying there on the floor, I reach over and gently pet the pup on her head.

Without a peep, Loki offers to show me around. We start in the master bedroom. On Sid's bed stand is a stack of rejection letters from some of the largest manufacturers in the world, all of them addressed to "Euraka Productions." Sid's been shielding me from the harsh truth: Ford, Timex, Lowe's, Chevrolet, Estée Lauder, Converse, Petco, Blue Nile, Nine West, Johnson & Johnson—not a single company has an encouraging word to say about our bladeless windshield wipers, tripod ladders, dog umbrellas, adjustable heels, pill rings, makeup applicators, or side-access sneakers. I lay the letters back on his bed stand and continue my search.

First Sid's dresser. Then Cookie's bureau and bed stand. Before long, Loki and I are rifling through the Brewster closets and breaking into boxes. Nothing.

The large cherry cedar hope chest at the foot of the bed calls out to be searched. I tip the lid open and the large mirror on the reverse side makes me jump. My reflection reminds me: *You shouldn't be doing this.* Organized neatly inside the ancient ark are old photographs, child immunization records, birth certificates, diplomas, a wedding veil, a silk baby pillow, cotton blanket, baby shoes, and even a terrifying clear plastic baggie of baby teeth and hair—it's hard to estimate how many children are represented in this Ziploc.

It is inside the hope chest that I find the original Western Union Sid sent Cookie at 10:10 A.M. on September 27, 1945. In the London telegram, Sid asks Cookie whether she'd like to have dinner with him in New York City later that week. Clarice Schwartz and Sidney Brewster's marriage certificate is rubber-banded to a thick stack of letters. The water-stained one on top is postmarked March 4, 1943, and is stamped Tripoli, Libya. The answer to my question may very well lie in these letters, but I won't dig through them: breaking into their house and rummaging through their most personal belongings is enough; I can't bring myself to read their private, most intimate exchanges.

Just short of declaring this hope chest hopeless, I find what I'm looking for: a small square manila envelope addressed to Sidney Brewster from an Air Force base in Bolling Field, Maryland. The envelope contains a brown plastic index card with "Army of the United States" printed across the top in white lettering. Underneath the military seal it reads:

This is to certify that

SIDNEY SILVIO BREWSTER 25 344 154

AVIATION TECHNICIAN THIRD GRADE H B G 376 12TH A F

is hereby discharged under other than honorable conditions from the military service of the United States of America.

The discharge papers are dated December 5, 1945, and signed by Colonel Theodore M. Singleton. On the back side is all of Sid's personal information, including a Brooklyn address, where he went to school (Lincoln High School), physical description (green eyes, dark complexion, notation of a half-inch scar on his left ring finger and a blemish on the anterior of his right shoulder), service locations in Africa and Europe, and his monthly salary when discharged: $96.00. The location designated for his thumbprint is blank, as are the travel allowance section and the area reserved for "Decorations, medals, and badges."

" 'Other than honorable conditions,' " I tell Loki, rereading it.

Loki is as puzzled as I am. But then, in not so many words, she suggests we move on and get something to eat. I'm hungry, too, and Cookie will be home soon.

I carefully place everything back in the hope chest exactly the way I found it and we go to the kitchen. Loki's treats are in the cabinet above the sink, and I help myself to a salami and Swiss cheese sandwich using Cookie's last two slices of white bread and some soggy lettuce.

The Brewster kitchen might as well be a mini Day's Pharmacy. Lined along the counter are dozens of medications. Cookie and Sid use blue and pink plastic pillboxes marked with the day of the week to remind them of what to take when.

Chewing on my sandwich, I survey the awesome collection. Some are empties. Others are duplicates. Most of the scripts are familiar. The labels on many of the plastic bottles suggest the contents are expired—in some cases the dates go back as far as the mid-1990s. But in all likelihood, most of the pills are new; Cookie and Sid are prone to recycle.

Dr. Yeardling wants to know everything Sid's taking, so on a scrap piece of paper I make a list of the few prescriptions that don't ring a bell—mostly stuff Gregory filled years ago.

When Loki hears something, she darts into the living room, leaping up and onto the couch. Unable to negotiate the plastic casing, she slides headfirst into the armrest. Above the pooch is that spectacular sepia-toned poster of Sid and Cookie. The sky-scraper, Sid's knee, Cookie's curls, that ring, the perfect proposal, the engagement story of engagement stories. I study the photograph with a renewed perspective. *Other than honorable conditions.* Maybe Sid's not wearing a military peacoat after all.

I examine the still, looking to Cookie for a clue. The twinkle in her eyes suggests something. That's when Present-Day Cookie pulls into the driveway. Loki's been anticipating her. I consider fleeing out the back door, but instead decide to take her head-on. Holding back the small dog, I walk out the front door.

Welcome home!

The eighty-two-year-old is still in the trunk of her car rustling up her groceries. When the screen door slams shut behind me, Cookie twirls around in shock. She points her cane at me with contempt. Chewing the last bits of my sandwich, I take two steps closer and slowly raise both hands like a stickup. Then before I can explain, she jabs the rubber tip of her cane right below my rib cage and I splutter salami and cheese all over the driveway.

"What's with you?" I cry, rubbing my chest.

"You're going to clean that up," she talks over me.

I reach down inside the trunk to bunch together her groceries and she thwacks me hard on the small of my back with her stick.

"You broke into my house!" she cries as I yelp in pain.

"I thought you were home!" I scream. "The front door was open!"

"Yeah, right. Tell it to the cops."

I follow Cookie inside. When she makes a move for the phone mounted on the kitchen wall, I block her path.

"Move!" she demands.

"Please just have a seat. You're entitled to be angry," I tell her.

Our faces are inches apart. We're both exhausted. She throws her hands up in frustration, limps over to the kitchen table, and delicately takes a seat. The plastic cushion lets out a soft sigh.

"I'll just call the authorities once you leave," she says, folding her hands on her tummy. "Unless you plan on killing me, too?"

"You and I both know I had nothing to do with putting Sid in the hospital."

"I wouldn't be so sure. Sid never went into cardiac arrest when Gregory did the pill fillin' around here."

Cookie's right. Sid's recent escapade has shaken my confidence. I'm constantly second-guessing myself. Every day I'm placing vulnerable men and women in heightened physical danger. Sid detonated, and the rest of our patrons are ticking time bombs. There are too many prescriptions; the pills look too much alike; no one is checking my work.

"After I report you to the police, I'm going to walk right across the street and tell that fiancée of yours everything," she threatens.

"Go ahead! I couldn't care less at this point," I say, walking over to her medicine counter. I grab a crusted-over eyedropper and shake it in her direction: "Half these prescriptions expired last century, you know. You love blaming me, but the two of you aren't exercising a whole lot of caution."

"How about you stop poking your nose where it doesn't belong?"

While we're on the topic: "Explain something to me, Cookie. When Sid was having his heart attack, why didn't he choose to go to the VA Hospital?" I ask.

"He was too busy having his heart attack."

"No, seriously. Sid told me he wasn't allowed to go there," I bluff.

"That's a lie," Cookie barks.

"What is? That he said it or he wasn't allowed?"

Cookie narrows her eyes and considers her response.

"Is it the same reason he doesn't use the Veterans Affairs Hospital to fill your prescriptions?"

Cookie continues with her frozen stare. Belligerence, hostility, anger, antagonism, scorn, contempt—I'm equipped to deal with Cookie's entire range of emotions, but not the silent treatment. She's starting to worry me.

"Hey." I wave my hand in her face to get a reaction and confirm she's still breathing. "What just happened? A minute ago you were reaming me out."

Cookie doesn't flinch.

"Hello?" I snap my fingers. "Was it my line of questioning? Forget what I said," I plead, pulling up a seat next to her. "Don't be mad at me, Cookie. Everyone's mad at me. I'm sorry."

Nothing.

"Say something—anything—and I'll leave. Then you can even call the police."

Cookie won't speak to me. She won't move. She wants me to go away and after another couple of excruciating minutes of silence, I do.

CHAPTER 29

Pacify Her

ON JANUARY 13, 1987, ten years and ten days after Gregory Day invented his "medicine-dispensing pacifier," two thousand miles away, in the tiny town of Dequincy, Louisiana, with a population no larger than Crockett, Jesse Clegg filed a patent application for a "medicine feeder." The pacifier depicted in Clegg's technical drawings could have been photocopied straight out of Gregory's composition notebook. Clegg's device shows a plastic nipple and a small squeeze bottle connected via a long plastic tube just like the one Gregory drew.

In describing the need for this "new and novel apparatus," Clegg eloquently wrote:

> *The task of feeding medicine to a small child or infant, especially when the latter is very sick or uncomfortable, is often a painful experience for both the child and the person attempting to feed the child. The spoon containing the medicine is generally always rejected, and often, due to the urgency of the occasion, force is used to open the child's mouth. This, aside from mental pain and anguish, sometimes results in bruised gums or lips, especially, as often is the case, when the child is awakened from sleep.*

("Mental pain and anguish." Boy, they knew how to write patents back in the eighties.)

Jesse Clegg eventually received U.S. Patent No. 3,426,755. It appears to be his or her first and only patent. It should have been Gregory's, but I should count my blessings. Even though Gregory didn't receive the patent for a medicated pacifier, thank goodness he invented it a decade earlier, or who knows what would have become of Baby Paige.

In the mid-1990s, a company by the name of Baby Me Products licensed U.S. Patent No. 3,426,755 from Jesse Clegg. Best I can tell from the prior art, the Clegg device triggered an explosion in the pacifier field. Inventors from around the world began proposing different ways of dispensing medication to infants, or as one inventor from Montevideo, Uruguay, in December 1995 described the potential consumer base: "small children still of sucking age."

My research takes me until dawn. I review all previous patents with one eye closed, terrified that someone, somewhere, at some point in history beat us to the punch, but alas the world has yet to see a pacifier like the one I have in mind.

By noon, our PMP is on file with the Patent Office. It takes three sheets of Euraka Productions letterhead to write out our story in longhand. Then I print "Personal & Confidential" across the front of the envelope, drop the pacifier proposal in the mail, and pray.

Twenty years ago, Baby Me Products took a chance on a first-time inventor. Maybe they'll do it again.

CHAPTER 30

Running, Out of Ideas

LARA hasn't shown up at the pharmacy since the Lemon Lolly incident and I give Belinda the day off. Flipping the sign on the front door, I make an executive decision: it's the Fourth of July, Day's Pharmacy is closed.

Sid never should have had that coronary, and I intend to prove it. Yes, he's old as dirt and blind as a bat, but he's also heavily medicated and in decent physical form. His cholesterol should be low, his heartburn virtually nonexistent.

There were dozens of prescriptions on Sid and Cookie's kitchen countertop, going back as far as fifteen years. I use the quiet time in the pharmacy to review all the drugs Sid was taking, to understand how they interact, and to arrive on an explanation as to why he ended up the way he did—flat on his back.

Sid's ticker: According to Janus's comprehensive computer database, Sid's anticholesterol and heartburn meds, taken together, pose all sorts of risks. But of the dozen possible side effects, "heart attack" isn't one of them.

Sid's tush: Sid takes special medication for an enlarged prostate, but Janus isn't aware of any "clinically significant adverse effects."

Sid's noggin: Sinus infections. All the nasal sprays come back clean. Glaucoma. I found five different eyedroppers in Sid's kitchen. Nothing troublesome jumps out at me, except for an expired vial of Metalol. Apparently, a common side effect of Metalol is a "darkening of the neighboring skin." This would explain Sid's raccoon eyes.

A bit further down in the Metalol entry of Janus's database is a list of the drug's active ingredients. The hyphenated word in the center of the page nearly gives me a coronary of my own: beta-blockers. *Metalol uses beta-blockers.*

I quickly write up my findings and drive to the hospital. Dr. Yeardling's shift doesn't begin for another hour, but the night-duty nurse promises to deliver my package to him as soon as he arrives. Before leaving, I check in on Sid, who is fast asleep. I'm told he had a rough night, but is now stable.

From the hospital in Vallejo, I cross back over the Carquinez and head home. But instead of stopping in Crockett, I pass right through. I'm on Eckley Drive, the very same road to hell that reunited us with our deranged high school principal, Harvey Martin. It was all downhill from there. That was the night Paige asked me if we could "wait" to get married, that Tyler reentered our lives, and that Sid invited me to join his drug gang. *If we stay on this road, we could be in Vegas by sunrise,* I told her that night. But instead we took a series of wrong turns, and here we are.

I'm working on less than two hours of sleep. Twice already I nearly drove Hulk off the road and into the Carquinez Strait. I'm in so much trouble. I went to all this effort to protect Paige, to preserve the memory of her father, to make peace with my former father-in-law, and for what? *More secrets. More trouble.* Sid and Paige are right: I invent cockamamy timepieces that can't tell time and high heels that crack in half. I'm no better a pharmacist, either: I hand out drugs willy-nilly. I killed my father-in-law, drove away the love of my life (more like dropped her off at the curb), and possibly put my best friend in the hospital.

I'm running. But the farther I get from Crockett, the more I realize I can't leave. I won't leave Paige, not in this mess. I've tried to help but only put more lives in danger. I've committed hundreds of felonies. Paige has had enough heartache and hardship. The last thing she needs right now is to inherit my rap sheet. I will find her and we'll talk. We'll figure this out one way or another. If it's over, then it's over, but I won't run.

I turn around and head home. When I arrive on our street, I stop one house short of Gregory's, just as I've done so many times before. Lara is home, but the Vomit Mobile is nowhere to be found. I call the news desk where Paige works, but she isn't on the schedule until tomorrow. I check Ollie's Auto Shop, but there is no sign of Paige's car. I try Manny on his walkie-talkie. He hasn't seen her either but suggests I try the Crockett Community Center— he made a delivery there this afternoon and thinks he caught a glimpse of her flipping burgers at the Independence Day barbecue.

The Community Center is closed and deserted. Next door is Alexander Park, where the parking lot is empty but for one car— a white MR-2 Toyota Spyder. The Vomit Mobile. Cold to the touch, the car hasn't been driven in hours.

The longer I search for her, the more convinced I become of the inevitable: Paige is with Tyler Rich on his floating bachelor pad. I picture the two of them naked in Tyler Rich's whirlpool. Fireworks go off behind them as they clink champagne glasses. As painful as it is, I need to see this for myself.

I take Loring Avenue to the Crockett Marina, a gorgeous one-mile stretch of road along the Carquinez Strait. Halfway down

Loring is the entrance to the construction site where Paige and I used to park. Underneath the Warner Construction billboard is a sleek architectural rendering of what the community is supposed to look like one day. The Waterfront Oasis is selling "30 completely renovated river-view lofts that provide the perfect blend of contemporary living and small-town vibe." The brick façades of the once-dilapidated C & H warehouse are newly sandblasted.

The Crockett Marina is dark and deserted. Stapled to the telephone pole at one end of the wharf is a red flyer touting this evening's celebration: "Join Us for Freedom, Flags, Fireworks, and Fun." I make my way down the barely lit pier of the teeny boatyard. Beyond the sailboats and Jet Skis are the houseboats. There are no security guards, and at most, a dozen small boats, so finding Tyler Rich's isn't difficult. The *Lobsta Mobsta* is farthest out.

Tyler Rich's gas-guzzling love boat is two-tiered. All the windows are tinted black. A small grill is bolted to the floor of the boat, and a bunch of flotation devices are strewn about the back porch.

I tiptoe closer and brace myself for cackles of laughter or moans of ecstasy, but all I hear is the sound of waves splashing up against the boat's hull. The *Lobsta Mobsta* is uninhabited.

In the far distance, I hear someone set off a few firecrackers. Then the high-pitched whistle of a bottle rocket. Paige is always saying that Lydia used to call these sounds "the hooligan fireworks," and she graded each explosion on its level of difficulty and danger. There is a deep boom. A five-finger blast for sure.

I take a seat on the wharf and speed-dial Paige's home number. If Lara picks up, I pray she takes pity on me and hands the phone to her sister. If Paige hangs up me, I can race back to her house before she manages to get too far.

Lara answers right away.

"Where the hell are you?" she commands.

"The marina," I confess quickly, my legs swinging off the dock.

"Oh, I thought you were Paige," Lara mutters. "You don't know where she is, do you? You've made a wreck out of my sister. I hope you're happy."

"Ecstatic."

I tell Lara where and in what condition I found the Vomit Mobile. Lara sounds worried. She doesn't have any good suggestions.

"I need to find her," I say with a hint of desperation.

"I'm so angry with you," she says plainly.

It's the Fourth of July. Families are barbecuing. Her parents are gone. Lara is alone, in a house filled with memories, and now her sister's missing.

"If you see her," we say in unison.

"Okay," we say, doing it again.

As a last resort, I try Paige's cell. Even if she's unwilling to see or speak to me, I need to hear her voice. I need to know she's okay.

Paige answers on the first ring.

"Don't hang up!" I plead.

"Fine, but I thought you and I were done," she says.

"Whoa, whoa, whoa. You're starting to sound as callous as your sister."

"This *is* her sister," Lara says, mostly entertained.

"Paige forgot to take her cell with her . . . again," I determine suddenly.

"Bingo."

We both laugh. Finally I feel like we're connecting. Unlike the last phone call, this time we say good-bye.

Driving along the Carquinez Strait, suddenly the sky lights up. The pyrotechnics originate from Vallejo. I pull onto the shoulder to take in the show.

I didn't wait when I was supposed to. And I waited when I shouldn't have. *Had I just done like Sid said, Gregory and I might have been friends. If we'd been closer, maybe Gregory would have confided in me or revealed the Day Co-Pay or hinted at the looming financial problems or told me exactly what it was that I was supposed to "wait" for. Or maybe when I asked him for his blessing, he would have just said yes.* I'd *love* to talk to Paige right now, but I *wish* I could speak with Gregory.

At some point, I drift off. My cell phone wakes me. The hospital pops up on the caller ID. When I answer, it's Cookie.

"Are you close? Can you meet me here?" she asks.

"I can be there in fifteen."

"I'll be waiting."

CHAPTER 31

With This Ring

SID'S enabler stands by his side, loading gingerbread cookies into his grandfather's mouth like he's feeding sheets of paper into a fax machine. There are chunks of cookie on Sid's gown. To see him sitting upright in his hospital bed, beaming from a sugar high, I'm overcome with joy and relief. Jordan is about to jam another pastry in Sid's trap when the two of them notice me.

"There he is!" Sid cries, his mouth still full.

Jordan comes at me quickly. His pretty young bride, Abigail, jumps up from her chair to watch her husband belt me in the kisser. I did nearly kill his grandpa. At the last possible moment, Jordan reaches out and rests his hand on my shoulder, smiling at me like we're old pals.

Sid calls Abigail over to him.

"Abigail is hands-down my favorite granddaughter," Sid informs me.

She gives me a shy wave hello. "Your *only* granddaughter," she reminds him, "and I'm not about to lose my second-favorite grandparent."

"Cookie does spoil you," Sid admits.

"We really appreciate everything," Jordan tells me.

Sid jumps in: "Wha? You appreciate him breaking in and ransacking my house?"

"About that," I begin. "I'm sorry I went through your personal belongings."

"The doc, here, told us everything," Jordan says.

"Very helpful," Dr. Yeardling agrees, as he enters the room. "There's no way we could have known Mr. Brewster was using an old bottle of Metalol to treat his glaucoma. We would have sent him home with a clean bill of health only to readmit him two eye-drops later."

"Or never at all . . . ," Jordan says somberly.

Abigail cradles her grandfather's face with both hands, and Sid smiles.

"A couple of months back, we got an alert at the pharmacy. It said one of the big drug manufacturers was recalling its hypertension pill because it potentially caused heart failure," I explain to the room. "Specifically because it contained beta-blockers. The story was all over the news," I say, recalling the night the news broke, the very same night Paige earned points by miraculously inserting the word *kumquat* into a live television report. "When I realized that Metalol also used beta-blockers, I suspected trouble."

"Metalol was never specifically recalled," Yeardling adds, "but a number of similar glaucoma drops got yanked after the *New England Journal of Medicine* connected beta-blockers with serious drops in blood pressure, fainting spells, and yes, in rare cases, cardiac arrest."

"Andy, you're like that genius doctor on *House*," Jordan says.

Yeardling rolls his eyes.

"Thanks to you, small fry, they're also changing my cholesterol meds," Sid adds, chewing on another cookie.

And the gingerbread man figures into your high cholesterol how?

Sid tells us he feels twenty years younger—a youthful sixty-three.

"I've got something else here I really think you're going to enjoy," I tell Sid, fishing both articles out of my front two pockets.

Sid's face drops. His heart monitor captures the anxiety. The last time I did this, only a few feet from where I'm standing, I introduced him to the ill-conceived, much-maligned "Cookie Cane."

"Stick out your hands," I instruct him.

He hesitantly complies. In one hand I place a baby pacifier and in the other a Red Rocket candy ring.

Sid studies my props as I describe the concept.

"So how do you make a baby takes its medicine? It is a challenge that has baffled doctors, pharmacists, and inventors for generations. That's where Gregory Day comes in. In 1977, his six-month-old daughter, Paige, got sick, and the compounding-pharmacist extraordinaire needed an easy solution. He filled a rubber squeeze bottle with medication, connected it to a souped-up pacifier using some thin plastic tubing, and popped the device between Paige's beautiful bee-stung lips. It worked. Simple, elegant, useful. A true trailblazer in the field of medicated pacifiers."

Sid nods in agreement.

"I thought we might try and patent Gregory's idea, but I discovered that someone else—Jesse Clegg of Dequincy, Louisiana—eventually beat us to the punch many, many years ago. Clegg even licensed the idea to a company called Baby Me Products. Medicine-dispensing pacifiers have come a long ways since then, but according to everything I've read, most of them still suffer from the same problems: spillage, leakage, and waste. In short: baby isn't getting her proper dosage.

"So the other day I'm in the pharmacy," I whisper excitedly. I point at Sid. "Your wife has a headache because Ruth Mulrooney's grandson won't stop giggling his little head off. I'm looking for a way to salvage a batch of Gregory's famous medicated Lemon Lollies when I come across that drawing of his souped-up pacifier. I snap up the closest thing that looks like a pacifier—one of those Red Rocket candy rings—and I shove it in Arnie's mouth. In the silence that ensues, it hits me—my 'Euraka Moment,' so to speak. One way to guarantee baby gets the perfect dosage of medicine every time . . . a lozenge." .

Sid shakes the Red Rocket ring in my direction. "So this essentially goes in that," he says, holding up the pacifier.

"I totally get it," Abigail cries.

Music to any inventor's ears.

Jordan nods his head in agreement.

"By combining Gregory's device with his lollipop formula, you get a pacifier that can receive a medicated lozenge. I love it," Sid screams. His voice is hoarse. "We'll need to make sure the nipple is porous yet resilient enough. And we can't have that lozenge falling out and becoming a choking hazard." He flips the pacifier around. His mind is racing. "We'll definitely need some sort of child-safety cap."

I nod my head, taking mental notes.

"So I'm to thank for all this," Cookie brags.

She's been eavesdropping for a while.

"Yes, if you didn't bring a four-year-old boy to hysterics, I probably never would have put two and two together," I say.

"You're coming with me." Cookie beckons me with her finger.

I follow her out of Sid's room and down the hall.

"Sit!" she commands.

I do, faster than her own dog. Cookie takes a seat next to me, resting her cane on the wall.

"When I was in intermediate school, my mother used to work at a fabric manufacturing warehouse in the Fashion District. After school, she'd make me baby-sit my brother, Sammy. He was five. One day, I'm chasing Sammy around the house, and I completely black out, clocking my head on the hardwood coffee table."

Cookie pulls back some thinning gray hairs to reveal a long, deep scar.

"I used to be a skinny little thing. But I was never one of those health nuts. I never aerobicized. So at first, we just figured I couldn't catch my breath and passed out because I needed more exercise. You see, in 1945, there was no such thing as 'hypertrophic cardiomyopathy.'" The terminology rolls off her tongue. "They eventually did more tests and figured out there was something wrong with my pumper. The official name came later when I learned that the walls of my heart muscle were abnormally thick—something I inherited from my mother, along with her migraine headaches and her consummate diplomacy. It was scary for a while."

I remember hypertrophic cardiomyopathy from pharmacy

school. The thick walls of the heart need more oxygen than an ordinary heart, and it's this lack of oxygen that causes shortness of breath, dizziness, and the occasional heart attack.

Cookie Brewster—the woman with the abnormally large heart.

"Like me, my mother was absolutely smitten with Sidney," Cookie continues. "I think she felt guilty about passing along this congenital heart condition; plus she felt responsible for introducing me to the man of my dreams right before they shipped him off to Libya. In all my letters to Sidney, I never burdened him with my problems. He had bigger fish to fry, like not getting killed. But my mother was a stubborn lady. She wanted Sidney to know I was sick. That I needed him. I begged her not to, but she wrote and told him everything.

"Sidney received Mom's letter *after* the A-bomb. Japan had already surrendered and the war was over. He was scheduled to return to an air force base in Maryland right before Christmas. All he had to do was stick it out for *three more months,* but that wasn't soon enough for Sidney," Cookie explains. "We'd had *two* dates. We weren't married. Not even engaged. His commanding officer couldn't justify letting him go home early. But Sid left anyway. To be perfectly honest, I didn't even realize he was dishonorably discharged until many years later. We never really spoke about it, but I know Memorial Day was always tough for him, especially when they kept coming to him to be grand marshal of the parade. It got easier after Sid recommended Gregory do it."

"Do you still have blackouts or chest pain?" I ask her.

"I'm ancient. Everything hurts, Andrew," Cookie says. "But the symptoms with my heart happen less and less. Medication helped, too. Drugs are a wonderful thing," she marvels. "As a precaution, of course, I had all the kids and grandkids tested when they were born. Then I made them all get retested after my baby brother, Sammy, died of the same heart condition."

Cookie pauses to regain her train of thought.

"My son, Oliver, got it," she says regretfully, "but he's fine. We get him checked all the time. My grandson at the other end of the hall is safe, thank goodness. The only person who ever knew about my health problems or Sidney's military record was Gregory," she makes clear. "With him in Korea and Sidney in World War II, Gregory always looked up to Sidney, helping us whenever and wherever he could. Just like you."

I thank her.

"Don't thank me so quick," Cookie says, taking a deep breath. "After you broke into my house and scared me half to death, and before you magically diagnosed Sidney's medical condition, I may have—in a moment of weakness—walked up to Paige at the Fourth of July barbecue and told her that you were illegally supplying sample drugs to the elderly. I may have also hinted that I planned on reporting you to the police."

I let out a nervous laugh.

"But you tell me where I can find the girl and I'll set her straight," she promises.

"Honestly, I don't know," I huff, inadvertently rubbing my bad eye. "I suspect she's with this guy we went to high school with . . . Tyler Rich."

"*That* two-timing weasel?" Cookie barks.

"Go on," I say, drawing out the words.

"Oh, Lydia couldn't *stand* the boy. Always flirting with both girls. Paige never liked him enough. Lara too much. If Paige didn't show him sufficient attention, he'd just switch to Lara, and back and forth. It drove Lydia crazy. At one point, Gregory had to pull the fink aside and make him choose. *Stop jerking my girls around,* he said. Boy, I loved Gregory. Tyler Rich picked Paige, even asked her to the senior prom."

"But he took Lara to prom," I remind her.

"Yes. Lara very much wanted to go with Tyler, and Lydia knew that, so when Paige asked her mom for advice, Lydia encouraged her to pass on Tyler's invitation. I don't think Paige was all that upset, really. She was more disappointed she'd have to wait two more years to buy her prom dress."

That's my Paige.

I'm so happy I want to plant a big wet one on Cookie's cheek.

"One more thing," Cookie says, "while we're having this whole heart-to-heart and all. I want to show you something I had specially made for Sid to celebrate our sixtieth wedding anniversary. I think you'll appreciate it."

Cookie reaches into her purse and takes out a blue velvet jewelry box. The taped-on bow is all crushed. She cracks it open, and there sits Sid's anniversary ring—the one that we disassembled in his garage—but all in one piece.

"Looks like new," I tell her. "You replaced the topaz."

"Not on your life. That ring cost me a pretty penny," she says, all offended. "After you two numskulls trashed it, I spent the next day and a half on my hands and knees in the garage searching for that stone. But when I found it, I started thinking that maybe your invention wasn't so stupid after all, considering my heart condition and Sid's health.

"Look," she says, taking the gold ring from the box. She touches something on its side and the whole top elegantly springs open. My eyes nearly pop out of my head. There, inside the tiny well, is a solitary pill.

"Don't get your panties in a wad," Cookie says, "it's just an aspirin . . . for effect. I'm going to ask that young doctor of ours to prescribe something that saves Sid's life in the event he ever has another heart attack."

I take the ring from her and examine it. My heart is racing. This is the first time I've seen a finished, working prototype of one of our inventions, and it's a total beaut. I try opening and shutting the top of the ring a few times, and it works smooth as butter.

"This is exquisite," I exclaim. "How'd you manage to find someone who could make this?"

"That was the easy part," Cookie says. "Sid knows this Russian fella who is a jeweler in San Francisco—the best in the business. Our whole family uses him. I sent him the pieces and he put it together, special order." *Igor Petrov strikes again!* "The hardest part was paying for it. That little enhancement cost me more than the original ring—but Sid's worth it. He's everything to me."

I delicately place the ring back in its velvet blue box and Cookie snatches it right out of my hands, snapping the case shut, nearly catching one of my fingers. Then she stuffs the gift back in her purse, squishing the bow even further.

My two-way Motorola radio bleeps. I unhook it from my belt.

"Andy, Manny, this is Manny. Over."

Cookie leans over and gives me a soft kiss on the cheek.

"Andy, Manny. Over."

I want to hug her, but she's already up, cane in hand, on her way back to see her husband.

"Go!" I tell Manny. "Any sign of Paige?"

"No, but I just got this strange call from Ruth Mulrooney. She didn't sound so good, speaking real slowlike. She says she needs to talk to you right away. She's experiencing some sort of problem with her medication. I promised I'd send you over."

Sid isn't even out of the hospital, and already I've found him a roommate. I consider what Ruth's taking: antidepressants—the ones I pushed on her. I was the one who swapped Prevos for Paxil.

"Oh man, I think I broked it," Manny says over the radio.

"Broke what?" I yell back into the transmitter.

"Oh good, you're there," Manny says, finally. "I dropped my radio on the linoleum in the kitchen and was worried."

"Ruth lives on Francis, right?"

"Yeah. You need me to come?" he asks. "I'd rather not leave my mom. The Vallejo fireworks are done, but we have a better view of the ones from Martinez."

I take a deep breath. "No, I'll go it alone," I say.

"Call me if things get screwy."

On my way out of the hospital, I stop outside Sid's hospital room. Cookie is standing by his bed, tenderly wiping away a few loose hairs matted to Sid's forehead. I do my best to stay out of sight, but it's no matter—the two lovebirds are absorbed in their own world.

CHAPTER 32

Medicine Woman

ALL the lights are on in Ruth Mulrooney's riverside estate—all of them. There are no cars parked outside her house. No movement inside.

I haven't seen Ruth since her implosion and subsequent explosion. Ruth's grandson wasn't the only one a bit shaken by Grandma's erratic behavior.

You don't treat a customer with a life-threatening illness the same way you treat someone with a mild sinus infection, but "pain is pain," Gregory always told me. "Everyone has something, and whatever your something is, when you're in pain, it's the most important, frightening, debilitating thing in the world."

I take the steps to Ruth Mulrooney's front door two at a time and rap three times. I don't know what's waiting for me on the other side of this door, but tonight I will channel the Ghost of Gregory Day and try to help ease this woman's pain. *Just let her be breathing. Let her be lucid.*

"Yes!" Ruth screams as she eagerly opens the screen door. "I knew you'd come. I *so* knew it."

Ruth is once again a redhead. She's wearing an attractive gold-colored silk blouse and white pearls. She grabs my cheeks and gives me a smack on the lips.

"Are you okay?" I confirm.

"You've made me so happy," she cries. "I'm *so* happy!".

It's only now that I realize that I've been duped. I've been invited here tonight to keep a lonely widow company on the Fourth of July.

I follow Ruth through the center of the house toward the back deck.

"I was driving on Loring Avenue tonight," I yell over, "and I see you're making some nice progress on those lofts."

"Yes, yes, yes," she hollers back. "You can see them from here. Harold wanted to call the building complex 'The Waterfront,' but it was my idea to add 'Oasis.' Since changing the name we've received four new offers. The first family moves in October 1."

Ruth then tells me to hurry up and meet her out back.

Standing on the patio is the loveliest woman I've ever seen. I want to cry tears of joy, but Paige is a step ahead of me. She blurts out a laugh that sounds more like a cough; even Paige and Ruth seem surprised at just how perfectly their plan came off.

"I'm getting you some lemonade," Ruth informs me and marches inside.

Paige stands up.

"Hi," I whisper, breathless.

Paige's thick, dark hair is in an updo; loose strands hang over her forehead. She's got on a simple fitted black T-shirt and red skirt.

We both take two steps closer. Our faces are now inches apart.

"What happened to you?" she murmurs, gently patting my puffy eye.

Our lips are nearly touching.

"Drug dealing carries its share of inherent dangers," I whisper back.

"Why can't I just settle down with a nice guy?" Paige teases, her mouth hovering ever so closely as she studies my face for additional bruises and scars.

I kiss Paige right below her left ear. She moans. I wrap my arms around her waist and we give each other a big, long squeeze. Then we sit on the porch swing and Paige starts telling me about her afternoon in Alexander Park.

She was handing out hot dogs and hamburgers to the first graders when this cranky volunteer walked right up to her, jabbed her cane in Paige's face, and started screaming something about illegal prescription medication, sample pills, and of course, everyone's favorite Fourth of July topic: "attempted murder." Cookie was in rare form, Paige tells me, and not making a lot of sense. She tried to calm Cookie down, but it was too late: one little boy in face paint started crying, and then a little girl, and then another, and another. Parents swept in like commandos. Before long, Paige broke down as well.

"It was so humiliating," Paige recalls. "Ruth found me behind the pool house, bawling. She handed me a soda, gave me some motherly love, and promised everything would be okay. When the barbecue was over, I stayed and helped clean up. Then my car battery went dead. That's when Ruth insisted I come home with her, so I did."

I clasp Paige's hands.

"Cookie might have acted and sounded like a madwoman, but she was telling the truth," I tell Paige. "Minus the 'attempted murder' part."

"I know. Over a couple of glasses of wine, I put it all together."

"I'm sorry," I tell Paige. "I tried to do what I thought your father would have wanted me to, but everything happened so quickly," I say, rubbing my forehead. "I thought I could find a way to get him—us—out of this mess. I got it stuck in my head that telling you about the pills would somehow tarnish his reputation. But it's so obvious now: I should have been up front."

"Me, too," she says, dropping her voice.

Paige takes another long pause. She's making me nervous.

"I love you," I squeeze in there right before she tells me something unforgivable about Tyler Rich.

"Sample drugs were never a big deal in my family," Paige begins. "I remember when I was twelve, Daddy would bring home sample packets all the time, and on the weekends, the four of us would sit around the dining room table and sort them into different jars. It was a game. Lara and I used to compete to see who could do the most pills in the shortest amount of time, and Daddy would give the winner one of those Nestlé Crunch chocolate bars."

"You and your sister competitively sorted drugs in exchange for candy in grade school?"

"Middle school," Paige insists.

"For how long?"

"Ten, twenty minutes at a time."

"No, for how many years?"

"Five, maybe six, maybe more," she says. "I stopped in high school and I figured that was that. But it sounds like Daddy kept going."

"Did it ever occur to you that you might be placing people's lives in jeopardy, not to mention breaking all sorts of laws?"

"I was a kid. It wasn't a big deal. Mom always went over our work with a fine-tooth comb, and Daddy always told us how proud he was of us. For customers who couldn't afford important medication, now they could, he'd tell us. I never got into the nitty-gritty of how the finances worked, and it didn't even occur to me that it might somehow be a problem with the insurance people."

"You mean an insurance *fraud* problem," I correct her, gently. "It didn't occur to you or you didn't let it occur to you?"

"Look, Andy, you did it, too."

"I did it?" I shriek. "I did it because you started this cycle twenty years ago!"

"That's not true," she says. "You did it for the same reason I did—because you thought you could help people."

"Paige," I say, touching her softly on the knee. "An hour ago, I was still under the impression that I was the one who put Sid in the hospital by giving him the wrong medication. Then I get this frantic phone call from Ruth."

"I know," she says. "I'm sorry. I should have said something a long time ago. Maybe I was a little ashamed, too. Lara and I suspected Daddy's money problems had something to do with his 'charity work,' but I never dreamed it was so extensive, or that you'd somehow get wrapped up in it."

Only now do I realize that all my sneaking around was for nothing. Paige helped launch the Day Co-Pay.

"This thing is bigger than financial problems," I tell her. "We're playing with people's lives, and it's no longer little girls sorting drug packets around the dining room table."

I gently cradle her cheek. Paige leans in and closes her eyes. We rock quietly on the swing.

"There are doctors who could still lose their medical licenses, a drug ring that includes our neighbors, thousands of pills, and about two dozen customers who still live on the Day Co-Pay," I whisper. "Add in one relentless Blue Cross of California collector who is dangerously close to finding us out, and that spells trouble . . . *right here in Crockett City.*"

The two of us think.

"But I will admit," I say, "I *am* sort of relieved. I was convinced you were going to tell me that you and Tyler Rich 'did it' on his floating love shack."

"Are you crazy? Have we met? I would *never.*"

"Really? Because I was in Cookie's bushes spying on you with binoculars the other day, and I saw Tyler Rich pick you up at the house."

She looks at me sideways.

"It's a long story, but this is me being more honest."

"It was nothing. My car wouldn't start; I was late for work; one more time and the news director was going to fire me for sure; Lara was nowhere to be found; I was desperate, so I hesitantly accepted Tyler's offer," Paige admits.

"And is he still advocating a regime change?"

"No . . . yes . . . maybe . . . I don't know. I don't care. He drove me to work and I set the record straight. He kept going on about needing 'closure,' so I made it abundantly clear—that door is *closed.* You have nothing to worry about. We did not 'do it' on the *Lobsta Mobsta.*"

I'm relieved.

"Did you hear? We have to sell the pharmacy," she tells me suddenly.

I know.

"Lara had some of the pharmacy chains drop by and size up the place. She said it wasn't such an easy sell. Walgreens passed, but Longs Drugs offered us $10,000, and Lara managed to leverage that offer into a $15,000 bid from Rite Aid. They can take possession as early as October. Lara is quite the wheeler and dealer," Paige huffs. "It took my parents a lifetime to build that business. I hate to sell it, and for so little."

"Fifteen thousand. Our inventory alone is worth twice that," I estimate.

"I know!" Paige complains. She's so offended. "Rite Aid thinks it's doing us some sort of favor by taking all that dental floss and deodorant off our hands. As for the prescription drugs, by law, apparently the new pharmacy is only allowed to accept 'sealed, unopened' pharmaceuticals."

"Given all of our mixing and matching, maybe that's just as well," I suggest, gently.

Paige agrees.

"So if it's not our toiletries or drug inventory, what does Rite Aid get for $15,000?" I ask.

Paige takes a deep breath. "Our goodwill," she says flatly. "Lara says goodwill is code for 'customer records.' We hand over all of our customer records and then we promise Rite Aid that we'll encourage our patrons to shop there."

"And if they don't come?"

"It doesn't matter, so long as we try to convince them we're fine," Paige says, thinking about it. "I guess I always knew we'd have to sell the pharmacy."

I place my hand gently on the small of her back. "I'm sorry, I know what that place means to you."

"It does, but not for the reasons you think," she says. "Daddy loved that pharmacy. It gave his life such meaning, especially after Lara and I left, and Mom died. I know he secretly wished that it would stay in the family forever, and I've always felt so guilty that I couldn't give that to him. But I didn't want to run a pharmacy, and neither did Lara. I think that's why he allowed himself to get into such debt—because he knew that Day's Pharmacy was in its golden years, too. But then you came along, and everything changed. It was like a light switch went off in his head. You have no idea how impressed he was with you, sweetheart. He had plenty of pharmacy techs, interns, and apprentices over the years, but Daddy never reacted to any of them like you."

"But then *you and I* started dating . . . ," I conclude flatly.

"No, you're wrong. We started dating right away. He felt that way about you *after* he knew about us. Even after you dropped out of pharmacy school. In the beginning, Daddy didn't know what to make of you. But how could he resist someone who came so highly recommended," Paige brags.

She continues: "I kept tabs on you after high school. I knew you were back in town. I knew you were in pharmacy school. Daddy didn't really need an intern, but he took one. Like it was any coincidence that I visited him on your first day of work. My father could have let you go when you quit pharmacy school. But instead he hired you full-time. You were *it* for him. Just like you were *it* for me. You were going to run the place. You were going to be his son. You were going to take over someday and carry on the tradition."

"I feel like I'm always . . . always disappointing your father, even now," I say.

Paige takes my hand. "You're not hearing me. What I'm saying is, he loved you," Paige insists, her eyes welling up with tears. "He loved you."

We're both quietly crying now.

The Martinez fireworks are now under way and Ruth's porch swing provides the most splendid riverside view.

"I have fresh-squeezed raspberry lemonade!" Ruth announces as if she hasn't been eavesdropping.

I take mine from her.

"So what's with this wedding?" Ruth says, squeezing her butt between us.

"The costs are getting out of hand, and so far, we've received forty-two yeses, and zero noes. Actually, forty-four, Ruth is coming with a date," Paige informs me.

I give Ruth a kiss on the cheek.

"Maybe I can return the dress," Paige suggests, sadly.

I'm touched by the offer, but I tell her no way: "You're wearing that dress."

"We need to cancel the hall," Paige admits.

She's right. We'll lose the $500 deposit, but it will still save us a fortune, including the penalty fee we'd pay if we used an outside caterer.

"Maybe we can renew our vows there in twenty years," Paige dreams.

"One wedding at a time," I beg.

Ruth gives me a look, but it's of no use; I'm not committing to another wedding, to the same woman, twenty years after we still haven't had the first one.

"Have you collected on Rhonda Rally's tab?" Ruth asks.

Rhonda Rally?

"Her sister, Fay, hasn't got one red cent, but Rhonda's loaded and she owes you a bundle. And what about that little tart, Lucille Braggs?"

I don't remember seeing Rhonda Rally or Lucille Braggs on either Gregory's Co-Pay program or Lara's hit list.

"Where are you getting these names?" I ask Ruth.

"That young lady and I talk," Ruth says.

"When did Lara start recruiting?" I wonder to Paige.

"No, no, not her," Ruth insists. "I know who Lara is. I've been chatting with that adorable girl, the one with all the tattoos and the jewelry in her tongue. She knows what's what."

CHAPTER 33

Doughnut Bite

MARTINEZ is everything Crockett once hoped to become but never managed to achieve. The county seat of Contra Costa County is about twice the size of Crockett and ten times its population. People know the City of Martinez because it's the Bocce Ball Capital of the country, the birthplace of Yankee legend Joe DiMaggio, and the home of the original vodka martini. It is in Martinez, not Crockett, where you pick up Amtrak, where you take your driver's exam, and where Paige and I just finished filing for a marriage license.

It's also where you buy lingerie.

Paige takes me by the hand into the floozy bordello Frederick's of Hollywood. She says she needs something for her trousseau, and I have to help. This way I don't end up buying it back only to burn it later.

Everything about this place makes me uncomfortable. I don't want to risk overhearing a female customer explain to the salesclerk why the latest plunge-pushup bra doesn't accommodate her "ladies" or why she finds certain G-strings more comfortable than others. I don't need images of what all these couples look like fornicating. Sure, I can appreciate the inventive combination of underwire, gel packs, cups, pads, straps, spandex, nylon, satin, and silk that go into a Frederick's design, but I think buying lingerie should be a more private affair. This probably makes me a prude.

The more Paige and I browse the exotic array of underwear and bras, the more I realize that I'm a meat and potatoes guy. I pluck a pair of white cotton "hip-hugger" panties off the "2 for $25" table and dangle them in Paige's direction for approval.

"Those are so cute!" she says, with a polite but patronizing tone. "Don't you want something *special* for our wedding night? Maybe fishnets, or how about a corset!" she says, excitedly.

She holds up a teeny triangle-shaped piece of red silk attached on both sides by tiny strings and asks me what I think. I adamantly shake my head no. It leaves nothing to the imagination. This is that rare case where "more is less."

A scrawny, conservatively dressed man about my dad's age with a thick 1970s porn star mustache joins us at the panty table. His "lady friend" cozies up to him. The man picks up a frilly black pair of underwear with ruffles and enthusiastically presents it to his lover. She approves. These two intend to have sex, soon, possibly on this table. I'm ready to go home.

"So first the pharmacy and now the house," she says. "Tell me your honest opinion, Andy, there's no way we can save the house, is there?"

There is just no way. The Rite Aid offer came in at less than half of what I estimated we'd get. That alone sealed the house's fate.

"I don't think so," I say, kissing her softly on top of her head.

Paige leans her head on my shoulder.

"I was thinking about how hard you've worked to collect all that money," Paige says, browsing some more.

Paige points to the thigh-high stockings on the long-legged headless mannequin. I approve and she tucks a plastic-wrapped pair under her arm.

"Had we known, had we just sold the pharmacy and the house right from the start, we might have been able to use that money and whatever you collected to pay off some of our *own* bills and maybe even finance this wedding," she admits. "But if I had to do it all over, I wouldn't change a thing. I'll always love you for trying."

"There *is* a silver lining," I inform her, kissing Paige on the lips. "And you know how I know? Because *I have a chart*," I announce, pulling it from my pocket.

Paige shakes her head. "Of course you do," she laughs.

"But you've never seen a chart like this one. It's called a doughnut diagram," I explain. "Similar to a pie chart, a doughnut diagram can be used to show how proportions contribute to the whole, but in many ways it's *better* than a pie chart because you can compare two different series of data."

"Boy, you really know how to put a girl in the mood."

Paige unhooks a silky black number from the half-price rack. She drapes it against her body.

"This is called a teddy. Similar to a bra and panties, a teddy can be worn underneath clothing, but in many ways it's *better* than a bra and panties, because it has this little convenient snap on the bottom," she says.

Paige curtsies all proud of herself.

"Buy that," I bashfully tell her.

"Yay!" she says excitedly. "Now *that's* the honeymoon spirit. You now have permission to tell me about your delicious doughnut diagram."

"It's pretty simple, actually. The inner ring represents the money we have. The outer ring represents what we owe. That bite in the top left-hand quadrant of the doughnut represents the difference. Between the bills, collections, sales, and the Rite Aid offer, I estimate Gregory still owes about $30,000. But here's the silver lining: now that we're selling the house, we don't have to pay another dime. All that $30,000 becomes forgiven debt. Lara says there is a lien on the pharmacy and another on the house. We just let the creditors sort out the money from both sales. If any other money trickles in, we should try to keep that for ourselves. If only I could figure out a way to make this doughnut diagram solve our Medicare doughnut hole problems."

But Paige stopped listening a while ago. Her eyes are fixed on the man tapping on the storefront window. Tyler Rich waves his shopping bags hello, points to the entrance, and lets himself in the store.

"Pay Day!" he yells across the floor room. "Hey, you two!" he says, consolidating his bags in one hand so he can ignore me and give Paige a quick hug and kiss on the cheek.

I should probably be proud of the fact Paige wants to wear thigh-high stockings and a black teddy with me (and not him), but having Tyler Rich here, inspecting Paige's potential sex purchases, only makes me livid.

"How *are* you two?" he asks.

My heart is racing. Fists clenched. I've never been in a fight before. Paige gently touches my shoulder, but neither of us speaks.

"Well, I don't want to interrupt whatever you two were doing," he says finally. "I'll let you go. I'm sure we'll talk later, Pay Day."

Tyler punctuates his last sentence with a wink.

"Stop calling me that," she says coolly.

Tyler Rich wasn't expecting that.

"I'm confused," he whispers loudly. "Now he won't let you have friends?"

"How many times do we have to go over this, Tyler?" she says. "You and I are not actually friends. I'm not entirely sure we ever were. It's been ten years since I saw you last, and I think it's time for you to move on."

The three of us stare at one another amid the pushup bras.

"Sounds like 'closure' to me," I add.

Tyler bobs his head and slinks off without saying another word.

Before he's even out the door, Paige looks at me lovingly. Then she dramatically holds all of her purchases over her head and asks, "Do you think they'll let me wear these home?"

CHAPTER 34

Belinda's Bonus

PEOPLE love Paige's sugar cookies.

The key, she says, is you need to undercook them slightly. This way they're soft in the middle and crispy on the edges. It also doesn't hurt to use tons of real butter and loads of C & H white sugar. Lydia also taught her that a dab of cider vinegar cuts down on the sweetness of the frosting.

Paige spent all morning baking. She doesn't care that it's the fifth of July. She's made American stars and flag-shaped cookies, decorating them in painstaking detail. Paige has a definite flair in the kitchen. The baking skills come from Lydia, the creativity from Gregory.

We grab a few fresh batches and make the neighborhood rounds, starting with Belinda's mother, Marylyn, two blocks away.

I don't think Marylyn will ever forgive us for standing her up that day. Marylyn offered to cater our wedding *for free,* and how did we repay her? By not having the decency to drop the woman a quick phone call notifying her that no one would be eating her chocolate raspberry soufflé. It took me two days to work up the courage to leave her a discombobulated phone apology. I learned later that Paige sent Marylyn flowers and a kind note, but by then, it was too late. Marylyn was furious. Belinda delivered the official message to me at work: "The offer to cater your wedding is 'irrevocably rescinded.'"

Paige and I exchange encouraging looks. *We are a united front.* Paige holds the ribbon-wrapped plate of cookies up high like a peace offering. Then I take a deep breath and ring the doorbell.

A moment later Marylyn's daughter answers. Belinda looks healthier than usual, dressed down in jeans and a plain white T-shirt. Belinda's dyed her hair from pitch-black to a conservative shade of brown. She still has the lip ring and the silver barbell in her tongue, but no dark makeup.

As soon as she recognizes us, she quickly and quietly closes the door behind her.

"That's a nice gesture," she says of the sugar cookies, "but I think Mom needs more time. My family is famous for its grudges. Mom and I are still pissed at each other over something that happened three weeks ago. The topic escapes me, but she was wrong."

"Then *you* enjoy them," Paige suggests kindly.

Belinda hesitantly takes the plate.

"I'm glad to see you two kids patched things up," Belinda says.

"Patch what up?" I pretend, all shocked.

"Oh, I don't know, maybe it was the toothpaste and deodorant in the pharmacy bathroom or the inner tube and blanket in Aisle Nine. I mastered deductive reasoning in eighth grade, Andy. Which reminds me!" Belinda says, snapping her fingers. "I have a wedding gift for you."

She quietly slips back in the house with the cookies.

"You slept on the floor in the pharmacy?" Paige whispers, slapping me in the chest with the back of her hand. "You said you stayed on Manny's couch."

Thirty seconds later, the front door opens, but this time it's Marylyn, a vivacious woman, with silky dark skin. For a woman who looks to be in her midthirties, it's hard to believe she has a nineteen-year-old daughter. Marylyn holds open the screen door but doesn't invite us inside, preferring to watch us twist in the wind.

"We're so sorry," I say immediately.

"Forgive us," Paige pleads.

"Don't be mad," I add.

Arms crossed, Marylyn mulls over our pleas for clemency.

"I forgive you," Belinda yells on behalf of her mother.

Marylyn purses her lips slightly.

"Thank you for the flowers and these cookies. It really wasn't necessary. I realize that the two of you are under a lot of pressure and mistakes happen," Belinda continues from inside the house. "By the way, did I mention how brilliant my daughter is? Sometimes I'm jealous of her because she gets to lead what appears to be a carefree life, and all I do is work. My therapist tells me that I'm apt to express this frustration in counterproductive ways, but enough about me. The two of you should come inside and cool down."

Marylyn can barely contain a grin.

"Well, you heard me," Marylyn says, stepping out of the way. "You're just lucky I was so crazy about your mother," she tells Paige, kissing her cheek.

Belinda, Paige, and I sit down at the large oak table in the dining room, and I eat the cookies we just gave them. Marylyn brews some iced coffee and adds some homemade cupcakes with vanilla frosting to the batch of sweets. Then she goes back in the kitchen. Cookie is supposed to drop by later this afternoon to sample some of Marylyn's cooking in anticipation of the Brewsters' sixtieth wedding anniversary. Paige and I may have lost the most talented, reasonable chef in all of Crockett, but we're both relieved to hear that Marylyn has moved on.

"I don't think I ever told you how much I enjoyed working for your father," Belinda informs Paige, with uncharacteristic tenderness.

Paige thanks her.

Belinda twirls a white business envelope between her fingers as she speaks. "The Days have always taken care of me," Belinda reminisces.

"I take care of you!" Marylyn reminds her daughter from the other room.

"Yeah, where were you Christmas '96? Your 'Latchkey Parent of the Year Award' is in the closet," Belinda screams back.

"Like a steel trap, that girl's memory," Marylyn yells.

"I love your family," Belinda continues. "Every Memorial Day your mother would set aside one of those Red Rocket candy rings for me. That bossy sister of yours always found the time to baby-sit me. And your dad was *always* looking out for me. He gave me a job. He suggested I get tested for anemia, and sure enough, I needed iron supplements. Then he provided me with health insurance when my mother's business tanked."

"I sold that business *for a profit,*" Marylyn insists from the other room.

Belinda rolls her eyes. Marylyn's said this before. "To your dad." Belinda raises her glass, and then hands me the business envelope she's been playing with. I open it, and inside is a single sheet of paper containing a neatly typewritten double-spaced list. In the left column are a dozen names. Down the right side are figures ranging from $500 to $1,000.

"It adds up to about $7,000, give or take a thousand," Belinda says. "I've already made all the phone calls. Each of them will pay."

"Pay what?" Paige asks.

"What they owe you. Their outstanding tabs," Belinda explains.

"But didn't my sister already figure all this out?"

"Your sister based her calculations on existing paperwork—scripts filled, insurance forms filed, transactions recorded. When I started at Day's two years ago, I used to write everything down, right down to the last gumball. But then Gregory started getting annoyed. He said I was being too nitpicky, especially when all he wanted to do was give everything away. Every time one of his 'special customers' came up to the register, he'd wildly start waving me off."

I nod my head. I know this wave all too well.

"So I *stopped* . . . but I *remembered*," she says slyly. "Ruth Mulrooney, that sweetheart, helped me figure out the difference between the ones too poor to pay and the ones taking their piss-poor time. One day, these folks would put mouthwash on their tab, and the next day it was a bottle of aspirin. It added up. I kept notes. The people on this list *easily* owe you ten times what I have written down there. They've always had the money and I have no doubt that many of them eventually planned on paying—they just needed a gentle reminder, which I was only happy to deliver," she says with a smug look.

Paige and I are touched by the extravagant wedding gift. We both know that seven grand will really help right now, but it also doesn't change much, either.

"Why didn't you say something before?" I ask.

"No one asked me," Belinda says flatly. "You and Lara seemed pretty confident you had it covered with all your computers, charts, graphs, arrows, and whatnot. There were a couple of times I almost said something, but then Lara would talk down to me. It was only after I overhead one of those drugstore reps from one of the chains talking to Lara about buying the pharmacy that I realized how bad things had gotten. It would just break my heart to see Day's close its doors."

Paige stretches her hand across the table and places it on Belinda's: "Amen, sister."

Belinda smiles back warmly, and the three of us sit.

WE HAVE one more delivery. Paige hands me the last of the ribbon-wrapped plates of cookies and our paths diverge. I head for Sid and Cookie's house, and Paige checks our mailbox for wedding responses. If she gets her wish, there will be at least one more goddamn "accepts with pleasure" waiting to be retrieved.

The only thing more annoying than a yes at this point is a yes accompanied by some sort of cutesy personalized note: "Congrats!"

one guest wrote; "Can't wait!" printed another; "How fun?" (We suspect the question mark was a mistake). Just once, can't someone "decline with pleasure" or even "accept with regrets"?

I let myself inside Sid and Cookie's, this time through the front door. Cookie is in the kitchen. I hand her the plate of treats. Before accepting them, she confirms that Paige made them and not me. Then she points toward the den.

Sid is in tan slacks and a Hawaiian shirt, hunched over his keyboard, hunting and pecking. He hits the Return key and the Web page slowly loads. The Brewsters can't afford high-speed Internet access. As the words appear, Sid puts his nose right up against the large monitor so he can read.

"I can show you how to increase the text size on the browser," I tell him.

"Already did that," he says, not breaking his concentration.

"Have you tried changing the resolution of the screen?"

Sid looks at me. He hasn't. He turns around and gives me a warm smile. Seeing him safely back home at his personal computer makes me so happy.

"Looky here," he says, using a shaky finger to help him zero in on the relevant section of the screen.

Sid is surfing the California Department of Health Services Web site. He lifts up his shades and strains his eyes to read the tiny print.

"Says that if you're eligible for Medi-Cal," Sid explains, "then you're not subject to the Medicare doughnut hole."

This is news to me, but it makes sense that those on Medi-Cal have no gap in coverage. Medi-Cal is California's version of Medicaid—health insurance for low-income households.

"I think a few folks on our list should qualify for Medi-Cal," he concludes.

"They'll qualify, but will they apply?" I ask him. Both of us know that many of them have too much pride to claim such benefits, including Sid.

Sid doesn't respond, instead gracefully tabbing over to another site.

"The Medicare page on the Department of Health and Human Services is much better organized than this rotten California page," he tells me, pulling up a blue chart. "See here, if you live in our zip code, you qualify for forty-eight different Medicare drug plans. Some of these premiums and deductibles are reasonable," he says, rubbing his chin.

We look some more and notice that many insurance companies now offer Medicare plans with no gap in coverage—no doughnut holes.

"Ruth Mulrooney called over here to patch things up with Cookie," Sid says. "Ruth mentioned that you're giving up that fancy wedding hall of yours." Sid spins his chair toward me and starts whispering. "My wife thinks you should just combine your wedding reception with our anniversary party. I think it's a splendid idea. Think Paige would go for it?"

"I'm really not sure."

"Our kids and grandkids are paying for everything. We checked with them and they're fine with it. We've invited a hundred and fifty people. I imagine it includes most of the same folks on your wedding list and then some. Outside of Crockett, how many additional invites do you think you'd need?"

This is Paige's big chance to invite the entire town of Crockett to our wedding. I think about the possible add-ons: "Twenty?"

Cookie is standing in the doorway. Sid checks this figure.

"Fine," Cookie determines.

After a moment Cookie notices Paige sheepishly standing behind her.

"Just so you know," Cookie informs Paige, "next month, you're having your wedding reception with our sixtieth anniversary party at The Old Homestead."

"Okay," Paige says, barely audible.

"But you'll have to go and buy your own cake," she demands. "I want my cake, and every bride should have her own wedding cake."

"Okay."

That was easier than I thought.

Paige's face has gone completely pale. She hands me a letter. It is from the Special Investigations Unit of Blue Cross of California. I read the first sentence aloud to the group:

> Be advised that your noncompliance with Blue Cross's internal investigation into claims involving the matter referenced above is now being referred to the Healthcare Fraud Division of the California Department of Insurance and federal authorities for possible civil and criminal penalties.

CHAPTER 35

The "Wait" Is Over

I DOUBLE-CHECK. The liabilities clause in the Rite Aid contract specifically requires us to disclose any "outstanding tax liens or loans, delinquent property taxes, previous judgments, or pending civil and criminal investigations or legal proceedings." Those lawyers—they're always thinking.

The offer to buy the pharmacy expires in three days.

For weeks now, Lara, Paige, and I have been consumed with the possible financial repercussions of failing to pay off all this debt, but bankruptcy pales in comparison to incarceration.

I still can't believe she did it. Brianna McDonnell loved Gregory; she was as sweet as they come, and yet she narked. She's a narker. Maybe she was looking to move up in the company or she was getting too much pressure from her boss. Maybe she still held some pent-up resentment toward Cookie and the Aspercreme incident. I gave Brianna too few records. I gave her too many. Whatever it was, it was enough to turn us in.

Paige and I jump out of the Vomit Mobile like superheroes. Barfman and Hurl Girl. We charge inside the pharmacy. Lara is already behind the counter moving boxes. She's dressed for a fancy dinner, which ended abruptly the moment we informed her about the Blue Cross letter. Her hair is pulled back in a ponytail.

"There are about a dozen boxes we need to go through," she instructs us. "I've made a pile for each of us. Andy, there were four months of printouts sitting next to my computer. What'd you do with them?"

"I gave them to Blue Cross," I tell her and then consider seeking safety underneath the closest archway for fear of a magnitude 5.0 or higher.

But Lara shrugs it off. "Then I'll start over," she resolves quickly. "It's going to take me a couple of hours to reprint each prescription."

From Aisle Nine, I hear Paige let out a gentle sigh. She's found my inner tube, blanket, and clock radio.

"I've compiled a list and made three copies," she says, handing them out. "It includes every prescription the pharmacy's filled and every insurance claim we've filed with Blue Cross over the last two years. Right now, the audit only covers six drugs. I've gone ahead and highlighted those six with different colors. We need to find the *original* doctor's prescription for each and every highlighted item."

I have to commend Lara on her organization and swift thinking.

"Take Conrad Callahan's prescription on September 27. Dr. Platt prescribed him ninety pills of blood thinner," Lara says, waving the original prescription. "Day's Pharmacy provided Conrad Callahan with *exactly* ninety pills and filed an insurance form with Blue Cross for *exactly* ninety pills. If I'm not mistaken, Blue Cross shouldn't be able to tell that half those pills were probably free samples. Wouldn't you agree, Andy?"

This is Lara's first acknowledgment of the Day Co-Pay. Paige gives me a look that confirms they spoke. I nod in agreement.

"Good. I say we give Blue Cross copies of every prescription. So long as what the *doctor prescribed* matches what *we filled* and what *we filed* with Blue Cross, we should be golden," Lara concludes.

Paige and I exchange looks of relief. This is a solid plan.

For the next six hours, Paige and I hunt for and make copies of the original prescriptions, checking off each highlighted item, one by one. When Lara finishes reprinting the electronic records, she pitches in on the boxes. Just after 2:00 A.M., without uttering a word, Paige lowers herself from her stool, gives us both an exaggerated yawn, shuffles to Aisle Nine, and collapses on my inner tube.

Lara and I push on.

By 4:00 A.M., Lara and I are both dragging. I grab us a couple of sodas from the fridge and we start going through my stack of "undecipherables." Most of the scribbles are from about a year ago and appear to be written by the same mysterious doctor. We finally realize the name is Dr. Rodney Sutton, a pediatrician who retired shortly before I started with Day's Pharmacy. Not unlike her sister, Lara takes immense pleasure in crossing off the dozen outstanding entries.

Lara cracks open her soda, takes a sip and a deep breath.

"We're getting close," she whispers to avoid waking Paige.

"We are," I say, gulping mine down. "We've got two more boxes, but my instinct is the last ones won't turn up."

"Mills," Lara says, reading my mind. "He must have called in most of those prescriptions over the phone, and for whatever reason, my father didn't properly record them in the system."

"Brandon Mills is an agreeable man. He and I are *grand friends*. He'll only be too happy to provide us with the proper documentation," I assure her.

Lara laughs quietly to herself.

"Sleeping Beauty over there may have more success. I did Mills's taxes three years in a row, for free, because Dad asked me to, and to this day he still never thanked me. Should have got him audited," she realizes. "But Mills loves Paige. Everyone does," Lara boasts of her sister.

We both sip our drinks.

"That's what really did me in, you know," Lara admits. "I started this accounting business in L.A. and I kept giving all my first-time customers a break on their taxes. But I couldn't cover the overhead and I ended up taking out this massive loan for, oh, some-where around $20,386 and 23 cents."

"Twenty thousand three hundred eighty-six dollars and twenty-three cents?" I repeat back.

Lara nods her head with a smirk.

"My parents started saving when Mom got pregnant with me," Lara explains. "A hundred bucks a month, split between two bank accounts: $70 in the college fund and $30 for our weddings. In all those years, they never missed a payment. Not even after Mom got sick. Or when Dad went into debt."

Lara unlocks the file cabinet next to her computer and pulls out the thin brown bankbook I discovered in Gregory's notebook.

"Paige and I cleaned out the college fund years ago," she says, handing me the American Trust Company passbook. "But the in-terest kept compounding on our wedding account. By January of last year, Dad had just over $10,000 saved for each of us."

Lara thinks about it. "I guess I shouldn't have been all that shocked when Paige agreed to let Dad loan me the *entire* balance, but I was. I always figured it was all about the wedding for Paige, but I should have realized it was all about getting married. My sis-ter is such a romantic.

"I have some sisterly advice for you, Andrew," she continues. "Paige can be generous . . . to a fault. I remember testing her as a kid. She'd have a cookie or get a new doll for her birthday; I'd ask her for it right away, and Paige would just give it to me. I had to start telling her, 'No, that's yours. You want that. Don't give it to me. Don't give it to *anyone*.'"

I turn to the last page of the bankbook where it shows Lara's massive withdrawal.

"After Dad loaned me the money, he stopped saving. It must have been too overwhelming to start over from scratch. Plus he probably figured Paige and I were old enough to take care of our own weddings, and as best as I can tell, he was superdeep in debt."

Lara stops. She studies me and picks her next words carefully. "But then—go figure!—he started saving again."

She hands me a crisp new Bank of the West passbook. Printed on the inside cover is the account holder, Gregory Day. The issue date is November of last year.

"There's isn't much in there. Only a few entries," Lara says. "But I thought you might find the time stamps noteworthy."

"Very," I say, staring at them.

In the right-hand column there are seven $100 deposits, each one made at the end of the month. The last entry is dated May 31—the day after I proposed, the day before he died. I feel an ache deep within me—a bittersweet mixture of happiness and sorrow. Lara studies me as I pull the pieces together. He started saving for our wedding as far back as *November*. Gregory probably knew Paige and I were made for each other before we did.

"Never once did Paige hold that loan over my head. That money could have really helped us over the last month, but Paige never went there . . . I hope you won't hold it against me, either. I'm sorry."

"I apologize for poking my nose in your business," I tell her.

"It's your business," Lara says, referencing the aisles. "At least until we sell this place or go to jail."

Paige stirs in Aisle Nine and we temporarily cut off conversation.

"Did you get a chance to read the Rite Aid contract?" she whispers.

"Skimmed it. Almost vomited on it. We took Paige's car."

"That car," she groans.

"So there's a section in the contract that talks about *you*. Not by name, but by role," Lara continues. "Part of the deal is that we agree to 'transition the records.' I can try to help, but the truth is no one knows our customers like you do. Rite Aid will pay you for your time. I told them that you make about 50 percent more than Dad was paying you."

"Thanks, and of course, yeah, that's not a problem."

"There's also an option in there if you or Belinda want to stay on full-time. They're going to need people to work the register, plus a few good pharm techs, and I'm pretty sure you'd get seniority since you're the only one who can translate Dad's notebook and instruct their pharmacists," she says.

"Thanks, but those Lemon Lollies were a total catastrophe. It makes you appreciate what a genius your father was with medication," I tell her. "I'm still working on cracking a few more of the codes in that notebook."

"It's your notebook now. As executrix of his will, I'm officially bequeathing it to you," Lara says, flapping her hands. "Do what you will with it. But if you don't pass along that knowledge, the truth is, some of our patrons may die along with Dad's formulas."

The words linger.

"I'll help with the books, but can I think about the full-time gig?" I ask.

"Take all the time you need," she says with a smile. "But they need an answer the day after tomorrow."

CHAPTER 36

Cookie's Cure

THE outgoing message on Brandon Mills's voice mail wishes me a happy Fourth of July and informs me that the doctor will return in two weeks. For emergencies, patients may try his answering service.

Paige is in the back room brushing her teeth. Lara is fast asleep in Aisle Nine. The clock on the wall says 8:01 A.M. I grab the receiver and dial. The woman at the other end picks up on no rings.

"I'm calling for Dr. Mills. This is an emergency," I maintain.

"Are you one of his patients?"

Like that should make a difference if it's an emergency.

"What problem are you experiencing?" she asks, losing patience.

"I'm bleeding."

I want this woman to start taking me seriously, but I instantly regret saying this. "Not internally," I explain. "Just on the outside . . . a little."

"Sir, if you're bleeding, you need to go to the nearest hospital."

From the other room, I hear Paige tighten close the squeaky faucet.

"My phone is about to die," I pretend. "Please have Dr. Mills meet me at his Crockett office in the next half hour. Again, it's definitely an emer—"

For dramatic effect, I hang up the phone midword. I hope she has caller ID. *A frantic, bleeding person called from a pharmacy.* He even managed to get the word *die* in there. *Maybe this is one message the service will find worth passing along.*

Paige walks out from the back room and helps herself to a new hairbrush from the rack. She pats down her long, sopping hair with paper towels.

"Did you manage to reach him?" she says casually, tearing the plastic packaging off the brush with her teeth.

"If he doesn't meet us at his office, we'll pay him a visit at home."

We need Mills to complete our files. The clock is ticking. It may already be too late, but the sooner we can get Blue Cross the records they need, the better our chances of reversing the damage, as well as selling the pharmacy.

Dr. Mills's office is right around the block from Day's Pharmacy. Seated on the toasty stoop, I page through Lara's color-coded list. On every page, pink highlights represent all the unaccounted-for medication that Mills prescribed customers and that we filed with Blue Cross. Brandon Mills probably called most of these scripts in over the telephone and Gregory never bothered to record them; and even if that wasn't what happened, we need Mills to provide us with paperwork saying it was. Mills helped Gregory and our indigent patrons with one more loophole: whenever possible, Mills stocked his patients up with twice as much medication as necessary. To help get them through. It didn't affect the price Gregory's customers paid, but it did allow Gregory to receive double the reimbursement from insurance. Any one of these schemes could have tipped off Blue Cross.

Brandon Mills turns the corner in his black Jaguar. When he spots me, he hits the gas. Paige jumps to her feet and waves him down and Mills parks.

"You had better be bleeding," he tells me as he exits the car.

He looks disheveled; the flimsy white collar on his polo shirt is sticking up on one side.

"I appreciate you coming," Paige begins.

"Like I had a choice!" he hollers. "It's against the law what you did."

"I'm sorry, but this *is* an emergency," Paige insists. "Can we step inside?"

"Say whatever it is you have to say right here. I can't stay."

Paige is appalled. "So that's how it's going to be?" she cries, snatching the worksheet from me. "Our insurance company is demanding some records, and you're going to help us find them or we're all going to prison. We need to see your files on about sixty prescriptions you phoned into our pharmacy over the last two years," she says, paging through Lara's list.

"I don't have time for this," he informs us coolly.

"What entitles you to be so inconvenienced all the time?" Paige demands. "The fact that you provided our pharmacy with *free* samples after my father gave you thousands of dollars' worth of stuff?"

"Again with this absurdity! I don't know what sort of lies this guy is filling your head with, Paige. But if anyone owes anyone anything . . ."

"Yeah, yeah, yeah, Andy told me. We owe you a fortune for all that priceless medical advice of yours."

Remembering something, I whisper it in Paige's ear.

"I have a legal right to see my father's medical records," she insists.

"You've got to be kidding me."

"You want us to pay all these medical invoices; well, I want to know exactly what I'm being charged for," she informs him.

"Paige, your father was seventy-five, with chronic emphysema," Mills reminds her. "What more is there to know?"

Paige doesn't move a muscle. Mills is uncharacteristically speechless.

I whisper again in her ear. Mills is getting sick of this game.

"I need to know *exactly* what his cholesterol levels were right before he died," she says, repeating my words verbatim.

The three of us stare at one another.

"Fine!" he yells, jamming his key in the top lock to his office. "But I already know what it's going to say: between the damage to his lung tissue and the lack of exercise, Gregory was a high risk patient for a coronary—it's not brain surgery."

"Don't you mean heart surgery?" I ask Mills.

"Shut up," he says, flipping on the lights and marching into the back room.

Two minutes later, Mills comes charging out.

"Told you!" he screams. "Gregory's HDL was 35! His LDL 160!"

"I wouldn't be too proud of yourself," I remind him. "Those cholesterol numbers are awful, especially considering you were his primary physician."

"You can lead a horse to water, but you can't make him drink," he insists.

Mills waits for a response, but clearly we don't understand.

"I gave him good medical advice and prescribed him the best drugs," he says, defensively. "That's all you can do as a doctor. You can't blame me because he smoked for fifty years or because he didn't get regular checkups or because he never took his cholesterol meds."

That stops Paige cold in her tracks. "Is that what you think?" she says suddenly. "You think he was skipping pills?"

I take Paige's hand. Mills flips through Gregory's records some more.

"It's highly plausible," he concludes, studying Gregory's chart again. "He was prescribed a high-dosage statin. Statins are as close to miracle drugs as they come, and yet his cholesterol readings were way too high. These are not the numbers we associate with someone who is religiously taking their medication."

I study Paige. She stares blankly at the carpet. Mills slowly closes his file.

"Sweetheart, maybe your dad didn't feel like taking the pills," I suggest.

"Or maybe he thought someone else might benefit from them more," Paige responds softly.

"Listen, the files I have on-site don't go back two years, and I'm not pulling that crap out of deep storage," Mills says, reaching for Lara's list lying on the neighboring chair. "Not this week, not with my assistant out."

He flips back and forth between the pages of Lara's packet, grunting in agreement here and there. "These all seem accurate to me," he tells us. "I'll summarize it on letterhead. If the insurance company insists on seeing something more, let them send me a subpoena."

WHILE Paige and I were busy schmoozing Mills, Lara was at Mindy's Stationery Shop copying, collating, and binding the rest of the Blue Cross paperwork. When the three of us get back to the pharmacy, Paige gets directions while Lara and I load the Vomit Mobile.

"You're a creative fellow," Lara says, handing me another box. "Get creative this afternoon."

It takes every ounce of energy to get the last box in the tiny storage space behind the bucket seats of Paige's clown car.

"Listen, sister, inconsolable crying and relentless begging are not beneath me," I tell her, wiping away sweat.

Paige steps outside and hands me the directions.

"You're on your own with this one, grasshopper," she says.

Lara wishes me luck and heads back inside the pharmacy.

"No," I insist. "Come with. We're on a roll. We're a team."

"I think we need to go with our strengths here, and I have a feeling you'll do better without me. I've seen how this woman looks at you."

"You mean like a future felon?" I ask her.

"More like a future cellmate. Now do whatever you need to save our ass," Paige instructs me with a wink. "Even if that includes shaking yours."

"I'm just a sexual object to you."

"ILY," she tells me for the first time.

I can't believe she's deciphered my code.

"Yeah, I'm a genius," she says flatly.

Paige kisses me, long and softly, on the lips. Then I drive off into the sunset, even though I'm headed north on I-80 and it's lunchtime.

Between Blue Cross's proprietary charts, historical maps, and finely tuned mortality tables, these insurance folks can smoke out a swindler in an instant. These are the same people who can predict who's going to die of scurvy one day and get hit by lightning the next. If I don't present them with a simple, airtight explanation, they'll snap me like a twig.

The Blue Cross of California building is located across the Carquinez Strait in downtown Vallejo. I park underground and unload my boxes. It's going to take me two trips to get everything inside. With my arms full, the receptionist buzzes me in. Before heading downstairs for the second box, I tell her that Brianna McDonnell is expecting me, even though she isn't.

When I return, Brianna is waiting for me. She may have totally sold us out, but I'm still relieved to see that she has her job and precious medical benefits. I'm bracing for her to be contentious, angry, or plain annoyed, but she is as cheery as ever. Brianna invites me into the adjoining glass conference room.

"Do you need me to grab a box?" she asks, seeing that my hands are full.

"But what about your back?"

"I'll be fine," she says, bending at the knees before lifting.

We slide both boxes onto the long oak conference table. Brianna gently closes the door and politely asks me to have a seat.

"I've been meaning to call you," she begins slowly. "But I've been out of the office."

"I apologize if we put you in a tough spot. We got the letter. You probably hear this all the time, but this is all one big misunderstanding," I swear, standing up and pulling off the tops of both boxes. I hand her an unmarked copy of Lara's list. "For every insurance claim we filed with Blue Cross on the six drugs in question, I can provide you with a corresponding copy of the doctor's prescription. I also have a corroborating letter from Brandon Mills."

"Ah, Dr. Mills," she recollects fondly.

"It's all right here," I insist, patting the files.

"I'm sure it is," she says. "Please sit."

Brianna reaches into her black leather portfolio and takes out a small map of our county. Crockett is one of a half-dozen towns highlighted in bright red. Brianna leans in very closely and explains, "You're not supposed to see this."

Then why are we doing this in a glass-encased conference room?

"My territory is all of Contra Costa County, which covers about a million people spread out over forty-five cities and towns," Brianna explains. "Each location is color coded to reflect how heavily medicated the community is. The hot spots are in red. Sometimes a town lights up in red because the residents are exposed to a unique health risk: a nuclear reactor melts down or chemicals get dumped in the drinking water. But then other times, something else is going on. . . ."

"El Cerrito, San Pablo, Canyon, Blackhawk, Pleasant Hill, and Crockett," she says, referencing them one by one. "Part of my job is to figure out why so many people in those towns are popping pills."

"Does this map take into consideration demographics? Because you take a place like Crockett—the average age has got to be like sixty."

"It's forty-two," she says with confidence.

"Nuh-uh."

"Uh-huh. Like you, I was certain it was higher, too. I even pulled the latest census data to check. But sure enough, the median age in Crockett is 42.4 years old. Ten years ago, it was 45. Ten years before that, 48."

"Crockett, California?" I confirm.

"How many Starbucks do you have in town?" she asks.

"They just opened one on Second Avenue."

"Any other chains?"

"Potentially a Rite Aid," I say flatly.

"New construction?"

"Some new lofts along the riverfront."

I think about it.

"Crockett is undergoing a rebirth," Brianna continues. "The drugs people take can tell you a lot about a town. Our records show healthy, new couples moving in. And new families.

"Take it from me, Andy, when you spend all your time around elderly, sick people, you get a warped sense of reality."

I start thinking about all the people I went to high school with: the ones who stayed and the ones who came back, and the terrifying reality that so many of these delinquents have already spawned their own miscreants.

"Our partial audit of Day's Pharmacy only covered six drugs because those six represent more than 70 percent of all your insurance claims," she explains slowly. "When I wasn't getting what I needed from you, I needed something, so I began reaching out to your pharmaceutical suppliers. I spoke with reps at Merck, Simpson, J & J, and Pfizer, and . . . I saw a pattern."

I try to jump ahead of her reasoning. *Dear God, she knows.*

"I noticed a major discrepancy. Basically you were claiming two to three times as many pills as you were buying. In most cases, this means the pharmacy is padding its insurance claims, but not you guys. Your doctors were prescribing exactly what you claimed. It could only mean one thing: you were getting hundreds, maybe even thousands of pills from elsewhere."

Maintain your composure. Bluff Sid proud.

"Maybe you were buying them on the Internet or going to Canada, or given your money problems, maybe you were commingling legitimate pills with free samples and getting reimbursed by us for the lot. We see this from time to time, especially with the independent pharmacies. You then use the extra money to subsidize the patrons who can't afford to purchase medicine."

I don't know what to say.

"Your delays, Gregory's unwillingness to cooperate—it all started to make sense. You guys had always been so good to me, but I had a job to do, so I took the weekend to think about it. I determined that I needed to tell my supervisor. That morning, before heading into work, I had my final consultation on my back surgery. Sitting there on the examination table, waiting for my doctor to enter the room, something didn't feel right. You know that feeling you get right before you do something that, deep down, you know is a terrible mistake?"

I nod, soberly.

"I remember you telling me what a big deal back surgery is, so I decided, in the eleventh hour, to get a second opinion. I still had that referral thanks to Gregory. I told the doctor it was an emergency, and seeing as I knew Dr. Mills, she was willing to squeeze me in. She and I talked about when I was in pain, but she was especially interested in knowing when I wasn't. One occasion came to mind . . . about twenty minutes after that psycho lady slopped gook all over my back in your pharmacy."

"You can't be serious," I shriek.

"Less than twenty-four hours before I'm scheduled to go into surgery, this doctor gives me a simple blood test. Five minutes later, I'm diagnosed with rheumatoid arthritis. I'm twenty-six years old and I have RA," Brianna says with some disbelief. "Can you imagine if I'd gone in for surgery? In a bizarre way it was a relief: it explained why I'm always feeling so tired and achy."

"Rheumatoid arthritis is treatable."

"But not curable. My prognosis is very promising, though. Dr. Mayor has already put me on an immunosuppressant, and thankfully, our health insurance covers physical therapy. It's been a crazy week."

"So you're honestly telling me you have Cookie to thank for this?"

"Cookie! Of course, how could I forget that name," Brianna shouts. "Not just Cookie, but you, Gregory, Dr. Mills—you all took care of me. I couldn't recall anyone in El Cerrito, San Pablo, Canyon, Blackhawk, or Pleasant Hill doing anything like that for me," she says, pointing to each red city on the map.

"That right?" I say, picking up on her playful tone.

"I started thinking that maybe I should start focusing more of my energy on those five towns and less on Crockett. Plus, the word on the street is Day's Pharmacy is about to become a Crockett Rite Aid," she says. "Between your pharmacy closing, these records," she says running one finger across the files, "and my recommendation, I have a sneaking suspicion your case will disappear."

I can't believe it. "But the letter you sent said the matter had already been turned over to the authorities."

"As of right now, nothing's been turned over to anyone. That letter went out automatically and it accomplished what it's supposed to—instill the fear of God," Brianna says. "We generally give folks an additional two weeks after sending that warning letter before actually shipping everything off to Sacramento. Truth is, opening an official case with the State can be a real pain in the ass."

Brianna and I soak in the moment.

"Do you like weddings?" I ask.

"Yes, I love weddings."

"Would you like to come to mine? I mean, ours. I mean mine and Paige's."

"Certainly," she answers without hesitation.

"Oh, and do you need a date?"

"Um, I could probably scare one up," Brianna says, modestly.

"Of course you could," I say, realizing that's a stupid question. "No pressure, but I know this one guy who would be a great date. A total teddy bear. And he's hilarious. He also played lead tackle in high school. And did I mention he owns the biggest delivery service in all of Crockett?"

CHAPTER 37

Gregory's Gift

IN 1898, Caleb Davis Bradham was in the back room of his pharmacy toiling away on a new concoction. The North Carolina druggist was close to a major medical breakthrough, or so he thought. By combining kola nut extract, vanilla, and some rare oils, Bradham thought he could artificially replicate the digestive enzyme known as pepsin. "Brad's Drink" didn't work, but it sure was tasty. In 1902, Bradham renamed the carbonated beverage "Pepsi Cola."

At about the same time, German pharmacist Charles Alderton was busy in Waco, Texas, crafting a miracle potion of his own. This one was designed to prevent malaria. Alderton asked the manager of the local drugstore, Wade Morrison, if he wouldn't mind sampling the brew. Morrison took a swig, liked what he tasted, and began serving it to his customers. The carbonated beverage didn't prevent the deadly infection, but it did become a pharmacy staple. Some think the soda got its name from the "pep" it delivered. But I prefer the version of the story where Morrison named the drink for Confederate Army surgeon Dr. Charles T. Pepper—his boss and future father-in-law.

Had I just invented "The Gregory" soft drink before he died, I probably could have saved myself a lot of grief.

PAIGE is extremely superstitious about when the groom sees the bride come wedding day. To eliminate the risk of bumping into each other, I offered to sleep in Aisle Nine, but Paige insisted I crash with Manny. As it turned out, Manny's foldout couch doesn't hold a candle to that inner tube.

It was only after I arrived at his condo last night that I realized Manny and Paige were in cahoots. It was a surprise bachelor party. Manny's mother, Margaret, kicked things off, preparing one of the thickest, juiciest porterhouses I've ever tasted. Then she retired early so Sid, Stanley, Cleat, Manny, and I could drink port wine on the porch and smoke cigars. Sid didn't partake, but he did supply the Cubans, and the criticism: first Cleat cut the draw holes too large, then I was holding mine wrong, then Stanley chomped down too hard on his, and Manny inhaled when he should have exhaled.

Fifteen hours later, I'm clad, shaven, and properly coiffed. I've got on my new black suit, a crisp white shirt, and black necktie. I look a little like a magician, or better yet, a mortician.

Margaret Milken peeks her head in the room to tell me my ride's here.

"You're Prince Charming," she says, delighted.

In one hand, Margaret has a bouquet of white tulips, and in the other, my boutonniere. With a trembling hand, she firmly fastens the red rose to my lapel. I kiss her on the cheek and we promise to see each other in a couple of hours.

Harvey Martin is sitting curbside in his freshly waxed 1965 azure blue Impala, the same Impala that nearly ran Paige and me off the road and into a ravine two months ago. He is wearing full-on police regalia—dark shades, a short-sleeved khaki button-down, and a six-pointed silver badge. There is a walkie-talkie clipped to his shoulder. Sitting behind the wheel, his belly hangs over a black utility belt.

"Step on it, kiddo. While your best man is still breathing," Harvey warns me.

I squat down next to the car and sit my chin on the edge of the passenger-side window.

He leans over. "You ready for this?"

I nod yes, and he tells me and my flowers to take a seat in the back.

Who would have thought back in high school that Principal Harvey Martin would eventually come in so handy? Besides ushering me to my wedding and supplying the wine, the volunteer deputy sheriff has graciously agreed to officiate at our ceremony. He only had one precondition: Paige and I were required to write our own vows—something even Paige never expressed much interest in doing.

It was a reasonable request, especially given his gratis fee; it also didn't take us long. I just went online, found some language we could live with, and cut and pasted it into an e-mail. The short paragraph covered the basics, among them, trust, understanding, forgiveness, compassion, peace, and, of course, eternal love.

Ten minutes later, Harvey called my cell phone.

"This is hogwash," he screamed.

"What is?"

"These vows are balderdash."

"You can't *reject* our vows," I informed him, confirming this with Paige. "They're *our* vows."

"You think I'm an idiot?" he asked. "Find someone else willing to do this quickie wedding in your price range. I asked you to do *one* thing. *One* thing. Now, do it, again, and this time, *with feeling.*"

So there we sat, frustrated at the dining room table, hammering out vows we didn't want to recite. Seeing as our entire ceremony can't exceed a total of five minutes, all we really needed were two or three sentences each. Over the course of an hour, we swapped and critiqued each other's drafts.

"What do you mean you 'promise to hold my hand through the night'?" I asked here.

"I dunno," Paige said, embarrassed.

"But you've never held my hand through the night before."

"It's an expression."

"I've never heard that expression."

"Forget it."

"No, leave it in. But do I have to promise to do the same thing?"

"No, Andy. You don't have to promise to hold my hand through the night."

"All I'm saying is we've only got time for like five promises, and that one isn't at the top of my list. Plus, I suspect neither of us will really sleep if we're holding hands."

Paige and I revert largely to the language from our original draft, with enough revisions to hopefully satisfy Harvey; among the changes, we eliminate the part promising a "world filled with peace and love," and instead emphasize words like *honesty, respect,* and *support.*

"Avert your eyes!" Harvey commands me, as he turns onto Paige's street.

Once he confirms the coast is clear of my soon-to-be bride, I'm allowed to open them again.

My best man is waiting for us in his driveway, dashing as ever in tan pants, a checkered brown sport coat, a cream-colored dress shirt, and a brown paisley necktie.

"Cookie's going to sit this one out," Sid says, slowly lowering himself into the front seat. "She's too consumed with coordinating the party afterward."

"The less attraction we draw, the better," I say, relieved.

"But she wanted me to wish the two of you all the luck in the world over the next twenty-five years," Sid says.

"Just the next twenty-five?"

"She says the first twenty-five are the hardest."

For the wedding ceremony, we've stripped attendance to the bare minimum: Paige, Lara, Sid, Harvey, and me. That's it. Even my parents won't attend. They're going to meet us at The Old Homestead for the reception, just like everyone else, and they're fine with that.

Harvey heads south on I-80. No one speaks for most of the ride.

"Small fry, this arrived at the house for you yesterday," Sid says nonchalantly, handing me a business envelope over his shoulder.

Sid's already opened it. The letter is addressed to "Euraka Productions" from "Baby Me Products" in Arlington, Virginia.

The subject line reads: "RE: Pacifier capable of receiving lozenge." I race through the text. "Thank you for your submission . . ." Baby Me Products will "design, manufacture, and distribute" your pacifier. Another paragraph goes on to discuss "exclusivity" and "a patent application." Post-it arrows point to three different places where I'm supposed to sign and date the nondisclosure agreement and accompanying rider.

There is also a check inside made out to our company for $1,000.

"They've agreed to make it!" I scream, startling Principal Martin as he turns onto the University of California Berkeley campus.

"Quite the contrary," Sid remarks. "They've agreed *not* to."

I check again, and he's right. The letter states "in no way should this agreement be read as a commitment on the part of Baby Me Products to design, manufacture, or distribute the above-referenced device."

"Here's how it works: you get a thousand bucks every year that Baby Me Products *doesn't* make it," Sid explains. "For up to three years—the outside amount of time it would likely take to receive a patent."

"I'm totally lost," I admit.

"This is what they do," Sid explains calmly. "It's an option. Companies pay for the *exclusive* right to . . . *keep the door open.* They hedge their bets."

"So this is *worse* than a company rejecting one of our ideas. This time they're not only rejecting the idea, but also making sure that no one else rejects it?" I confirm. "For $1,000 a year, the idea gets shelved?"

"No, this is a *good thing,* Andy. Read the fine print. Baby Me Products is going to subsidize the patent application, and if it gets granted, *you* get to be the named inventor, as long as you agree to exclusively license the idea back to them if they decide to manufacture it. It could happen. They just aren't prepared to make too many promises right now."

"I don't know. It feels like we're selling out if we cash this," I say, studying the check. "They're treating us like second-class citizens."

"You bet your ass we're selling out! But second-class citizens? No way." Sid laughs. "This from the guy who just spent the last year pouring good money after bad getting 'Poor Man's Patents.' You've literally got someone at your doorstep willing to finance the real McCoy and you're still complaining. Snap out of it! I don't know what you wrote in that letter of yours, but it sure had the magic touch."

"I told them the truth," I say. "Well, as much 'truth' as possible without incriminating anyone. The invention stands on its own, but to seal the deal, I wrote about Gregory, his notebook, Paige, this wedding."

"The truth: what a novel approach," Sid admits, rubbing his chin.

We drive through Berkeley's lush campus. School's out, but it's summer. Cal students wear tank tops and shorts and look ready to be active.

"This place has got a damn good engineering program," I confirm with Sid, as I study the contemporary architecture.

"Best in the country," Sid brags. He quickly picks up on where I'm going with this. "What courses did you take in pharmacy school? Organic chemistry, calculus, physics. A lot of those are prerequisites for engineering, you know. I bet most of your credits from U.C.S.F. would probably transfer."

Harvey begins winding up the Berkeley Hills to the Lawrence Hall of Science.

"I was hoping they might. Even if I can't get into Berkeley, UC–Davis and UC–Sacramento have pretty decent engineering schools," I say.

Sid nods.

"I'd have to talk it over with the *wife,* of course," I say. This is the first time I've used the word, and it cracks me up to hear it. I sound like I'm pretending to be an adult or talking about somebody else's life.

"I think you should try for Berkeley. You'd be close, and if you needed money, I bet Rite Aid would keep you on part-time," Sid suggests.

I pull taut the large rectangular Baby Me Products check. Between the little bit of money Gregory put aside for us in his savings account, his pacifier, and this check, we might be able to cover the rest of the wedding costs. And for our first anniversary, Baby Me Products will send us another check. Maybe Paige and I will take a trip.

Gregory wanted us to wait so he could give his daughter a proper wedding. He managed and then some.

CHAPTER 38

A Shotgun Wedding

PRINCIPAL-turned-peace-officer Harvey Martin pulls up to the concrete plaza of the Lawrence Hall of Science so he can drop Sid and me off and park. I grab my tulips and check my watch. The museum closes in three minutes. Busloads of children exit the building—some buddied up, others holding hands in a human chain. Sid and I walk past the fountain and wait for Harvey by the ledge.

The visibility is even clearer than the day Paige and I booked this place. It's a completely unobstructed view from the Bay Bridge to the Golden Gate. This might be my favorite place on the planet.

"We'll always share the same wedding anniversary," I inform him.

"I'll be a big help to you if you ever go senile," Sid says.

I wonder to myself how many more anniversaries we have together.

Throughout the rest of the conversation, we rarely look at each other, our eyes trained on the gorgeous, serene scenery.

Some time passes in silence, and then I ask him: "Why do you think Gregory never phased out the Co-Pay program?"

"I know he was trying," Sid insists, thinking about it. "But I think he felt stuck. He talked to me about wanting to fix things, but we were never quite sure where to begin. Like most illegal drug rings, I suspect, it started off with a small group, but over the years, it snowballed, and after a while, none of us was sure who really needed the drugs and who just took them because they were free. Then the laws kept changing. Medicare made it so complicated. Some people die from eating too many doughnuts. If you ask me, I think it was the doughnut hole that did him in."

Sid mulls it over some more. "He never said it outright," Sid continues, "but I'm pretty sure he thought *you* were the one who could help get us on the straight and narrow. 'Wait and see,' he would tell me. 'Just wait.' "

I realize now that I never told Sid that Gregory asked *me* to "wait."

"I also think he found it very gratifying to help people. Gregory really was the Mayor of Pomona Street," Sid says, raising an eyebrow. "Getting so far in debt—I know it hurt his pride something awful. It's tough when you get to my age and you've been self-sufficient all your life: you don't want to file a paper with the government declaring yourself bankrupt. But we were being silly," he admits. "Cookie and I need medical coverage, and we're going to get some. I've decided I'm not too proud to sign us up for Medicaid."

I lay my tulips on the ledge and reach into my jacket pocket.

"If you're not too proud to do that, then maybe you'll consider this," I say, handing him a small wad of papers. "You don't have to look at it right now, but I printed it off the Veterans Affairs Web site. It spells out the difference between being 'dishonorably discharged' and being discharged under 'other than honorable conditions.' They sound alike, but they're not. A 'dishonorable discharge' is 'punitive.' It's a criminal proceeding where you go to court and a military tribunal court-martials you. But that didn't happen to you. You were discharged under 'other than honorable conditions,' which is much more common and much less severe. 'Dishonorably discharged' veterans don't get medical benefits from the VA. 'Other than honorable' veterans do."

Sid isn't sure what to make of this. I can see him thinking: there aren't too many ways I could know what I know. *Stay with me, Sid. Keep your cool. Remember where we are and what we're doing here. I'm about to marry the woman of my dreams. Sixty years ago* to the day *you were willing to sacrifice everything to do the same.*

"So you're saying they're not the same?" he checks.

I shake my head. He continues to stare.

"Who told you about me?" he asks.

"Cookie."

"No, she didn't," he says, definitely not believing me.

I know the whole truth will eventually come out, but for now, I need him to suspend reality. From the corner of my eye, I can see Harvey approaching.

"We better skedaddle," Harvey yells over, toting a boom box and a black moleskin notebook. "I just saw our girls in the parking lot."

Sid studies me through wraparound shades. He takes a deep breath.

"Ready?" Harvey says, reaching us.

I grab my flowers.

"We are," Sid says, shaking the VA papers in my direction. "Thanks, small fry. I can always count on you for solid medical advice."

Harvey lunges at me, throwing a sweaty palm over my eyes. This means Paige is close. Blindfolded this way, Sid takes my arm and the two of them slowly guide me inside.

"I AM so going to get fired for this," Sheila says, hustling us against the flow of schoolchildren traffic. Sheila knows full well that Paige and Lara are right behind us. "They are going to rehire me just so they can fire me again," she says, dipping her nose to smell her fresh new bouquet of white tulips.

Lawrence Hall of Science is now officially closed, but there are still about two dozen preschoolers milling about the Science Park. Sheila is definitely risking her job by letting us do this, but at a rate of about $100 per minute, it's hard to feel like a five-minute wedding is a huge favor. Today's price tag does not include a cocktail hour or a fancy dinner party. Our deposit simply buys us a speedy ceremony set against one of the world's most dazzling backdrops. Sheila gets nothing out of doing this for us except a sense of satisfaction. Never again will I underestimate the power of flowers and senseless begging.

"Montessori Preschool," Sheila mutters, studying the last lingering group. "They've got bus problems."

"Yeah, I saw it smoking in the parking lot," Harvey says.

"A replacement bus is on its way," she explains. "I'll be pre-occupied keeping them busy inside. I *need* you folks to stick to five minutes and leave, pronto. Okay?"

"In and out," I promise her.

Like a skilled dogcatcher, Sheila rounds up the strays: two teachers at the picnic tables, some little girls in the rock garden, a few little boys working the telescopes. She tucks the last of them inside, and just like that, silence.

I can hear my heartbeat.

Our photographer, Lonnie, a scrawny guy recommended to us by his film school classmate Cleat, directs us to a nice sheltered spot under a black oak tree perched at the edge of the property. He tells us the lighting is good here and yet shady enough for Sid to take off his wraparound shades.

While Harvey aligns himself with the trunk of the tree, Sid pops an audiocassette in the portable stereo and hits play. Harvey directs Sid and me to stand to his right, and he casually signals to anyone who can see him in the building that we're ready.

Louis Armstrong starts singing about "trees of green" and "red roses, too." The doors to the museum are motionless.

Thirty yards away, Sheila finally props open the back entrance to the museum, and the maid of honor, stunning in her long navy blue dress, steps up to the threshold. In the movies, this is the part when she dashes across the lawn to tell the groom about the run-away bride, but Lara's big smile assures me everything's fine.

"The wife picked this next number. Canon in D Major," Sid whispers. "Cookie says it's the song every woman secretly wants played at their wedding, even if they complain it's overplayed."

The soft, regal sounds of the harpsichord and violins begin slowly.

A precious young girl in a white dress steps out of the museum carrying a single white tulip. She can't be more than five years old. She follows Lara, who walks across the lawn in step with the building sound of the orchestra. Right behind that cute preschooler with the wild curly brown hair is her shy male classmate. He appears to be carrying something, too. Another flower girl is right behind him giggling. Boy, girl, boy, girl, the processional follows Lara down the long stone walkway. The line is twenty children deep.

When Lara reaches us, she steps to Harvey's left and begins doing traffic control: girls on one side of the lawn and boys on the other. Our impromptu guests are trying so hard to maintain composure, but the seriousness of the music is too much for many of them to take. The giggles are contagious.

The first boy then reveals what he's carrying. Before taking his seat, he hands me a small sapphire-colored crystal. I can only assume the stone is part of a collection Sheila found in the museum gift shop. If she loses her job, Sheila may have a future in wedding planning. I thank him and cup my hands so the remaining rock bearers can drop off their gems.

I'm so consumed with balancing my rock collection that I don't even notice Paige standing at the end of the aisle in the most exquisite strapless wedding gown I've ever seen. Tightly fitted at the top with a red sash across the waist, the white satin dress flares at the bottom, just barely brushing the floor. A short white veil hovers over her shoulders.

This is my beautiful bride.

I think that by not wiping my nose or patting dry my cheeks that I'm not crying, but I am. I take a long, deep breath. The music swells as the rest of the strings in the orchestra join in. I pour all the stones into Sid's shaky hands and Sid starts stuffing them in his pockets.

Paige has a look of wonderment about her. She's about to burst into tears or nervous laughter. When she finally reaches me, she asks whether I approve of her dress. I take her hands in mine and tell her that it was worth every penny.

Lara gently lowers the music and Harvey welcomes our one friend, Sid, our one family member, Lara, and all the distinguished guests of Montessori Preschool. This evokes some proud smiles, a few laughs, and a lot of rocking.

Harvey removes the elastic band holding his notebook closed and begins reading from his notes: "When people get married, they promise to stick together 'for better or worse, for richer or poorer, in sickness and in health.' But the way I see it, Paige Reese Day and Andy Gordon Altman have already had their fill of worse, poorer, and sickness. We wish them better, richer, healthier lives. Like I always say: if you're lucky, today will be the worst day of your lives."

Harvey Martin may have just ruined our wedding. Paige and I use the same blank space above our heads to figure out what Martin meant.

Lonnie snaps a picture.

"I know we're on the clock here, so I want to turn the ceremony over to the groom, who would like to recite some personal vows. Andy?"

"You have the vows," I politely remind him.

"You have the vows," Harvey whispers back.

"Remember: you made us redo them. I e-mailed you."

"Never got 'em. Maybe they got caught in my spam filter."

"Your spam filter?"

Martin shrugs his shoulders.

"You have a wonderful memory, Andy. Paraphrase," Sid suggests, handing me the two wedding bands.

I'm drawing a total blank. Paige takes my ring and then my hand and slips it on my finger.

"I promise to love and trust you," Paige begins, insisting on my full attention. "To laugh and grow together. To occasionally sell you my clothes, to award you points, and to invent new ways for us to play together. I promise to be your partner, your best friend, and your family."

I study her. "And I promise to respect and trust you," I say, calming down. I slip the wedding band on where the engagement ring used to sit. "I promise to tell you 'I love you.' To make you laugh at least once a day. I promise to hold your hand through the night. To be your ally, your best friend, and your family."

"Here's the deal," Principal Martin says, hamming it up for the crowd. "When they kiss, I want everyone to jump up and down, and make as much noise as possible."

The crowd leans in. A few pop up prematurely. Lara and Sid brace, too.

"Ready . . . set . . . you're married," he says like magic. "Kiss!"

We do, and as we hold that kiss, trying not to laugh, Paige and I take in the strangest assortment of animal chants, screams, and cries. *Ooh, ahh, ooh, bleh, blah, bleh*—Paige and I run through the crowd—we're married.

Waiting to take us to the reception is a shiny white Cadillac ambulance decorated in white flowers and red ribbons. "Just Married" is sprayed across the back window. Manny is tightly buttoned up in a light gray three-piece suit. Sporting a black limousine driver's cap for added effect, he opens the door for Paige. I meet her inside the delivery truck from the other side.

Wedged on the floor between the front and backseat is a sterling silver bucket packed with ice and a bottle of champagne.

Manny flips on the surround sound. "I've put together a special little mix tape, just for *lovers*," he says, dropping his voice. "Aw-yeah."

The clapping beat from the synthesizer kicks in. Paige starts grooving out, shimmying her shoulders. In rhythm, I begin to unwrap the champagne cork.

Marvin Gaye is "hot just like an oven," he "needs some lovin'," and apparently the only thing that's going to help that feeling? You guessed it.

Sexual healing.

Maybe it's the build of the car or the pitch of the Berkeley Hills, but the next turn comes up on us quickly. The three of us gently tip to the left with the music. I've barely got the wire restraint off the champagne cork when it fires, skimming my right temple and ricocheting around the cab.

The three of us let out a collective gasp.

"Get up, get up, get up, get up, let's make love tonight."

Paige and I stare at one another wide-eyed. I slowly reach up and touch my right eye to confirm it's still there.

"Almost bought the farm there," I say nervously.

"J'yeah," she snort-laughs. "You know what you need?"

"*And when I get that feeling,*" Marvin Gaye sings.

I nod my head, and tell her, "*I need . . . Chew-bacca, Chew-bacca.*"

"*Chew-bacca . . . Chew-bac,*" she and I then scream in unison.

Manny doesn't get it, but he's thrilled to join in.

EPILOGUE

GREGORY'S creditors managed to sell his home within forty-eight hours of placing it on the market. Brianna McDonnell was right—as one of the last affordable locations in the Bay Area, Crockett is experiencing true revitalization.

The creditors directly handled the sale, but because Paige knows all the real estate brokers in town, she was able to exert some influence. At least ten buyers came through the house that weekend, one outbidding the next, and yet Paige made sure the right family closed the deal on her childhood home. The Linders are from New Jersey. They have two little boys, Morgan, seven, and Harry, three. Mr. Linder is a carpenter. Mrs. Linder has been hired as the new social studies teacher at Willow High.

They'll make this their happy little home, Paige assured us.

Between what we paid the creditors, the money from the Rite Aid agreement, and the sale on the house, the bank and credit card companies will end up getting the bulk of what they're owed.

The Linders take possession October 1, the same day we move into the Waterfront Oasis lofts. As a wedding gift, Ruth Mulrooney agreed to sublet us one of the condos at next to nothing. It's on the third floor and looks directly out on the Carquinez Strait. I love the fact that our warehouse stands just feet from the very patch of sand where Paige and I first got to second base.

The new address will cut down on Paige's commute by three minutes. Paige should know in the next couple of weeks whether the news station will bring her on full-time. Her prospects look promising, especially seeing as she's now doing more general assignment work. Paige has already started looking at other local markets for TV work, too. We plan to stay in Crockett, at least for the foreseeable future. This is our home. This is our family. I'm still not sure who was more thrilled the day Ruth offered us this oasis on the waterfront, Ruth or Paige. The two of them literally grabbed hands and started jumping up and down together in a circle. Not even our wedding day may have compared.

Under the Rite Aid contract, we were permitted a "one-day fire sale." As a gesture of gratitude for everything he's done, I dusted off one of our sleek black knock-off Montblanc fountain pens and gave it to Manny. The replacement ink cartridges will cost him twice what the pen's worth, but Manny didn't mind. In return, Manny spent the afternoon selling everything else inside that glass display case, including the case itself. He's quite the salesman. I wish Gregory could have seen Manny in action. Just amazing. Everyone pitched in that day, including all four members of Sid's former drug cartel. Hundreds of buyers came from as far as Sacramento. The over-the-counter drugs, toiletries, candy, and magazines alone raked in about $3,000.

Pharmacy keepsakes and souvenirs brought in another grand. From a small chunk of the honeycomb floor to an antique glass bottle, from the soda fountain to that cherry red, four-hundred-pound, fifteen-foot "Days Pharmacy" sign (no apostrophe and all), nearly everything sold. Of the pictures on the walls, a few we gave away, but most of them we kept, including the one of Lydia serving daughters Lara, nine, and Paige, seven, root beer floats, as well as the one where you can spot my parents in the crowd at the Day's Pharmacy ribbon-cutting ceremony.

Right before the fire sale, Rite Aid came in and confiscated all of our sealed prescription drugs. For the remaining open inventory, federal law requires us to dispose of the drugs "in such a way as to render them unfit for human consumption." After barely escaping criminal prosecution by Blue Cross of California, we probably shouldn't have pushed our luck, but given our comfort level with felonies, we decided to forgo "full compliance." We handed out the remaining drugs to the two dozen or so stragglers who still needed weaning off the Day Co-Pay program.

While Sid tries to help each of them find an affordable insurance program, we plan to help subsidize the remaining hardship cases with the money Belinda identified. Even if they're forced to pay full price for some of their drugs, Lara estimates that $7,000 could cover at least 150 prescriptions—that's an average of four prescriptions per straggler over the next three months. We'll see if it works. We've begun calling the new, completely legal interim drug plan "The Belinda Bargain."

Come the end of the day, guilt got the better of Brandon Mills, and he forked over $1,000; but even that money, combined with the estate and fire sales, didn't quite cover everything. It was the Baby Me Products check that covered the last of the wedding costs.

I applied to engineering school last week. Sid wrote me a recommendation. If admitted, I start next spring. Applying to college meant declining Rite Aid's full-time offer, but I was able to refer another eminently qualified pharmacy technician: Stinky Stanley. It was my way of returning the favor after he deejayed our wedding. So long as the hiring manager catches Stan on a relatively rank-free day, the gig is his for the taking.

Belinda passed on a Rite Aid job, too. She's decided that she's done doing drugs (her words). Belinda and Cleat plan to spend the next two months driving cross-country. Cleat says he wants to film every step of the deterioration of their relationship, if and when that happens. He's already writing his acceptance speech for Sundance. When they return, Belinda says she may get her certification in public accounting. Switching professions was actually Marylyn's idea. Lara's been able to offer Belinda plenty of career advice.

Lara went back to Los Angeles right after the wedding to resuscitate her small accounting firm. She says she's hiring and needs good, cheap labor. I relish the vision of Belinda and Lara back in business together.

While I'm not accepting a permanent job with Rite Aid, I will spend the next few months transitioning the company over. That mostly means bringing the new staff up to speed on our quirky yet lovable clientele. Given that they're keeping our street address *and* our customer records, we expect most of our patrons to stay on. Working three, maybe four months at Rite Aid is what it's going to take to pay off what I still owe on Paige's engagement ring.

At the new pharmacy I'll also spend some time training the younger pharmacists on the lost art of compounding, thanks to Gregory's notebook. I'll do it for the sake of our patrons, for future Crockett generations, for Gregory, but mostly for me.

United States Patent [19]

Day et al.

[11] **Patent Number:** 7,079,454

[45] **Date of Patent:** July 7, 2009

[54] **MEDICATION LOZENGE PACIFER**

[76] Inventors: **Gregory A. Day**, 342 Alhambra St., Crockett, CA 94525; **Andrew B. Altman**, The Waterfront Oasis, 45 Loring Ave., Bldg. B, Apt. 24, Crockett, CA; **Sidney S. Brewster**, 341 Alhambra St., Crockett, CA.

[73] Assignee: **Baby Me Products**, 56 Fairfax Drive, Arlington, VA 22202

[21] Appl. No.: **10/741,524**

[22] Filed: **November 14, 2007**

[51] Int. Cl. **A61J 7/00**; A61J 17/300
[52] U.S. Cl. **606/231**; 606/233
[58] Field of Search 215/11.1-11.6; 606/222-238; 604/99

[56] **References Cited**

U.S PATENT DOCUMENTS

3,426,755	5/1989	Clegg	128/360
4,786,648	1/1989	Cease	606/236
4,862,159	9/1989	Lindenberger	606/236
5,109,482	4/1992	Bohrman	606/236
5,123,915	6/1992	Miller	606/234
5,176,705	1/1993	Noble	606/234
D375,835	2/1997	McGovern	D24/194
D380,290	6/1997	Reiter	D24/194
6,121,578	1/2000	Trimble	606/236
6,197,644	3/2001	Clay	606/236

FOREIGN PATENT DOCUMENTS

1103008	9/2005	France	606/236
0761251	4/1996	Italy	606/236
0513666	1/1991	United Kingdom	606/236

Primary Examiner—Steven R. Kosach
Assistant Examiner—Owen Thompkins
[74] *Attorney, Agent, or Firm*—Allan Fanucci, Winston & Strawn LLP

[57] **ABSTRACT**

A medical pacifier constructed to receive and administer a lozenge medication (11). The device comprises a nipple of porous yet resilient material (10) with a reservoir chamber (13) used to hold in place and contain the solid and excess liquid form of the drug. The back of the mouth guard (23) serves as a base for the child safety cap (26) that secures the back end of the reservoir (28) as well as prevents the lozenge from becoming a choking hazard. The device ensures the infant or child is delivered a steady flow of the proper dosage while avoiding spillage, leakage, and waste.

6 Claims, 3 Drawing Sheets

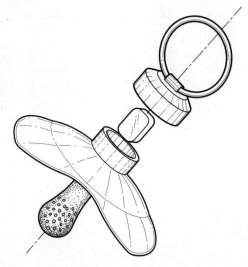

Inventors Appendix

IF I know you, and you're like me, you spend most of your spare time trolling government Web sites in search of newly issued patents covering notably peculiar gadgets. Some of the inventions I came across in my many years of scouring the Internet made cameos in this book, while others—e.g., the bladeless windshield wipers, the automated plant watering system, the talking cane, and the adjustable heels—were products of my imagination.

A quick shout-out to a few true inventors and fellow soul mates:

Candy ring
U.S. Patent No. D242,646 for a "Combined Candy and Ring" (similar to the one in Chapter 1 and throughout) was issued to Arthur T. Horin of New York, New York, and Stan Hart of Beverly Hills, California, on December 7, 1976 and assigned to Topps Chewing Gum Inc.

Tripod ladder
U.S. Patent No. 6,874,598 B1 for an "Ergonomically Improved Tripod Stepladder" (referenced in Chapter 5) was issued to William H. Baker of Oklahoma City, Oklahoma, on April 5, 2005.

Wearable dog umbrella
U.S. Patent No. 6,871,616 B2 for a "Pet Umbrella and Combined Pet Leash and Umbrella" (referenced in Chapter 5) was issued to Irina Zhadan-Milligan and Yuri Zhadan of New York, New York, on March 29, 2005.

Side-access sneakers
U.S. Patent No. 6,874,255 B2 for "Side Entry Footwear" (also referenced in Chapter 5) was issued to Noam Bernstein of Omer, Israel, on April 5, 2005.

Tactile watch
On July 18, 2006, I was issued U.S. Patent No. 7,079,454 for the type of tactile timepiece pictured in Chapter 13.

Pill ring
U.S. Patent No. D451,422 S for a "Ring Incorporating a Compartment for a Pill" (the inspiration for the ring in Chapter 20) was issued to Florence E. Wenrich of Mechanicsburg, Pennsylvania, on January 4, 2001.

Pill-water thermos
U.S. Patent No. 6,419,081 B1 for a "Combined Pill and Water Container" (referred to in Chapter 22) was issued to Edward N. Ross of Fiddlewood, Louisiana, on July 16, 2002.

Medicated pacifier #1
U.S. Patent No. 3,426,755 for a "Medicine Feeder" (similar to the pacifier in Chapter 22 and quoted from in Chapter 29) was issued to Jesse M. Clegg from Dequincy, Louisiana, on February 11, 1969.

Medicated pacifier #2
U.S. Patent No. 5,123,915 for a "Medicated Pacifier" (along the lines of the patent in the Epilogue) was issued to Lawrence and Jeffrey Miller from Oldwick, New Jersey, on June 23, 1992.

Medicated pacifier #3
U.S. Patent No. 5,176,705 for a "Medication Dispensing Pacifier" (also similar to the patent in the Epilogue) was issued to David E. Noble from Sewickley, Pennsylvania, on January 5, 1993.

For a closer look at some of these inventions as well as others I abandoned for one reason or another (and why), visit me at AlexWellen.com or EurakaProductions.com.

Acknowledgments

Top billing goes to The Oracle, who read countless drafts and offered brilliant, critical, thoughtful advice and edits every step of the way. This book would have been impossible without my mother's insight.

To Kris, the kindest person I know. Thank you for the boundless support and endless sacrifices. I wish I could write faster. I appreciate you not divorcing me. Some people don't realize it, but if you rearrange the letters in "Paige," subtract the P, A, G, and E, and add K, R, and S, you get "Kris"—my inspiration.

To my late father-in-law, Robert, and my sister-in-law, Sharon, two of the loveliest people I've ever known. You immediately welcomed me into your family and I love you.

To Shaye Areheart and Jenny Frost, my publishers, who challenged and encouraged me to embark on this first book of fiction. To Kate Kennedy, the wisest and most dedicated of editors; she immediately understood the message of the story and the sensibility of the characters. She has made me a better writer and this novel a far better book.

To Richard Morris, my agent and consigliere. Everyone needs a champion and partner; we truly have a ball writing books together.

To Po Bronson and The Writers Grotto. I feel so nostalgic and grateful for those magical two years in San Francisco, working full-time at the writer's collective, feeding off such brilliant authors.

Because people say this, and I may never get an opportunity in this lifetime: I would also like to thank the Academy and the Hollywood Foreign Press Association.

Last, but not least, everyone else. Writers, readers, editors, and cheerleaders alike: Hugs and kisses to The Optimist, Nathaniel

Cash, Mike and Laura, Carolyn Disbrow, CNN, Joshua Rubin, Karyn Lu, Kelly Byrom, Maryanne Ortel, Vendela Vita, Jake Morrissey, Sally Kim, Dave Rubin, Allan Fanucci, John Trimble, Olen Creech, my pharmacist advisers Alan Weickert, Neil Spector, and Diana Leong, and the charming and welcoming residents of Crockett, California.

About the Author

ALEX WELLEN is a writer, inventor, and Emmy Award–winning television producer for CNN who lives in Washington, D.C., with his wife and son. He is a *New York Times* contributor and has written for numerous national publications and appeared on a wide range of syndicated television and radio programs. On September 18, 2006, through an act of God, Wellen won the much-revered *New Yorker* Cartoon Caption Contest.

He is the author of the critically acclaimed nonfiction memoir *Barman. Lovesick* is his first novel.